THE PICADOR BOOK OF

Contemporary Chinese Fiction

Born and educated in Hong Kong, Carolyn Choa read English and Drama at the University of Hull. She subsequently trained as a dancer at the London Contemporary Dance School, and continues to work as a choreographer for theatre, television and film. Carolyn is also a film producer and lives in London with her husband and son.

David Su Li-qun was born in Chungking in 1945. He graduated in acting from the National Academy of Drama in Beijing and from 1980 to 1984 was the resident playwright at the National Union Theatre. In 1984 David Su emigrated to London and since 1987 has taught at the School of Oriental and African Studies at the University of London.

THE PICADOR BOOK OF

Contemporary Chinese Fiction

Edited by Carolyn Choa and David Su Li-qun

PICADOR

First published 1998 by Picador

This edition published 1998 by Picador
an imprint of Macmillan Publishers Ltd
25 Eccleston Place, London SW1W 9NF
and Basingstoke

Associated companies throughout the world

ISBN 0 330 35264 4

1 3 5 7 9 8 6 4 2

A CIP catalogue record for this book is available from
the British Library.

Typeset by SetSystems Ltd, Saffron Walden, Essex
Printed and bound in Great Britain by
Mackays of Chatham plc, Chatham, Kent

For Anthony and Max

*

For Wei San and Henry

Contents

Contents

Some Information

The idea in compiling this anthology was that it should be a bridge into the heart of Chinese culture, focusing on modern-day concerns.

Looking back into the history of Chinese literature, it is apparent that fiction written in prose is a relatively recent development. Up until the Yuan dynasty (AD 1280–1388) poetry mostly dominated the territory of Chinese literature. The novel as a literary form gradually evolved through the Yuan into the Ming dynasty (AD 1368–1644) when such works as *The Water Margin*, *The Monkey* and *Jin Ping Mei*, all well-known folk tales, were written down. It was not until the Qing period (AD 1644–1911) that the novel came into its own, producing classics such as *The Scholars*, *The Strange Tales of Liao Zhai* and perhaps the best-known and best-loved novel, Cao Xuequin's *The Dream of the Red Chamber*. Apart from this last masterpiece, which was as complex in narrative as it was in characterization, and as exquisite in form as it was profound in its philosophy, these epics were narrative led. However colourful and inventive, however romantic, heroic or tragic, the characters which inhabited these pages were essentially narrative in function. Interest in psychological complexity did not really become the major concern until the twentieth century.

Character-led fiction was an important development in modern literature, the 1920s and '30s producing a plethora of outstanding writers such as Lu Xun, Lao She, Ba Jin, Shen Yan Bing, Xie Bing Xin and many more, most of whom have been widely translated. After 1949, the emphasis in fiction swung once more towards the political at the expense of the personal standpoint, and it was not until after

Some Information

Mao's death, towards the end of the 1970s, that writers felt able to explore the plight of the individual with a renewed sense of freedom. For the past two decades, they have been testing the water, so to speak, of political change, and continue to do so with growing confidence.

I am so glad, as a Chinese writer settled in London, to be able to introduce my country and my people to English-speaking readers, and to embrace the freedom that allows me to do so.

I'd like to thank Jung Chang for her support and friendship and I'd like to thank my colleagues at the Language Centre at SOAS.

Finally, I'd like to thank my wife Wei San and my son Henry who give me love and support for everything.

DAVID SU LI-QUN

A Few Words

To select a few examples of work out of the wealth of material on offer is a daunting and necessarily subjective exercise. However, relatively few contemporary writers of Chinese fiction have been translated in the West so that thankfully there is no real danger of covering old ground.

We tried to bear two things in mind when assembling this anthology. First we wanted pieces that are representative of the people and culture of China today, hence most of the stories included have been written over the last twenty years. Our second aim was to present work which cuts through to the heart of the human condition without sacrificing the wide-ranging social concerns that have always characterized post-revolutionary literature.

This collection ranges from the purely whimsical to the serious-minded, from romance to politics. Regional voices are represented as well as those working in the mainstream of the classical tradition in Beijing and Shanghai. Apart from David Su, who resides in London, the rest of the authors all live and work in their own country. As a result, they have been able to observe the habits, dreams and preoccupations of their compatriots from the point of view of the insider. These artists offer incisive, unflinching critiques of their own times, but the spirit is compassionate. Interestingly, this new probing of emotional depths is often accompanied by an intentional simplicity of language.

From small town to big city, these men and women approach their writing very differently, yet each is a clear product of the same long, rich and confident heritage which is distinctively Chinese. None of them strive to be fashionable, nor do they emulate the West without taking into account the sensibility of their indigenous culture, least of all are they manufacturers of latter-day chinoiserie targeted at a commerical market. What is fascinating to note is a developing common interest in the voice of the outsider, in the courage of the individual stance, repeatedly shown to have the power to effect changes in the face of collective judgement. 'Black Walls', 'The Window', 'The General and the Small Town', and 'One Centimetre' all centrally explore this theme.

The writers included in the anthology are well-established in China and a handful have had their works translated in the West, notably Wang Meng, Su Tong, Cheng Nai-shan, Shi Tie-sheng and Wang An-yi. It is our particular pleasure to introduce some others who are as yet unfamiliar to a Western audience. Some are young, some are not. Most have been through periods of disappointment, even to the point of despair, but all have maintained a sense of optimism, looking to the future with a playful spirit and a capricious sense of humour. We salute these writers who bear witness to the endlessly metamorphosing China of our age.

Finally, I would like to thank Peter Straus for suggesting this project to us, David Su Li-qun for his scholarship and for his help in the labyrinthine copyright negotiations in China, Christine Kidney for her enthusiasm and editorial support, SOAS for giving us access to their treasure-trove of a library, my agent Judy Daish for her invaluable insight and practical assistance, and my parents for making me learn Chinese at school.

CAROLYN CHOA

David Su Li-qun

from *Beijing Opera*

Jane was particularly excited today. She received a letter from her father saying that her brother Steven had just been posted to China to work for the British Embassy. The whole family was in London celebrating his twenty-fifth birthday, which doubled as a farewell party.

Before leaving London, Steven was first to attend a course in Chinese Culture and History, arriving in Beijing in just over a month, in October.

Jane hadn't seen him for more than two years. Like his sister, Steven had spent most of his childhood in China and only returned to England for the last two years of his secondary education. He was a pupil at the famous St Paul's School for Boys, going on to Oxford University to read Philosophy, Politics and Economics. On graduation he had spent a year and a half doing a Masters degree on Chinese History. As a student, Steven was a great squash player, representing both his school and his university at County level. After Oxford, he went through a political phase and even stood for Parliament. Around the same time he was working for a bank as their Chinese political consultant, earning a considerable salary. Steven was therefore generally regarded by his contemporaries as a high flyer. Later, he had grown increasingly fond of Oriental culture and decided to become a diplomat. His first assignment was an eighteen-month stint in Japan. The transfer to China was a promotion – to become the second in command at the British Embassy in Beijing. He had never been an opera fan like his sister, but Steven had always loved, and was becoming quite an expert, on other aspects of Oriental art. In particular, he had spent time studying Chinese literature, antiques, painting and calligraphy.

He wrote a post-script in the letter to Jane:

It was wonderful to get your letter, and to hear that you are thinking of studying Chinese opera, perhaps even becoming a professional! I was surprised, of course, but I do admire your determination. My ignorance of the subject is almost complete, but I did accompany Father to a few performances when I was little. You must forgive me for not understanding why it was considered so special! In comparison to what we have in the West, Beijing opera seemed childish and vulgar. As you know, we used to do Shakespeare at school and to me that will always remain the highest form of theatrical art. Still, I will always support you in whatever you choose to do – if this is your passion, then why not pursue it?

   Your brother who loves you,
      Steven

Jane had always known that Father would respect her opinion but she never expected Steven to give his support, so this was a wonderful surprise. Unfortunately, she also had to get the approval of her guardian before proceeding any further.

At first he shook his head, saying: 'There is a lot of difference between Chinese and English culture. However skilled you might become in time, I don't think that a local audience would ever tolerate a "foreign devil" in the midst of their traditional theatre.' But Jane was not to be put off and he finally had to give in, at least to the extent of allowing her to write to her parents to solicit their opinion.

Before Jane had even begun the letter she knew that Father would not object. He was, after all, an opera fan himself. Mother, however, was extremely unlikely to say yes. Jane's mother was a member of the English aristocracy, and had always valued status above everything else. Entering the theatre was not what she had planned for her daughter. Fortunately, there was a tradition of democratic decision-making in their household, where majority opinion always held sway – Steven's support was crucial and now that she had it, Jane knew that half the battle was won.

One other person was to be instrumental in shaping Jane's destiny – the owner of Lan Ling Guan, Zai Chao.

But before going to him Jane decided to confide in the poet Lin Wen-qiao. She told him that she had already secured her parents' approval.

Lin's reply was straightforward: 'This is the dream of a lunatic and the whole thing is utterly out of the question.'

Jane asked: 'Is it because I am not good?'

Lin shook his head: 'If you are not good you can always work to improve. You can get a top class teacher. No, that is not the problem.'

'Is it because you think I am too stupid to learn?'

Lin shook his head again: 'How could that be true? You are more hardworking and intelligent than almost anybody I know.'

Now Jane smiled: 'It's because I don't look right, isn't it? Because I have pale skin and blue eyes, and my nose is a little higher than yours.'

Lin was exasperated: 'If you know then why do you ask?'

'This is only your prejudice speaking,' Jane replied, a little less polite than she should have been. 'Who doesn't know that opera is for the ears and not the eyes! Those who stare at the stage with their eyes wide open are not the real opera-lovers. Even if someone came to look rather than to listen, do you really think that they could tell the colour of my skin under all that wig and make-up?'

Lin was silent.

'Look at this photograph.' Jane produced a picture of herself in full costume in the role of Huang Bao Chuen.

Lin took it from her hand and examined the photograph with close attention. She was right. It was impossible to tell this was a foreigner. He turned towards Jane and took a good look at her profile. Her nose was in fact not much higher than that of an average Chinese girl. With the help of make-up this could easily be disguised. Still, the matter was beyond contemplation. He could not agree to such folly.

Jane would not take no for an answer. She insisted on being taken to Zai Chao for a second opinion. Eventually Lin reluctantly agreed.

When they arrived at Lan Ling Guan, two guests in court attire were already seated. They had come to ask for a piece of Master Zai's calligraphy. When they saw Lin enter with a blonde woman, the gentlemen were at a loss whether to stand up and greet her or to discreetly retreat from her presence.

Zai laughed: 'Honoured guests, please do not be alarmed. This lady is a close friend of Master Lin's. She is also a regular amateur performer here at Lan Ling. You should see her in *The Exile of Su San*. Miss Jane is every bit as good as Master Lu Rain!'

The two officials marvelled.

Jane quickly added, 'Please do not listen to our host, he is too gracious! I have less than one per cent of Master Lu's talent.'

When the two men heard Jane speaking such excellent Chinese, they looked at each other and said in unison: 'This lady is truly a magical creature!'

Lin asked: 'What kind of scroll would the gentlemen like today?'

The fatter of the two replied: 'To tell you the truth we have not come for our own pleasure today. We are here on behalf of the Ambassador to England. Apparently the British Museum has requested a sample of Master Zai's calligraphy, to be hung above the entrance to the Oriental Wing.'

Zai added: 'Ah, this was the suggestion of Master Hang Yau Wei and Master Chiang Dzi Yuen. The Ambassador wants to raise money for the new railway. As you know I am still half a monk, and earn my living selling opera tickets, so politics is hardly my milieu, but if my unworthy efforts could be of help to the country, then I am more than happy to oblige. What should I write? Master Lin, you are the scholar here, perhaps you would like to make a suggestion?'

Lin thought for a moment and said, 'To present the word "Luck" would seem somewhat commonplace. If we are looking for something to suit the occasion, emphasis ought to be on the relationship between the two countries ... Why not make a gift of the character "Eternity"?'

The two officials and Zai all applauded the suggestion.

'Excellent! Master Lin, you never fail to live up to your distinguished reputation! This is exactly what I shall do! Housekeeper, please bring two pieces of paper in the largest size.'

The housekeeper disappeared. Zai walked over to the corner of the room and took down his biggest brush which was hanging on the wall. He turned to Jane and said, 'Miss Jane, it is for your country and mine. The task of grinding the ink must fall on your shoulders today!'

Jane had never seen such a large brush before. She found this all very amusing and happily agreed. With the help of Lin she began to grind the ink.

The housekeeper now reappeared with two sheets of paper, each measuring about a metre square. Zai took one look and said, 'This is not nearly big enough, bring another two!'

When the housekeeper returned with more sheets the two officials were given the task of pasting them together. Now the paper covered the entire floor of the living room.

Zai tucked away the tail of his long robe, rolled up his sleeves, shook off his shoes, and stood silent at the centre of this vast expanse of white.

Jane did not understand what was going on, so Lin explained: 'Before one puts ink to paper the mind must merge into a single point. Without this focus the strokes will appear diffused. Once the brush makes contact with the paper there must not be any breaks until it lifts off the page at the end. The number of characters is irrelevant, the important thing is for the energy to flow from first to last in a single breath.'

Jane now turned her gaze towards the two court officials. They were standing reverently with arms hanging by their sides, so still they appeared not to be breathing.

Lin whispered in her ear: 'Observe carefully later how the brush makes contact with the paper, how it travels, pauses and comes to a halt. The energy flows from deep within the artist. I haven't made a scroll this big in years, let alone attempted a single character! It is common knowledge that the fewer strokes there are the more difficult the task. In this way calligraphy is comparable to building a house – the less material at one's fingertips, the harder it is to construct a frame. Without a solid structure, all the skill of execution is in the spirit!'

The ink was almost ready. Suddenly, Zai awoke as if from a deep sleep and said: 'Good, let us have another sip of tea.' His whole demeanour once more relaxed. Approaching Jane's side, he dipped his forefinger into the ink to test its consistency: 'A little bit longer, if you please, it is difficult to wring energy out of a dry brush.'

Jane was once more perplexed. Again Lin came to the rescue: 'Master Zai would like the ink to be thicker.' Then lowering his voice he said, 'He was unable to locate his spirit. He will drink some tea then try again in a little while.'

The tea was brought, everybody sat down again. Zai said: 'Master Lin, did you know that contained within the character for "Eternity" is every facet of Chinese calligraphy? Let me entertain you with a little story – there are, of course, eight different strokes in the character.' He gestured to Jane to come to his side.

Zai dipped his finger into his tea and drew on the side table: 'The first stroke is a dot. The brushwork here resembles a boulder bouncing off the face of a cliff, plunging down without pause or hesitation; the second stroke from left to right is a thousand miles of flowing clouds, light in substance yet full in form; the third stroke through the centre is as an ancient bark, alive with moisture without a hint of dryness; the hook aspiring skywards unleashes a hundred arrows, focused in aim, explosive in power; to the left the brush across is as waves smashing against a steady rock; the next stroke down must hold the strength to tame a wild beast in water; the seventh from right to left is shallow in appearance but searches deep towards its roots; the eighth and final stroke is as the ocean swelling up to chase the thunder.'

Suddenly Zai felt his spirit rising and said: 'Quick, fetch the brush, I'll do it right now!'

The fat official presented the huge brush. Zai seized it out of his hands, ran towards the ink stone, and plunged the sable into the black, viscous liquid. Lifting his hand a little, Zai let the ink seep down so that it sank to the tip but without dripping. He collected himself for a brief moment then immediately began. Zai was holding the giant brush with both hands – first it looked as if he was rowing, turning his oar this way and that, negotiating the currents; now he was a warrior brandishing a long staff, riding the wind. Wrist, shoulders, waist, focus all moved together as a rhythmic whole, suffused with energy...

Zai finally came to a stop and everyone shouted 'Hao!' in unison. Jane was stunned into silence. The ink seemed to have expanded to fill up every corner of the room. Jane felt sure it was going to burst through the walls and reach out into infinite space...

Examining the brushwork, Jane could see how each stroke was perfectly balanced, in lightness and intensity, moisture and dryness. Where the ink was heavy it resembled the concentrated blackness of unmined lead; where light, a cloud shimmering in the reflection of a new moon; where dry, the bottom of a disused well; where moist, like dew on the tip of a new spring branch. The frame of the character was lean as steel, the intricate corners delicate as carved jade. Within its power reposed a deep sense of calm, out of its strength a careless grace emerged. Here was a gaze direct yet mysterious, a beauty conscious of itself yet unimpressed by the attention it drew.

The two officials were overjoyed. The minute the ink was dry they picked up their treasure and left with overwhelming gratitude.

It was only now that Lin brought up the subject of Jane's intention to become an opera singer.

Zai thought for a moment and said: 'Female liberation is in the air. Even the Health Department has just issued an edict for women to unbind their feet. In Shanghai there is already an opera company featuring women only. These are changing times and perhaps Miss Jane's ambitions are not totally out of reach. What I worry about is whether or not she could put up with the hardship of an actor's life. This young lady has been raised like a beautiful flower in comfortable surroundings. How is she to endure such tough regimes? Miss Jane, first you must realize that most actors come from ordinary families, and usually end up on stage because their parents cannot feed them. Secondly, historically speaking, actors are not unlike prostitutes in one respect – once you have entered the profession it is almost impossible ever to extricate yourself. All day long you will be in the company of actors – not only are your parents likely to object, you yourself might find it limiting after a while and begin to regret your decision.'

'Master Zai, I love the opera. I want nothing else from life and I am willing to take the consequences. If you would only give me some guidance I would be grateful to you forever. Please indulge my sincere request.' At these words Jane dropped to her knees and bowed low to the floor.

Zai helped her up at once and sighed. 'I can see that your mind is made up. In that case we must think carefully where best to send you.'

Zai allowed himself a moment's thought: 'How about the Shiao Yang Troupe? The director of the company, Yang Tien, is a good friend of mine. He is a reliable man and I would not be so worried if I knew that he was looking after Miss Jane.'

'The actor from Shanghai?' Lin asked. 'I hear he is as famous as can be in the south, but that this is the first time he has come to Beijing. Perhaps he means to conquer the capital as well!'

'That is indeed the man I refer to. He is the prized and only pupil of the actor Hong Fang To. His martial arts skills are quite incomparable. Unusually he is also blessed with an excellent singing voice. Yang is one of those rare actors who can tackle both disciplines with equal accomplishment.' Zai continued, 'When I was in Shanghai I saw some dozen operas in his repertoire and I said to him at the time, "To be the best in Shanghai is not enough. You must have the courage to conquer Beijing. Beijing is like a dragon, Tientsin, a tiger. Until you can ride the dragon and subdue the tiger you have not reached the pinnacle of the opera profession." In fact he was here last year to "steal" from us. He must have seen more than eighty operas and stayed here with me for four months. He loved to talk late into the night. Yang thinks that midnight is the witching hour when all the spirits of heaven and earth congregate. Everything becomes clear to him at midnight. He wrote to me recently, asking me to draw up a plan for his visit.'

'That's perfect,' said Lin. 'I wonder when he is thinking of making his dèbut?'

Zai replied, 'It is not yet decided. Yang is not only hugely talented but also very ambitious. He is not like the average actor. All this time he has been quietly putting a company together. It would appear that he is not concerned with making a big splash overnight. He would rather start small, learn slowly and establish his reputation in time. This way he can build a solid foundation. Here is a man who has thought carefully about how to shape his career. If Miss Jane were to train under his auspices, her future will be assured.'

Jane found it hard to contain her excitement. She knelt down again and bowing her head all the way to the floor she said: 'Thank you, Master Zai, Master Lin!' She did not know what more to say, so the young English girl kow-towed to the two Chinese masters three more times...

Translated by Carolyn Choa

Cheng Nai-shan

Hong Taitai

Everybody called her Hong Taitai.* Fifty years ago that name was celebrated throughout Shanghai society. A party marking a baby's first month of life, a wedding banquet or a birthday all fell short of perfection if Hong Taitai was not in attendance. There was a period after 1949 when the words 'Hong Taitai' seemed redolent of mothballs, as if they had been shaken from a camphorwood chest. But within the circle of the few rich families in Shanghai, for example, they still carried a good deal of weight right up until the 'great proletarian cultural revolution' of the 1960s. In Shanghai, one had one's own little circle of happiness. And no matter how the storms raged outside, as long as one had three meals a day and stuck to one's own affairs, and thanks to the government policy of buying out the bourgeoisie, one could rest assured of eating at the Park Hotel today, the Maison Rouge or Jade Buddha Temple tomorrow. No one would interfere. It was a very active period for Hong Taitai. The managers of both the public and private sections of the big restaurants and hotels all knew her; she was a very warm person. If Hong Taitai came forward to do the honours for a banquet on some special occasion, it would be reasonably priced, but ample. And the food would be something special, quite out of the ordinary.

My first impression of her dates from my tenth birthday.

* Taitai is the traditional term for Mrs or wife, which fell into disuse after 1949 for being considered a very bourgeois title and was severely discouraged during the 'cultural revolution'. The Chinese term is retained here, rather than replaced with the English 'Mrs' to call attention to this connotation which the term 'Mrs' lacks.

I was the ninth child in the family, nicknamed 'Jiujiu', or 'Little Ninth'. My parents were in America. When they left they had been afraid that I was too small to make such a long trip and would be in the way. Then the situation had changed, unexpectedly and so greatly, and I was left behind in Shanghai for good to live with my eldest brother and his wife. My brother was twenty-one years older than I and often joked that he could have fathered a child my age. He did spoil me as if I were his own daughter. Fatherliness in an eldest brother has always been the Chinese way.

The day of my tenth birthday they did things up a bit on my account, though it was nothing more than noodles and a few dishes. In those days my brother and sister-in-law were rather careful of appearances. They couldn't have competed with Hong Taitai at any rate; she was the wife of a bourgeois. Brother and his wife, no matter what, were subject to their work units, and they had to be careful. So they did no more than invite the brothers and sisters still in Shanghai over for an ordinary family dinner.

We had just sat down – we hadn't even got around to pouring the wine – when there was a knock at the door, and a voice, vivacious and sweet, was heard, 'I've come to beg a bowl of birthday noodles.'

'It's Hong Taitai!' My sister-in-law gasped, startled, and pushing back her chair she fled into her room to change her dress.

'That's how thoughtful she is.' My brother hastened to open the door; sisters and sisters-in-law busied themselves getting an extra bowl and chopsticks, bustling and rushing about. Thinking back on it now, this Hong Taitai's entrance into my life was strangely like that of the domineering Wang Xifeng in *A Dream of Red Mansions* who always announced her arrival on to the scene with some arresting remark like: 'So sorry I'm late welcoming visitors from afar!' The exact words were different, but the effect was the same. Her voice was so confident and hearty; she had an air of being completely at home.

'Hong Taitai!' The family stood to greet her.

'Ah, I made it on time,' Hong Taitai said, removing her white kidskin gloves. She wore a square of checked wool on her head, the ends so long they fluttered with her every movement, adding immensely to her charm. When she took off her full-length cashmere coat, she was wearing a claret-coloured *qipao** underneath, a phoenix embroidered in gold thread down the front, dazzling in its brilliance. In the 1950s such elegance had become a rare sight for anyone, let alone a child such as myself who had as yet seen nothing of the world. This sudden manifestation of such a gorgeously dressed beauty took my breath away.

She sat down next to me and pressed a red envelope into my hand. There was a shining golden character glued to the envelope – longevity – but because it was in the traditional, complicated form, it took me a moment to recognize it. At that time such red envelopes, used for giving presents of money to children on special occasions, were no longer on sale. Hong Taitai said she had glued it together herself out of red paper; the character was also her own handiwork.

'Hong Taitai, really, you shouldn't put yourself out of pocket over Jiujiu's birthday. She's a child.' My sister-in-law had changed and come back out, and though she was much younger than Hong Taitai, she looked faded beside her. The only thing one noticed in that whole room was that brilliant combination of red and gold: dazzling, but pleasingly so!

'Mr Hong and I are old friends of your parents. I went to see Jiujiu at the hospital the day she was born. She was so alert and bright-eyed, such personality, not like most babies. When the nurse brought you in you were as pink as a glutinous rice dumpling.' She described it vividly, and I was enthralled.

'At first your parents planned to come for you after a while, but now look... They must miss you terribly. I pity you that your mother

---

* Traditional high-necked, close-fitting Chinese dress.

isn't here. So though I pay no attention when one of your brothers or sisters has a birthday, Jiujiu is different; I have to come to celebrate your tenth birthday, to stand in for your mother and raise a glass to you, wishing you long life!' Her words warmed my heart.

After the meal, my brothers and sisters put on some music, *A Rose for You*, a Xinjiang folk-song quite popular at the time, and the brothers and brothers-in-law all surged toward Hong Taitai. But she frowned, and with a graceful flick of the hand in which she held a cigarette, said, 'Put on Bing Crosby. Us old folks like the old songs.' When that bewitching voice was heard, she laid aside her cigarette and began, tripping lightly, to dance. As she danced, the side slits in that claret *qipao* rose and fell, now hiding, now revealing her graceful legs. I really hoped I might grow up a bit faster and be all that she was: full of life, charming, beautiful.

When all the guests had gone, I took out the red envelope she had given me and counted: forty yuan! Forty yuan in those days!

'A grand gesture. Mr Hong is the only one who could afford her,' Sister-in-law said, pouting her lower lip. 'What a memory she has. How could she remember Jiujiu's birthday, let alone that it was her tenth!'

'That's her stock-in-trade.' Having said that, brother added sympathically, 'Her lot is a hard one, too. If she'd been born into a good family and got an education, she'd certainly have done well, an intelligent person like that.'

Only later did I find out that Mr Hong was in the raw silk business and when Mrs Hong took up with him, he was already quite successful. He had a wife and family, but he rented a small house in the western district of Shanghai and lived there with Hong Taitai. She it was he took everywhere with him, thus in everybody's mind, she was 'Hong Taitai'. But there was talk, both out in the open and on the sly, some of it not very complimentary. As for the true facts of Hong Taitai's background, no one was able to find out. Even the Hongs' housemaid, Ah Ju, knew only that one night, carrying a white leather bag, she had arrived with Mr Hong and had been there ever since. It was said that Hong Taitai was a good cook, and Mr Hong had grown pink and stout under her care. Almost overnight she became well-known; Mei Lanfang* and Zhou Xuan† both were guests in the Hong family parlour. For a time, the house was filled with important guests every day. It seemed that this Hong Taitai had 'arrived' in society the same way – a white leather bag in hand. And with her arrival, Mr Hong's business expanded.

My second meeting with Hong Taitai occurred while I was in senior middle school, at Mr Hong's memorial service. Elder Brother was the natural representative of our family, he took me along on the strength of my having been the recipient of Mr Hong's forty-yuan birthday gift. The service was held at the International Funeral Home. There were leading comrades from both the Chinese People's Political Consultative Conference and the Association of Industry and Commerce present. As we entered, I saw Hong Taitai dressed in a black taffeta *qipao* with close-fitting sleeves, wearing a pair of the black leather pointed-toe shoes that were extremely popular in the sixties. Though there were indications that she was putting on weight, her graceful waist made her appear as lovely as ever. She walked composedly among those who had come to pay their condolences, greeting those who ought to be greeted, nodding to those who needed nodding to. The grief weighing on her made her seem even more dignified and noble. On the hairnet holding the thick tresses was a spray of pure white orchids, giving her a very refined air. As soon as her glance fell on us, she hurried to greet us.

'Jiujiu, you've become a young lady.' Her gentle voice dispelled the dread I felt in this venue of eternal parting. 'You're the next generation. Wear a yellow flower.'‡ Her soft white hand fastened the yellow bloom

---

* A Beijing opera star.
† A popular film star.
‡ Flowers, real or artificial, are worn as symbols of mourning.

to my blouse. She began to speak of all Mr Hong's good qualities, and as she spoke she grew sad and dabbed at the tears in the corners of her eyes with a flaxen handkerchief. By comparison with the main wife, weeping and wailing to one side, she appeared to be more highly bred, more worthy of the title Mrs. Yet in the end it was mere similitude, for when the formalities began, she conscientiously peeled off to one side, a mourner who knew her place.

'Hong Taitai will suffer now! This is really difficult for her!' the other mourners commented surreptitiously among themselves.

'Yes, Mr Hong was a man among men. But was he willing to entrust the family property to Hong Taitai? Naturally, it was safer with his wife. With him gone, Hong Taitai is left with nothing, not even a last word. It's hard for her.'

Hearing such talk, looking at the lovely black-garbed Hong Taitai, I thought of Chen Bailu in Cao Yu's play, *Sunrise*.

Once Mr Hong died, we saw little of Hong Taitai. In the adult's eyes, she was, after all, a woman of uncertain past!

In a twinkling, I was twenty years old. The celebration was still a family affair. Recalling the gaiety of ten years ago, I couldn't help thinking of Hong Taitai. I accused Elder Brother of being a snob, but he said I was naive. As we locked horns, there was a soft knocking at the door. It was Hong Taitai's maid, Ah Ju, a woman about thirty years old from Shaoxing. She was carrying a red-lacquered tray which held a specially prepared duck. Attached to the duck was a glittering gold *shou* character – longevity – exactly like the one I had received ten years before.

'Hong Taitai's indisposed, so she sent me to convey her best wishes to Jiujiu. She prepared the duck herself,' Ah Ju rattled off as instructed. One could see she had learned it by heart before she came. Everyone asked after Hong Taitai, and Ah Ju stammered. 'The house has been let out. Hong Taitai has a second-floor room with a balcony and a room on the first floor for me and the kitchen. It's enough for the two of us; it's fine, just fine. Goodbye now.' With that she made her escape.

Everybody began to inspect the duck. It lacked nothing in appearance, fragrance or flavour. It was then the three hard years of natural calamities. A duck such as this one would cost at least ten yuan on the black market. At the same time that we were saying what a crime it was to eat Hong Taitai's food, we were all scrutinizing the duck. It was lean. It was quite possible that it was one Ah Ju had stood in line all night to buy, in which case it wouldn't have cost much more than two yuan. Since it had been personally cooked and sent over specially, it seemed to be worth much more than that. But the gift was small after all, so she didn't appear in person. 'She's a very capable woman!' everyone agreed.

Not long after, the tempest* blew up in 1966 and people could hardly fend for themselves, much less worry about Hong Taitai.

Two years passed and things became relatively quiet. I happened to be walking by Hong Taitai's one day, and looking up at her balcony without thinking, I suddenly spied the old familiar curtain fabric. Spurred by this, I headed upstairs. A young man wearing a work overall with 'work safely' printed on it barred my way and asked in a rough manner, 'Who are you? Who are you looking for?'

'I'm looking for Hong Taitai,' I stammered out. I regretted that as soon as it was out. To call someone 'taitai' in those days was to invite criticism.

Unexpectedly, he sang out, 'Hong Taitai, someone to see you,' and led me upstairs.

'Jiujiu!' Hong Taitai welcomed me with surprise and pleasure and wiped away tears, moved. How rare in those days, a genuine sigh and embrace. I leaned against her bosom and cried.

The room was still furnished with French-style furniture. The

---

* The 'cultural revolution'.

mirror was covered with pictures of leaders, the best method of protecting mirrors in those days. Ah Ju brought tea, and I had just said, 'Thank you, Ah Ju,' when Hong Taitai corrected me softly, 'Call her Sister Ah Ju. I've adopted her. That man on the stairs was Ah Ju's husband.'

Hong Taitai was wearing a blue Chinese-style cotton jacket. With her hair cut short, in revolutionary fashion, she looked much like someone who would be principal of an elementary school.

'Thanks to their moving in with me, no one dares bother me. The house was ransacked till there was not even one yuan left and I was half-dead myself. As I was crying over it, Ah Ju came and said we should bring her man to live with us; he was a worker and no one would dare bully me then. I said I didn't want to involve them in my troubles, but she said, "Anyway I'm a servant. Even if worst came to worst I'd still be a servant. I'm not afraid." I'm so grateful to Ah Ju and her family!'

'Hong Taitai,' Sister Ah Ju cut her short, embarrassed.

'I've told you before, don't call me Hong Taitai. Call me mother.'

'Ah.' Ah Ju laughed ingenuously. 'I can't do it. I'm not used to it.'

'I get only eighteen yuan a month for living expenses, so I have to depend on the two of them to take care of me, and they have two children of their own.' Hong Taitai sighed deeply. 'Ai, how could I have come to this! If I had only gone out to work earlier on, I wouldn't have got into this predicament, no income at all!'

Hong Taitai kept me on to dinner. She hadn't been able to break that habit. With Ah Ju, her husband and their two lovely innocent daughters, plus Hong Taitai and myself, there were six gathered round the square table. It was a home-style meal of two dishes and a soup with an additional plate of scrambled eggs in my honour. The bluish glow of the eight-watt fluorescent tube shone gently on us. Hong Taitai now and again put some food into the children's bowls with her chopsticks, very grandmotherly. I thought I heard them call her

'Nanna', and I found it very strange. 'They mean mother's mother,' Hong Taitai explained. 'I like them to call me that.' The children, seeing their opportunity, purposely raised a chorus of 'Nanna', and Hong Taitai beamed. I sensed that she had never before laughed so contentedly. Her son-in-law stolidly scooped in his food without saying a word. But when I was taking my leave he dashed ahead turning on the stairway lights all the way down. 'My son-in-law hasn't any education; he's a bit rough, but he's a very good man,' Hong Taitai told me softly. 'There's no need to be afraid of him.'

When I got back and told my brother and sister-in-law what had happened, they expressed great admiration for Hong Taitai. 'That Hong Taitai, she can take the bad with the good. What an incredibly capable woman!'

Later I got married. Tied down to housework and child, I hardly made the effort to see my brother and sister-in-law, let alone Hong Taitai.

In 1982, my parents made their first visit back to Shanghai from the US. All the old friends gathered; and of course Hong Taitai was invited as well. During the 'cultural revolution' many of them had lost touch with each other, and they were glad to renew relationships, but though it grew quite late, Hong Taitai still didn't appear.

'Where's Hong Taitai? We're waiting for her reappearance in society.'

'Ah, didn't you know, she's a famous slowpoke.'

Just as we were really growing anxious, she arrived, accompanied by Ah Ju. She was wearing a downy mohair coat over a close-fitting black satin jacket, and though her hair was raven black, you could tell it had been dyed. Yes, she had aged some, but she was as graceful and refined as ever. The company rose to greet her, but she pushed Ah Ju forward. 'My adopted daughter.'

When it came time to eat, no place had been set for Ah Ju.

'Ah Ju, go out and have a bowl of noodles and come back for Hong Taitai in two hours,' we suggested.

'Just squeeze together a bit.' Hong Taitai pulled Ah Ju to the table and asked the waiter to bring another bowl and chopsticks. The others were rather startled; the atmosphere grew somewhat embarrassed. Though society as a whole had changed, such circles still clung to iron-clad rules. Before all the hot dishes had been served, Hong Taitai got up to leave, saying she had something to do.

The gathering fell to discussing her.

'How could she take a servant into the family? She must be crazy!'

'Well, it's not so surprising. Her own background is more or less the same.'

'That's what happens when one lives with servants. You become petty and overlook etiquette.'

These dreadful comments, served up with the food and drink, dropped airily from their mouths. I hastily gathered up my child and left.

A few days ago, a woman friend of mine moved by chance to a place in Hong Taitai's lane, and I dropped by to see her since I was in the neighbourhood.

She welcomed me happily. 'Jiujiu's come!' Her silver hair made her look kinder than ever. She said she no longer dyed it. 'I'm getting old, and it doesn't turn out well any more,' she said, patting her hair. Sister Ah Ju politely brought tea and sweets for me.

'Jiujiu thinks of me. Of the old crowd, you're the only one who thinks of coming to see me. How big is your son now?'

'Ten.' As I said it, I remembered my own tenth birthday and told her how struck I had been by her beauty.

She smiled wanly. 'That's past.'

She told me that in the beginning a few old friends still came to see her. Now everything was back to normal after the 'cultural revolution'. There were even mah-jong parties and dancing, but she was done with it all because her stiff old legs couldn't manage it now.

'Actually it's all a waste of money and time. Ah Ju is so busy. I can't do much to help her, but I can knit a few sweaters, to thank her for being so good to me. They're extremely frugal themselves, but they know my delicate appetite, and there's always one dish especially for me at each meal. There aren't many daughters – even natural-born ones – like that.' She touched my sleeve, speaking emotionally, while her hands never ceased their work on the small sweater she was knitting.

'Mother Hong, what are you making?' A passing neighbour stopped in.

'My granddaughter's having her baby any day now. I'm knitting it a little sweater.'

'Well! The fourth generation! You're very lucky, Mother Hong!'

'Yes, I am,' Hong Taitai replied contentedly, and she smiled.

Translated by Janice Wickeri

Shi Tie-sheng

Fate

1

Now to talk about myself: to talk about why, because I was one second late, or because I was unable to be one second later – you might also say because I was one second early, or could not manage to be one second earlier – I became a lifetime paraplegic. According to my prognosis prior to that one second, from whatever angle I looked at it, I should have had quite a beautiful future.

Prior to that one second, about thirteen people had already offered me eighteen marriage proposals, eleven of them sending along photographs, of the young women, and all eleven of them were very pretty. This may, to some extent, explain why I have been confident in my 'beautiful future'. But I wasn't thinking about marriage at the time; my ambition was much greater. 'No,' I said, 'I'm not thinking of such things now.' My erstwhile matchmakers were not without regret. They said, 'Mo Fei (Mo Fei is my name), we want to see what kind of a goddess you marry.'

Later on that one second arrived. Later on that one second passed. My once strong and healthy legs were instantly transformed into two sticks of useless furniture; they withered day by day into two sticks of exceedingly ugly furniture. All this meant that cruelty and misfortune had taken a fancy to a man named Mo Fei and clung to him for the rest of his life. I cried like a baby for several years and then, having absolutely no alternative, was reduced to a man who writes fiction for a living.

A woman reporter once asked me how I happened 'to take the road of creativity?' I thought for some time before replying. 'Having reached an utter dead end, I sank to this level.' The woman smiled so charmingly. 'You're really modest.' She really said so.

2

Practical reality has nothing to do with modesty.

Who knows, maybe those half-understood, half-real, half-illusory recollections of Tenth Uncle were originally premonitions from my childhood. They say children's eyes can penetrate to the bottom of many mysterious things and events, but grown-ups lose that ability.

All that is, of course, unimportant. What is important is that my legs cannot move and have no feeling; this is not a half-understood, half-real, half-illusory recollection; it's a crystal clear, absolutely indubitable reality. And from the looks of it this reality will remain a reality as long as I go on living.

I never used to curse people. I now feel the absolute necessity of all the curses ever invented in the world. A necessity, they are, and sometimes even a necessary conclusion.

3

It was only an accident of one second's duration. To talk about it now is of little interest. It was a summer night, cloudy; the moon was pale, the stars few, and pedestrians were already very scarce. A night soil cart came by mingling the rich perfume of night soil with the sweet scent of evening dew – a rare odour. I was riding my bike home, so happy that I had naturally begun whistling a tune. I was whistling the famous pedlar's aria from *The Pedlar and the Maiden*. I had just been to the opera. I really believed my luck was pretty good. I was soon to go abroad to study; my thoughts were concentrated on that, on the other side of the world; not just on that side, of course; the world is very large. My wallet was already crammed full with my passport, visa, plane ticket, and a wad of related documents – the fruits of one year and eleven months of difficult struggle. This wallet was firmly attached to my belt; unless somebody ripped off my trousers, it would be quite impossible to lose it. May the designer of this wallet be richly rewarded in this life and the next – that's what I was thinking at the time. The temperature fell gradually and a slightly cool breeze began to blow. In the buildings along the road someone was cursing loudly while another one was softly playing a nocturne by Chopin. The out-of-town street vendors were spreading their baggage out in the shadows, yawning broadly, making a racket as loud as an ancient nightwatchman's.

An ordinary summer night. I whistled a tune. The world is very large. I think I'll go to visit the Grand Canyon in Arizona on one of my vacations, and Niagara Falls on another. If I earn a little extra money and live very frugally most of the time, maybe I can also go to Egypt and visit the Great Pyramid of Cheops; to Venice to see St Mark's Cathedral; to the Louvre in Paris, the Tower of London, Mount Fuji in Japan, and the wild game reserve in Tanzania … I will see them all; it's such a rare opportunity. I'm full of energy and as sturdy as any camel; I could even walk across the Sahara Desert and go camping at the foot of Mount Kilimanjaro. I wouldn't shoot the lions, though, those wonderful lions.

I whistled a tune, not very well, but that tune was so moving. I don't believe in asceticism. Mo Fei is not an ascetic; he will surely have to have a wife. She'll be very pretty and kind-hearted, very intelligent, very healthy, very romantic and generous, very gentle and tender, and she'll love me very much; when we're alone she'll just naturally think of an infinite number of amazing little loving names to call me.

Compared to her I'll regard everything else in the world as light as a feather, but in comparison to her I'll probably seem stupid and clumsy, only able to call her dear, or my dearest, making her so angry she'll give me an extraordinarily loving slap on the face. A real man should have at least one opportunity to demonstrate his weakness. Afterwards he will not, however, feel that his 'heroic ambition' has been undermined; quite the contrary, he'll be even more outstanding in the future and make his wife proud for the rest of her life! A pleasantly cool summer evening arouses a person's emotions, makes his thoughts run riot in praise of the beauty of all creation.

Prior to that one second you could rightly say that Mo Fei was not dreaming. I rode my bike and whistled that pedlar's tune. I was figuring how I'd return home after four years with my Ph. D. and work for our ancestral homeland. I would never be 'so happy I forgot my home in Shu,' as the proverb goes – Mo Fei was not that sort – Heaven and Earth are my witnesses, you know what I was going abroad to study? Education. Our country's education is in urgent need of reform and talented people to bring it about. Mo Fei didn't lack the ability to study astrophysics or genetic engineering, but Mo Fei had his heart set on his country's education – right up to that one second I had been teaching in a middle school.

I turned my bike into a rather narrow street; I had to take this road to get home; the shadows of the trees were dancing across the road surface – later on it will be proven that the dancing of these tree shadows may rightly be compared to someone being cut to pieces by a thousand knife blades.

I was still whistling. I was an innocent person. I thought when I return in four years I can have a son (of course I have to have a wife first) or maybe a daughter; if government policy permitted it I could have a son and a daughter; I didn't even consider which should come first and which second – I think men and women should be equal – and only hoped my son would look like me and my daughter like her mother, only hoped the reverse would certainly not be the case. Was it wrong to think that way? I can't see what was wrong with that. I was an innocent person on that summer night and all the time prior to that summer night. I was an innocent person. Innocent, without sin, at least that is true.

I whistled that most celebrated tune from *The Pedlar and the Maiden* and rode my bike closer and closer to that ultimately evil second. At the same moment a young taxi driver whom I was fated to meet was also hurrying speedily toward that one second.

4

In the general scheme of things that was a totally unimpressive summer night; or would have been if someone had not dropped an aubergine on the street. I was whistling that pedlar's tune when my bike wheels ran over that aubergine; afterwards I knew that the aubergine was very large, very slippery, and very hard; this aubergine caused my wheels to swerve violently to the left, the shock threw me two or three metres ahead, propelling me directly into what had to happen in that one second. I heard the loud screeching of a car braking and my good luck came to an abrupt end. All the wonderful things mentioned in this story so far were transmuted into a heap of nonsense. They would remain forever a dream.

There could have been an end to it then and there – the problem is it didn't kill me outright, but only snapped my spinal cord in two. After that everything simply vanished into thin air, vanished into thin air like smoke and clouds, and after the smoke and clouds vanished, the world turned around and showed me its utterly inhuman backside – I mean showed it to me, to Mo Fei.

5

I often recalled later a battery-powered toy hen running animatedly along the ground until it ran into a pebble, turned a somersault, landed on its feet again and kept right on running animatedly forward, only its direction was completely reversed (it probably turned one revolution forward with a one hundred and eighty degree twist).

6

I lay in the middle of the road. When I tried to roll over and stand up I couldn't. That young taxi driver mentioned above ran over and asked me how I felt. I said I felt pretty strange, like I better rest a minute. Then the driver took me to the hospital.

I asked the doctor, 'When will I be well? I'm going abroad soon and don't have much time to waste.' The doctor and the nurses grew very still; I thought they didn't understand what I meant. They stripped me and took me to the operating room; I told them to watch out carefully for the wallet on my belt; I even told them the date on my plane ticket. A woman nurse said, 'Aiya, look what time it is!' I thought to myself it really isn't too early; I said, 'It really isn't too early, but I'm here for an emergency treatment.' The woman nurse stared at me without moving for half a minute. Then I realized they could not understand me in such a short time, could not understand my ambition of many years and the course of my laborious struggle, could not understand the hardship I had gone through in the past one year and eleven months either, and thus could not possibly understand what that wallet meant to me. I encouraged the doctor not to tremble but to work as boldly as possible; if I, Mo Fei, let out one peep then it just wasn't me. The doctor gripped my hand and said, 'I hope from now on you can always maintain your present courage.' At the time I didn't understand his unspoken message.

7

The true situation was soon apparent: I had already been planted in a sick bed, like a 'perennial' sprig of ivy that's been planted in a flowerpot. As far as that sprig of ivy is concerned, right up until the day it dies its entire world will consist only of a flowerpot, the corner of a wall, or a thin strip of sky. I'm a little better off than it is. Mo Fei's a little better off than it is. 'Mo Fei, we certainly want to see what sort of a goddess you marry' – that kind of a Mo Fei, he's better off than a perennial ivy plant. At the thought I looked up and wailed unconsolably; I sounded just as though I'd returned to my childhood and I looked like nothing more than a great big fool.

I have an elder sister; she hurried to my side from far away, held me tightly in her arms and called out my childhood name just like when I was little: 'Hush now, don't worry, don't worry, don't do this, don't do this, no matter what, I'll take care of you all your life.' ('Don't cry, don't fuss, the grasshopper flew away, Sis will catch you another one tomorrow.') But this wasn't my childhood; the grasshopper didn't fly away; there wasn't even any grasshopper. A perfectly good spinal cord had flown away. I pushed my sister away, extracting my hand from her icy cold grip: 'Go away! Go away! Everybody leave me alone!' Sis held me close again, her strength suddenly grown extraordinarily great. I glanced up at the sun; it was still the same old sun. And the sky? It too was still up there above the earth.

Mother did not come, we didn't dare to let her know. Father was like a huge shadow lacking the power of speech; coming in without a sound, going out without a sound. He bought many good things to eat and set them on the table; then he went out and came in again without a sound and bought still more good things to eat and placed them on the edge of my bed. I screamed and Father started a moment and then moved out of the way. I knocked the flowerpot into the spittoon, threw the tea cups into the chamber pot, smashed my wristwatch and tossed it into the waste basket, swept everything within reach onto the floor and then I started to curse: with my hands behind my head, staring at the ceiling. I railed at the world as hard as I could, repeating every dirty word I knew several times, with tears streaming down until the day grew dark; then I was exhausted, my heart a useless shrivelled mass, pulp from a tree that had been rotting for a thousand years. I jabbed stealthily at my thigh; there was absolutely no feeling. I quickly pulled my hand away, afraid I had poked someone else. How the hell is this going to end? In the long, slow stillness, pigeons were cooing outside the window ... vast, empty, with seemingly no place to rest in heaven or on earth.

How is this going to end? No one was willing to tell Mo Fei.

8

A policeman explained the accident to me. That young driver was not at fault. 'No one could have anticipated that you would swerve into the centre of the road so suddenly. The driver wasn't speeding, he wasn't drunk, and he put on the brakes just in time; if he had put on the brakes one second later,' the policeman emphasized, 'forgive my bluntness, but you would be dead now.' I thanked him and he said there was no reason, it was his job to tell me what had happened. I asked him if I was in any way at fault. My sister said not to be rude. The officer said I was not at fault either. 'You were riding in the bicycle lane and keeping to the right; you're a good citizen who conscientiously respects the traffic rules, but nobody riding along would necessarily be watching out for an aubergine, and, besides, that stretch of road was very dark.' I said the shadows of the trees were dancing about the road.

'What's that you say? Right, there were many shadows from the trees; from the looks of the accident scene, you certainly did not deliberately run over that aubergine.'

'No kidding!?' I said, and my sister said, 'Mo Fei, really!'

The officer sighed. 'But you were tossed into the road just at the wrong time; if it had been one second earlier, the car would not have hit you. The doctor said the same thing: "Such an unfortunate coincidence, the spinal cord was snapped in two and nothing else was even injured."'

'The way you put it makes it sound like it was my fault.'

The officer said, 'I didn't say that. I just said the road was dark and it was understandable you didn't see that aubergine.'

'Then whose fault was it?'

'Mo Fei—!' exclaimed my sister.

I said, 'Sis, can't I even ask whose fault it was?'

'Comrade Mo Fei, that's an unreasonable request, and furthermore, you should watch your attitude toward an officer carrying out his duty,' said the officer.

'If that's the case,' I said, 'you have an obligation to explain to me who is ultimately at fault.'

'The aubergine,' said the officer. 'If you think it's a worthwhile question to ask, well then, that aubergine. Why did you have to run over it at that precise moment?'

9

The days just went on like that. All I saw every day was the morning and evening sun outside the window. The documents in my wallet were still there, silent as an ancient tomb preserving the records of innumerable heart-rending legends.

It is humanly impossible to re-attach a severed spinal cord, and so the days just went on like that. The medical college interns often came and stood around me while the teaching physician told them why I was a typical example of paraplegia: 'You see how robust the upper body is while the lower limbs are completely atrophied.'

The days just went on like that. My digestive system was astonishingly healthy, unhesitatingly taking in various kinds of fragrant things, which, when they reemerged, were all marvellously transformed into a uniformly smelly mass. The days just went on like that.

The sunflowers were harvested. The seeds fell from the tuberoses and were blown into the ground by the wind. The sky hung with kites for a few days, just for a few days, and then one by one they disappeared. The snow fell silently. Children ran about noisily in the snow chewing on fresh hot baked yams. I sighed. 'Ai, baked yams.' What I meant was the world really had not changed, baked yams were still the same old baked yams. My father's tall skinny shadow followed the sound haltingly across the snow in the direction of that yam vendor's charcoal stove...

The days just went on and on like that. Heaven above knew how unjust it was that Mo Fei should exist this way. I cried a while and thought a while, thought a while and cried a while; it seemed like that cop's final question was the only thing that made any sense.

10

Gradually I remembered. About two hundred metres from the accident site I had run into an acquaintance. I remembered: I was whistling that pedlar's aria when I saw him; he was fanning himself as he walked along the side of the road, and I shouted, 'Hey!' He looked around to see who it was and shouted, 'Oh!' I asked, 'Where are you going?' He said it was cool enough and he was going home to sleep. 'You coming over for a while?' He lived in a big apartment building about fifty metres away. I said, 'No, see you tomorrow, I'm going on.' We waved at each other and went our separate ways.

Although I did not get off my bike, I did squeeze the brakes while I was talking, no doubt about it, I did squeeze the brakes a little. How much time did I lose squeezing the brakes? One to five seconds. Right, if I had not wasted one to five seconds talking to him, then I would have run over that aubergine one to five seconds sooner. Of course, of course, the aubergine would no doubt have caused my bike wheels to swerve to the left and I would have sprawled out in the middle of the road as before, but everything that happened later would have been changed. When the driver of any car saw a fellow laid out in the middle of the road, no matter who he was, is it possible he would not stop? No. The car would have stopped. It would have been only one inch away from me but that would have been enough. Right now I would be at the Grand Canyon or some place else in the world and not planted in this sick bed. No. I would certainly not be planted in this sick bed. That old Mo Fei. That old Mo Fei whom everyone thought would marry a goddess.

11

Let me tell you another thing by the way. To this day there are still only thirteen people who have proposed marriage eighteen times to Mo Fei, and eleven of them have sent along a photograph. These three numbers will never increase, and they are a further indicator that today's Mo Fei is a totally different person from yesterday's Mo Fei.

Heaven and earth have been turned upside down and the human comedy has followed suit.

I have no other reason for saying all of this except to note that Mo Fei is completely innocent and without blame.

On the other hand, the young women are also quite innocent. It is not a young woman's fault if she wants to live a free, romantic, rich, full, and in short, perfectly wholesome life. It is not the fault of any young woman's parents that they want their son-in-law to be the pride and good fortune of their later years as he stands beside other people's sons-in-law. It can be deduced from analysis that the failure of these three numbers to ever increase is not any individual's fault; it is not my friends' fault, it is not anyone's fault. As sure as heaven is high and earth is thick, without question a donkey is bigger than a dog.

12

Mo Fei's suffering resulted from that one to five second delay.

We have to ask and we have every reason to ask: what was it that caused Mo Fei to meet up with that acquaintance about two hundred metres from the site of the accident?

At this point I again remembered something: somewhere between three and five minutes before I met that acquaintance, I ate a steamed bun at a little restaurant. I was hungry, not just greedy but genuinely hungry; when someone is hungry and he passes by a little restaurant, eating is a necessary action. If God punishes me on that account, then there's nothing I can say. I went into that little restaurant, got in line behind six other people, becoming the seventh person waiting in line to buy steamed buns. 'When will the steamed buns be ready?' I asked. The sixth person in the line told me, 'You came in at exactly the right time; they're about to come out of the steamer; I got here just when the last batch came out and I've been waiting half an hour already.' So I waited a while; I figured if I went home this late there would not be anything left to eat, and it was nine hours since I ate lunch.

The steamed buns were ready quite soon, and the old lady selling them counted them out onto the plates. Some of the first six people ate four *liang* and some bought five *jin* to take out; by the time it was my turn, the old lady said there was only one left. I looked into the basket and asked, 'Are there any more in the kitchen?' 'No,' said the old lady, 'just this one, do you want it?' I asked if she was going to steam any more, and she said tomorrow she'd steam some more, but that was it for today. I looked at the big clock on the wall: ten-thirty. So I ate that single steamed bun.

Now let's do a little calculating: if I had eaten five steamed buns (I originally intended to eat five) instead of just one, if it took two minutes to eat one, I would have left that little restaurant at least eight minutes later. At the time I met that acquaintance, you remember, he was on his way home and was only about fifty metres away from home; any normal person would certainly not take eight minutes to walk fifty metres. And he was quite normal; I can vouch for that. All this means if I had arrived a little earlier at the little restaurant and joined the line as the fifth or sixth person, I would certainly have eaten five steamed buns and would not have met up with that acquaintance. I would not have called to him, would not have said those few words to him, would not have had to squeeze the brakes a little, would not have wasted one to five seconds, and would not have had my spinal cord severed – today's Mo Fei would be on the other side of the world studying for his doctorate of education and not here, certainly not sitting in a wheelchair.

13

By now the problem is already rather clear. Please pay particular attention to the words of the sixth person in line at the little restaurant: he said he had already waited there for half an hour since the last batch of steamed buns came out. That means if I was unable to arrive at that little restaurant half an hour earlier, then I had to be the seventh in line, had to eat only one steamed bun, had to run into that acquaintance, had to waste one to five seconds, and had to have my spinal cord severed – today's Mo Fei would still be sitting in a wheelchair.

We have to believe that it was all fate. Why? Because the opera *The Pedlar and the Maiden* was over at exactly ten o'clock. No matter how close that little restaurant was to the theatre, and no matter how fast I rode my bike, I could not reach that little restaurant one half hour before ten-thirty. It's a question of simple arithmetic. This all means that at the moment I got on my bike to go to the opera God had already arranged Mo Fei's future for him. When you're doomed you're doomed.

14

Now let's see how God arranged it that Mo Fei should go to see that opera.

I said before that I had been teaching for some time at a middle school. The day of the accident I was supposed to get off at six-fifteen; that was the usual time, and we cannot see God's hand in that. The fourth afternoon section was my physics class; at exactly six-fifteen I promptly called out, 'Class dismissed!' The students filed out in a bunch, and I walked out, too. I went out into the yard to look for my bicycle; I was planning to go straight home; I was hoping to spend a little more time with my parents before I went abroad. Just then I heard a student ask me: 'Teacher, may I go home now?'; I suddenly remembered that I had sent this student out of the room as a punishment during the fourth section.

This is what happened. Half-way through the class, this student suddenly started laughing out loud. He was sitting in the back row next to the window; he was usually an extremely well-behaved student; sometimes I even wondered if he wasn't a little below average intelligence. I asked him to stand up. He stood up. I asked to explain why he was laughing. He put his head down and remained silent. 'OK,' I said, 'sit down and pay attention.' He sat down, but went on laughing. I asked him to stand up again. He stood up again. 'What's so funny?' He didn't speak. I could see from that he was trying very hard to restrain himself from laughing; he covered his mouth with his hand the way girls often do; I always suspected that his intelligence was on the low side. 'Sit down,' I said, 'and don't laugh any more.' He sat down again but was still unable to keep himself from laughing; the classroom order was breaking down as the more mischievous students took advantage of the situation to start laughing along with him. All I could do was ask him to leave the room. 'Please go outside and calm down,' I said, 'the rest of us cannot hear the lesson.' He walked out obediently. By the time class let out, I had just about forgotten him; I was certain at the very least he must have some sort of personality problem. The poor kid.

'You can go home now,' I said, 'but from now on pay attention to classroom discipline.' He started laughing again, went right on laughing. By this time I was getting a little angry. 'What's so damned funny anyway?' I questioned him like that for about twenty minutes with absolutely no success; he continued to laugh but refused to answer.

Just then our most respected old lady principal called me. 'Mo Fei, there's a ticket to the opera, do you want to see it?' I asked what was playing. '*The Pedlar and the Maiden*, you want to see it?'

'Why do you want to give it to me? Aren't you going?' She said she wanted very much to go, but she had just received a phone call from the Department of Education; she had to attend an emergency meeting. 'You want to see it or not?'

'OK,' I said, 'I'll go.'

I have already told you what happened after that.

15

After a while I was released from the hospital. The hospital is not far from our home. I sat in a wheelchair while my parents took turns pushing me along the street. The poplars were once again laden with blossoms, and far off in the clear blue sky some cuckoos were calling out 'sobitter, sobitter' – it gave me a feeling of estrangement from the world. The breeze blew and the birds' cries gradually faded into the distance. I heard someone calling me. 'Mo Fei, Mo Fei! Is that you Mo Fei?'

I said, 'That's right, it's me.' One of my female classmates at college was standing in front of me.

'How–, Mo Fei, what are you doing here?'

'Where do you think I should be?' I asked.

'Didn't you go overseas to study? What happened to you?'

'If you're asking me, then who should I ask?'

Her eyes opened wide as though she had just noticed my legs. 'How did it happen?'

'It's very simple; it's the easiest thing in the world.'

She blushed. I used to say that to her quite often in college when she could not figure out a math problem. My mother could not restrain her tears; she pulled my father over to stand some distance away.

'It was a question of five steamed buns,' I said, 'or one aubergine.' Then I told her the essentials of what had happened.

'Really–, really–, ai–!' she said.

'We have to recognize that it was my fate,' I said.

'Mo Fei, you mustn't think that; Mo Fei, you have to be strong.' Tears were streaming down her face. 'Mo Fei, you have to go on living.'

My far away sister said the same thing in her letters: 'You have to go on living.' Nobody said how long to 'go on living' meant; it must mean live until death, but who doesn't live until death? My sister said not to worry, that if she had only one loaf of bread, a quarter of it would be for me (the other three fourths would be for her, my brother-in-law, and my little nephew). But I was worried about a few things more important than bread, things that my kind and virtuous sister could never give. Thus I began to write fiction. And thus when that woman reporter interviewed me I told her I'd sunk to this level because I'd reached an utter dead end. Just like becoming an outlaw.

16

For many years now I've been secretly wondering why that student sitting in the back row had suddenly started laughing. That was the turning point in my life and fate. That kid certainly was a little stupid, but he laughed in such an unfathomably obscure manner, just like the profoundly mysterious workings of fate. Maybe children's eyes really do have clairvoyant powers of observation? I wonder what he saw at that time? I think if I could paint an accurate portrait of his laughing expression, I could then exhibit the God of Fate's true countenance for all of you to see.

If it had not been for that mysterious laugh, I could not have received a ticket to *The Pedlar and the Maiden*; and today Dr Mo Fei, Ph.D., would have long since returned home in fame and glory to live with his wife and a flock of children.

17

In those difficult years I started to enjoy sleeping. I placed enormous hopes in sleep; perhaps when I woke up the situation would have changed. Covered in cold sweat, I'd look at the stillness of my bedroom by moonlight and rejoice that it was only a nightmare; with my heart pounding under the covers, I'd kick my legs and rejoice that it was only a nightmare; the moon would go down, the street lights would go out, the alarm clock would go off, and I'd straighten up my luggage, walk out into the fresh air, and hurry to the airport in time to catch my plane . . .

People who have nightmares should be considered the luckiest people in the world – because they can wake up from them; in that way they are much more fortunate than people who never have nightmares.

Every time I woke up in those days; however, I discovered that I'd had a beautiful dream of waking up from a nightmare. Having a beautiful dream is the most deceitful thing in the world – because you have to wake up.

To wake up from a nightmare or to go on sleeping and having a beautiful dream, both of these are enjoyable. But in my case the situation was exactly the opposite.

After lying in bed for two years, I started to write fiction. This was in order to eat, to drink, to dress, to pay the rent, and also because this profession provides the same satisfaction as sleep, but it offers one advantage over sleep – freedom. If you want to wake up from a nightmare, then you wake up from a nightmare; if you want to sleep and have a beautiful dream, then you sleep and get it; you have complete freedom of control. Thus, although we once dwelled at opposite ends of the earth and were totally unacquainted, now as we wander the rivers and lakes together, fiction and I mutually sustain each other. It has nothing to do with modesty.

One day I finally met that student again; that student whom I always regarded as a little stupid. He read one of my stories in a magazine and rounded up a group of students from those days to pay me a visit. These children had all grown up, they had bristly beards, and two of them were about to be married. They were all quite happy laughing and talking and remembering things they'd done in the past. One of them said, 'Let's drink to Mr Mo's becoming a writer.' Then I remembered to ask that student, 'Why couldn't you stop laughing that day?' He still looked very sheepish and said it was nothing. I took another tack and asked him, 'What did you see then?'

'A dog,' he said.

'A dog? A dog made you laugh like that?'

He said, 'That dog...' when he got that far he started laughing again and couldn't stop, but finally he restrained himself and calmed down; he had grown up after all.

'That dog,' he continued, 'aimed right at the big slogan on the front gate of the school and farted; I heard it and I saw it; it was very loud but muffled.'

Nobody believed him; they said he probably heard it wrong, but then he asked me, 'Do you believe me, Mr Mo? I didn't hear it wrong, really, I didn't hear it wrong. It really was because of that dog's fart. Mr Mo, you believe me?'

After a long time I said I believed him. The expression on the boy's face was that of a prophet.

18

No matter what I'm doing these days I always hear that muffled sound pounding in my ears. It occupies my entire space and time, prolonged and unrelenting; and it will continue to shake Mo Fei's entire life with its prolonged and unrelenting vibration.

Why why why? Why did there have to be that muffled sound?

There is no why.

God said the world must have that muffled sound and that muffled sound came to pass; and God said it was good, and things simply came to pass; that was the evening and the morning; and thus were all of the days after the seventh day.

Translated by Michael S. Duke

Wang An-yi

Life in a Small Courtyard

Just as we returned from our tour, the new building of the Municipal Song and Dance Ensemble had at last been completed. Meanwhile, the houses in the old, small courtyard near the East Railway Station, which had originally been our headquarters, were now to be used as accommodation for our families. Moreover, it was rumoured that the station square was to be enlarged and our small courtyard was just within the limit of those houses marked for demolition. It meant that in the near future the authorities would reallocate us new living quarters. The future looked good.

Within a couple of days, the rehearsal hall, together with the small stage in the courtyard, had been divided into more than ten separate rooms; the building used for storing the sets was also divided into four rooms. Even the kitchen was transformed into two rooms. No reason to turn up your nose at our untidy small courtyard; it allowed some young couples to get married, and had also enabled a number of families of three generations crowded into a single room to separate. As a result, A'ping and I were given a room in the former rehearsal hall. Though it was by no means large, neither was it too small. When the new living quarters were allocated we would be able to get a small flat. Before long, all the rooms in the courtyard, except an eight-square-metre room beside the lavatory, were occupied. Thus, the housing problem of the Municipal Song and Dance Ensemble was, at last, solved. Even more, the two sunniest and biggest office rooms, which could be exchanged later for a suite of three rooms and a kitchen, were now being occupied by Huang Jian, the son of the director of the Cultural Bureau, and his wife Li Xiuwen, who were not members of our troupe.

Originally, these two rooms had been left vacant. Perhaps we all realized that such good rooms could not belong to us. Even if we had occupied them temporarily, we would sooner or later have had to move out. An inconvenience. Wiser to make a more modest choice from the very beginning. As was expected, a week later, Huang Jian and his wife had moved into the two best rooms in our courtyard.

On the first night, Xiuwen forcibly dragged me to her home. I stopped dead in my tracks at the door, unable to recognize our old office room. From the centre of its light blue ceiling hung a chandelier. A suite of natural-coloured wood-grain furniture appeared both simple and tasteful. A spring-mattressed bed was covered by a dark green and black rhombus-patterned bedspread. Over its head was a white wall light. Between a pair of small armchairs stood a floor lamp with an apple-green lampshade, casting a soft green circle of light on the floor. It was like a miracle.

The scene reminded me suddenly of the little room in which Xiuwen and I had lived together in the past. There, four beds had been placed side by side. The one nearest the wall had a bedspread made of handwoven cloth and a rattan suitcase at the side. It was Xiuwen's. Next to hers was mine. We had just been transferred from the countryside with a wage of eighteen yuan per month.

And now, wearing a pair of red thick-soled slippers, Xiuwen gracefully paced up and down the light green room. After turning on her large television set, she handed me a cup of milk and a dish of cakes. She had become prettier, almost enchanting. Of course, she had always been attractive. At first, she was a member of our chorus. Later on, due to some problem with her voice, she could no longer sing. The ensemble kept her as an announcer. When she first stood before the microphone, the audience whispered, commenting on her appearance. Huang Jian was one of her ardent admirers. However, Huang Jian's first love had not been Xiuwen but … How far my thoughts had drifted! I shook my head.

'Does the milk taste bad?' Xiuwen asked in amazement.

'Oh no, it's fine.' I awkwardly tried to gloss over my blunder. 'But, I don't really want it. I've just had supper.'

'Then, have some fruit?' Picking up a big pear from the fruit tray, she peeled it slowly with a stainless knife and cut it into slices, which she stuck on some toothpicks. She handed them to me.

'Your room's lovely!' I exclaimed sincerely, full of praise. I reached for a second slice of pear. I was not used to this dainty way of eating fruit. In the past, I could have gobbled down four large apples at one go, when the ensemble distributed fruit bought cheaply from an orchard. Xiuwen could devour even more than I. Now she merely nibbled at a slice.

'Although Huang Jian isn't from Shanghai, he has good taste. Whatever I like, he always tries his best to get for me.' Her smile was self-satisfied. 'I haven't seen your place yet! A'ping and you are both from Shanghai, so your home must be beautiful!'

'Some home! When we're on tour, our home goes with us.'

'That's true. You should try to change your job. Do you want to be a dancer all your life?'

'Of course not. When I'm too old to dance, the troupe will find something else for me to do.'

'Then it'll be too late. Look at me, I'm now working as a typist in the Cultural Bureau. It's an easy job. In fact, typists are badly needed in several other places too. Try to find some way to get transferred.'

'Easier said than done!' I sighed, reaching for my fourth slice of pear, and saying to myself, Who can compare with you? The daughter-in-law of the bureau director.

Suddenly the window was pushed open with a bang, as three little heads and six staring eyes emerged above the windowsill. Following their line of vision, I saw on television a fierce fight going on. Turning my head again, I recognized they were Jiang Mai's children. Having graduated from the Provincial Art College in 1967, Jiang Mai had joined us as a trombonist. Some said Jiang Mai had once been a stylish fellow, and there had been a number of young girls madly chasing after him. Carried away by this, he overdid things. His handsome looks quickly faded. All his girlfriends ditched him. When he was thirty, he finally found a young girl worker called Xiao Zhang, who agreed to marry him. Their domestic bliss was brief. Xiao Zhang insisted on having a daughter. But unfortunately, she gave birth to three sons in succession, and if our leader had not hinted enough is enough, she would surely have given birth to a fourth or fifth. Owing to their tight financial situation, the couple quarrelled and grumbled frequently. Though their neighbour for only a week, I was already accustomed to their constant bickering. You can't imagine how they sniped at each other!

Going over to the window, Xiuwen smiled at the three boys and invited them in. The children, however, were not used to such hospitality and shyly disappeared. I remembered how Xiuwen disliked being disturbed. On tour, when some of our colleagues brought their children with them and the kids cried or made a noise at night, Xiuwen would complain bitterly. Now, she had changed completely. How a comfortable life can improve one's tolerance of others!

Huang Jian returned. On seeing me, he halted, seemingly embarrassed, but quickly recovered his composure and went to wash his hands. Why be like that? Let bygones be bygones. Ever since he became friendly with Xiuwen, I had left him alone. But it seemed he still hated me. I often had a laugh over it. But now, I also felt somewhat uneasy. Before swallowing the last slice of pear, I stood up and hastily took my leave.

Passing a room that had originally been used as a dressing room, I heard someone saying, '... She's not pretty at all. Granted she has large eyes, yet they're expressionless. She has a high nose, but it's a snub one.' The speaker was Ren Jia, wife of Hai Ping. She was well known for her jealousy. Ren Jia was afraid her husband was too handsome and she was too plain. It made her very nervous, and that, in turn, made all of us very nervous too. One of her methods was to attack other girls. At this moment, I didn't know who she was going on about. Xiuwen's eyes were both large and beautiful. As for me, people said that my nose was high, but only A'ping considered that it was a bit retrousse. Was Ren Jia speaking about Xiuwen or me?

As I entered my 'Home', I saw A'ping ecstatically practicing conducting before a mirror. He used to talk a lot about music and poetry before our marriage. How I had been fascinated by such unworldly things!

*

The next morning, I saw Xiao Ji, a carpenter with the state design group, squatting at the entrance of the lavatory and brushing his teeth. I was puzzled. It took me three or four minutes to make it out. He must have moved into the small eight-square-metre room. Its door formed a right angle with that of the lavatory. But I had still no idea when he had moved in there. He hadn't made any noise. The stage design group of our ensemble was, as a matter of fact, regarded as the most unimportant section, and its carpenters were practically anonymous. Furthermore, Xiao Ji was, by nature, a simple, taciturn man. Nobody ever took any notice of him.

We were having breakfast when Xiao Ji stepped into our room. As he was a rare visitor, we stood up to welcome him. Smiling shyly, he handed us two packets of sweets. Waving his hand, A'ping said, 'No need for that!' Xiao Ji's face turned red. I realized what they meant and immediately took them, saying, 'Congratulations!' Xiao Ji turned and left, while A'ping was still saying, 'No need for that!' What an ass! Only after I had held them up for several minutes so that he could read the 'wedding sweets' printed on them, did he exclaim, 'Oh! he's got married!'

'You're such a nitwit!' I scolded.

This irritated him, so he explained, 'The change was too sudden. I wasn't prepared for it.'

I ignored him, but thought to myself that there was some truth in what he said. We were not prepared at all. There had not been the slightest warning. Xiao Ji always did things quietly. But, who was his bride?

Having finished our meal, we locked our door and went to fetch our bikes. Jiang Mai, Hai Ping and his wife also got theirs. We all glanced simultaneously at Xiao Ji's room. He was just locking the door. Beside him stood a young girl dressed in a purple jacket, with a dark grey scarf round her neck. Her braids were coiled up on top of her head. Her forehead and mouth were both very broad. She wore a pair of spectacles. They came over to us. Xiao Ji gave a nervous smile but the girl was relaxed and accepted our curious glances.

'She seems a very lively girl,' Old Jiang was the first to comment.

'Stands like an artist,' added A'ping.

'She's got a kind of dignity,' concluded Hai Ping. His remarks were usually accurate. I gazed at Ren Jia anxiously. She sneered. 'She looks too serious. Not sweet enough.' How harsh she was! I wondered whether she was also as exacting with her students.

'Their sweets were the cheap kind, so they can't be well off.' Old Jiang was always very sensitive about the question of prices, a result of his being hard up. I looked at him pityingly.

Having reached the ensemble's headquarters, I saw that the leaders were collecting money from everybody to buy presents for Xiao Ji and his bride. But the bridegroom was doing his utmost to stop them, declaring loudly that the reason why he hadn't breathed a word to anyone about the marriage was to save his colleagues spending their money. No one listened to him. It was a tradition that whenever anyone got married, we gave presents. It helped to make us feel like one big family.

I was chosen to give Xiao Ji the present from our group. Soon after supper, I went to his room.

The door was unlocked. I heard the sound of hammering from inside, so I knocked several times. There was no response. I pushed open the door and stepped into the room. Xiao Ji was nailing up a picture; there were already several lying here and there on the floor. The bride was hanging one on the wall. Three walls were already full of them, making the place look quite beautiful. Turning their heads at the same time, the newly-weds greeted me. 'Welcome! Sit down, please!'

But the only stool in the room was being stood on by the bride, so I had to sit on the edge of their bed.

Putting down his hammer, Xiao Ji went to make tea for me while his wife got down from the stool and hurried to bring me a dish of sweets. I looked around the room: only a table beside the bed, a kerosene stove, a pot and some enamelled bowls. With a dish of sweets in her hand, the bride came over to me, asking, 'Does our room seem very shabby?'

Should I nod or shake my head?

'But, actually, it isn't!' Pointing to the pictures, she went on. 'Look, we have magnolias, bamboos, mountains, rivers and the sun...'

Smiling, I turned to Xiao Ji and scolded him. 'Why don't you introduce her to me? I can't just call her "bride"!'

Before he could open his mouth, his wife said, 'Let me introduce myself. I'm Lian Zhu. I just graduated from the fine arts department of the provincial art college. I'm now working as a teacher in the first middle school.' She spoke the Beijing dialect with a strong provincial accent.

I then introduced myself. 'I'm Songsong, one of the dancers.'

'Were you an educated youth from Shanghai?'

I nodded my head. I gazed at her. The more I looked at her, the more I felt Ren Jia's remarks were unfair. In fact, Lian Zhu was very charming. It was just that she rarely smiled.

'I'm from the seaside.'

I chuckled, drawn to her more and more. I realized from her accent that she came from the area around the port of Lianyun.

An outburst of noisy quarrelling interrupted us. Amazed, Lian Zhu stood up and walked toward the door. Xiao Ji and I followed her. I told her, 'You'll get used to it after a week.'

Opening the door, I spotted the shadow of someone moving toward us from the darkness and calling my name. It was Xiuwen! I remembered that, although she had been living here for more than a week, she was still curious about each quarrel. She would listen to it, enquire what it was all about and then spread the news.

'Xiao Zhang sent Old Jiang to buy half a pound of meat, but Old Jiang bought a whole pound. Now they're at each other's throats. Listen, it's getting worse. Let's go upstairs and try to patch things up between them!' Her big eyes glistened with excitement. I was immediately aware that what she suggested was not so much aimed at patching things up but at watching the fun. Feeling disgusted, I remarked indifferently, 'No need. Let them sort it out themselves.' Although they had quarrelled for more than six or seven years, even fiercely, they had no wish to divorce.

Lian Zhu agreed. 'No couples want outsiders to interfere. Everyone has some self-respect.'

Turning her face to the bride, Xiuwen looked her up and down. She urged, 'Let's go and have a look at their room.' Grabbing me by the hand, she dragged me there.

All of a sudden, her room and furnishings emerged before my eyes. I tried to hold Xiuwen back, but she had already rushed inside and was standing in the centre of the almost empty room. She winked at me. Fearing that she might blurt out heaven knows what kind of criticism, I hastened to divert her attention.

'Are you going to watch television tonight?' I asked.

'Television?' She gazed at the bed on which lay two thin, old quilts, replying vaguely, 'It's silly to look at television every night.'

'What about listening to your cassette tapes?'

'You can't listen to the same music over and over again.'

'Where's Huang Jian?' I uttered the name I was unwilling to mention.

'Gone to have fun,' Xiuwen answered unhappily.

As it happened, Huang Jian's voice sounded in the yard. 'Xiuwen! Xiuwen!'

'He's come back. Go home quickly!' I pushed her, relieved that she would have to leave. She moved toward the door slowly, saying, 'We've nothing to talk about.'

Finally she left the room, and the noise of the quarrel in the upstairs room also died away.

Looking up, Lian Zhu enquired in a soft voice, 'Do they always quarrel?'

'Yes. They're often short of money.'

'Really?' Turning around, she stared at me and then at Xiao Ji. In spite of her thick glasses, I could still see a look of doubt in her eyes. That was natural. Newly-weds only thought about love. Love ... How had they fallen in love? I couldn't restrain my curiosity and asked them.

The corners of Lian Zhu's mouth moved slightly, until she gave a rare yet moving smile. She gazed at her husband, who smiled back at her. Who would ever have noticed that this silent young carpenter had eyes like deep pools?

'How we fell in love? Where to begin? ...' Lian Zhu felt embarrassed.

'Say whatever you like,' her husband encouraged her.

'Oh, it's very simple,' Lian Zhu began at last.

'No, it's very complicated, in fact,' the young man countered.

'We waited and waited. Shortly after we had been transferred here from the countryside, I went to study at college. He had to wait again until my graduation. It was always wait, wait. What about you?' Having nothing more to say, Lian Zhu launched into a counterattack.

'Oh, we're an old married couple now.'

'Nonsense! You're the same age as I. Twenty-nine, right?'

'Twenty-eight. It was really nothing special. He just kept pestering me with poems and music.'

'And you didn't chase after him?'

'No, of course not!'

'What?' Lian Zhu seemed sorry.

'Didn't you also send him a poem?' Xiao Ji suddenly asked.

'How do you know that?' I cried out.

'Oh, my dear Songsong!' Putting her arms round me, Lian Zhu giggled and soon I did too.

I sat there till after ten o'clock, then happily said goodnight. As soon as I reached my room, my joy evaporated. A'ping told me that the leader of our ensemble had just telephoned him to say that rehearsals would begin tomorrow and we would go on tour again the following Monday. I refused at once. 'I won't go!'

Putting down his pen, A'ping stood up and reached out his hand to console me. I pushed him aside, walking toward the bed. 'I won't go! Why should we go again? We only came back two weeks ago! I won't go!' I threw myself face down on the bed. To go on tour meant packing in a hurry, loading and unloading our luggage, setting cold stages and living together in a big room with many of our colleagues ... I was on the verge of tears.

Coming over to me, A'ping embraced me and said comfortingly, 'I'll be there to help you ... Fill your hot water bottle.'

'Is that all you can say?' I yelled angrily.

'What else do you want me to do?'

51

'I want you to get me transferred to another job. I don't want to dance any longer. I need a stable life, a settled home. I want ... I want a baby!' The tears ran down my cheeks. Xiuwen's comfortable room appeared before my eyes. Ah, how much I wanted...

Upset, A'ping stroked my hair awkwardly.

*

To leave on schedule, we had to work overtime. It was already very late at night when we returned home. In silence, we squeezed into the former janitor's room to leave our bicycles. After that, without saying good night to one another, we all hurried to our respective rooms. Most of our colleagues had some hot soup and warm rice ready, whereas A'ping and I ... How I longed for some hot soup! A'ping held my hands tenderly. Though I had worn two pairs of gloves, my hands were still cold. He put them into the pockets of his overcoat. I drew them out at once. I didn't want such tenderness. What I needed badly was a stable family life, not embraces and kisses!

Involuntarily, I stooped in front of Xiuwen's window, through which the apple-green light dimly shone. How cosy to be bathed in such a mild light. What was Xiuwen doing at this moment?

Several voices whispered below the windowsill – Old Jiang's three boys.

'Doesn't Aunty Li like to watch television?' It was Old Jiang's youngest son, only three years old, speaking in a childish treble.

'Why doesn't she like to watch television?'

Xiuwen's silhouette could be seen at the window; the soft light made her face even more graceful and charming. I unconsciously touched my own cheeks, but because of the weather and stage make-up, my skin had become rougher.

The door was suddenly pushed open and Huang Jian came out. On seeing me, he smiled unexpectedly. Why did he smile at me? Was it because he no longer hated me? Or was he mocking my refusing him in the past? My heart ached. I wanted to get away, but my feet wouldn't move.

'Let's go,' A'ping said, biting his lips. His deep eyes flashed. He looked unwell. I started to move.

As soon as we reached our room, I threw myself on the bed, wanting to lie there for ever. But my stomach was rumbling with hunger. A'ping had bought me two stuffed steamed buns from our canteen, but, as I was angry with him, I had refused to even look at them. I hadn't eaten anything for nine hours. I got up from the bed, took a bowl of cold rice and filled it with some hot water. Just as I was about to eat, A'ping snatched it away from me. 'Why let yourself get run-down?'

'I'm hungry!' I shouted, stretching out my hand to grab the bowl.

'Don't you see that I've already begun to cook a meal!' Having put aside the bowl, he continued to cut the cabbage.

'I can't wait!' I stamped my feet irritably.

'Have a biscuit then.' Putting down the knife once more, he handed me a can of biscuits.

'They're too dry. I don't want them! I won't eat them!' I pushed away the can. It slipped from his fingers to the floor.

'You just want to pick a quarrel? I . . .'

'It's you!' he interrupted me roughly. 'You . . . you regret you made a wrong decision. If you had married him, you could also have become a wealthy lady and led a comfortable life!'

'You!' I was speechless with rage and shock.

Flushed with fury, he continued, 'What were you thinking? I told you clearly I had no money, position or ability. I said you'd suffer if you married me! I warned you, didn't I? I was afraid all along you'd regret it. And as I expected, you do!'

Not knowing why, I suddenly slapped his face. Turning around, I flung myself onto the bed, sobbing. After a time, I fell asleep. When

I woke up, I discovered I was lying under my cotton quilt, a hot water bottle at my side. The room was empty. Where was A'ping? Where had he gone so late?

I felt I was suffocating as if there were a heavy weight on my chest. I was very hurt. How could he say such things to me? I had suffered so much by marrying him, yet he said that I regretted it. If I had taken a lift in Huang Jian's jeep that night, then I would … but, instead, I had chosen to hitch a ride on the back of A'ping's bicycle. Why had I done it? I was thinking that he could always play the piano at dancing practice: that he could conduct the orchestra to follow the steps of my solos. I was thinking of the endless stories he told me about Beethoven and Tchaikovsky. Because of this, my parents became angry with me, as did Director Huang of our cultural bureau … Now A'ping said that I … Tears again ran down my cheeks. Had I ever regretted it? Did I envy Xiuwen for her good luck? No, I had never envied her. On the contrary, I looked down on her because she was so cheap. When Huang Jian declared his love for her, she immediately accepted him. All the young girls looked at her with disdain.

My watch had stopped. I didn't know what time it was, but I was sure it was very late. There was not the slightest sound in the courtyard. Suddenly the noise of a car engine broke the silence. Huang Jian stepped out from the car. He went out almost every night, leaving Xiuwen alone. How strange when they had such a comfortable room! Why was he unwilling to stay at home and sit and talk with his wife? How we longed to sit carefree at home and chat about things! But we had neither a comfortable room nor the time to talk.

The car headlights were finally switched off. Huang Jian entered his room and silence reigned again. Where was A'ping? Why had I been in such a foul temper? I began to worry about him. Putting on my cotton-padded coat, I quickly got up and opened the door. I hurried along the passage formed by the sets. Almost every room was dark except Xiao Ji's, where a lamp still shone brightly from the window. There were also faint sounds of voices. A pair of young lovers had, of course, a lot of things to talk about.

The gate of the courtyard was lightly pushed open, and a slender figure slipped in. He had come back finally. Unwilling to let A'ping discover that I was waiting for him, I rushed back home.

Just as I got under my quilt, he stepped into the room and came over to the bed. I pretended to be asleep, but my eyelids moved. Then he sat down at the table, holding his head in his hands. The bowl of cold rice and slices of half-cut cabbage remained on the table. So he hadn't eaten his supper. Where had he been?

*

It was Sunday, the next day. After breakfast, A'ping went out immediately with some music scores under his arm. I didn't ask him where he was going. I didn't care a fig for him!

It was a fine day without a cloud in the sky. The sun shone warmly, making our small courtyard, which was usually crowded and untidy, appear large and bright. The yard was crisscrossed with clotheslines from which were hanging cotton-padded quilts and mattresses. A group of kids were playing hide-and-seek among them. Old Jiang's three sons were shouting at the tops of their voices. I brought out my trunk to air our clothes in the sunshine. Generally speaking, the climate in the north was very dry, yet, as we had been on tour for two months, our clothes could get musty.

Xiuwen was also busying herself airing their clothes. I saw that they had a lot: overcoats – long, medium and short – of wool or other material. Xiuwen loved dressing elegantly; she never wore trousers that hadn't been well pressed or shoes that were not well shined. In previous years, owing to financial difficulties, she had not been able to indulge herself, but now she could have anything she wanted. All of a sudden, she bent down and started to vomit. I ran over and held her arm. 'Are you sick?' I asked. She nodded.

'Does Huang Jian know?' I glanced at their room, but there was no sign of him.

'Yes, he knows. He bought me some medicine.'

'Oh,' I said no more. It would have been better if he could have kept her company more often.

I left Xiuwen and went back. At this moment, I saw that Lian Zhu was also busy with her clothes. In her trunk, apart from clothes, there were several parcels wrapped up in newspaper.

'What treasures have you hidden there?' I said, pointing at the parcels in the trunks.

'Letters,' Lian Zhu answered in all seriousness.

'Letters?' I was at a loss. Picking up one, I saw written on the newspaper: from the municipal ensemble to Sanpu Commune, 1975.

'That year, Xiao Ji had been transferred to work in your ensemble and I was still living and working in Sanpu Commune,' explained Lian Zhu.

Another parcel was marked: from the provincial art college to the municipal ensemble, 1977.

'Those were the letters we wrote while I was studying.'

One had only 'Sanpu, 1970' written on it.

'They were the letters we wrote when we were both living in the same village.' Smiling for a while, she took the parcel from my hand and laid it in a corner on which the sun shone directly. From her expression, I could guess that she treasured those letters the most.

Counting them, I found there were ten parcels altogether. So they had written to each other for ten years! I exclaimed in surprise. 'You were friends for ten years?'

'Yes.'

'How was it in those years?'

She straightened her back, and said as if to herself, 'Every day we ate coarse food and worked hard from early morning. But we managed because we had each other.'

'It can't have been easy.' I sighed.

'Of course there were difficulties. You know the kinds of problems educated youths had when they fell in love.'

'Yes, I know.'

'If one was transferred to work in the city, the other had to wait. We waited years. At first, I feared I'd be a burden to him. Later on, when I entered college, he feared I'd refuse him.' She smiled ironically. 'We were always doubting.'

'Did you ever waver?'

'She shook her head slightly. 'It wasn't easy, finding each other. We shared good and bad times. It would be unthinkable to start all over again with someone else.'

Hearing this, I felt an ache in my heart.

'What if, in the future, well ... when you have some difficulty again, and this difficulty is quite different from ones in the past. Perhaps just an everyday problem, that is to say...' I muttered, striving to find the right word. 'For example, just like Old Jiang and his wife, who quarrel over a few cents. Of course, it's ridiculous, but if you are really short of money then...'

'Oh, I see,' she said, putting one hand on my shoulder and stretching out the other to twist a strand of my hair. She gazed up at the sky. 'Material life is also very important to us. I can't be sure that we wouldn't quarrel or grumble over money. Still we can always remember what we went through together. Then I think we can probably manage to get over such problems.'

I bent down my head, avoiding her eyes. Like them, A'ping and I had also found each other and faced life's troubles together.

Lian Zhu continued, 'It seems ages ago now, but it will always mean something to us because ... because that's love. Without our love, we might have become depressed or lost hope during those years. But how can I preach to you old married couples?! I'm determined to protect our love, to cherish our marriage. But that's not so easy to do.'

For us, it was also not so easy. I sighed sadly.

'Why the sigh? Would you like to have lunch with us today?' she enquired, looking at me attentively.

I nodded my head.

The meal was very simple, but I ate quite a lot, probably because I hadn't eaten the night before. I noticed that most of the pictures on the walls had been put into frames. Not every family could possess such riches. With many things to prepare for the coming tour, we parted after lunch.

A'ping still had not come. Where was he? When would he return? I felt miserable because he hadn't eaten for a whole day. I hastened to prepare a meal for him. Having washed some onions, I sliced them and then broke some eggs. I'd cook rice with fried eggs. Before I had finished, Lian Zhu called me to go out with her.

Xiao Ji and Lian Zhu argued over every purchase so it was evening before we finished shopping.

It was already dark and the streetlights lit up either side of the river and shone on its surface. While we were walking slowly along the bank, Lian Zhu remembered her hometown: 'How beautiful it was with blue waves, golden sun, shells, sandy beaches and seagulls. Standing on the shore, I felt I owned that vast world. Our life was so beautiful and we were so deeply in love. So we're not poor at all.'

'We're only short of money,' Xiao Ji added drily. We all laughed.

Back in our courtyard, the news on the radio reminded us it was already seven o'clock. Xiuwen was washing clothes and waved as soon as she saw us. When we went over to her, she asked Lian Zhu in a low voice, 'Did you chat with Hai Ping yesterday?'

'Hai Ping?' Lian Zhu, baffled, looked first at me, then at her.

'That tall man with wavy hair.'

'Ah, you mean that handsome one? Yes, we talked a bit while I washed clothes here yesterday.'

'Good heavens! He and his wife had just had a fight about it. Didn't you know his wife's very jealous?'

'That's ridiculous!' Xiao Ji said angrily and pulled Lian Zhu away with him.

Opening her mouth awkwardly, Xiuwen didn't know what to do. I felt sorry for her. To smooth things over, I said casually, 'So we'll be off again soon. How I envy you!'

She forced a smile. Xiao Ji had embarrassed her. She bent down to pick up the wooden tub, but couldn't lift it. I realized that she was pregnant and asked, 'Where's Huang Jian? Why doesn't he give you a hand?'

'He's bought a washing machine for me, but it hasn't been connected yet. It can't be used for the time being.'

I helped her carry the tub to her room. Huang Jian had money; he could buy a lot of things, but money can't buy everything. At her door, I put down the tub and was about to leave when she said suddenly, 'When you go away I'll feel lonely again.'

'Then don't let Huang Jian gad about so much. You must make him stay at home with you.'

'We don't seem to have much to say to each other.' She had expressed this many times, but now she seemed depressed. I wondered whether she had been upset by the unpleasant scene or whether, because I had only admired her, I hadn't noticed her unhappiness before.

How to comfort her? Huang Jian and she had fallen in love with each other at first sight. Perhaps it had been a bit too easy. They had never experienced any difficulties; their romance had been quite smooth. After a while I said, 'No, you won't feel lonely. You have your television set, tape recorder and...'

'I'm tired of them,' she said, shaking her head.

The gate of the courtyard was suddenly pushed open for a car. Huang Jian threw out a parcel which Xiuwen caught. She quickly unwrapped it and found a new short jacket in the latest style. With a cry of joy, she left me and rushed into her room to try it on. This would keep her amused for the moment. When she grew tired of it, Huang Jian would buy her a new one. But what if he could no longer produce something new, or she tired too quickly of his presents? What would happen then? The apple-green light could not be a substitute for love.

This made me long for A'ping. What was he doing? I went home, but there was no light on and the door was locked. When I went in I saw the onion slices and bowl of eggs untouched on the table. Where had he gone? I got on my bike and rode along the main street.

Where could I find him? First of all, I went to our new building. Perhaps he was practising there. But there was no sign of him. Then, I headed for the municipal cultural centre, in case he was chatting with his buddies. But it was in darkness. Then I thought of his students. I hurried to their houses but he hadn't been to the first two I called on; so I went to the third one. This was the home of Doctor Zhang, who worked at the municipal hospital. His daughter was taking piano lessons from A'ping. Doctor Zhang told me that A'ping had just left there an hour earlier and that he had already signed a sick-leave certificate for me, which A'ping had taken. I was at a loss to understand. Doctor Zhang said, 'He came yesterday evening and said he desperately needed it. This morning he came again to urge me to write it, so I promised to give it to him this evening. I gave it to him because he never asked any favour from me before.' So that was it! I left without a word. Racing home, I nearly knocked down some pedestrians. How impatient I was to find A'ping!

Riding over the Huo Ping Bridge, I saw a familiar figure standing under a streetlight. A'ping! The dim light cast a faint shadow on the ground. With both hands, he was holding the railing looking at the river. What was he thinking about? I wanted to call him, but I was too excited to utter a sound. Putting down my bike, I ran over to him.

On hearing my steps, he turned his face, stared at me silently and produced a sheet of paper from his breast pocket. I took it, folded it and slowly tore it into pieces.

'What's wrong with you?' he asked in a daze.

'Nothing.' Tears ran down my cheeks.

'What's the matter?' He removed the pieces from my hands.

'If I remain here, how can you manage?' Sobbing, I grabbed the pieces again and threw them into the river.

With his eyes shining brightly, A'ping embraced me tenderly.

'What were you thinking about here?' I asked him in a soft voice.

'I was thinking about how we stood here the first time. Do you still remember? It was precisely here that I said, "I love you!" I'd been in agony for ages, afraid that you'd reject me. It was clear that you could lead a more comfortable life if . . .'

I covered his mouth with my hand, but he took it away and continued, 'But you said you loved me and told me, "I only want you. I want no one else but you!"'

*

It was time to set off again. The leader of our ensemble decided to arrange for the bus to pass by our courtyard. Early in the morning, we gathered together in the yard to wait for its arrival and say goodbye to our families.

The parting conversation between Old Jiang and his wife was filled as usual with calculations.

'Mail me twenty yuan next month.'

'I'll send you thirty.'

'Nobody asked you to send so much,' snapped his wife, ignoring her husband's kindness. 'You'd better pay more attention to your meals during the tour.'

'I'll mail you thirty.'

'No, I need only twenty.'

I couldn't refrain from laughing. They still loved each other. They were only short of money.

Ren Jia and Hai Ping stood face-to-face. Ren Jia fixed her eyes full of worry and fear on Hai Ping. Hai Ping said something to her, which I couldn't hear distinctly, probably to set her mind at ease. To tell the truth, apart from his being handsome, there was nothing to give her cause to doubt him. It was not easy for Hai Ping to endure the jealousy of his plain, narrowminded wife. If he didn't love her, then why did he suffer so? Yet she was too anxious to keep his love to herself. She simply wouldn't share even a tiny bit.

Xiao Ji and Lian Zhu hadn't appeared yet, and the cause was obvious. They had so often been apart before and now they were to be separated again. Xiao Ji was unable to find himself a comfortable job. How long would they have to write letters to each other?

All of a sudden, I felt very happy. At least A'ping and I were always together. I turned to look at A'ping. He held my hands tightly; as usual they were as cold as ice. He put my hands into his deep overcoat pocket. It was very warm because he had put a hot water bottle in it. What a silly, dear fellow!

The bus arrived. After we had all stowed our luggage on the racks and sat down, I noticed the apple-green light was still shining in Xiuwen's home, pale in the dawn. Huang Jian was gazing at me from the window. Before he would do anything, I smiled at him.

The bus was carefully driven out of the gate. Our small courtyard was not so poor after all.

Translated by Hu Zhihui

Wang An-yi

Between Themselves

Bicycles sounding their bells shuttled in and out of the lane, a two-way lane used as a thoroughfare. It was lined with smart modern houses, but at one end people had built many shacks. None of these had gas installed, so firewood crackled and smoke belched as they lit their stoves. A boy seated in front of one smoky stove was eating pot stickers. First he ate the pastry, keeping back the meat stuffing. He put those pitifully small meatballs in the bottom of a large bowl, then ate them one by one.

'Did you never eat meat in your last life?' swore Grandad. Grandad was eating a big bowl of thick gruel.

The boy chomped the meat stuffing.

'That child chomps like a pig,' said Granny, across the way. She was lighting her stove, her tattered fan wafting up wreaths of black smoke.

'I've not stinted him of meat. The wretch must have starved to death in his last life!' Grandad angrily rapped his chopsticks on the back of the boy's head.

Ducking, the boy chomped more loudly.

'Damn it! The meat stuffing in these dumplings has shrunk to a piddling speck.' Grandad picked one up from his grandson's bowl, then dropped it back in disgust.

A woman on a small-wheeled bike rode out from the lane and shot through the smoke. He spat at her, his gob of spittle landing on her back carrier. He was expert in spitting far and accurately.

Soon all the meat stuffing was gone. The boy got up, put his satchel on his head and raced off. In his hurry he trod on Granny's foot. She screeched, 'Are you blind, young devil!'

Grandad chimed in. 'Drop dead, you wretch!'

By now the boy was out of sight. His school was just around the corner, close enough for him to run home in the ten minutes' break to gobble a ball of cold rice.

Satchel on his head, he dashed forward as he made a hooting noise with his mouth, like an automobile horn. He trod on someone's heel so that his shoe came off, knocked over a child, fell over himself, got up again, rubbed his knees, and sprinted on. When he reached the school gate two of his classmates stopped him to see if he had brought a handkerchief. He produced one, grimy and black but neatly folded. After some hesitation they let him pass, as it undoubtedly was a handkerchief.

Having run his blockade, he dashed on, knocking right into someone else who staggered without falling over. Shouts went up near by.

'Wang Qiangxin's bumped into Teacher Zhang. Bumped into a teacher!'

He pulled up.

Still stunned. Teacher Zhang turned to smile at him. 'Never mind, it wasn't deliberate.'

At that, as if reprieved, he ran on.

'Wang Qiangxin, say "sorry". Hurry up and say "sorry"!' shouted the children behind him.

Teacher Zhang stood steady to adjust his glasses and straighten the books in his hands, then went on his way.

'Good morning, Teacher Zhang!' two girls greeted him.

'Good morning,' he answered rather awkwardly.

'Good morning, Teacher Zhang.'

'Good morning.'

He nodded repeatedly all the way to the staffroom. When the bell rang, footsteps thudded and pandemonium broke loose, then the playground quieted down. With a sigh of relief he produced from his bag an unwrapped loaf he had bought in the grain shop, poured himself some boiled water, and started to eat. His class wasn't till the second period.

'Your breakfast?' a colleague asked.

'That's right,' he answered, gulping down a mouthful.

'You really rough it,' remarked another colleague.

'Hmm,' he mumbled, his mouth full.

'Thick gruel makes the best breakfast, I think,' someone else commented.

'Hmm.' He gave up eating, wrapped the remaining half of his loaf in a piece of paper, and put it back in his bag.

The sun lit up the level playground where the gym teacher was drawing lines with white chalk. These lines and the white stripes on his track suit gleamed in the sunlight. A sparrow was hopping along. From one classroom came the sound of children reciting a lesson in unison. They were dragging it out, knowing it by heart.

*

The bell rang. Pandemonium. Children poured out from every classroom, converged in the playground, then surged out of the school gate.

Picking up his books and box of chalk Teacher Zhang went back to the staffroom where Teacher Tao, the teacher in charge of Form Four, was lecturing Wang Qiangxin.

'Stand here and think seriously about your behaviour in class today.' With that she went off to the canteen with her bowl and chopsticks. Wang Qiangxin, left in front of her desk, kept shifting from his left foot to his right, from his right foot to his left. He scratched himself, sticking his hand up his back beneath his jacket or down his collar to scratch. He couldn't keep still for a second.

Zhang opened his drawer and took out his bowl. As he passed Wang Qiangxin he heard the boy's stomach rumble. He stopped and lowered his head to ask, 'Are you hungry?'

Wang Qiangxin said nothing, and simply grinned at him.

'Were you rowdy again in class?'

The boy smiled and said nothing, hanging his head sheepishly.

'Can't you keep quiet?'

The boy smiled awkwardly, fidgeting all the time.

Zhang went back to get the half loaf of bread from his bag and offered it to the boy.

Wang Qiangxin eyed it as if afraid to take it, but finally he took it. He bit off big mouthfuls and chomped them, looking vigilantly around.

A wizened, bent old man stumped in, his shoulders hunched helplessly forward, his arms unwillingly thrust up behind, as if doing an exercise to radio music.

'So the young devil's been kept in again!'

'You must be his grandfather,' the teacher guessed.

'What's the young devil done this time?'

'Own up, Wang Qiangxin,' said Zhang.

'In our Chinese class I fidgeted and talked,' he mumbled with crumbs on his cheeks, his head tucked in defensively.

'Damn you!' The old man slapped his head.

Zhang had grabbed the old man's hand in dismay. But the old fellow, proving stronger than the teacher, pulled his hand up so that they both hit the boy.

'This won't do. This is no way to treat him.'

Having worked off steam with a few whacks, the old fellow told the teacher, 'All right, now that I've whacked him, let him go home for his meal.'

That put Zhang on the spot. This wasn't for him to decide. He wished he had left before to keep out of trouble.

'If he makes a row again, Teacher, you must beat him. You can beat him to death and I won't hold it against you.'

'What an idea! It's better to reason with him.'

'Well, I'll take the young devil back; you teachers are very busy.'

'Go along,' was all Zhang could say.

The old man dragged his grandson off. Zhang picked up his bowl and chopsticks and left the staffroom. At the door of the canteen he met Teacher Tao. He passed her, then decided to turn back and tell her, 'Wang Qiangxin's grandfather has taken him home.'

'Taken him home?' Her bulging myopic eyes stared through her glasses.

'That's right.' He hung his head guiltily.

'You gave permission?'

'His grandfather came...'

'I wanted to talk to his grandfather.'

'I...'

'Fine, so you came to his rescue. You're playing the hero – I don't want to play the villain. I wash my hands of him. You take him over.' She went off in a huff.

With a sigh of exasperation, he stomped out of the canteen, his appetite gone.

Meanwhile Wang Qiangxin was wolfing down his meal. Granny, across the way, looked up from the basin of clothes she was washing and saw the boy eating, and heard him chomping away.

'Isn't it disgusting the way that child eats,' she said to her neighbour, Maomei, who was sitting on a stool knitting.

'His face is disgusting, too,' agreed Maomei. 'His ears are too small and his eyebrows and the corners of his mouth turn down as if he were crying.'

'That's right. That child cried nonstop from the day he was born. Cried his mother to death. Then, strange to say, he stopped crying.'

'Doesn't even cry when his grandad beats him up.'

Wang Qiangxin was full now. He put down his bowl. Lifting the lid from the wok, he scooped out some rice crust and munched it.

*

Bikes passed in both directions, their bells ringing. Cars came and went, their horns honking.

Teacher Zhang rushed to the bus holding a pancake and fritter, and managed to squeeze onto a bus. The door shut, catching the back of his jacket.

'Comrade, my jacket's caught in the door,' he said.

'Please buy tickets or show your monthly ticket,' the conductor called over the microphone, drowning his voice.

He kept quiet. At least his bottom hadn't been pinched.

'If you're not getting off, comrade, let's change places,' suggested a woman, squeezing up to him.

He tried to move forward but failed, his jacket caught fast. He apologized. 'I'll get down first at the next stop.'

The woman moved onto the step above him, her white neck just opposite his face. Her wide-open collar showed an angora sweater, and under the round, woolly collar of this lurked a sparkling golden necklace. His heart palpitating, he turned his head to avoid staring at her.

There was a sudden commotion. One of the passengers had lost a purse.

'Hand it over at once, whoever took it!' yelled the conductor. 'Otherwise we'll drive to the police station.'

'Give it back quick! Give it back quick! We don't want to be late to work!' other passengers shouted.

'Look on the floor, everyone, to see if a wallet's been dropped.'

They jostled one another, looking on the floor.

His heart beating faster than ever, he broke into a sweat and his face turned pale. He forced a smile, a most inappropriate smile. The glance the woman threw at him made his heart contract. Sweat trickled down his neck.

'It's all right, I've found it,' someone called out, stooping to pick up the purse. The others pressed forward.

'Look and see if anything's missing.'

Nothing was missing.

He relaxed. The woman glanced curiously at him again. The door opened and he nearly fell out. She got off the bus and looked closely at him again before going off.

Reaching school, he saw Wang Qiangxin at the gate. He called, 'Wang Qiangxin, I've something to say to you.'

The boy stopped and started scratching himself, first reaching under his collar then up his back.

'Can't you keep quiet in class?'

The boy said nothing, smiling cryptically.

'Do you have to make such a noise?'

Still smiling, he sniffed hard, as if to sniff everything up into his head.

'Yesterday when I let you go home for lunch, your teacher was angry with me.' Zhang had to tell him this frankly.

He looked up as if puzzled.

'If you go on misbehaving, you'll make it awkward for me.' This said, Zhang casually stroked the boy's head and then walked on.

Someone in the staffroom told him, 'The head wants to see you. Wants you at once.'

'The head wants me?' His heart missed a beat. Forgetting to put down his things, he hurried to the head's office.

'Ah, Teacher Zhang, please take a seat.' This politeness reassured him to some extent.

'Did you want me for something, Head?' He perched on the edge of the seat.

The head opened a drawer and took out a sheet of stiff paper, which he handed to him. 'First read that.'

It was an official letter from the unit in which his father had worked twenty years ago, stating clearly in black and white that his father, who had been labelled a Rightist in 1957, had now been cleared. He stared blankly at this document, unable to work up any sense of elation. To him, his father was a stranger who had long ago left home and died of oedema on a farm in Yancheng. His father's colleagues had told him, 'Your old man was quite different from you. If he'd been like you he wouldn't have got into trouble.' And from his childhood onward, in school, in the street, wherever he went, people pointed at him behind his back and said, 'His old man...'

'His old man...'

'His old man...'

'Congratulations.' The head, who doubled as Party secretary, sprang up to shake his hand. Zhang hastily stood up but staggered, not standing firm till the head had sat down again. 'We're going to remove from your dossier all the material on your father. I hope you'll buck up and work hard, without letting this weigh on your mind.'

'Of course, that's ancient history now,' he replied.

'It's past and done with; let's look ahead,' the head urged.

He went back to the staffroom to pour a cup of tea. Not till he sat down did he realize that his underclothes were all wet. The bell rang, followed by what sounded like the galloping of a cavalry. In a flash, the empty playground was full of children. Girls skipped over ropes or rubber-band chains, boys dashed here and there helter-skelter. Teacher Tao came in, her face grim. His heart thumped; he stopped drinking tea. Without so much as looking at him, she went straight to her desk and sat down without a word. Not daring to question her, he watched from a distance as he sipped his tea. When he finished he got up to go to the toilet. Seeing Wang Qiangxin dashing about, his head covered with sweat, he called him to halt.

'Wang Qiangxin, did you make a row again in class?'

'No!' The boy looked up in surprise, the droop of his eyebrows more obvious.

'Teacher Tao is angry,' he whispered.

'Not with me. She praised me in class.'

'What did she say?' Zhang suspected that the boy had mistaken sarcasm for praise.

'Teacher Tao pointed at me and told Zhang Ming, "Even he's kept quiet, but you're making a row."' He was spluttering, gulping back spittle, his front and back teeth, above and below, so jagged that his mouth seemed full of teeth. He looked so ludicrous one couldn't help but pity him.

*

Zhang overslept. As soon as he opened his eyes he saw from his old-fashioned chiming clock that it was already seven. Having no time to buy breakfast, he ran to catch his bus. When he reached the school, it was empty. He asked the janitor why and discovered that it was only half-past six – his clock was a good hour fast. As he put his things in the staffroom, he felt a sudden craving for dumpling soup, so he hurried to a small restaurant next to the school. It was crowded with customers, some concentrating on eating, some bored with waiting, and these inevitably stared at him.

He stood at a loss in the doorway, not wanting to shove his way in or to withdraw. Tentatively taking a few awkward steps in search of an empty seat, he felt more eyes on him, so he beat a hasty retreat.

A few more steps took him to a stall selling pancakes and fritters, where two fair-sized lines had formed, one to buy bamboo counters, the other to exchange these for fritters. As was only right, he went to the back of the line for counters and took from his wallet some small change and grain tickets.

'Teacher Zhang!' someone called.

Looking up, he saw Wang Qiangxin in the line, two counters clutched in one hand and one chopstick in the other to pick up fritters. He had nearly reached the wok.

'Teacher Zhang get your counters, quick.'

Zhang nodded at him with a smile, though knowing that this was easier said than done.

Wang Qiangxin, standing in the line, clamped his chopstick between his lips then rotated it so that it rattled against his teeth.

'Take the chopstick out of your mouth, Wang Qiangxin, or it'll hurt your throat,' Zhang felt constrained to warn him.

The boy did as told, repeating, 'Buy your counters, quick, Teacher Zhang.'

There were still three people ahead of Zhang in the line.

Wang Qiangxin reached the stall. He slowly handed his counters to the girl selling fritters, but didn't reach out to take them, just staring at the specks of oil on them.

'Take them, quick!' the girl urged.

'Too hot,' he said, procrastinating.

'Not after all this time,' snapped someone behind.

'I'm small, afraid of hot things,' he replied brashly, then called to Zhang again, 'Hurry up!'

'You can't buy for other people,' those behind objected, squeezing him out of the line. Only then did Zhang realize why the boy had been stalling. He said with feeling, 'I'll take my turn; there aren't too many people.'

'Have one of mine, Teacher Zhang, I'll line up again.'

'No, no.'

Wang Qiangxin thrust a fritter at him, smearing his jacket with oil. Zhang had to take it and wrap it in a pancake. Walking off, he turned back and saw the boy lining up again while eating. His method was to bite one end of the fritter and hold it in his mouth, pulling it farther in after each bite. The fritter disappeared slowly, as if swallowed whole.

During the break the door of the staffroom burst open and two girls helped in a third, who was crying. A group of boys behind marched Wang Qiangxin straight up to Teacher Tao's desk. These boys had pushed over the girl, then fallen on top of her. Now she couldn't raise her arm, which was badly hurt. Teacher Tao had no time to investigate. Instead she took the girl straight to hospital, coming back at noon to announce that her arm had been broken, the bone splintered.

After school that afternoon, Teacher Tao called those boys to the staffroom to find out what had happened. Since Wang Qiangxin was one of them and Zhang suspected that he was involved, he sat somewhat apart to listen intently.

'Why did you knock her over?'

'We didn't mean to.'

'Why were you pushing and shoving?'

'Just for fun.'

'What fun is there in that? Was it a game? Who started it?' Tao's voice was stern.

'Wang Xin shoved me.' Zhang Ming was the first informer.

'Zhu Yan shoved me,' said Wang Xin.

'Feng Gang shoved me,' said Zhu Yan.

'Luo Hong shoved me,' said Feng Gang.

'Meng Xiaofeng shoved me,' said Luo Hong.

'Wang Qiangxin shoved me,' said Meng Xiaofeng.

'Zhang Ming shoved me,' said Wang Qiangxin.

So they had come full circle. Teacher Tao had to laugh.

'But who started it?' This was as impossible to find out as what first put the earth into orbit. So the hospital expenses had to be divided among them. Teacher Tao paid one share as she was in charge of that class and responsible for it.

'Go home and tell your parents, understand? When the time comes I'll give you the receipts to take back and show them. Off you go!'

Once outside the staffroom the boys raced off, slinging their satchels about and teasing one another.

Zhang followed them out and stopped Wang Qiangxin.

'So you've landed in trouble again. You had me on tenterhooks.'

The boy grinned, very thick-skinned.

'Can't you stop making trouble?'

He just smiled.

'Your grandad will wallop you again.'

Still he smiled.

'Can you pay the medical fees?'

That wiped the smile off his face.

'Shall I help you explain to your grandad?'

'No use. Anyway we can't pay.'

'Why not?'

'Yesterday he went to ask my dad for money, but Dad gave him very little. Grandad came back cursing.'

'How can your dad act that way?'

'His wife's a terror. And he's in a bad position, so he has to do as she says.' This was said most phlegmatically.

'What a know-it-all you are!' Zhang frowned.

'What's strange about that?' He smiled enigmatically.

'If you really haven't the money, I'll pay your share for you.'

'Honestly?' His drooping eyebrows went up incredulously.

'Honestly. As long as you're told, and stop making trouble.'

'All right.' Agreeing readily, he started off, as if afraid the teacher might change his mind. He turned back abruptly to say, 'Want to eat mutton hot pot, Teacher?'

'Why ask?'

'I can queue up for the tally for you. I often go in the morning for a tally, then make forty cents by selling it in the afternoon to someone who couldn't get one. I won't charge you anything.'

'Living on my own I don't eat mutton hot pot,' said Zhang.

*

After school Wang Qiangxin's grandad tugged him back there by one ear, and in the other hand held a pole for hanging up clothes. The boy, his head on one side, took short, rapid steps to keep up with the old man. He knew that if he struggled it would be the worse for him. The old man, who knew Teacher Zhang, went straight up to him.

'Teacher, help me beat this young devil. With one foot in the grave I can't beat him hard; you must help me.' He bawled this out, panting. All the teachers in the staffroom turned to stare.

'What's happened? Do take a seat.' Zhang felt embarrassed.

'I'm at my last gasp, can't move. When I told him to wash the rice, the young devil refused. Dashed off with me chasing behind. I'll do him in!' He struck out with the pole. The boy jumped over it as if jumping over a skip rope.

'Come here, Wang Qiangxin,' ordered Zhang. 'Hurry up and apologize to your grandad. Say you're sorry.'

'Sorry,' muttered the boy, inching forward.

'What farting use is it to say sorry? Help me wallop him, Teacher. I won't hold it against you if you kill him.' The old man thrust his pole into Zhang's hand. Zhang took it, not knowing what to do with it.

'All right then, Grandad, he's acknowledged his mistake. Wang Qiangxin say "I was wrong!"' Zhang's voice rang out as if he were pleased with himself.

'I was wrong,' the boy droned, like a mosquito.

'See, he's owned up honestly. Let him off this time. If he does it again I promise to help you teach him a good lesson.' At last he saw the old man and boy out and came back for his things. A colleague said, 'Wang Qiangxin seems to listen to you, Old Zhang.'

'Oh no,' he disclaimed.

'He behaves like your son.'

'Oh no.' Despite these modest rejoinders, he felt pleased. On leaving the school it occurred to him to call on the boy's grandad since he was ill. He went for a stroll, bought a bottle of royal jelly tonic, then headed for their lane.

Wang Qiangxin, holding a big bowl of noodles, had squeezed into a neighbour's doorway to watch a fight. Zhang called the boy out and went into his home with him.

Their place was a wooden shack built against the brick wall of a house. The old man was eating noodles too, with pickles. In the boy's bowl, apart from pickles, was chopped pork.

'Wang Qiangxin, why can't you show your grandfather more respect? He's so good to you.' Zhang felt touched.

'From some sin in my last life, I owe him a debt I can never pay off in this one,' replied the boy.

That shocked Zhang into silence.

Another row had started outside. Unable to sit still, the boy sprang up and rushed out.

'That damned little devil lost his mother when he was three. I've brought him up. I've no money, but I'm better than a stepmother. Only I'm afraid I'm not long for this world.'

'That's no way to talk, Mr Wang, you're still hale and hearty.'

'Once I close my eyes and pop off, he'll have a thin time.'

'It won't be so bad; everybody will help out.'

The old fellow, glancing sideways at Zhang, grunted. 'Some time back I started saving up for him. With money there's no need to be afraid.'

'Not necessarily.'

'I've muddled along all my life on the Shanghai Bund, thirty years in the old society and thirty years in the new. I've come to see that men are like fish, money like water. A fish out of water is done for.'

Zhang had to keep silent. He knew the old man was wrong, but couldn't think how to refute him. If he thought of a good refutation he'd still have to find the right metaphor for it.

When the row outside stopped, Wang Qiangxin came back to announce, 'Our group leader has come.'

'I must go.' Zhang stood up.

'See your teacher off.'

The boy followed Zhang out. A small crowd had gathered around the opposite gate.

'What's the quarrel about?'

'Maomei and her brother keep squabbling. He blames her for not having a job. But that's not her fault.'

'No, that's not her fault,' agreed Zhang.

They walked to the main road together.

'Now go back.'

'Doesn't matter.' he walked on with the teacher.

'You must behave better in class, Wang Qiangxin, eh?'

'Hmm.'

'And outside school too, eh?'

'Hmm.'

They walked for a stretch in silence.

'Why don't you get married, Teacher Zhang?'

'Eh!' Zhang turned to look at him in surprise.

'Has no one introduced you to anyone?'

Zhang's cheeks burned: he was speechless.

'Actually, you ought to marry Maomei.'

'What's that!' Zhang was staggered. His head reeled.

'Actually Maomei's not bad except that she has no work. And her bottom's too big.'

'How can you talk like that!' His face turned as red as a lantern.

'Why not? Have I said anything wrong?' The boy sounded surprised and looked with concern at his teacher.

'Aren't you too small to meddle with such matters.'

'It's you I'm thinking of. Though Maomei has no job, she's young. You wouldn't lose out.'

'You mind your own business.'

'I'm thinking of Maomei too.'

'She doesn't want you butting in either. Just mind your own business.'

They walked another stretch in silence.

'Wang Qiangxin, you really must behave better in school, eh?'

'Hmm.'

'And out of school too, eh?'

'Hmm.'

The streetlights cast their shadows on the ground one long, one short.

*

When school ended, the gym teacher took Wang Qiangxin to Teacher Zhang and said, 'Teach this boy a lesson. He kicked up such a rumpus in my class that he spoiled it for everyone.'

'Wang Qiangxin, what have you been up to this time?'

The boy said nothing and just smiled.

The gym teacher went on, 'When it was time to line up, he wouldn't stand up straight but flopped this way and that. Leaned against a classmate or flopped onto the ground, as if all his bones were broken.'

'Is that right, Wang Qiangxin?' asked Zhang.

He smiled and said nothing.

'See, this boy won't sit properly or stand properly. Won't listen to anyone, except you, Teacher Zhang!'

Wang Qiangxin, indeed, wasn't standing properly. One of his legs was straight, the other bent, one of his shoulders was higher than the other; his neck and head were askew, his eyebrows crooked and his eyes screwed up.

'Wang Qiangxin, stand properly,' snapped Zhang.

The boy shifted to the other foot, still with one leg straight, the other bent, one shoulder higher than the other. He had simply switched around.

'Wang Qiangxin, don't you know how to stand?' asked Zhang patiently.

He shook his head; whether stubbornly or sheepishly wasn't clear.

'Is the boy going through some physiological phase that he's so hard to cope with?' said the gym teacher.

'Stand properly, Wang Qiangxin,' Zhang was losing patience.

Still the boy slouched, squinting at him as if playing a game with him.

'Wang Qiangxin, stand properly.' Zhang was really angry.

'I won't,' he had the impudence to say.

Zhang raised his hand and slapped his face.

Everyone was flabbergasted. The gym teacher grabbed Zhang's arm. 'You mustn't beat a schoolchild, Teacher Zhang.'

The boy suddenly started bawling. 'You hit me, you hit me. Bugger you.'

Zhang stared in a daze at Wang Qiangxin, his mind a blank. It struck him that the character for 'sob'* with its two 'eyes' was a perfect picture of sobbing.

The boy walked sobbing to the door and no one stopped him. They watched him leave the staffroom, then turned their heads to look at Teacher Zhang.

Zhang was thinking distractedly of that character 'sob'.

Before long an old man in the posture of a setting-up exercise came in and bore down on Zhang.

'Bugger you, you hit my grandson! How can teachers hit school children? This is the new society. You're not a teacher in an old-style private school, able to cuss and beat kids whenever you please. Bugger you!'

* Chinese character 哭

The other teachers managed to stop the old man from butting Zhang's chest. Zhang, sweating and dazed, could only bow with clasped hands.

'I'm going to find your boss, your headmaster!' yelled the old man.

'I'll go with you.' Zhang had found his tongue at last.

They went together to the headmaster's office. There, Zhang apologized to the old man before the head.

The next day, Zhang went to Teacher Tao's Fourth Form and apologized to Wang Qiangxin before the whole class.

The third day, in a meeting of the staff trade union, he made a self-examination and accepted the criticism of his colleagues.

The fourth day, Zhang called on the head in his home to relinquish the promotion for which he was due.

The fifth day, the head withdrew a report to the Education Bureau recommending outstanding teachers.

The sixth day was Sunday.

The seventh day was Monday.

The eighth day was Tuesday.

The ninth day, when Zhang was going from his classroom to the staffroom, Wang Qiangxin rushed up, his head sweating, his red scarf back to front as if he were wearing a bib. Three or four metres from the teacher he stopped abruptly.

Zhang stopped too.

Wang Qiangxin looked at him.

Zhang looked at the boy.

Neither said a word.

Zhang turned and walked off.

Wang Qiangxin veered and walked off.

Both were rather flurried.

Translated by Gladys Yang

Su Shu-yang

Between Life and Death

Ah, here you are. Sit, sit. How about some tea? It's brewed, just ready to pour. What a rare pleasure this is. No other writer has ever bothered to come and sample our life here. Our unit deals with things that make people's skin crawl, I'm afraid: everything in this building is destined for cremation. Anyway, nobody ever visits, since we are only associated with the business of dying. Those of us who work here are generally deemed unworthy to enter the higher echelons of art and literature. There is a fear, I suppose, that we carry with us the stench of death wherever we go, so powerful as to overwhelm the delicate fragrance of flowers and chase away the Goddess of Creativity, as if even her lute will end up in the fire – cremated alongside the corpses.

Most people find our work crass and lowly, not fit to be embraced into the mainstream of life. We are limited to keeping company with the God of Death. All anybody wants to write about are hospitals and doctors – I have no objection to that, of course, but hospitals and us are close companions – what they can't cure end up on our doorstep. So why is it that they get praised sky-high, while we are somehow less than worthless, our work thought to be devoid of sound philosophy? Philosophy to the arts is like a soul is to the body, I grant you. But these people don't know what they are talking about! Life and death are both full of mystery and surely all religions deal with the relationship between this life and the next. Religion is by nature philosophical! How can there not be philosophy inside a crematorium? Only an outsider could have such cranky ideas! Frankly, people look down on us. They think that just because we spend all our time with corpses we are half-dead ourselves. The Old Society used to call us 'pall-bearers', the lowest of the low. I regret to say this hasn't changed much, even though sooner or later every writer ends up being part of our 'business'. Just now, however, they'd much rather keep their distance. In fact, we have looked after more writers and artists here than you can count. I dare say the numbers are large enough to form a film studio on the other side, not to say an orchestra, a dance troupe, a theatre company and on top of that a huge writers' union, no less influential than what you might find in this world. Don't you believe me?

Anyway, you are here, that's good. So you almost chose our profession yourself! Don't look so surprised, we have our ears to the ground. Some time ago we were exchanging information with the crematorium you were going to join – to see if we can improve our work in this unit. There are young people here too, you know: men, women, educated people. Standards may not be very high, but we do have quite a few high-school graduates among our staff. In fact, you are looking at one right now.

Our colleague from the other unit pointed at your name one day and asked me: 'Do you know so-and-so?' I said yes, of course.

'He almost came to work with us, did you know? He is a proper writer now!'

I knew your name, although you were down on your luck at the time. A crematorium can produce good writers too, as well as poets, artists, musicians, scientists. It is not impossible. Who can figure out why we are so despised?

Ai, I've talked such a lot of rubbish and still haven't got round to the main theme. I guess you are here to ask me about my family, my wife, things like that?

Where should I begin?

Let's start with my father. He spent his entire life servicing the dead, yet he has never complained. He used to say:

'Everyone has to die one day. To be good to other people is the same thing as being good to oneself. In life, we may be divided into aristocrats, professionals, beggars, whatever; but the minute we close our eyes, everybody is equal. Over on the other side, it is not fashionable to show off and behave like a bully. Anybody who wants to climb over other people's heads and stand on their shoulders is not going to have an easy ride, there are quite a few revolutionaries over there as it happens. All they have to do is to get on a platform, summon the crowds, and start a campaign. It would be much easier to build a socialist society in the other world I can assure you!'

Can you deny my father's words are full of philosophical wisdom, imagination and poetry?

He used to say: 'Being kind to the dead is also to comfort the living, so that those who survive can concentrate on getting on with their own lives. In this way we too contribute to the welfare of the state.'

Is this without perception? I don't deny he was also somewhat superstitious. Just before he died – and we looked after him here of course – he said to us: 'Don't be sad, dying is just like a light going out. I have lots of friends on the other side. I may be going alone, but once I'm there my friends will band together and rekindle my light.' When my father went he went with a smile.

What was there to worry about? His conscience was clear. Whenever he saw a dead body which was over-dressed, wearing a beautiful watch, or a nice pen, he would say to the family:

'Keep the good clothes for yourselves, it isn't cold over there, and nobody cares how you dress. Keep the watch too, and the pen. Over there time-keeping is automatic, and everybody uses a typewriter. After all these are things to remember him by, and you may find some use for them later on. Burning everything would be a waste.'

During the ten years of the Cultural Revolution we were inundated with people who had been persecuted, dying without justice, often with violence. My father was equally kind to all of them. He would give their faces a good scrub, erasing any trace of maltreatment. Don't think there was no interference though! He was occasionally admonished:

'Don't you have any kind of standpoint on our class struggle?'

My father would look up to the ceiling, and speak with a soft voice: 'Don't shout, his soul is still here. All this shouting might persuade him to follow you home and stick to you night and day. Is that what you want? You must realize this is our work, and we have our own standards. If you don't agree with what we are doing, you are more than welcome to do the job yourself. In any case, what exactly is the nature of your objection? When your time comes, would you want to go with a dirty face?'

I don't know what you writers think of people like my dad. Was he a good man? Was his soul beautiful? Is he worth writing about?

Another time he was engaged in a debate with a notable pen-pusher at the time. This philosopher had come to supervise the cremation of a man unjustly branded as an 'Old Opportunist'.

My father said: 'The boundary between a living and a dead man is no more than that of a breath. There are inumerable cases of people who are alive but don't breathe at all and people who are dead but full of spirit!'

This made the philosopher stop short. He ordered an immediate investigation into my father's ancestry, to see if he had come from 'bad stock'. The foreman said: 'He is descended from three generations of undertakers. All his family ever did was burn the dead. No need to investigate.'

This was what they called 'revolution' at the time, can you imagine! And they couldn't even refute my father's simple ideas. What do you think? If you look carefully at this world and the next, you're bound to see the truth in what he says – over there, there are many who have died who will always remain in our hearts, and yet a lot of the so-called living are stone-cold inside.

Me? There is nothing interesting about me.

I was a high-school graduate. I didn't manage to get into a university. My old man said to me one day:

'You might as well follow in my footsteps. Nobody is willing to do what we do nowadays. If it carries on like this, sooner or later there won't be anyone left to take care of the dead. The socialist doctrine can't only benefit the living, while the others are left to wait in long queues! It isn't as if we are a body bank, looking for an overabundance of corpses. No, they must be sent on their way as soon as possible. Our task is to be a comfort to both the living and the dead. Believe me, young man, it isn't such a bad profession – you are a member of the youth group, show the way...'

At that time my head was full of revolutionary fervour, so I wasn't too happy about the prospect of following my father into the crematorium. I had a girlfriend too, a graduate of middle school, who collected old junk for a living. She was very pretty, and always smiling. Her name was Er Ya. If you will permit me to borrow a Western phrase – this seems to be the fashion nowadays, and no doubt using it will elevate my status – the smiling face of my girlfriend looked just like the *Mona Lisa* by Leonardo da Vinci. She had a kind of eternal mysterious smile. We used to sit side by side, and got on extremely well. Nothing obvious was ever said between us, but in the manner we spoke together, the way we looked at each other, things were perfectly understood. I loved her, and she liked me too.

You are still young, you must appreciate the sensation of a first love. Flames and sparks are meaningless adjectives. The way I felt could only be described as bitter sweet, I can think of no better way of describing it. There was always something tugging at my heart, all day long I ached to see her shape, to hear her footsteps. I could happily have spent all my time walking with her silently through the rain, just walking. There was an infinite number of things I wanted to say to her, yet whenever we were with each other, I would become tongue-tied, staring at her like an idiot. There is a Japanese song called 'The Sailor': 'When I think of my baby, I am filled with melancholy...' Ai, melancholy, that is indeed an apt description. Just imagine, here was a warm and pretty girl who was capable of inducing melancholy in my heart – how was I to rest? I trusted her. I trusted that she wouldn't be petty or materialistic. I trusted that she knew everyone must die eventually, and move on to the next world, and that somebody has to be there to pave the way, improve their looks, give them some peace. Such a day will come to her too. Surely she would not despise those who will be of help to her in time? I made up my mind. Choosing between work and love, I put my work first, believing that romance and cremation need not be mutually exclusive.

I was wrong.

When I told her I was going to work at the crematorium, she told me at the same time that she had had an offer from a film studio to become an actress. She could not accept my decision. She could not begin to imagine how a film star and an undertaker could walk side by side on the street, let alone go to the park and look at roses and peonies, or row a boat under the weeping willows. Clear breeze, drizzling rain, fresh flowers, green grass, poetry and music are all associated with life, the dead are only permitted darkness. Just because I keep company with the dead, people think that I, too, must be half dead, and not to be associated with beauty. Anyway, she didn't say much else. There were some tears, of course, but not enough to stop her from leaving. We said goodbye.

You see, a person's fortunes are often determined in the spur of a moment – the very moment she was invited to star in a movie she changed completely – from a poor girl who earned her keep collecting rubbish into a glittering movie star. As for me, it only took a moment as well, not much longer, to make the decision to become a man who burns dead bodies for a living. In that split second, I toppled from the fairly respectable position of an educated man to being the scum of the earth, undeserving of literature, art, or philosophy. And yet nothing had really changed. Not my education nor her beauty; nothing had altered in our appearance – our bodies, down to the length of our eyelashes, remained exactly the same. But our worth, and the whole way we were perceived by others had turned upside down. Before that crucial moment, we were ideally suited, after that moment, our destinies diverged and sped in opposite directions. What can it all mean? Today her picture adorns the pages of calendars. People spend an entire month in the year looking at her image. Meanwhile, during the course of the same month, I would have said farewell to many of our contemporaries and waved them off to the next world. You writers love to talk about life. Tell me, how did our lives come to be fractured in this way?

No, I am not so small-minded as to be envious of other people's fame, nor do I want to drag them down to my own level. Neither am I suggesting changing the pictures on our calendars. It is perfectly understandable that people would rather look at a pretty film star than one of us in here! What fool would pay good money to ogle at idiots like us month after month? All I'm saying is that a person's destiny is often determined in a flash, down to the nobility of our minds, or the hour of our death. Sometimes we simply find ourselves standing at crossroads, like trains arriving at a junction. Some go east, some go west. Is it really necessary to call the one going east a rocket, or the one going west a pile of twisted old metal? Society needs different skills to function, without us, dead people will have nowhere to go. Anybody who wants to dispute this can try dying themselves, see if they still disagree.

Come, let's take you as an example. Say you really did join that crematorium as a member of staff, and let's say the foreman is a stubborn old fool, and that whatever fancy essays you might have written, he refuses to let you leave. Where would you be today? Would you still be welcomed everywhere with applause? Or would people treat you the way they treat me – holding their noses, rubbing their chests in fear of the smell of death? Whether you are a worker in a crematorium or a writer adored by the public, does your worth fluctuate in any significant way? Of course not! Your height remains the same, although it's true you might not be as fat. Life has its own rhythm-dynamics, its own way of proceeding. Since sociologists have no answers, why should we all spend so much time worrying about status and power? Those who are successful turn up their noses at the rest of us and those who fail – perhaps we shouldn't even call it failure – often try to put an end to their lives. They hang themselves, drink bleach, creating havoc for us here. The important thing surely is to know yourself, respect yourself. That must be enough.

See, I have been getting on my high horse again.

Let's talk about her, my old girlfriend, the movie star. Sometimes we would run into each other. If there was nobody around she would stand three feet away and say two words; if she was not alone, that beautiful neck of hers would suddenly change direction showing me the back of her head. I never take any notice of her, whatever the circumstances.

I hear she has gone through three or four boyfriends. Like choosing a chicken in the market, she would pick one up, give its neck a thorough appraisal then decide whether or not to buy. Two years ago she finally got married, maybe he was the sixth in line. I don't know. I've got to give it to her, she sent me an invitation on the day. At first I didn't want to go, but my mother kept on at me.

'Shu Ren, go and have a look. At least Er Ya hasn't forgotten you. She still remembers her old friend at the crematorium. Go and congratulate her, don't let anybody think we are small-minded, or that we have suddenly shrunk in stature. Go on, put on your good wool suit, let everybody see that you are every bit as handsome as the man on the movie screen. Take a good present too, I don't want people to say we have to skimp.'

This was the pride of old people talking. I couldn't contradict my mother, so I did as I was told, and went along to congratulate Er Ya.

The wedding wasn't big but it had style. Every guest seemed to have arrived from some foreign beauty contest. Let's just say if you were not at least a metre seven in height, with a sweet dimple on either cheek, eyes the shape of an almond, brows like a new moon, you'd better not be there. When I went in, the bride, Er Ya − I'll call her by her nickname as I'm sure she wouldn't want me to reveal her identity − introduced me to her Number Six with a smile. This man had a big bottom, sturdy waist, thick eyebrows and huge round eyes − the hairy heroic type. He took my hand and boomed at me: 'Ah, my friend, so which company are you with?'

I was perplexed for a moment and thought to myself, I am not a soldier, why would I belong to a company? Of course! He meant a theatre company. In his eyes acting was probably the noblest profession on earth.

'He is a poet,' Er Ya interjected quickly.

'Oh, a poet!' the groom said.

'No, I am not a poet,' I said. 'I work at the crematorium. I burn bodies for a living.'

'Really?' The groom was somewhat taken aback, withdrawing his hand.

'Yes, I rub shoulders with corpses every day.' I was deliberately nonchalant. 'Actually everybody is in regular contact with dead bodies. The fish, duck, chicken and beef about to be served up on these tables are all corpses of animals as you well know. Allow me to wish you both every happiness for your future, goodbye.'

I left, deliberately spoiling their appetite. Did I make too much mischief do you think?

Er Ya said I wrote poetry. This was not entirely without foundation. I write poems and songs in my spare time. Obviously I don't write about our profession, however worthwhile I might think it is. Dead flesh disintegrating in a furnace is not what most people want to read about. Perhaps I should write about the way the make-up is applied? But that doesn't seem popular as a poetic theme either – in fact, it appears to be something of a taboo. We might work with the dead, but in our hearts we celebrate life. We celebrate the spring, the wondrous effervescence of our days, the warmth of the sun, even down to a blade of grass, or a wild flower – nothing is too insignificant to be the subject of my poetry. I see tears every day, black muslin and white flowers, the power of death, the weight of grief. But these are not the things I focus on. I write about happiness, smiles, how children learn to walk on the lawn, the embrace of lovers under a tree. I write about love, babies, mothers, vitality which goes on generation after generation, undefeated by death.

All the young men who work here learn to write, paint, sculpt, garden, compose songs, play music or chess; they also enjoy ball games and love to swim. We are the guardians of the last exit, but we prepare the dead as if they are about to make their first entrance. Ours is the final frontier between life and death. If you believe there is another world, then death on this side merely coincides with birth on the other. Perhaps this is mere idealism, and that neither heaven nor hell really exists. What we do know is that both life and death are mysterious, subjects which inspire constant fear and interest. Consider this: once, Tom, Dick or Harry didn't exist, somehow, for some reason, they become sentient, they begin a life, they manifest themselves in the world. They are happily going along, then just as suddenly and inexplicably, they don't feel anything any more, they become an inanimate object. How many philosophers and writers have explored this question, yet nobody has written about our work – how we turn tangible shapes into a phantom militia marching into the next life. Our work is full of mysticism and yet it is thought to be commonplace. Wouldn't you agree that's odd?

Did you ever consider some of these things before you came to see us? Where we are is like a garden. Despite our daily contact with death, we urge our youth leaders to value life, to go on living with renewed courage. Why must we be the butt of so much antagonism? Those departing are given their final solace here.

I say this not because I want you to take up our profession once again. I only want to point out that this job is just as valid as any other. We shouldn't be despised, that's all.

You ask about my wife? Ah, we met at the Cultural Centre. I belonged to the literary group and she was in the music department. I wrote some lyrics, she liked them and set them to music, and we performed the piece at the local concert. She played the strings, I sang. We won a prize. We went to celebrate afterwards. That was how we got to know each other.

She said my lyrics were good, full of a passion for life. I wrote about a small wild flower, how it sprouts in the spring, blossoms, is trodden underfoot, and yet continues to bloom, giving out its own unique fragrance for all to enjoy.

She asked me: 'Your observation seems so acute, so full of feeling. How is that?'

I said: 'Because I look into the face of death every day.'

She was shocked, she didn't know I worked at the crematorium. But I knew what she did. She had just graduated from the university – she was a gynaecologist.

After that time, she didn't talk to me for quite a few months. When we rehearsed at the Centre she would just stare at me. I loved her, but I had to disguise my feelings. Those of us who work here are condemned to a single life. I couldn't tell her I was in love, that would have been disrespectful to Wei Xue – that's her name – and I didn't want to upset her. I had to leave her to make up her own mind. If she didn't love me, I wouldn't have complained. The full pressure of society on the back of a single young girl would have been too much to bear, and it might well have crushed her under its weight. Besides I had a little self-respect too. Er Ya had bruised my heart, and I couldn't let another girl break it completely. I felt I had to give myself to my country, to society, to hundreds and thousands of families, look after the dead, console the living. After all my heart was only the size of a fist. I thought that perhaps there wasn't enough of it to go round.

Eventually one day Wei Xue invited me to accompany her on a walk in the park. Under the newly renovated pagoda, looking into the setting sun, she asked me gently:

'What exactly do you do?'

'I make up the corpses.'

'Aren't you afraid?'

'I was frightened in the beginning. Not only frightened, but repulsed. Often I was not able to eat after work. But I don't want to describe their faces and make it even more difficult for you. Anyhow, I got used to it by and by, and began to look upon the corpses as empty canvasses, or sculpting material, and then it was fine.'

'Is there extra bonus in this line of work?'

'No. The wages are the same as everyone else's. I earn less than you do.'

'What is the value of the work you do? Don't you find it irksome?'

'I don't want to spout philosophy at you – it's all so much hot air. All I can say is, when a family sees their relative lying there peacefully, as if they were merely asleep, it makes them think that there has been no suffering, and they get enormous comfort from that. Many people thank me with tears in their eyes.'

She didn't say anything, her eyes fixed at the clouds in the evening sky.

'Since you have this skill, why don't you do make-up for people who are alive?' she asked, not unreasonably.

'Because somebody has to do this job,' I said. 'I happen to do it well. I also do re-sculpting work. Those with broken noses get new bridges, collapsed cheeks are refilled, wounds are carefully disguised. I also shut the eyes, mend lips which have been torn. In this way the dead can make their exit the same way they looked when they were alive.'

'But what is the point of it all? They are already dead!'

'You are right, my exhibits never last more than three days, then they all end up in the furnace. Nonetheless, in those three days I often experience the most incredible love and gratitude from the survivors, and sometimes it seems to me that even the bodies want to sit up and thank me! My heart would be full to bursting.'

'Don't say any more, I can't bear it,' she said softly.

'Aren't you regularly in touch with death too?' I asked her.

'Yes.' She sighed. 'Sometimes I think that the most ineffectual science in the world is medicine. Death always wins in the end.'

'This is a little too pessimistic,' I chided her. 'You deliver babies! Babies are born all the time. No matter how many people die, nobody can stop others from being born. It may be true that medicine is in a race against time with death, but it also helps bring life into the world.'

She tilted her head to look at me, then laughed, 'If we became friends, what do you think people will say? Life comes through my fingers, death runs through yours!'

I laughed too. 'We often say that crematoriums and hospitals are intimately linked. Like boats on the same river. You paddle upstream, we paddle downstream. That's all.'

Later I said: 'You welcome life, I give death a proper send-off. You and I are guardians of the two gateways of a lifetime. When we are born we are all equal, when we die we are equal once again. What we do are similarly respectful of the true worth of people.'

Tears were streaming down her face: 'I feel very confused, very confused indeed. Why did I have to meet you?' She was sobbing now. 'Can't you lie to me, and say you are a poet? Don't you write poetry? Haven't you published a lot of poems?'

'But I am someone who makes up dead bodies. That is what I do

93

every day. I can't lie to you. This work is not incompatible with writing poetry, a poet is not worth more than a mortician. Really they are not.' I grabbed her shoulders, and said with feeling: 'Think about it carefully before you make up your mind, I won't blame you whatever you decide.'

I left. The evening sun threw my shadow on the ground, it was long and slender, and I thought to myself, the poet is my shadow, the mortician my true self, but my shadow is worth more than myself in the eyes of others. If you stand a corpse on the ground, it too would cast a shadow. The shadow might even be that of a hero, straight and strong. But there is no life in a corpse. To think that even the shadow of something without life might be admired, and yet I, so full of vitality, can only cause misery and confusion. Tell me, why is that? Attitude? Yes, you're right. It is to do with attitude. Here is an attitude which clearly doesn't do anybody any good, and yet people continue to defend it. You don't believe me? Go and do a survey in the streets. Ask the question: 'Can a beautiful woman doctor marry a man who burns the dead?' Answer: 'No.' At least ninety per cent will say no. I am willing to lay a bet.

Spring had gone, summer arriving hot on its heels. Then all of a sudden it was time for folks to go and look at the turning leaves on Shiang Shan.

Wei Xue invited me to go with her.

We stood on the top of the mountain, waves of red spreading underneath our feet. She was sad again.

Letting out a sigh she said: 'Why can't your profession be different? I am not someone who is interested in money. I don't need only to make friends with university graduates – a scholar who is shallow is far inferior to an uneducated man who has soul. But you, a beautician for the dead...'

'That's not so good, is it?'

'It's not so easy to accept, I must admit.'

I didn't speak, perhaps more accurately, I had nothing to say. There was a breeze blowing through the leaves. I listened to the sound for a while, and then spoke.

'Look at these mountains, those trees. When we are dead, they will still be here. But even in nature the new is constantly substituting the old. Nothing escapes the ever-changing cycles of living and dying.'

'You seem to be something of a philosopher.' She sighed again.

'Let us part then!' I said. 'Let's not see each other again.'

'No, no, no!' she screamed. 'I couldn't bear that, can't you give me some encouragement? How can I face society's pointing finger on my own? Why don't you say something? Why don't you launch an offensive? Don't you think you are being terribly selfish?'

My brain exploded all of a sudden. She loved me for sure. But she couldn't face the prejudice of the entire world. She was right, how could I let her deal with this alone? If I didn't shield her, then I was indeed being selfish. I was waiting to have everything brought to me on a plate. Love is something that occurs between two people, and in order to earn its rewards, one must be willing to fight, to wrench it from the hands of the opposition.

I took her in my arms and said with gratitude, 'I love you. Nobody will ever take your place in the world. Even though I deal with death, I am not dead myself. I have just as much passion and energy as the next man. I won't let you go. I shall make you happy. I may not earn very much, but happiness is not dependent on money. Look at me, Wei Xue, my chest is broad enough to give you shelter.'

She threw herself into my embrace, through tears she said, 'I love you and I am going to marry you. One who enables birth can marry one who facilitates death. We shall have a family which lives between these two enormities.'

'Nonsense, in our family there will only be life, because every day we shall shoo death away.'

That Chinese New Year, we were married. All my workmates came – old, young, men, women. Our friends from the Cultural Centre, the newspaper and the hospital came too, they all laughed, they laughed so much tears ran down their faces.

My wife is very good to me, there is only one rule: I have to have a bath before I go home. When I get there, she insists I rinse my hands twice more with clean water. I know why of course, she doesn't want me to stink of corpses. But actually it is she who smells of Lysol. In any case I always tell her I like the smell.

It's lucky you came today, she has just given birth to our baby yesterday. A little girl every bit as good-looking as her mother. Morticians' daughters are no less beautiful you know!

On the same day, by coincidence, Er Ya's husband died, his body was brought here. He was drunk when he decided to go for a spin in a cheap car. I don't need to tell you how his face looked. I'm sure you can imagine. On the table next to him was a young man, someone who had been sentenced to hard labour twice in his lifetime. He died rescuing a baby who had fallen into the river.

I did the make-up for both of them. Er Ya's husband was too high-born or too privileged perhaps, and lost his life in his empty pursuits. The youth who saved the baby had a tough life, but at the moment of death he was elevated to a state of grace. I am pondering a poem in his honour. Apparently, a famous artist has drawn his portrait, and now a sculptor also wants to make his image, to be erected at the place where he made his sacrifice.

The two corpses and I were all in the same little room. I looked at them both, and felt quite moved. Number Six had looked down on me once, but now waits for me to clean away the evidence of his recklessness. The young man I didn't know, but apparently he had been the target of a lot of prejudice, and had taken one or two wrong turns in his life, but then he was able to prove his worth in death. He will always remain in people's memory, just as Number Six will disappear without a trace – perhaps even while alive he wasn't all that different to a corpse. In my eyes the two men are equal now. As a matter of fact I was far more meticulous with Number Six, since his face looked a lot worse.

Er Ya came. She could see that I had repaired her husband's face, and turned to me with red, grateful eyes. I asked her to go closer and take a good look, say goodbye properly. But she ran off crying. She was frightened of him now. What about when he was alive? Did she ever really love him? Just you wait, Number Seven will be along shortly.

I had just finished working on those two when I got a call to say my daughter had arrived.

So you see, I had barely said farewell to death when life was already round the corner.

I walked through the streets looking at the lights, the cars, the people. I thought to myself, how many people have turned to ashes today? Probably only I knew the answer. But how many were born? I had no idea. Whether you think that death is ridiculous or solemn, it can never put a stop to the never-ending flow of life. People will always remember the achievers, and recount their history for future generations. But it is the insignificant deaths which demonstrate to us how, in the final equation, we are all the same. The way we die hardly matters, one instant and it's all change again. All we can do is to respect our own lives, or the new-born will surely come along and shove us into the furnace!

Ai, why haven't you drunk your tea? What I have been saying, you must promise never to publish...

Translated by Carolyn Choa

Su Tong

Cherry

To Yin Shu the postman, Maple Wood Road has always been special. The road is actually a hilly path, winding under a canopy of trees. It is very long and very steep. If one was to ride a bicycle from the big clock tower without using any brakes, it would only take two minutes to get from the top of the slope to the bottom. Generally speaking, however, a postman only needs to go as far as the hospital before turning back. This whole area is almost solely dominated by the high walls of the Maple Wood Hospital and its medical school. There are few residents besides, and most of the mail is destined for the hospital.

The postman who used to work this area was an impetuous youth prone to speeding down the hill on his bike like a shooting star. Once he ran straight into an old man with a walking stick trying to cross the road, and was thrown off his bike. After that incident the post office was naturally keen to put someone else in his place. That was how Yin Shu's slender, leisurely silhouette came to appear on Maple Wood Road.

Everything about Yin Shu is slow and meticulous. His physical appearance matches his personality perfectly – there is no spare flesh on him anywhere. His colleagues at the post office regard him as something of a weirdo. He only speaks when absolutely necessary – otherwise his cool gaze holds everyone at bay, forestalling any possibility of idle chit-chat. Also, he has some strange habits. Each time before setting off on his round, he would ask for a whole bunch of elastic bands. His post is not only sorted by names and addresses, but also by colour and size. This unnecessary and time-consuming activity has inevitably become something of a joke at the post office. Further, before getting on his bike, Yin Shu would clip the bottom of his trousers with two wooden pegs, despite the fact that his trouser legs are extremely narrow and that this was a completely superfluous exercise. Still, Yin Shu is Yin Shu, and nobody would dream of interfering with his routine. After all, what he does doesn't really affect anyone else, even though he would insist on keeping his very own piece of pale yellow soap, kept under lock and key, which he has bought with his own money.

Yin Shu never minds what anyone thinks of him. He knows that his so-called weirdness is only a product of his loneliness, a subject often probed in the newspapers these days.

Every morning, at precisely eight forty-five, Yin Shu would ride past the ancient clock tower, glittering in the splendour of the early morning sun. The hands of the clock are always pointing to ten past seven. Yin Shu would lean forward, peddling at full speed up to the top of Maple Wood Road. Looking down, unwinding in front of him is a path full of phoenix trees, and red maple and winter pine. Everything is peaceful and clean. The air here is tinged with a faint whiff of medicine, but even this smell conveys a sense of cleanliness and peace. In his heart Yin Shu knows that this extraordinary place is his own favourite patch.

It had been raining that morning, the path was slippery with puddles and fallen leaves so Yin Shu decided to push his bike. When he approached the side door of the hospital, he noticed that this door which remained permanently shut was rotting, a thin layer of moss creeping from behind the hinges. Suddenly, it opened slowly, as if pushed by an unseen hand.

A girl in a white dressing-gown appeared from behind the door, and stopped right in front of his bike. Yin Shu was taken by surprise, and instinctively swerved to avoid her, but the girl lightly skimmed over to block his way again. She was young and pale, her beauty and sadness causing Yin Shu's heart to skip a beat. She stretched out her right hand from under the wide sleeve of her dressing-gown – a hand as delicate as white jade. Her black eyes looked up at him moist with hope and longing.

What do you want?

A letter. Is there a letter for me?

What is your name?

White Cherry.

Sorry?

White, as in snow. Cherry, like the tree. Perhaps the letter is addressed to Cherry. That's me. I am the only person called Cherry here.

Yin Shu thought that this name was both strange and beautiful, but he didn't say anything. Quickly looking through the post, he could see that there was nothing for Cherry. So he said, there is nothing for White Cherry, nothing for you.

How come?

She slowly withdrew her hand, a shadow flitting over her beautiful face. How come there isn't a letter for me? I have been waiting such a long time.

She was still blocking Yin Shu's bike. He rang his bell and said, Excuse me, could you let me pass? The bell gave the girl a shock and she jumped back to the edge of the wall.

In confusion Yin Shu quickly pushed his bike away. A few paces along, he looked back just in time to see the girl disappearing through the side door, pulling it shut creaking behind her. The creeping vines along the top of the frame trembled a little. Yin Shu found this incident a little odd, but then he reckoned patients must occasionally sneak out to take a walk, or have a look at the scenery, so perhaps it wasn't so strange after all. The girl in the white dressing-gown must be a patient at the hospital but he couldn't begin to guess what was wrong with her.

The autumn days were now getting cooler, the song of crickets had died away. Maple leaves were turning red, and foliage from the other trees started to shed, covering over the moist ground underfoot. The leaves would either flutter in the wind or lie pasted to the earth, rotting away silently. From high above, this autumn scene on Maple Wood Road appeared full of warm layers of reds and yellows, making most passers-by forget the existence of the hospital behind its high walls, and that not a few yards away lurked a kingdom of illness and death.

Yin Shu the postman liked Maple Wood Road in the autumn.

His wheels crunching on dead leaves sounded like soft whispers. Yin Shu raised his head and looked around. Beneath a wide clear October sky new leaves were clinging to old branches. At times like these his breath seemed to coincide perfectly with that of nature, and his heart would fill with joy. Nobody understood why Yin Shu was always happy in the autumn, just as nobody could understand his impenetrable sense of isolation during the other three seasons. The beast in the postman's heart was known only to himself, and he never had the urge to let anybody else near it. Yin Shu started humming a folk song from his native North East, but his warm rasping voice came to an abrupt halt.

The girl in the white dressing-gown was there again, standing by the door, holding a length of vine torn from the wall. She seemed to be waiting for somebody. Who? Almost immediately Yin Shu realized from the expression in her eyes that it was him she was waiting for.

White Cherry. The name popped up from the back of his mind. He automatically started searching through the post bag to see if there was anything for her. But he need not have bothered. He already knew that there was nothing addressed to White Cherry. That there had never been anything addressed to White Cherry.

Postman, is there a letter for me?

No. Yin Shu shook his head. He wanted to steer his bike past her, but her sad and urgent gaze forced him to stop. He fanned open all the letters so that she could see for herself. He said look, all the post for the hospital is here. Your name is White Cherry, there isn't a letter for you.

They all call me Cherry. She peered closely at the letters, her slender jade fingers flicking through every envelope. There was still a tinge of hope in her voice – perhaps they just put Cherry.

No. You can see. Nothing for Cherry.

She let out a long melancholy sigh which made Yin Shu examine her face properly for the first time. A sigh laden with so much unhappiness ought to have come from someone who had been through all the vicissitudes of life, and yet the girl standing in front of him was so young, so beautiful, her soft black hair streaming down, glistening with the sheen of youthful vitality. She was tracing the wall lightly with her fingers, her eyes moist with tears. No letters for her. Never any letters for her. Yin Shu felt a warm current course through his veins, melting his cold heart. He was suddenly filled with an overwhelming sense of pity for this young girl called Cherry.

You are always standing here waiting for a letter, he said. Could you tell me whose letters you are waiting for?

I am waiting for a letter from my mother. I have been waiting every day for a year. But she has not written to me.

Yin Shu was intrigued. You have been in hospital for such a long time, how come your mother doesn't know? Hasn't she been to visit you?

She is somewhere far away. I know that she is thinking of me every day, and I think about her every day, but why doesn't she write to me?

Perhaps she doesn't know your address, or the letters might have got lost on the way. These things happen all the time, Yin Shu said.

Cherry's sobs were becoming more distinct. Autumn sunlight streamed through the twining vines to fall on her face and white dressing-gown, forming intricate patterns of light and shade. The girl was sobbing, leaning against the wall, her every gesture drenched with deep sorrow.

Try and be patient, perhaps your mother is already on her way to you. Yin Shu awkwardly waved his bundle of letters, not knowing how to comfort her. He coughed a little. Apart from your mother, is there anyone else who might write to you? If you tell me I'll try to look out for their letters. Is there anyone else?

Da Chun. Da Chun ought to have written by now. He knows I'm here. The girl raised her wide sleeves, half hiding her tearful face. There seemed to be more to her story. Da Chun's letters should have arrived by now. I gave him everything. I have suffered so much because of him. Other people might forget me but he won't. Why hasn't he written?

I don't know, perhaps his letters are on their way. All of a sudden a white ambulance sped down the road and disappeared through the front gates of the hospital reminding Yin Shu that he must be on his way. I have to go, he said apologetically. A wind had risen, making the girl's dressing-gown billow up around her, but her tears were still wet. Yin Shu pushed his bicycle a little way, then looked back and said, it's getting cool, you should put on something warmer.

Yin Shu's colleagues at the West Side Post Office noticed some tiny changes in him lately, the most obvious being the smile that occasionally flickered on the corner of his lips. Most people imagined that he must have found a woman. Unusually, Yin Shu now went over to the sorting department every day to offer help. Although he spoke little, it was soon obvious that he was not there because of any great passion for sorting letters, but because he was looking for something. One day, somebody decided to be direct and asked, Yin Shu, whose letters are you looking for? He hesitated for a moment and then said, have any of you seen a letter for White Cherry, addressed to the Maple Wood Hospital?

Who is White Cherry? they enquired. Is she your girlfriend? Confronted with their crass questioning Yin Shu again fell silent. The smile on his lips became distant, mysterious.

Yin Shu was still Yin Shu and his strange encounter that autumn remained his own secret.

Autumn is a rainy season with falling leaves – the rain would cleanse the town overnight, and the leaves would fall in the rain. Yin Shu noticed that the girl called Cherry always appeared on mornings after a wet night. She would be leaning against the wall, her white dressing-gown and her body giving out a faint scent of rain and leaves, full of sorrow and poetry.

The girl was there again, wearing the same thin white dressing-gown, spotlessly clean, as white as snow, as ice. Yin Shu approached with a mixture of excitement and anxiety. There were no letters for her, still no letters for her. He walked right up to her side, but dared not look into her eyes.

There are still no letters for you, he said, his foot lightly kicking up the rotting leaves on the ground. Don't be impatient, wait a little longer, something will turn up.

No, my patience has run out. The girl's voice seemed less sad than before. She was standing between the door and the dangling twines of vines, combing her long hair with her fingers. Yin Shu felt her gaze linger on his face for a long time. He raised his head and saw her eyes, deep as autumn pools, full of mystery and gentleness. The girl said, I am not going to wait for the letters any more. I was waiting for you.

For a moment Yin Shu was puzzled. He scratched his head. Why? If you are not waiting for your letters, surely I cease to be of any significance.

I want to talk to you. The girl broke off a length of vine and started to pick at the tiny leaves. Her every gesture made an indelible impression on Yin Shu. She said, I want to talk to you. In the hospital nobody ever talks to me. Nobody likes to talk, I am so bored I could die. I am going crazy with loneliness.

Yin Shu sensed a change in the circumstances. The expression on the girl's face made him feel bold. Talk? All you want to do is talk? Yin Shu stared at her awkwardly. With a wry smile he said, talking happens not to be my strong point.

But every time I sneak out you happen to be here.

You are a patient at the hospital, shouldn't you be talking to your doctors? Yin Shu said. They are supposed to care for you. Why don't you talk to them?

They never listen to me. They don't want to listen to me. You are different, I feel that you are the only person I can talk to. The only good person in the world.

Why do you say that? You don't even know me.

No, I do know you. The girl gave him a fleeting smile. She crossed her arms and cuddling herself, looked down at her white dressing-gown. I wear this all year round, whether it is cold or windy or snowing. I often feel cold. Nobody has ever said to me, it's getting cool, put on something warm. Only you said that.

Yin Shu found himself blushing inexplicably. A little embarrassed, he muttered, it is turning cold, why are you still in something so thin?

Because this is all I have. I don't have anything. There are lots of things I want to tell you, do you want to hear?

Yes I do, but I am a postman, and I still have my round to finish.

Yin Shu saw disappointment flit across her face, tears already welling up in her eyes. He wanted to stay but needed to go. Thinking as fast as he could he said, with all the sensitivity he could muster, tell me the number of your bed, I'll come and see you on my day off.

Ward nine, bed nine, very easy to remember. The girl turned towards the high wall of the hospital, repeating the numbers with her sorrowful voice, Ward nine, bed nine. You won't forget your promise, you will come and see me?

I never break a promise, I will come. Yin Shu rode off but he had only gone a short distance when he felt a breeze behind him, trailing a string of tiny footsteps. The girl had caught up with him, barring his way. She was looking at him in a slightly odd way.

What is it? Yin Shu had to stop. He said, I won't lie to you, I'll come and see you.

I believe you. The girl was suddenly shy. Looking down she said, can you give me something? Anything. Something on you right now.

Anything? Yin Shu asked, not understanding. First he touched his cap, then the keys in his pocket. Neither was appropriate. His voice was full of apology, I'm sorry, but I am in my uniform and I haven't got anything with me I could give you.

Anything will do. I don't want a present, just something of yours. The girl sounded urgent and sincere.

Finally Yin Shu took out a handkerchief from his pocket. It was a man's handkerchief with blue and grey checks. Will this do? It's not very clean but it's all I've got.

Yin Shu still remembered the way the girl looked when she took the handkerchief from his hand. She was full of happiness, content-ment even. Clasping her souvenir she ran like a deer through the side door of the hospital, waving the piece of square fabric in the air, letting it flutter, her white dressing-gown dancing gracefully in the light October breeze.

The following few days were beautiful and sunny. Every time Yin Shu passed the hospital on Maple Wood Road the side door remained firmly shut, the moss on the hinges and the rust on the locks testifying to its scant usage.

The girl in the white dressing-gown didn't come out any more. Yin Shu the postman found this strange, as strange as her sudden appearance when he first set eyes on her. Craning his head to look back at the closed door, he felt puzzled and somewhat disappointed.

Yin Shu did not forget his promise. One Sunday morning, he took off his green uniform, and walked into the hospital in his ordinary clothes. The man at the reception recognized him and asked, have you come to visit a patient today? Yin Shu nodded but offered no explanation. He wore his distant, mysterious smile.

This was a big hospital. Yin Shu walked across what seemed to be an infinitely large patch of withered grass smothered in dead leaves.

Finally he stepped out of the garden and into a maze-like corridor filled with the scent of medicine. Wandering back and forth, Yin Shu began to feel intrigued. As a postman he could usually find his way around, but whatever he did today he was unable to locate ward number nine. Where could it be? Eventually he stopped a couple of nurses rushing past. Is there a Ward Nine here? Their answer gave Yin Shu a shock and made him wonder if he was in the middle of a nightmare.

One of the nurses said, Ward Nine doesn't exist any more. It has been converted into a morgue.

The other one pointed to the woods at the back. If you go through the woods there is a building with a red tiled roof. That's the mortuary.

Yin Shu can't remember how he made it through the woods towards the red building or how he managed to summon his impetuous courage.

In front of the door there was a man repairing a cart for transporting corpses. Yin Shu asked him, is there a girl here called White Cherry? Yes, the man replied, I think she's number nine. Yin Shu asked again, do you know when she died? The man said, I have a feeling it was last summer. She has been lying here with no one to claim the body, I don't know why. Who are you? Are you a relative? No, Yin Shu said, I am nobody, I am a postman. I just wanted to come and see her.

Yin Shu's face was white as a sheet. With his hand clutching his chest he walked gingerly towards bed number nine. There he saw once more the girl in the white dressing-gown, her beautiful face almost alive, her lonely expression just as he had always known it. Yin Shu looked down at her right hand, delicate as white jade, tightly clutching a blue-grey checked handkerchief.

Translated by Carolyn Choa

Su Tong

Young Muo

A woman called Shih-feng came to Cedar Street one day, making enquiries about Dr Muo of the United Clinic. Hurrying, her face clouded over with anxiety, the other women in the neighbourhood did not at first notice her great beauty.

Someone passing by told Shih-feng that the United Clinic had shut down the year before and had since been turned into a scrap merchant's, but that Dr Muo still lived in the building. They asked if it was a consultation she wanted. Shih-feng was carrying a red nylon bag and was nervously twisting its handles. Stuffing the vegetables further down she looked up and down the street and said, no, it's not me who is ill. It's my husband.

As usual, the scrap-yard reeked with the stench of rubbish, the most pungent of which were chicken feathers, sold before they had properly dried out in the sun. Shih-feng walked through a pile of feathers, instinctively holding her nose with one hand. Some workers pointed her in the right direction. Go right in, they said, just give the doctor a shout.

Shih-feng stood in the middle of the courtyard and bellowed, Dr Muo, Dr Muo. Windows on either side of the building were thrown open in response. It sounded as if a voice was answering from behind each one. Then a bearded man chewing something leant out and looked her up and down. Shih-feng turned towards the west window but nobody was there. All she could make out was an old-fashioned redwood bed with a mosquito-net hanging over it. The net seemed to shudder a little, then fell silent again.

Are you Dr Muo? Shih-feng asked, turning back to face the man with the beard.

What seems to be the problem?

My husband is ill. Everybody says Dr Muo has a secret formula for his condition. I have come all the way from the northern part of town. It took me some time to find this place.

Where is he feeling the discomfort?

Er ... Shih-feng hesitates, her fingers still twisting the handles of the nylon bag. It's ... he fell ill after drinking some cold water.*

Drinking cold water eh? The man behind the window was scrutinizing Shih-feng's face, his eyes seemed to light up for a moment. Almost immediately he said, I'll come with you to have a look, I have to fetch my case, shan't be a second.

Shih-feng waited a short while in the courtyard, then Dr Muo appeared in his white coat carrying a medical bag. Shih-feng was still holding her nose against the stench of the chicken feathers and old shoes, burning with impatience. She heard Dr Muo leaving instructions with somebody behind the other window. Stay in bed, have a rest. Shih-feng didn't wonder who was inside the house, nor did she perceive the difference in appearance between this young man and the legendary Dr Muo, because her husband was groaning with pain at home, because her heart was in turmoil.

Without exception the locals on Cedar Street loathed Dr Muo's son. He was bone-idle, feigning illness most days which enabled him to stay home in bed. In the spring he would loiter, in the summer he fished, in the autumn God only knew what he got up to, and in the winter he hibernated like a big black bear. The discrepancy in moral character between father and son was so pronounced that people in

---

* Traditionally in China, it is believed that drinking cold water after sex is extremely dangerous and can cause serious illness, hence Shih-feng's embarrassment in expressing the nature of her husband's illness.

the town hailed Young Muo as a prime example of the degeneration of modern youth.

Nobody could figure out why Young Muo went home with Shih-feng that day, only that the doctor had flu and had spent the day in bed. Perhaps Young Muo's outrageous behaviour stemmed from his concern for his father's health. But medicine was not a game, and whatever his motive, Young Muo should never have gone.

It was a beautiful day in July, sunny after the rains of the plum season. Young Muo and Shih-feng walked side by side through the noisy Cedar Street, one relaxed and confident, the other anxious and tense. Young Muo was chatting away, hoping to lighten the mood of his companion. Occasionally Shih-feng would flash him a smile, displaying that charm peculiar to young married women.

By the time they were crossing the open ground next to the local railway, the midday sun was beating down remorselessly. Please wait a moment, I have an umbrella. Shih-feng fished out a folding umbrella from inside her bag and opened it. That was how Young Muo and Shih-feng came to share an umbrella on their way to visit the patient.

Shih-feng's home is on Cloth Street to the north of the city. There is only one room: the bed, the stove, the night-stool were all here one next to the other. Shih-feng's husband was reclining on the bed, his hands on his belly, his forehead covered in beads of sweat. When he saw Shih-feng enter with Young Muo, his lips moved a little, muttering something which sounded like 'doctor' then he began to groan again.

Young Muo stood by the door, casting a couple of sidelong glances at the man on the bed, when his smile suddenly froze. All of a sudden it occured to him that he was supposed to do something useful, and panic crept into his eyes.

Shih-feng fetched a flannel from the wash basin, wrung it dry and started dabbing at her husband's forehead. She said, does it still hurt as much?

The man said, it's a little better. It feels like a weight, like a sharp piece of stone pressing down.

Young Muo sat on the edge of the bed as if deep in thought, one hand reaching out clumsily to feel the lower abdomen of the sick man. Does this hurt? Did you say it's like a sharp piece of stone?

The man frowned. Yes, it hurts, like a sharp stone.

Have you had your appendix out? Young Muo enquired.

Yes. Shih-feng interrupted. But it was the cold water. He was thirsty, he drank cold water.

I got out of bed and drank a bowl of cold water, the man added, obviously not inclined to elaborate. He said to Young Muo, we understand this condition is your specialty.

Young Muo's expression went a little blank. Falling ill after drinking cold water? He muttered to himself. I know you got ill after drinking cold water, the question is how is it possible to get ill by drinking cold water? Engrossed in his own thoughts, the patient in front of him suddenly seemed rather comical. Casually he said, you needn't tell me any more, I know exactly what this is. I'll write you a prescription. After three doses you'll be right as rain.

Young Muo was very nervous when he opened up the medical bag to look for the prescription pad. The names of several herbs flashed through his mind – scutellaria bailkalensis, angelica, bellflower, plantago seeds ... In any case these common herbs couldn't do anyone any harm. Young Muo took out his father's prescription pad and laid it out on top of the greasy, messy table. To his surprise and delight there was a prescription already written out on the first page. He had no idea for whom this was intended. Young Muo let out a sigh of relief, composed himself and copied it word for word onto the next page.

After fanning it dry, Young Muo departed. Shih-feng thanked him and saw him out. Dusk was already encroaching when they stepped onto the street. Young Muo stifled a giggle and asked Shih-feng a strange question.

Is that your husband?

Yes, why? Shih-feng didn't see what he was driving at.

Is he really your husband?

Yes, of course. Frightened and perplexed, Shih-feng looked at Young Muo. Dr Muo, what are you trying to say?

Nothing. Young Muo's fingers drummed on the medicine bag. Pulling a face he said, here is what one might call a fresh flower planted in cow dung – it's a terrible shame that's all.

Without waiting for Shih-feng's response, Young Muo had already bounded over to the opposite side of the street. Shih-feng hadn't expected the doctor to be such a tease, somehow it didn't seem to go with his reputation or status, but she had no time to reflect, she must hurry to the herbalist before they closed.

Naturally, the first problem arose from the prescription. The next morning, Young Muo was idly playing chess with somebody or other in the scrap merchant's courtyard, when he saw the woman called Shih-feng hurrying towards him. At once the colour drained from his face – the game he had embarked on the day before was beginning to scare him now. His first instinct was to run, but then that might make matters worse. He decided to brazen it out. Standing up he walked towards Shih-feng.

How is it going, is your husband better?

The pain is gone, but he's got terrible diarrhoea. All night long he suffered. I am afraid he will not be able to stand it much longer. Shih-feng was panting. Overnight her pale peachy complexion had turned sallow. She grabbed hold of Young Muo's shoulders and pleaded with him. Dr Muo, I beg you to come and have another look at my husband.

Young Muo was relieved that the worst had not happened. At least the man was still alive! What could a few herbs possibly do in any case? He surmised his father's prescription must have been a laxative.

How do you treat diarrhoea? He didn't know. He wasn't sure if he shouldn't end his charade there and then, go home, confess, and seek his father's advice on the correct prescription. But circumstances did not allow this course of action. Shih-feng was looking at him with such hope, such helplessness. Moist with tears, those eyes now seemed specially beautiful and affecting. Unable to control himself, he patted her on the shoulder and said, Don't worry, I'll come with you straightaway.

The second time Young Muo went to Shih-feng's home on Cloth Street, he wore khaki trousers and a white dacron shirt, a tune on his lips, a pair of plastic slippers on his feet. Nothing in his appearance in any way resembled a famous doctor of medicine, but Shih-feng and her husband were in too much of a panic to notice that anything was amiss.

The cramped, untidy house was stale and rank. Shih-feng's husband was sitting on the night stool, holding his head in agony. He looked weak and drained. Occasionally the man would drop his hands and look up forlornly at Young Muo, his expression full of shame and desperation. It was as if he wanted to speak but ended up merely sighing and shaking his head.

It's good to let it all out, Young Muo lit a cigarette and said. This is a natural healing process. All sufferers of this illness go through this stage. Once everything has come out, you will be well on the way to recovery, you'll see. You have already expelled the sharp stone.

But I am worried that he can't bear this much longer, Shih-feng said. Dr Muo, is there any way you could put a stop to this?

Stop the diarrhoea? Young Muo thought for a moment. There is no need to do anything else. Just stop taking the medicine and it will stop quite naturally.

That day Young Muo spent the whole morning at Shih-feng's house. Strangely enough, the diarrhoea gradually subsided. Shih-feng's husband sat up in bed, thanking Young Muo with his words and with his eyes, telling his wife to cook something special for lunch. Young Muo did not refuse. He stayed and ate a simple but delicious meal. Shih-feng even brought out a bottle of white wine. Young Muo didn't drink normally, but he wanted to drink that day. He poured the wine down his throat, while Shih-feng's husband cheered him on from the bed. The wine chased away any shadow of anxiety he might have had before. He was boasting now. If you have any peculiar illness in the future, don't hesitate to call on me, I guarantee you instant recovery. Then he picked up an old harmonica, and performed a tender moving love-song for the benefit of Shih-feng.

At first nobody on Cedar Street was aware of Young Muo's house calls on behalf of his father. This tomfoolery had, by accident, ended rather well, as was often the case in life. Young Muo was well-known on Cedar Street for his dissolute behaviour, and indeed he soon forgot about the whole incident. Furthermore, he was certain his father had no inkling of what he had done. Young Muo continued to revel in chess, swimming, loitering the streets, sticking his head into gatherings of girls, and generally fooling around. In short, his routine remained largely unchanged.

*

What happened later started on the first day of autumn. This day, on his way home from a gathering at a friend's house, Young Muo found himself in front of Shih-feng's house on Cloth Street. There was the familiar peach-coloured blouse airing on the clothes-line. Suddenly he had the urge to go in.

He dismounted from his bicycle and walked through a narrow alley partitioned off by wooden boards. As luck would have it, he found Shih-feng sitting on her doorstep shelling soya beans.

Shih-feng recognized Young Muo at once. Pleased and flustered, she almost kicked over the bowl of kernels. Young Muo, on the other hand, was calm as can be. Having exchanged a few pleasantries he sat down to help.

Is he not home from work yet? Young Muo asked.

No, he gets off at six, Shih-feng said.

I guess he's all right now?

What?

I mean the illness. It doesn't trouble him any more?

Oh, the pain stopped a long time ago. Shih-feng felt a little shy and turned away to toy with the beans in the bowl. After a while she said, it's such bad luck but his health is no longer the way it used to be.

Has he some other ailment?

Actually it's not what you might call an ailment exactly. Shih-feng hesitated, her face turning bright crimson, her eyes fixed on the yellow and green husks on the ground. Let's not talk about this anymore. She tried to change the subject. Dr Muo, won't you stay for supper?

A minor illness can become serious if not treated properly. I know what's wrong with him now. Young Muo was watching Shih-feng's expression, a trace of a smile hovering on the corner of his lips. This kind of illness is not difficult to treat. It all depends on whether or not you really want to treat it. I have a ready-made remedy right here.

Shih-feng's eyes remained firmly fixed on the husks on the ground. Slowly she moved from Young Muo's side. Would you shell these for me, please? Shih-feng picked up the bowl of beans and went over to the stove, a strangled sob escaping from her throat as she rose. I am so unlucky. She flung the beans into the pot and sobbed. Why am I so unlucky? Sometimes I feel as if my life is completely pointless.

Hey, you haven't opened the door on the stove, how are you going to cook? Young Muo remained seated where he was. He thought he might as well point this out.

Shih-feng squatted down to open the ventilating door on the stove.

Hey, you haven't put any oil into the pot either, Young Muo added.

Shih-feng stood up to go and fetch the oil jar from the table. The jar was empty. Damn, damned damnation! she grumbled to herself, shaking the jar with agitation.

I'll go and get some for you. Tell me which is the nearest shop. Young Muo raised himself up from the floor.

Shih-feng stood holding the jar. When she lifted her head and looked into Young Muo's face, her eyes were already brimming with tears, burning with desire. With one hand she skilfully closed the kitchen door behind her. What Shih-feng said then was a surprise to him, Young Muo told people later – he was not at all psychologically prepared for what happened next.

He comes home at six, she said.

Soon the news of the affair was all over Cedar Street, because a woman who worked at the scrap-yard had seen them emerge from the bushes by the city moat. Whenever Young Muo passed through the scrap-yard, the women would regard him with interest and shout out, Young Muo, are you on your way to burrow in the bushes again? He would give them a wave and reply, sure, why not, why waste the opportunity? If the bush is waiting, why shouldn't I go burrowing?

This was the season of autumn winds and falling leaves. Young Muo of Cedar Street was immersed in an unexpected game of romantic intrigue. His daily movements had become unpredictable, his aimless wandering now a rare sight in the neighbourhood. Meanwhile the esteemed Dr Muo was kept completely in the dark. He had guessed his son was in love, what he didn't know was that the object of his desire was a married woman named Shih-feng who lived on Cloth Street.

The women working at the scrap-yard predicted that sooner or later disaster would strike. Sitting in their ringside seat in the shop, they were soon rewarded with a wonderful bit of drama. One day, three livid, heavily built men stormed into the courtyard, looking for Dr Muo. The women pointed to the building behind. The men leapt over the rubbish screaming obscenities, one of them sweeping up a broken broomstick *en route*. By the time the women realized they meant trouble and rushed over to see, a fight had already started. What shocked everyone was that these men were attacking Dr Muo. Old Dr Muo and his wife were caught in the middle of the fracas – Madam Muo was screaming, Dr Muo had turned a deathly white, a gaping bleeding wound on his forehead, too stunned to speak.

The women rushed up to separate them, shouting for Young Muo at the top of their voices. There was no response from the east window – Young Muo must have gone out. It suddenly occurred to the women that these people had got the wrong man. It was the son not the father they were looking for. So they all yelled, stop, stop beating him, you've got the wrong man.

Fortunately the three men stopped at once, they too could see that old Dr Muo didn't look like the person they were looking for. They dropped the broomstick, wiped their hands and said, we thought it was a little odd too, why would Shih-feng go with an old man? Then full of suspicion they asked Dr Muo, if you are not him, then who is that scum Dr Muo?

Old Dr Muo was furious and refused to answer. Perhaps he had guessed by now that he was taking punishment for his son. The doctor tried applying some Yunnan ointment on his own head wound, but the incident had left his hands shaking, unable to perform a function so familiar to him. In fury he threw the bottle on the floor and screamed at the thugs: get the hell out of here! Get out!

Dr Muo spent the entire afternoon on his redwood bed, swearing at his son, his wife weeping by his side. The old couple strained to hear Young Muo's footsteps. At midnight they heard a sound outside. Dr Muo screamed through the window: get out, get the hell out! But it was only the neighbour's cat.

Young Muo did not come home all night.

The following day Young Muo sneaked into the courtyard,

drenched from head to toe. The women noticed his wet clothes and crept over to have a peek through his window. Young Muo slammed shut the window and said, what are you peering at? I am changing my underpants.

When Madam Muo saw that her son had returned safely a weight lifted off her chest. But she couldn't understand why he was so wet. Knocking on his door she enquired: What happened? Did you fall into the river?

No, I didn't fall, I jumped, Young Muo replied.

Why did you jump for no reason?

She made me, so I jumped. She didn't know I could swim, Young Muo said.

Madam Muo was horrified. Her voice began to tremble. Where is she? How is she?

I don't know, I fished around for her in the water for ages. At one point I almost got hold of her hair and then it slipped out of my hands again. After that I lost sight of her.

Somebody had died! Madam Muo saw stars and passed out.

There was chaos in the courtyard. Thankfully the women rallied round to help, so that Young Muo was able to apply some restorative musk oil to his nerve-wracked parents and settle them down to rest on their redwood bed. In the midst of the commotion a woman came looking for a prescription. Young Muo screamed at her, what sort of timing do you call this to come looking for a cure? I'll give you a couple of grams of arsenic!

This was how Dr Muo came to have a stroke. The famous doctor who had been respected all his life now lay in his redwood bed, staring angrily at his son, unable to utter a single word. It was only now that Young Muo woke up as if from a dream. He picked up the wet clothes on the floor, and the image of Shih-feng's body bobbing on the moat flashed by in front of his eyes. Suddenly he turned to the group of women and asked, you don't think I'd be charged for murder do you?

Don't be silly. It wasn't you who killed her was it? She wanted to die herself. In matters like these both parties must be held responsible, one of the women consoled Young Muo.

Says who? Another chipped in, hiding a smile with her hand, she wanted to tease Young Muo a little. If you don't get life you will be sure to get the death penalty, either way your game is up.

•

The hearse from Cloth Street slowly wound through Cedar Street. Everyone stood up from their lunch to take a look at the corpse and the mourners. This was the first time most people had seen the woman called Shih-feng. Her face was bouncing up and down with the rhythm of the cart, swollen, pale, yet still beautiful. Shih-feng's name had become familiar to the residents of Cedar Street over the past few days, and now finally she was laid out for all to see, a drowned body.

The hearse stopped in front of the scrap-yard. Shih-feng's husband and family were intent on laying out the body in Dr Muo's house, in order to expose Young Muo's crime. According to ancient custom, this was the most effective way of demanding justice. The Muo family were unable to put up any resistance. Young Muo had escaped to a relative's in another town, and the old couple had no choice but to lie in bed waiting for whatever fate had in store for them. Life and death no longer held any meaning. Their hearts had turned to ash.

So it was that Shih-feng's body stopped at Dr Muo's house for three days. The women at the scrap-yard and their customers were full of complaints about the increasingly foul stench – this was one reaction on Cedar Street. Then there were those who came by holding their noses to sneak a quick look at the body and still holding their noses, swiftly depart again.

Apart from the chance to look at Shih-feng, one was given the opportunity to take in her poor faithful husband at the same time. There he would be, telling anybody who would listen how Young

Muo had deceived and then killed his wife. We thought he really was Dr Muo. Who could have guessed he was a con-man? Shih-feng's husband repeated endlessly, who would have thought he was a good-for-nothing scoundrel, a lout, a layabout?

This was the season of autumn winds and falling leaves. The focus of almost all the gossip on Cedar Street had to do with Young Muo. It was impossible not to go back to his childhood, when all anybody could remember was idle bad behaviour and waste. Ever since he was a child, Young Muo had not done a single thing worthy of praise in his life. His association with a death like this was therefore hardly surprising. If he had to go to court one day he would have fully deserved it. The person to feel sorry for was Shih-feng. A moment's confusion had led to the sacrifice of a young and beautiful life.

One of the women at the scrap-yard who dabbled in witchcraft remembered the first time she saw Shih-feng. Apparently she had known immediately Shih-feng was heading for disaster. When she moved, the woman said, I saw a red light trailing behind her...

Translated by Carolyn Choa

Mo Shen

The Window

1

In March of last year I was on a train heading home after finishing my press assignment in another province.

Seated opposite me were two middle-aged peasants deep in a discussion about something. After a while I realized they were going to get off at Xi'an and were worrying whether or not they could catch the long distance bus for Huxian that same day.

Suddenly a clear voice from a seat near the window interjected: 'Don't worry! The bus leaves at two p.m. There'll be plenty of time for you to catch it.'

We all looked in the direction of the speaker, a young girl about age twenty-five, with large shining eyes and plainly dressed. She had been reading quietly and nobody had taken any notice of her.

She sounded so sure of herself that another passenger then asked: 'Do you happen to know if there is a long-distance bus to Yaoxian this afternoon?'

'Yes, there is one at three o'clock,' the girl replied.

'What about an earlier one?'

'Yes, but...' she hesitated. 'I'm afraid you may miss it.'

'What time does it leave?'

'At one o'clock.' After a moment's thought she added, 'Look, this train is due to arrive at Xi'an at twelve p.m. I'll draw a map for you. Once you reach the station, continue up that road until you come to the number eight bus stop. Take a bus from there to the long distance

bus terminal. If you hurry, you may just catch it.' Then she sketched out the route on a scrap of paper and handed it to the man.

'Thank you very much, comrade,' he said with gratitude as he looked at the map. 'Do you often travel on the long distance buses?'

The girl smiled and shook her head. 'No. Never.'

'Oh, do you live in Xi'an?'

Again she shook her head.

Puzzled, the man persisted: 'Then you often go there?'

'Not frequently.'

By then all the listeners were interested and another passenger asked out of curiosity: 'Then how can you know the place so well?'

This made the girl blush. Then she smiled modestly and murmured: 'I ... I just know it, that's all.' At this she lowered her head and resumed her reading.

Since everyone's curiosity had been aroused, we all hoped she would say more, but she remained silent until she got off the train thirty minutes later.

Shortly after my return to the press, we were contacted by the railway bureau about a mass emulation efficiency drive. They had organized a team of highly skilled workers to demonstrate various aspects of their work and the opening demonstration would be that day. They would like to have it reported in the press to help boost their campaign.

The demonstration had already begun when Old Shi and I arrived at the large hall which was packed full. The audience enthusiastically clapped or praised the performers, who were the best chosen from among nearly ten thousand workers and staff of the railway bureau. Some were elderly, others middle-aged. The last to be introduced was a girl, whom to my surprise I recognized as the one on the train.

A booking clerk at another station, she could give the distances and the fares of journeys between all the main stations in the country.

Her supposed passenger making the enquiries was a young man.

Glancing disinterestedly at the girl, he asked in an offhand way: 'How far is it from your station to Yinchuan and how much does it cost?'

Without hesitating the girl promptly replied: 'It's 1,460 kilometres, and costs 25 yuan 80 fen.'

Astonished, the youth became more interested and picking up a railway map he enquired: 'How about to Zhuzhou?'

'1,900 kilometres, and the fare is 29 yuan 30 fen.'

The audience applauded. Then an old man, who for many years had worked as a booking clerk, stepped forward. He asked with interest: 'You certainly know all about the main stations, but what about the branch lines?

'I'm not so sure.' Then blushing she added shyly: 'I'll try.'

'How far and how much to Xihekou on the Yingtan-Xiamen line?'

'It's 1,682 kilometres and costs 28 yuan 30 fen.'

'To Ranjialin on the Guiyang-Guilin line?'

'1,100 kilometres at 23 yuan 6 fen.'

Delighted, the old man, his head to one side, asked: 'What's your name?'

'Han Yunan.'

'And how long have you been working?'

'Three years.'

'Well, I'll be damned! Three years!' Amazed, he turned to the head of the group who confirmed it. Then facing the audience and raising his arms, he exclaimed: 'Amazing! This is the first time in my life that I've met someone who can challenge me.'

Before the audience could clap, the director announced: 'Comrade Han can also tell us the arrival and departure times of trains at all the first and second class stations administered by our bureau. So let's carry on now with the demonstration.'

Another round of applause broke out.

Han's performance not only astonished us laymen, but also the old railway workers. Her knowledge went far beyond the limits of her job.

Everyone could just imagine how many hours she must have spent learning all those thousands of dull numbers. We wondered how she could have done it and if the long distance buses in Xi'an had anything to do with her work?

Eager to find out more, Old Shi and I returned to our office. We reported all this to our chief editor and discussed our plan with him. With his approval, we visited Han two weeks later.

Old Lei, secretary of the station Party committee greeted us warmly and took us to the booking office where the clerks were busy at work.

As we watched young Han, we discovered that she was exceptionally fast selling tickets and that her method was rather unusual. Apart from her answering normal enquiries, she would sometimes hold out a card for a passenger to read. Once she even answered a passenger in his own dialect which we found very difficult to understand.

After an hour she closed her window for a break. Knowing that we were reporters from the press made her very shy. It was only after our repeated assurances that we would not publish anything without her approval that she relaxed and talked to us.

She began:

I started work as a booking clerk in 1974. Many people thought it was a good job, but I wasn't satisfied. There were all sorts of little things to attend to and I was terrified of making mistakes with so much money passing through my hands each day. However, that was the work. As I was completely green and slow at the job, the passengers would get exasperated. Trains and passengers pass through here from all parts of the country and by night you are hoarse from talking. But some passengers who've never travelled before drive you mad. You tell them the express train does not stop at small stations and they demand to know why. Once an old man, hearing the announcement that train 83 would be delayed until 19:00 hours, came back to return the ticket he had just bought. When I told him the train would arrive in about an hour, he became furious and yelled: 'You are supposed to serve the public, yet you are cheating me. The announcer said the train would be delayed for nineteen hours!'

Such incidents were not uncommon and I grew more and more fed up with the passengers. Gradually my attitude towards them also got worse.

In the summer of that year, a middle-aged man wanted to book a ticket to Huaxian. I informed him that train 54 did not stop there.

'Eh?' he replied as if deaf.

I repeated the information, but his response was the same. After the fourth or fifth time, I was fuming. 'What's the matter with you? Please move aside.'

He looked rather taken aback and then handing over his money again said: 'I want a ticket for Huaxian.'

I almost lost control of myself, but seeing all the passengers lining up, I simply tilted my head and said: 'Eh?'

'A ticket for Huaxian, please.'

'Eh?'

Everyone burst out laughing.

Flushed with anger the man complained: 'What a terrible attitude!'

'Nonsense! My attitude to you is good,' I retorted. 'You acted like that several times, I only said it twice. Yet see how impatient you are!' And so saying I slammed the window shut.

I honestly felt he was in the wrong and sat sulking behind my window.

Three days later I had a row with a passenger going to Sichuan, who wanted to pay his fare in small coins wrapped up in a handkerchief. I told him to go to a shop and get banknotes, but when he refused I would not sell him the ticket.

A fierce quarrel ensued.

The following day was Spring Festival. My boyfriend, Lu, had arranged to come to my home.

His full name is Lu Bingxiang and he is an assistant locomotive driver. We'd been in love for more than six months, but felt too shy to tell our families, so we arranged that he would come to my home first on the holiday and then I would visit his home on another holiday.

Early that morning I got up feeling a mixture of happiness and nervousness and told my mother about Lu's coming. She became very upset and complained that I should have told her earlier, but when Lu came she relaxed and bustled about preparing a meal. As she was cooking, she discovered she'd run out of soy sauce and sent me to buy some from the store.

Since we needed it urgently I dashed into the store only to find the shop assistant chatting animatedly with an old acquaintance. I waited patiently for a while and when she made no move to serve me, I finally called out: 'Comrade, please can I have some soy sauce?'

She just glanced in my direction and then ignored me.

I repeated again: 'Comrade, I'd like some soy sauce...'

Before I could finish she had stalked over, glaring, and snapped at me: 'Since you haven't even bothered to take the lid off your bottle, how can I fill it?'

Stung by her rough tone, I replied: 'Look here, comrade, I didn't come to have a quarrel with you...'

'Did I choose to pick a quarrel with you?'

'What do you mean? What an attitude!'

'If my attitude is not good, I must have learned it from you!'

'Why you!... You!...' Words failed me. Then an argument started over the counter.

When I was on duty the next day I related the story to my colleagues who all agreed I had been badly treated. As we were talking, Secretary Lei entered and so I told him about the incident.

After I'd finished, he gave me a serious look and said: 'Young Han, I'm glad you hate that sort of attitude. Both that shop assistant and you are serving the public, so in the future you can remember the affair as a mirror which not only reflects the behaviour of others but also your own.' Then he took out a letter from his pocket and asked me to read it.

Puzzled I took the letter, which was from a worker at the Lueyang Steel Plant. He'd written:

... Early in March this year, my wife gave birth to a child. I wired my mother to come and help us out. Two days later I received a telegram that she was already on her way.

A week passed but she had still not arrived. Then another week. Anxiously I sent another telegram asking what had happened and the reply came that she should have arrived over a week ago. I wondered what could have happened to her.

Since my mother had never travelled by train before, my brother wrote her destination on a scrap of paper and gave it to her in case she made a mistake changing trains. When she disembarked at your station, she went to the booking office to buy a ticket. The clerk at window number two, a young girl with two short pigtails, asked her where she was going. My mother replied she was going to Luoyang, but perhaps the clerk did not care. Anyway the girl took the money and carelessly threw her a ticket for Luoyang. My mother then remembered the paper in her pocket and was about to show it to the girl, when she slammed the window shut. Although my mother knocked on the window several times, the girl ignored her.

As a result my mother travelled all the way to Luoyang in the opposite direction. At Luoyang she traipsed about for a whole day until she finally discovered she was in the wrong place. Being old and having high blood pressure, when she heard that she was more than 500 kilometres from her destination she fainted from worry and fatigue. She was rushed to hospital, where she lay in a coma for twelve days, her life in danger.

Only when the hospital at last contacted us, did we understand what had happened. Then I went immediately to Luoyang...

This caused my family great distress and it has made me think deeply. I've often been guilty of carelessness and irresponsibility in my work. Now I see how I should behave. After all, whatever work we do in this country, we do it to serve the people. All our actions affect the masses. It is to be regretted that so few people seem to realize this so far. I don't know who that clerk was, nor do I wish to know. Who is to blame? She's only partly responsible. I just wonder why our standards and morality have declined to such an extent in the past years. Why have so many good comrades been affected? I ask myself these questions all the time. I hope that your station leadership will not criticize that comrade too much. Rather, if possible, please let her read my letter. It may help her understand more about the responsibilities of a booking clerk...

Unable to continue, I buried my face in my hands and wept on my desk. I felt so ashamed and I would have felt better if that comrade had called me some names, but instead of blaming me, he had tried to excuse me. From his letter, I knew he was a very thoughtful man with a high political consciousness. Then I thought of myself, and of all the foolish things I had done...

When my fit of crying had passed, I raised my head and biting my lips admitted: 'I'm sorry. I was very wrong. Secretary Lei.'

Seeing that I was genuinely upset, he said in a gentle voice: 'Tell me, Young Han, what did you do wrong?'

'I should never have treated the passengers like that.'

'Anything else?'

I tried to think of something to say but couldn't.

'Young Han,' he continued, 'maybe what I'm going to say isn't correct, but I think the main problem is that you do not understand what it means to be a booking clerk. Why should you be so impatient to our passengers, when normally you're quite an even-tempered sort of girl? Our passengers are people going to be reunited with their families after long absences or those helping to build up our country.

Just think of their dreams and hopes as they eagerly line up in front of your window. Everything you booking clerks do is connected with our country's construction and the lives of our people.' He paused and still looking at me seriously continued: 'Take those peasants from the mountain regions. You get annoyed with them because they have not done much travelling and ask you all sorts of questions, but have you ever thought how in the old society they could never have travelled by train? Today they can. You may not be able to tell, but in fact they have undergone some profound changes. Through our work, we can show them the warmth the Party and Chairman Mao have towards them and that they can take pride in being the masters of the state. If we do a bad job we may hurt their feelings. So tell me, Young Han, what have you done for them?

Despite his gentle tone, I felt ashamed to the core. Tears filled my eyes when I considered his words.

That night my remorse kept me awake.

From then on, my attitude towards my work changed. The next day, a passenger enquired about a ticket to Dalian. 'Twenty-nine yuan 9 fen,' I stated. Instead of giving me the money, he leaned forward and repeated his question. I again replied but he still failed to catch what I had said. I repeated it loudly a third time but he kept holding the money in his hand.

The day before I would have flared up. But now I resolved not to lose my temper no matter how often he asked. Finally I wrote down the figure on a piece of paper and showed it to him. He immediately gave me the money.

Once he got his ticket, he still hesitated to leave.

'Is there anything else I can do for you, comrade?' I asked.

Suddenly he poked his head in through the window and said gratefully: 'You've been so kind, young comrade!' Then pointing to his ear, he added: 'I suffered from an ear disease and my hearing is bad. Other people usually get very impatient with me, so thank you for your kindess.' He fumbled in his bag for a large red apple, which he presented to me, while the other passengers cheered.

No passenger had ever been so friendly to me since I first began working. I thanked him but gave him back his apple. Tears moistened in my eyes.

After that I was very strict with myself. I discovered that quite a few passengers had bad hearing. To find out the reason I went into the booking hall to become a passenger myself. To my surprise I found the hall very noisy, so that although one could hear the passengers speaking clearly behind the window, they could not hear the replies distinctly.

This really upset me, because I had thought that many passengers had deliberately pretended not to hear me, whereas in fact they could not. My own subjectivity had landed me in a lot of trouble!

Once I changed my attitude towards work, all sorts of ideas about how to serve the passengers better sprang to my mind. For example, names of some stations sound alike, so I wrote them on cards and would show these to passengers. Whenever they could not make out the difference between Xiangfan and Xiangtan, or Xinan and Xi'an, I would show them the card. Passengers come from all over the country and pronounce the names of the stations in dozens of different ways. I tried to learn to speak and understand various dialects.

Young Zhu, another clerk, helped me on her own initiative. The youngest member of our staff she was very enthusiastic and had been in a literary and art group. She could speak a little of the Shanghai and Guangzhou dialects, and so each day she gave me lessons.

In our free time we practiced calculating on the abacus, drawing a railway map, writing labels with the distances and prices covering the main network of stations. These we put up around the office and recited in our breaks. I loved practicing, reciting them as I got up or when I went to bed, even on the bus to and from work.

Before this Lu and I had always gone to see a film or walked by the River Weishui on our days off. Now I begged him to help me memorize the figures, by asking me questions while I tried to answer. My mother thought things had gone a bit too far and so she scolded me. 'Are you crazy, you silly girl?' She said, 'How can you relax and enjoy yourselves with you talking all the time about kilometres or millimetres!'

After three months my work became much easier. By the end of the year I had sold 20,000 tickets without making one mistake. One day, Secretary Lei came to me with a bundle of letters and said: 'Your letters, Young Han.' Startled, my heart beat fast. Perhaps something had gone wrong again because of my carelessness. But all the letters were full of praise.

'Well, Young Han,' he said beaming, 'try not to get too big-headed.'

I grinned sheepishly.

Zhu punched me and laughed.

2

Young Han paused for breath. Spotting the cup on her desk, I poured her some water.

'So you had no more problems after that?' Old Shi asked. She was silent for a while and then continued.

It was in March 1976 that under the influence of the 'Gang of Four' everything was turned upside down and right became wrong. Some people at the station put up a big-character poster criticizing Secretary Lei as a 'capitalist-roader'. I said I didn't agree and so some people began to attack me.

The main attack came over my application for membership of the Youth League. It had been approved by our booking office branch and referred to the main branch for discussion at a meeting. Unbeknownst to me, the secretary of the station's Youth League committee had secretly conspired with some members to attack me. I went to the meeting very excited, taking my notebook to jot down their opinions. Within ten minutes after it began, I could no longer write anything down. The first speaker said I had only a vague understanding of the political situation and so I didn't dare to go against the tide. The next criticized me for not concentrating only on politics but on trying to become a bourgeois specialist at my job. The third went even further. He asked if Secretary Lei had shown me a letter from a worker in the Lueyang Steel Plant. He declared it was a counter-revolutionary letter slandering public morality by saying it was no good and that our standards had declined in the past years. He said only those who were against the revolutionary order of the time would claim that. He alleged that by showing me the letter Secretary Lei was involved in counter-revolutionary activities and accused me of being an accomplice of this 'capitalist-roader'.

It was so obvious that the whole show had been rigged. I was trembling with rage. Several Youth League members unconvinced by these attacks took the floor on my behalf. Pointing at my accusers, Young Zhu said: 'I think you are jealous of Sister Han and so you are trying to attack her. All the passengers praise her and don't notice you. That's why you hate her.' But she couldn't go on, she was choking with tears of indignation.

Early next morning I saw some big-character posters attacking me and mentioning Young Zhu. One claimed there was a sinister person manipulating us. There was also a cartoon of a girl with short plaits, her head raised while reciting a list. On her forehead was a lump as a result of having bumped into a lárge boulder, and written on the rock were the words: 'Wrong way!' Behind the girl, another with long pigtails, was encouraging her: 'Not wrong! Bump again!'

I could hardly bear the pressure. Whatever my many faults, I did not think it was wrong to try and serve the people. Ignoring everyone I turned away and rushed back into the office, tore the labels with the station names on them off the walls, threw them to the floor and stamped on them. Secretary Lei came into the office just as I had nearly finished.

I found it hard to stop the tears streaming down my face. Finally I cried out: 'That's the last time I'll ever do such a stupid thing again.' Angrily I stamped on some more cards. 'I worked like an ox day and night ... And what do I get? Nothing but criticism! It's just asking for trouble. Oh, hell! Why did I ever try to be an ox?'

All the time Secretary Lei smoked, wrapped in thought and saying nothing until I had calmed down a bit. Then he raised his eyes and said matter-of-factly: 'Young Han, do you think everyone should clap their hands and sing your praises just because you've done a good job?'

His remark jolted me.

In the same tone, he continued: 'If that's what you think, then you're very wrong.'

Then he began to pick up the cards one by one, dusting them while he spoke: 'You say you won't be so stupid again, that you'll never again be like an ox. Well, I'll tell you a story ...

'Before Liberation, there was an outstanding revolutionary fighter who threw all his energies into revolution to liberate the people. He crossed the snow-covered mountains, waded through marshlands and endured unimaginable hardships.

'After Liberation he devoted his life day and night to the interests of the people. Everyone says the light often burned all night in his office and he never got enough rest. One day his staff and attendants ganged up to write a big-character poster demanding that he take better care of his health and rest more. Having read their opinions, he agreed but said that as he was getting older, he had to do more work for the Party.

'He said he was the ox of the people, and that is how he had worked genially all his life. For years he had relished work and insisted on shouldering the most tiresome, the hardest, the heaviest loads, whole-heartedly and without complaint, making great efforts to pull the plough and sow the seeds of happiness for the people ...

'Finally he became seriously ill through overwork. Rumours about his illness spread among the people and all expressed the one hope that after some time he would be cured. Young Han, how the masses loved him and hoped he would be ...'

I was moved by the quiver in Secretary Lei's voice.

After regaining his self-control he went on: 'But actually his case became worse and knowing that he had not long to live, he worked even harder. Even when he was too weak to speak, his thoughts were for the people and he hummed *The Internationale*. When his pain was intense, he told his nurse: "Please go and look after some other patients. You can do no more here!" Later ... later after his death had been announced, eight hundred million Chinese people wept as one throughout the whole country. They all said ... such a man will never die ...'

'Of course, Premier Zhou!' I exclaimed, standing up. 'Our beloved Premier Zhou!'

Secretary Lei made as if to continue but could not as tears welled in his eyes and, covering his face with his hands, he remained thus for a long time. Then his voice came as if from far away: 'Young Han, you're still ... too young to understand. I've been a Party member for thirty years, but when I think of Premier Zhou, I feel as if I'd never even qualify.'

Wiping my eyes with my handkerchief, I was about to answer when a voice called for Secretary Lei from outside the door. It was Young Zhu. She must have overheard our conversation. Racing into the room, she grasped Lei's hand as tears flowed down her cheeks.

Then she suddenly turned and rushed towards me saying: 'Sister Han, I want to be an ox for the people too.'

Hugging each other, we both wept.

That day changed me. I seemed to have grown up, talking less. Everyone noticed it. Young Zhu also changed from a laughing girl, fond of singing, to a meditative one who spoke not a word. I knew she was gathering her inner strength. It added a depth to our lives. We secretly started an emulation campaign, to see which of us was more considerate to passengers, who was more competent. We carefully studied the needs of the passengers and discovered that they had three main worries. First they were worried lest they should arrive at their next destination at an inconvenient time. Next they were anxious in case they missed their connections. Lastly they were concerned that they wouldn't be able to find their units or a room in a hotel. So we learned not only all the timetables for trains run by our bureau, but also all the bus timetables in all the province's main cities. Then we learned the directions to all the large hospitals, factories, colleges and universities in Beijing, Shanghai and Xi'an. It wasn't going beyond our duty. For the sake of our passengers, I was willing to learn all kinds of information.

I'd arranged to visit Lu's home on May Day. On 28th April, he came to see me. As soon as he came into the room and saw me memorizing the timetables, his face darkened.

'What's the matter with you?' I asked.

He sat their sullenly and only when I pressed him did he reply: 'Yunan, please stop all this nonsense.'

'Why?'

'Stop pretending!' he answered irritably. 'They've been putting up big-character posters criticizing you. Yes, you've been making enormous efforts, but you'll end up being labelled as a bourgeois specialist. Don't invite more trouble for yourself.'

'But Lu...'

He interrupted: 'The secretary of your Youth League committee has cited you in a speech at a branch meeting as a typical negative example because of your activities in "Encouraging the Youth to Go Against the Political Current" and it has spread throughout the whole bureau. Yet you're still in the dark.'

Amazed at his anger, I asked: 'But, Lu, whatever others may say, the important thing is, am I taking the correct path or not?'

'It's no good,' he shook his head. 'All the newspapers and magazines are full of that stuff.'

'But are they correct?'

'Who cares?' he suddenly exploded. 'But if you don't watch out you'll get into a whole lot of trouble.'

Even though he had a hot temper, he'd never been so angry with me before. I was very upset. 'I know, Lu, I've caused you some trouble too.'

He leaped up and burst out: 'Me? I'm not afraid of anyone! Look at me, I'm as tough as can be. They can do what they like to me.' He banged his fist on the table and paused before continuing: 'But I don't like them getting at you, Yuan!' He wheeled round and went out slamming the door.

The Weishu River was near my home, its banks wide and quiet. That afternoon I went there by myself. The pebbles reminded me of the times Lu and I had thrown stones into the water for fun. At the big locust tree I remembered the day I had told him about my problems with the passengers, complaining that some were unreasonable. He had smiled without commenting. All these memories made me feel worse. I tried to shut them out and wandered about aimlessly. I raised my head and saw in the distance the Qinling Mountains in a blue haze. The Weishu flowed rapidly south as far as the eye could see, the sunlight shimmering on the water. Eagles soared high above the horizon. It was a beautiful sight.

Sometimes nature's grandeur refreshes one and causes one to reflect. I seldom do that. But at that moment I thought of the endless flow of history, the revolutionary cause, mankind's ideals. I stood there transfixed gazing into the blue distance. It was over the rivers and mountains and land of our country, like this river and land, that the ashes of Premier Zhou were scattered. He dedicated his life to serving the people and working for future generations, and his spirit lived on in our hearts guiding us. He had owned nothing. He had had no children of his own. And his ashes had been scattered in accordance with his selfless ideals. What pressures and problems could I not withstand when I thought of Premier Zhou?

That brought me back to earth as I dashed back to my office, saying aloud to myself. 'No! Not over my dead body. You won't allow me to serve the people? Well, I won't take it. I won't!'

3

So I carried on serving the passengers as best I could like before. If I had some free time, I would help the old people, not for praise but because it was my job and I didn't care about the criticism. One Sunday Young Zhu and I went to Xi'an to sketch a map of the city's principal units. Then we memorized it.

On May Day I did not see Lu nor go to his home in case I embarrassed him. I often longed to see him, but I tried to push such thoughts to the back of my mind and threw myself ever more into the work.

In the middle of July, I was working on the night shift. It was raining and there weren't so many passengers in the booking hall. At about half past eight, an old peasant more than fifty years of age suddenly rushed into the hall. He leaned his head towards the window and panted: 'Comrade, which is the fastest train to Xi'an?'

Sensing his urgency, I immediately replied: 'Number 46 express train at 21:03.'

Handing me the money, he turned to his anxious companions and said: 'There's no time for a meal as the train will be here soon.'

I asked what was the matter as I gave him the tickets. He explained that they were commune members from the Five Star Brigade in the Qinling Mountain region. A school graduate from the city working in their place had accidentally poisoned herself while spraying insecticide and now she hung onto life by a thread. They had set off the previous evening carrying her by stretcher to the station without stopping. Now they were rushing her to Xi'an for emergency treatment.

Seeing the anxious looks on their perspiring faces, I asked an old worker to keep an eye on the tickets while I went to the duty room to get the key to unlock the platform gates to let in the stretcher before the train arrived. Then I rushed back to my office to fetch a raincoat to cover the girl. Perhaps those commune members had never travelled before; anyway they kept thanking me over and over again.

The girl was certainly in a serious condition, delirious and tossing about. Worried about her, I saw her face when one of the peasants lifted the quilt and was startled. It seemed so familiar! Yet when I looked again carefully, I was sure that I did not know her.

The train arrived, and so I hurried to buy some cakes. I gave them to the old peasant. 'Here, uncle, you must be very hungry. Please have these when you're on the train.'

Accepting them, he replied, his voice choking: 'You are so kind to us. We peasants of the Five Star Brigade will never forget you!'

'Now, now, uncle!' I felt very touched by his words. 'It's you who've suffered so much to save this girl's life. How can I ever forget you?'

He was going to say more, but as the bell signalled the train's departure, I urged him to get in.

The train was about to leave when I suddenly thought of something. It would arrive at Xi'an at 23:31 and the last bus to the hospital left at midnight. Since they'd never been to Xi'an before, they could easily lose time finding the way. And time meant that girl's life! So I quickly drew a map for them with my pen on a bit of paper. Then I held it against the window of the train and explained it to them over and over again until they were quite sure of the route. Only then did I feel at ease.

The train started to pull out and I jumped back behind the safety line. The peasants waved to me from the window until the train was quite a distance from the station.

Lu suddenly flashed into my mind. If he knew how the timetables and maps could help to save a young girl's life, surely he wouldn't be so angry with me? Stubborn as he was, he still was a very sensible fellow. I wondered how he was now.

To my great surprise, a dozen peasant representatives from the Five Star Brigade came to our station a week later with letters of praise. All the passengers were curious and appreciative when the old peasant told the story of that night. News had somehow got around that I was being attacked and so many of the passengers, indignant about the episode, got together to write a big-character poster headed: 'To Attack Comrade Han for Serving the People Is Wrong.' As I was off duty that day, it was not until I came to the yard the next morning that I saw it pasted on the wall with letters of praise. And many passengers had added their own comments in ink, such as:

'Learn from Young Han!'

'Comrade Han is like one of our family!'

And some remarks were even more pointed:

'Those who persecute Comrade Han are opposing Chairman Mao's teachings on serving the people!'

'Comrade Han's spirit in serving the people is correct. Those who go against this will come to no good end!'

I was so overcome that I wept. No one had ever given me such support and encouragement as those people. To serve the people filled me with joy, and I told myself that come what may I would do this all my life. That would be my only aim.

Time sped on. It was nearly the end of August before I had time to realize it. One day, when I had just finished selling some tickets for the express train number 46, Secretary Lei came to tell me there were two passengers outside who insisted on seeing me.

Puzzled, I went out to find none other than the girl student and her father. They both warmly took my hands in theirs.

'How can I ever thank you, comrade,' her father began. 'Xiaolin would surely have died but for your help.'

I explained: 'It was nothing. The people you should really thank are those commune members who brought her here.'

'No. We want to thank you all!' Xiaolin chimed in. 'The doctor said I had a narrow escape. An hour later and that would have been that. When they heard that, all the peasants said we must thank you first. But for you they'd have lost two hours.'

Feeling embarrassed I changed the subject and asked the girl if she was better.

'Fit as a fiddle!' she beamed. 'Sister, my father said that the moment we got off the train, we must come to thank you.' She held my hand tightly all the while, innocently insisting on calling me 'sister'. She positively sparkled with health and I thought what a lovely younger sister she would make.

'You know, you look vaguely familiar to me,' I said. 'I'm sure I've seen you somewhere before.'

'Really?' She looked at me ingenuously. 'But this is the first time I've seen you. Where do you think you saw me?'

I tried hard to recollect but finally gave up. Then we talked about other matters, until I noticed that it was time to return to my work.

'You go back first, Dad,' she said to her father. 'I'll wait here for sister and then I'll bring her home for supper.'

I protested but she refused to listen and so helplessly I went back to my office.

Actually I always felt awkward with strangers for I was shy, but because this family had invited me so earnestly and sincerely, I felt unable to refuse. So when I finally accepted their invitation, Xiaolin's joy knew no bounds. She took both of my hands in delight.

Her mother was waiting at the doorway when we arrived. As I entered, she took me by the hand to the middle of the room and, patting my head, looked me up and down. She kept praising and thanking me. I just stood there in embarrassment, not knowing whether to stand or take a seat.

Xiaolin had disappeared and then strode in with someone who hung about the entrance, reluctant to come into the room.

Surprised at this, Xiaolin urged: 'Hurry up! Come and meet big sister. What's the matter with you today?'

Her brother moved forward dragging his feet. One look at him and I was struck dumb, for it was none other than Lu!

He stopped in front of me staring at his feet, wishing to look at me, but afraid to. His face was red as a beet.

'The moment I heard what had happened,' he stuttered, 'I guessed it could only be you ...'

Both his parents and sister were confused. The girl kept asking: 'Do you know her then, brother?'

Not answering her, he turned to his father and stammered: 'She is ... well, we had arranged ... for her to come ... on May Day ...'

Raising his eyebrows, the truth dawned on Xiaolin.

She threw herself on me and hugged me: '*Aiya* sister ... I mean sister-in-law!' She broke off, jumping with glee and clapping her hands. 'Oh, now I see! Now I see!'

The feeling of family intimacy grew stronger. Then the mother grinning widely was ordered by her husband to stop standing about and hurry and get some food ready for their guest.

I stayed with them until after eleven o'clock, when Lu escorted me home. Instead of catching the bus we chose a quiet path. Lu turned to me as we walked along: 'Yunan, you know ... all these days I've been longing to see you, but I was afraid...'

'Afraid? What of?' I asked.

'Of you, that you'd snub me. Oh, Yunan, are you still angry with me?... Well, what I want to tell you is that I was wrong.'

My heart was beating madly. 'Oh, Lu...' I said softly, and then could find no words to express my feelings. As I looked at him I wanted to laugh, but for some reason tears filled my eyes.

That night I returned home very happy, very excited.

A blush appeared on Young Han's cheeks and her long lashes swept down passionately.

Entranced by her story we were abruptly brought back to earth when she cried out as she looked at her watch and rose to her feet declaring: 'My goodness! I'm almost late for my work!' With that she dashed shyly out of the room.

We did not try to delay her by saying goodbye. She opened her window, smiling an apology, then turned to face the passengers with a friendly and earnest expression.

When we reached the entrance, both of us halted inadvertently, and with feelings of respect gazed back to her window for a while...

Translated by Kuang Wendong

Wang Meng

The Lovesick Crow and Other Fables

The Discommoded Frog

A frog contracted dysentery after a binge of eating unripe grapes. Cramps wrung his bowels, and his appetite disappeared. His gorge rose to his chest, and his head spun dizzily. He lay on his belly in a harvested rice field, gasping and sighing as he surveyed the world with bleary, unfocused eyes.

A timid but studious rabbit scampering through the field heard his moans and wondered what philosophical profundities, what breadth of experience, were implied in these sounds. He looked at the frog's slightly shuddering frame and wondered what farseeingness and maturity and restraint such trembling represented. He respectfully asked to be instructed: 'Great teacher, please do not keep your wisdom and learning to yourself. I may not be worth much, but teach me something. Redeem my obstinate, benighted spirit with the brilliance of your all-embracing compassion and thorough enlightenment!'

The frog spluttered in outrage: 'The Apocalypse is at hand. You at least are an educable young man. Look at that sky: it must have gorged itself sick. You can see little specks whizzing back and forth, and there are mirages of grapes everywhere. Look how bloated it is and how it sags. And look at this land. It is caving in; it is constipated; it has the runs; it is in spasms; it is racked with cramps that make it shake uncontrollably. And look at the sun: it has lost its brilliance too.

143

It is wavering and will probably fall out of the sky soon. When it hits the ground it will start a big fire and dry up the rivers. And there are no ripe heads on the rice stalks in this field. This field is a wasteland, and it exudes the stench of an animal with loose bowels. Those things flying overhead are nothing but a bunch of flies: measly, lowly, droning, no rhythm, no harmony, no classical training...'

Just then a lark flew through the sky over the field and started to sing.

'Master Frog, look! There is a lark,' said the rabbit.

'You think I can't see it? You think I can't recognize it? Do you think it's a lark just because it looks like a lark? What do you know? Even if it looks like a lark, it is really a transformed fly. Can't you tell?'

The frightened rabbit crouched in a foetal position. Suddenly the frog let out a pitiful yell: 'The world is falling apart!'

The rabbit's vision darkened as he plunged into hopeless despair. But only ten minutes later he opened his eyes and discovered that the sky was still the sky; the land was still the land; there was certainly no danger of the sun falling; and on the nearby threshing floor, farmers were threshing the grain. The lark was singing more joyfully than before. But the honourable dysenteric frog had passed into the void.

Boiled Eggs and Radio Calisthenics

My father was a man of wide reading and many talents and he never tired of teaching what he knew. For many years he groomed and trained me, hoping to make a genius of me.

He taught me literature. His favourite book was the *Three Hundred Poems of the Tang Dynasty*, and he tutored me until I could recite them straight through. Any time I tried to read a new book he would lose his temper and harangue me irascibly: 'Do you think you have mastered the whole *Three Hundred Tang Poems*? Do you think you can integrate and apply the marvels, the techniques, the rhymes, the antithetical matching, the word choice, the fitness of idea, the poetic imagery, the realms of thought, the shades of meaning and everything else in this book? Do you think your poems are better than Li Bai's, Du Fu's, Meng Haoran's, Wang Wei's, Li Shangyin's or Du Mu's? Have you surpassed the saints and immortals of poetry? Do you think that Tang poetry is outdated?'

He taught me to sing. His favourite song was 'Su Wu Tending the Sheep'. Any time I attempted to learn a different song, he would question me angrily: 'So you think your singing of "Su Wu Tending the Sheep" is fine, do you? Do you sing it like a master? Would you be graded 110 per cent on it?'

He taught me calisthenics – Set No. 1 of radio calisthenics. Whenever I wanted to study the five new sets, he asked compelling and very logical questions: 'Do you think you've done the first set long enough, and you don't need to improve or keep in form? Isn't the first set good enough for a 160-centimetre runt like you? Do you think...?'

He gave me boiled eggs to eat. When I asked if I could switch to fried eggs or cake made with eggs, he shouted me down: 'Do you think you don't need boiled eggs now? Boiled eggs provide you with calories, animal protein, and vitamins A and C: Don't tell me you want to give them up?'

Due to my father's eloquent rhetorical questions, to this day I have read only one book – *Three Hundred Poems of the Tang Dynasty*. I can sing only one song – 'Su Wu Tending the Sheep'. I can do only one routine of calisthenics – the No. 1 Set of radio calisthenics. I have eaten only one kind of food – boiled eggs.

The Thousand-*Li* Horse in its Dragon Lair

Five years ago I had the fortune to make passing acquaintance with a thousand-*li** horse in a cow stall down in the country. Hunger and exposure to cold had left it beaten down, withdrawn, drooping and reticent. It could only run as fast as a cow; even donkeys did not want it among them. Harnessed to a plough, it fell far short of a cow in strength, so even though it was kept in a cow stall, it was a 'reject' among cows.

Later a few men came who were good judges of horses, and with their knowing eyes they spotted this thousand-*li* horse. They fed it two scoops of oats, and it immediately showed its strength by galloping a few circles, to the amazement of the cows, donkeys, mules and pigs.

Then it rejoined the horse herd. The horses held an impressive reception to welcome its return to the group.

Later it took first place in a horse race. For this it was asked to leave the stable. A special dragon's lair was made for it – anybody knows a horse that can cover a thousand-*li* in one day is really a dragon exiled from heaven. Instead of oats and grass it ate bodybuilding mix, pearl rice, fish-liver oil and calcium with dextrose. Every summer it was watered from an artesian well of beer, and in the winter it drank Maotai and Five Grain Liquor.

Once a common horse went into the dragon's lair by mistake and was driven out with one well-placed kick.

The horse gradually grew fat. Its neighing became loud and coarse, and its stomach was distended. Of course it could not gallop any more.

I can see its future already – smoked horsemeat at the slaughter-house. It makes me shiver at the mere thought of it.

---

* A *li* is approximately ⅓ of a mile.

I Am One of Your Kind

As a nightingale was singing his song one evening, a snake read an essay aloud to it, proving that the snake was one of the nightingale's kind. The article stated that the snake's egg had once been lined up in the same row with the nightingale's egg. That is to say, they were from the same district. Besides, the same sun had shone on their eggs prior to hatching, which proved that they were members of the same clan. Thirdly, they both liked to sing at night, and their singing, from the snake's point of view, was quite similar. Fourthly, they both enjoyed doing things in the garden. Fifthly, neither of them liked the snow and ice of winter. Sixthly, they both liked roses, which proved they had common interests. Seventhly...

The nightingale said in exasperation: 'Even if your article had a thousand items of ironclad evidence, I would not admit that you are a nightingale instead of a snake.'

Then the snake pulled out another article which proved that he was not a snake, and that other snakes could not be his kind. His evidence was, first of all, that his colouration differed from other snakes. Secondly, his measurements differed from other snakes. Thirdly, his body shape differed from other snakes. Fourthly, his fetishes differed from other snakes...

The poor nightingale grew so drowsy from hearing this line of reasoning that he fell into a rosebed and went to sleep.

The snake slithered over, and with one bite he gulped down his fellow creature.

Pretty at First

My first impression of my female neighbour was not bad. But it was a shame she was so fond of dispensing theories on what is and is not beautiful. For instance she often said to me: 'I just don't like noses that stick out. We're Chinese. People with noses that stick out are nothing but xenophilic lackeys. An elephant's nose is very large, but does that make it look good? Most people with big noses don't give a damn about anything, and they think they're better than everybody else...'

Because she said this over and over, I could not help taking a good long look at her nose, and I discovered that it was really somewhat flat.

She also liked to say, 'Hair that is too black does not impress people. Why do I say so? Dyeing hair is popular now. If your hair is dark and glossy, people might think you dyed it. And overseas you see all sorts of wigs everywhere. Just pay a little money, and you can have any kind of hair you want on your head. You can have it coarse or fine, sparse or thick, red, black or yellow.' Then she added in afterthought: 'And that's why I say, the time when you could judge a woman's appearance by her hair is already past.'

She spoke too much. I could not help focusing my attention on her hair, which was actually on the sparse side. It was dry and had a brownish tinge, like buckwheat infected with rust blight.

Another thing she said was: 'I don't believe the folk saying that says, "A good pair of shoes beats a shirt." Shoes are basically secondary to a person's appearance. The Red Army men wore straw sandals during the 25,000 *li* Long March. They didn't have the chance to go to Wangfujing to buy high-heeled leather shoes. The quality of a woman's shoes is not as important as her gauze mask. A snow white mask shows that a woman is civilized, sanitary, thoughtful, concerned

148

for other people, discerning, well-provided for, modern, informed about science, modest, optimistic, judicious, objective, self-restrained and cautious. And what does a pair of good shoes show? It is a sure sign that a woman is banal, superficial, free with money, pretentious, fake and flirtatious.'

Her theory made me notice that though she wore a gauze mask as white as snow, her shoes were quite drab and poorly fitting. There was an awkwardness in her walk, probably because she was splay-footed and had fallen arches.

As she held forth with her aesthetic theories, I finally realized that her looks did not deserve much in the way of compliments.

The Singer who Always Won the Day

Once a singer received no applause after her performance. At a meeting afterwards she said: 'Applause doesn't mean anything. Is the sound of hands clapping beautiful? Is it art? Is it precious like gold? How much can you sell a kilo of it for? Some people get a little applause, and they're walking on air; they forget who they really are. They are chosen to be singing stars and get to ride on airplanes and to cut phonograph records. What a farce! This is corruption of the soul. If you don't believe me, I'll swing *my* rear end and sing dirty songs: see who gets more applause then!'

She also suggested doing an analysis of the audience and lining it up in groups by category to prove whether or not applause had any value.

At another performance the audience gave her thunderous applause. And so she spoke effusively: 'Songs are for people to listen to. No matter how good the lyrics and melody are, it is useless if people don't like to hear them. The eyes of an audience are crystal clear, and listeners have a balance scale in their hearts. If you depart from what the audience likes to see and hear, you become elitist rather than populist, and you deviate from the proper orientation. This leads to isolation, self-congratulation, narcissism, ivory tower obscurantism, despair and degeneration. It is not just the sound of hands clapping that I hear in the music hall: it is the beating of each passionate heart!'

After a while, musical workers held a meeting to discuss unwholesome trends in musical performances and the need to channel the audience's interest and raise its level of appreciation. She brought up the time that her audience had not applauded her as an example and proclaimed: 'I took a stand! I took a stand! I took a stand!'

More time passed, and the musical workers held yet another meeting, where they spoke of the lack of songs and performances which were welcomed by the masses. This time she made an example of her performance that had received thunderous applause and proclaimed: 'I've already done that! I've already done that! I've already done that!'

Comedy of the Ducks

After the publication of Andersen's story 'The Ugly Duckling,' a disturbance arose in the flock of ducks.

'I've been saying for a long time that I'm really a swan, but I've been ignored, looked down on and misunderstood,' said an old male duck. 'My youth has been wasted. Give me back my youth. Give me my swan's feathers and wings. Give me back my swanly pride and honour!'

'This is all because of the farmer's shortsightedness,' quacked a female duck. 'And the turkeys are jealous of anyone with ability! Because of them we are poverty stricken, we are down and out, and we are called "ducks". And what does "duck" mean? The Chinese people think that the main characteristic of ducks is stupidity. Are we really stupid? I may not know what one plus two is, but is that my mistake? Has anyone given me training? Has anyone sent me to university?'

'I believe I've already turned into a swan. I'm going to make sure by looking at my reflection in the lake.' A moulting duck walked to the edge of the lake and looked in, but the graceful shape of a swan was not what he saw. He racked his brains for a while, and finally discovered the truth of the matter. He cried loudly to the others: 'The water in the lake is not fair. This water gives special breaks to some birds! This water has accepted a bribe of toad meat from the swans, and that's why their reflections look so wonderful, and ours look so dull!'

'Down with the lakewater! Down with the farmer! Down with the turkeys. Down with the Chinese people!' The ducks cried in unison, getting more and more angry.

The farmer walked over and hit the leading drake with a bamboo pole. The ducks quieted down immediately.

The swan, who actually had once been an 'ugly duckling' flew overhead through the blue sky, conversing with the white clouds.

After Becoming a Swan

On the other hand, what happens when an ugly duckling transforms into, or perhaps it is better to say, is recognized as a swan?

His life as an ugly duckling was poignant, moving and noble-minded. It drew people to him.

After his reputation was made, and he was given the title and privileges of a swan, was his life still so wonderful and touching?

Suppose he got 'puffed up' and looked down on his duck brothers? He would go around with a fat cigar in his mouth and make a habit of shouting at people. He would demand the best food and proclaim

151

everywhere he went: 'I am a swan. I was once treated as an ugly duckling. I am a swan! The bastards thought I was an ugly duckling!' What would happen then?

Maybe he was an authentic swan, but why did he have to rub it in?

Lovelorn Sister Crow

Sister Crow fell in love with Brother Crow. They were never apart, flying wing to wing and singing duets as if they were joined by an invisible thread.

'How blue is the sky, how gentle the wind, how buoyant the clouds!' Their song was a delight to the ear.

'How blue is the sky, how gentle the wind, how buoyant the clouds!' A group of young crows flew in circles around the admirable couple, singing happily.

Who would have expected Brother Crow to be influenced by the 'new tide' from the West and its 'sexual liberation'? He left Sister Crow in the lurch and didn't even say goodbye.

Sister Crow was heartbroken. She sang, 'Gloomy the sky and dark the land, dreary the wind and bitter the rain. His heart is a wolf's and his liver a dog's. He and his hypocrisy. In this whole crow's world there is no beauty, goodness, truth, youthfulness or justice!'

'Gloomy the sky and dark the land. Dreary the wind and bitter...' The young crows sang after her, but not as resoundingly. Though they had plenty of sympathy, they could not completely understand Sister Crow's feelings. Besides that, their increasing years had brought certain subtle Freudian notions.

Soon the young crows were splitting off in pairs, and when they got intimate they started billing and cooing like on the movie screen, all they heard from Sister Crow was a string of curses: 'Damn you, damn you, damn you!'

'Look at this emptyheadedness! Look at this false beauty! Look at you living in a dream. Don't you know that passion is emptiness and emptiness is passion? That is a truth that cuts through everything!'

'Love is a prostitute! Love is a thief! Love is a were-fox! Love is a witch. You have to be above love if you want enlightenment.'

'Love is a demon! Love is a sea of suffering! Love is poisoned wine! Love is a dirty rag! I don't see any worth in such vulgar pursuits!'

'So you're flying now; you're pairing off and singing. Do you think your flying and courting and singing are anything special? Don't fool yourselves. I had a grander time then. You've been diddling around all this time, and you haven't come up with anything original. It makes me laugh so hard my molars fall out! It's more of the same old thing. It's all the same delusion I went through years ago!'

'Damn you! Damn you! Damn you!'

At first the young crows were shocked and puzzled, but later they got used to it. Before this they had not known the bitter taste of love, but now they showed a fair amount of sympathy for Sister Crow. Still they were absorbed in flying, courting, singing, and nibbling, and could not spend time thinking of Sister Crow's affairs. They were too busy.

A Story I Heard

Below is a story I heard. I was told it is a translation of an African fable which appeared in a magazine published in the Sixties. It is so perfect, and it gets across its message so well, that I just had to write it out here. It is not my creation, and I hope the editors will not count this story when they count up the number of words to pay me for.

A man who found fault with everything lay beneath a walnut tree, sighing and venting his spleen. 'How unfair this world is! You try to find what sort of justice or right there is, but it's like picking through filth. There is nothing but a load of modern superstitions and primitive ignorance. Look at this tall-standing walnut tree. It has deep roots and a straight trunk; its foliage is luxuriant. It stands here, imposing and dignified, but the walnuts that it bears are not as big as the eggs of a chicken. This is ridiculous! It's moronic! It's an affront to the honour of all trees. An insult is what it is! And look at that pumpkin over there – a limp, spindly vine. It has no spine, no upstanding character. It lacks the distinction of growth rings or a woody stem. A creeping thing like that, down among the mud and dog turds, could never be a rafter or a beam … But somehow the gleaming golden pumpkins that grow on that vine are three times bigger than my head!'

As he cried out at the way fate had treated the walnut tree, and attacked the pumpkin for its upstart plumpness, a slight breeze loosened a walnut, and it fell – 'bop' right on his head.

He jerked back in fright and his heart skipped a beat. It was a good while before he regained his wits. He felt his skull, and it was as sound as ever. There was no cavity or concussion or wound. There was not even a little goose egg.

He found himself giving praise from the bottom of his heart: 'Praise to all-knowing and omnipotent heaven; glory to the Lord! In such a just and equable world as ours the wisdom and grace of heaven are everywhere. Just think, if the walnuts on this tree really had grown as large as pumpkins and one of them had fallen down, it would have smashed my gourd. For me that would have been the end to all eternity!'

Translated by Denis C. Mair

Chen Shi-xu

The General and the Small Town

In a small town like ours, miles from anywhere, the slightest change attracted great attention.

'Hey! Does anyone know why they're putting up a new house near the prison at the foot of Ringworm Hill? Who does it belong to? Are they enlarging the jail again?'

Ringworm Hill, about two *li* from the town centre, was actually a large rocky mound.

'You're all so dim!' The owner of this mocking tone popped his head out from behind the door of a shop. He was the barber. He was bald on top, though his few remaining hairs on the sides of his scalp were carefully oiled and combed.

Known as a newsmonger, he was an important figure in the small town. Though confined to his shop, he seemed to have his fingers on the pulse of the town and was the first to know of any new development. When passing on news, people often started with, 'According to the barber...' The barber liked to add a touch of drama to the news. If he heard something important, he never announced it in his small shop. He would, like now, step out and go to the crossroads where there were all kinds of stalls.

'I bet you've no idea. The house is for a general who will soon come here to live.'

'What? A general? Come to live with us?'

The news caused quite a stir. In a backwater like ours, the coming of a general was sensational news. It was indeed a great honour bestowed on us.

The barber cleared his throat and warned, damping their enthusiasm, 'But don't raise your hopes! In fact, it's nothing special.' The listeners craned forward, their curiosity aroused, asking why.

'Why? Humph! Listen, but this is for your ears only. Don't let on. Strictly confidential! The general's been dismissed! He's been exiled here!'

'Exiled! Why?'

'He was a renegade.'

People gaped in astonishment. Like a bolt from the blue it struck at their vanity. They were disappointed and downcast.

'In name he's a retired officer.' An ingenious propagandist, the barber regained the listeners' waning attention. 'He still keeps his rank of general.'

Then he continued in a low voice, 'He was allowed to keep either his army rank or his Party membership. I may as well tell you all about it. People like us are just ordinary citizens, that's all. But he was an officer and a Party member. Now why do you think he chose to remain in the army?' He stopped abruptly, letting them ponder over this question. Holding their breath, they looked at one another, not knowing what to say.

Then a young porter from the transportation team, having put aside his barrow and elbowed into the crowd, broke the silence. 'In my view, he should have kept his Party membership. It's an honour!' Quite a few people seconded him.

The barber pursed his lips disapprovingly.

'No, it's better to remain in the army,' an old tailor observed prudently. 'A man has to eat. Where can he get money from if he is demobbed? What can he live on if he's no income? He's probably no skills and you can't expect an old man like him to till the land, can you?'

'Right, you've got a good financial brain,' remarked the barber, patting him hard on his shoulder. Excited, the tailor grew red, feeling greatly flattered.

'That's just what the higher-ups thought too, so they pensioned him off, allowing him to wear his army uniform.' He paused to glance at the young porter and went on, 'Don't you know, as a high-ranking officer he gets a fat pay?'

People exclaimed in admiration. But talking of money reminded the barber that he hadn't started work yet and he hurried back to his shop.

But someone caught his coat tail, asking, 'Tell us, when will he come?'

'Haven't you anything in that thick head of yours?' He was obviously impatient. 'Don't you see that house? When it's completed, he'll certainly move in there.'

Reluctantly, people scattered, murmuring their guesses and predictions or sighing over the ill-fated general, taking the news to all the corners of the town.

*

Now, with the listeners departing, let's have a look at this lovely little town.

The town had two streets only wide enough to allow the passage of one jeep. Six hundred metres long altogether, they crossed at the centre of the town. The streets were paved with flagstones here and there, while paint peeled from the jutting-out buildings. All these showed its antiquity.

A stream, only ankle-deep, meandered around the town. Unfortunately, on its banks were heaped piles of rubbish and debris.

It was really surprising! People gaped when they first set eyes on the general. Everybody thought the same. 'No wonder he was dismissed. An old duffer like him doesn't deserve to be called a general!'

What would a general look like then? Though we'd never met one before, he didn't fool us. A general should have grey hair, straight eyebrows, and perhaps a paunch. He must be tall and strong, looking impressive and awe-inspiring like in the films. But this man was small, wizened and wrinkled. Moreover, he was slightly hunched and lame in one leg.

Far from being broken by his unlucky circumstances, he paid great attention to his appearance as if to make up for his poor physique. Whenever he walked in the streets, his uniform was always well ironed without any creases, and he held himself straight like a soldier. The red star on his cap and his two red collar insignia stood out brightly. No matter how stifling the weather, he kept his jacket collar buttoned. Though lame in one leg from an old war wound, he walked steadily. However, all this unfortunately reminded us of his disgrace.

We often watched him, not in awe or contempt, but out of curiosity. He didn't seem to mind at all. On the contrary, he walked about, though with some difficulty, the second day after his arrival.

Leaning on his shining wooden stick, he limped from one end of the street to the other. Or sometimes, he strolled along the dry stream bed strewn with litter. Someone said, tongue in cheek, that the old man kept moving habitually because he had walked all over China!

After a short period, he began to make some unfavourable comments about our small town, in which we had lived happily for a long time. He asked, for instance, 'Why don't you spend some money on putting a tarmac surface on the two streets?' or 'Why don't you dig a large pit on the other side of the stream for your rubbish so that it can be made into compost?' Our sophisticated and clever local cadres would excuse themselves saying, 'Where can we get the money for it? Our salaries are pretty low!' or 'We're simply too busy!' Their listeners would chuckle, catching that dig at the general.

Our feelings towards this queer general were rather mixed. Though disgraced, he still got a decent pay. We all felt his criticisms and suggestions were well meant, yet no one was willing to befriend him.

Apparently, he soon noticed our mood, for he stopped making any more embarrassing criticisms. Instead, he found himself a place at the crossroads. There under an old camphor tree, whose top had once been struck by lightning, just opposite the barber's shop, he stood upright sometimes for hours, supported by his stick. Blinking his bleary eyes, he stood musing silently. No one knew what was in his mind.

His posture was really amusing. Vendors nearby raised their heads to glance at him from time to time, and even passers-by lingered to look at him before continuing on their way. Behind the glass windows of his shop, the barber gazed at him standing in the dusty street and joked cheerfully, 'What do you think he looks like?'

'A sentry?' someone said.

The barber shook his head.

'A traffic policeman then,' said another.

He shook his head again. After some further exchanges, the barber said matter-of-factly, 'Have you ever been to Hankou? At one end of Sanmin Road, there's a bronze statue of a figure standing erect and holding a walking stick. Just like him. Exactly!'

Gradually, people got used to seeing the general standing there, like a bronze statue. He became like the coppersmiths, cobblers and tinkers at the corners of the crossroads. If you didn't see one of them for a couple of days, you would feel there was something missing.

But he was not a statue, he was a man, and one with a shrewd mind moreover. And one day people would discover that he was also possessed of a hot temper.

One Sunday, there was a great commotion in front of the butcher's, as some young rascals with baskets on their backs fooled around, enjoying making a racket.

The general stood as usual viewing the scene, while his hand holding the stick trembled slightly and the veins in his temples swelled in anger. Suddenly he limped across, raised his stick and tapped a soldier on the back. Wet with sweat, he was squeezing his way through the crowds and shouting boisterously. Turning his head abruptly, he met the old man's blood-shot gaze. He withdrew from the throng at once and asked, 'Anything I can do for you, sir?' Though a new recruit, he decided that the old man must be a high-ranking officer.

'Tidy yourself up before speaking to me!'

Darting a timid, worried glance at the general, the cherubic-faced soldier quickly righted his cap, did up his collar buttons, rolled down his sleeves, and finally lowered his head, staring down at his shoes.

'Which unit are you from? What's your job?'

'I'm a cook in the mess of the garrison stationed here.'

A few brief seconds of silence followed.

'Attention!' the general suddenly shouted. This professional harsh order immediately silenced the noisy crowd. Heads turned to look at the two soldiers, who seemed oblivious of everything around them.

Panting, the old man gave a second order, 'Turn left! At the double! Quick march!'

Still holding himself erect, the general breathed heavily, gazing at the retreating figure.

All was very quiet now at the crossroads. As though checked by some strange power, the jostling, noisy crowd automatically fell into line. At that moment, they felt the might of the old man, who had once commanded thousands of troops.

*

Not long after, another incident shocked the small town, making those who were inclined to side with the weak realize that something was wrong with their present situation.

It was inevitable that the old general, who had been through hard times, had had his health impaired. Apart from the care of his wife, once a head nurse in a large hospital, the general was permitted regular check-ups in an army hospital some fifty *li* away. A sign of charity perhaps. He could also go to the town's hospital in an emergency.

One day, he became pale and ill, breaking out in a cold sweat. As he was entering the local hospital, supported by his wife, a country woman who had been sitting on a bench by the consulting room suddenly tugged at his coat, begging, 'Please save my child! I hurried over thirty *li* to get here before dawn, hoping to see the doctor as soon as possible, but...'

Inside it was so dim that they could hardly see each other. The general felt the boy's forehead, then started. 'Hurry up!' he shouted. 'Take him to the doctor at once!' Then he tore into the consulting room and said to the doctor seated at a desk, 'Doctor! Here's an urgent case!'

Sitting behind the desk was the doctor, the wife of the town mayor and head of the hospital. Her occupation, social position and the way she carried herself served to demonstrate that she was the most important woman in the town. At that moment, she was listening to the heart of one of her distant relatives and chatting with the patient about her daughter's dowry. She was so engrossed that she forgot to remove the stethoscope. Interrupted by the general's cry, she glared at him and said, 'Register first.' Then she turned back to her relative, all smiles.

'He registered ages ago!'

'Then you'll have to wait... Yet, it's worth having a daughter.'

'But he was registered first.'

She turned abruptly and asked, 'Little Wang, did you call number one?'

'Of course!' replied a young nurse bent over giving an injection.

'See,' said the doctor and, turning to the peasant woman, she added, 'you weren't here when your number was called. You'll have to join the queue again.'

'But I was here! Our village doctor told me that my boy was suffering from acute pneumonia...' The woman, carrying her child in her arms, broke off, out of either nervousness or disappointment.

'She probably didn't hear you clearly,' said the general.

'Then she can learn a thing or two about our regulations. A country has its laws and a hospital its rules. If we don't stick to the rules, there'll be chaos, won't there?' Throwing her stethoscope on the desk, she shot the general a reproachful glance.

'But this is an urgent case! You can't be so rigid! Now, what number was this patient?' asked the old man, pointing to the relative.

'H'm! So you've come to make trouble today, eh? Are you the kid's father or grandfather?'

'You should be ashamed of yourself!'

'What? Ashamed? You old fool! Why should I be ashamed? Am I anti-Party or a renegade?'

The general raised his stick.

The cocky woman screamed, protecting her head with her arms.

It was so quiet that you could hear a pin drop in the room. Her relative was flabbergasted. Nobody came out to grab the general's stick. It remained quivering in mid-air. People hoped it would strike the doctor's snub nose.

But the stick did not fall. Instead, the old man stretched to grab the other end and snapped it in two.

Turning with difficulty, he asked his wife, 'Is there any medicine at home?'

She nodded, knowing that he meant medicine for pneumonia.

In a trembling voice, he asked the peasant woman, 'Do you trust me? Then follow us!'

The news of this incident soon got around. Now even timid people dared to show their dissatisfaction.

It was true that we were rather cut off from the world and, as a result, we were rather easily cowed. But it was precisely this that made us rely on our own judgements. If a 'renegade' helped others in difficulty while a 'Communist' bullied the people, shouldn't their titles be exchanged?

For a couple of days, there was no sign of the general under the camphor tree. People began to anxiously whisper about him. It was said that his condition had taken a turn for the worse. And since the incident in the consulting room, he had been deprived of the right to use the town government jeep to go to the military hospital.

Late one night, some fine young men led by the porter came to the general's house. They put the old man on a stretcher and hurried him off to the military hospital.

*

1976 began terribly. It was bitterly cold. Overhead the clouds were hanging thick and heavy, while the ground was muddy and slippery. Our little town looked more desolate than ever.

As if favoured by fate, despite the bad weather, the people in the town had the monotony broken by some encouraging news.

Just after the New Year, the barber came to the crossroads with an air of importance. No doubt, he had something vital to announce. People gathered round him at once. Having cleared his throat, he began, 'You know what, the general's no longer a renegade! His case has been cleared!'

'Are you sure? How do you know?'

'You don't believe me?' chided the barber, glowering at the questioner. He never tolerated any doubts about his information. However, he went on, 'If you don't believe me, ask him.'

'I told him,' admitted the porter, elbowing his way forward. Not used to speaking in public, he blushed. 'When we were in the hospital, two men from the general's original army came and said that the general's record before he joined the Red Army had been cleared. He never betrayed the revolution.'

'Humph! Ridiculous to have wronged a veteran revolutionary for such a long time,' the barber butted in with his comment. 'I said long ago that the general was every inch a damn good man! Indeed...'

'Indeed, sufferings test a man.' People sighed, sympathizing with the general.

'Then he'll soon leave us, won't he?' the tailor raised his question hesitatingly.

A far-sighted man! When the inevitability of this was forced into their minds, the townsfolk again became depressed.

'Well,' the barber said after a sigh, scratching his bald head, 'It's only natural. Ours is a small town. How can a little temple house a big Buddha?'

People felt sad. It was always the same: you realized a thing's worth only when you had to part with it.

'What a mean lot you are!' the porter snapped in anger. 'The Party and the State need him badly. You always wished him good luck. Now it's come, you're miserable. Isn't that selfish?'

Yes, it was. The general had his work to do, which was of vital importance. After all, we couldn't ask him to be our mayor, could we? So his leaving would be something worth celebrating.

People looked expectantly in the direction of the hill, hoping that the general would come and stand under the camphor tree as before. They longed to see him, and if possible, have a chat with him.

The desire to see the general grew stronger. Then someone suggested that everyone should go to call on him, since he had come back the previous day and was still unable to walk about.

Why not? So the crowds headed for Ringworm Hill.

The desolate, rocky hill became a lively spot. Normally people steered clear of it, if they could. There was neither wood to collect nor grass to graze cattle. Moreover, for centuries, it was where those executed had been buried. If you had to pass this ominous hill, you'd certainly give it a wide berth.

But now, the house beside the prison was like a sacred place for pilgrims.

As they were swarming around the door, they saw the general inside, hunched over and looking thinner. They halted, not daring to cross the threshold, filled with shyness and awe. Even a wag like the barber was lost for words. Only when people nudged him did he mutter in a fluster, 'General!' But it was inaudible, even to himself.

For some time, the general did not know what to say either, his eyes wide open in surprise. But when he soon realized their intention, tears brimmed over and streamed down his lined face.

Although Ringworm Hill was not far from the town, this was the first time that people had seen it joyfully. They were also astonished to find rows of pits for planting trees on the slope behind the general's house.

'Are you going to plant so many trees, general?'

'Yes. I hope to change the colour of this mound before meeting Marx in the nether world. It's a pity that fruit trees won't grow here. Still, we'll make do with pine trees.'

'Do you mean to live here as a hermit?'

'Hermit?'

'Yes.'

'What an idea Ha! Ha!' The general laughed heartily until he was seized by a fit of coughing. Then he went on: 'My aim is to safeguard the small trees until they've grown big enough. When you've some time, we'll divert the stream too, build some irrigation canals and a reservoir. This will help your fields. The hills will be green and the stream will retain water all year round. If we plant some flowers, and keep some birds and animals, we'll have a fine park. I'd like to be the park keeper. And you, young man,' he patted the porter on his shoulder, 'can bring your beautiful wife there and have fun. I assure you I won't close the gate ahead of time!'

'Then promise not to hit them with your stick if you catch them kissing each other behind your house,' the barber teased, as the people roared with laughter.

*

'How shall we say goodbye to him? What shall we give him as a keepsake? How can we keep in touch with him?' Those were the questions everyone in the town thought and discussed. Some even quarrelled over the order of inviting the general to dinner.

But all of a sudden, the town was overshadowed by the death of Premier Zhou. He died at a time when he was most needed. The morning that his death was announced, the general, supported by his wife, suddenly appeared under the camphor tree at the crossroads.

The sun was up, pale and dull. It was extremely cold. The small town looked more bleak and gloomy, silent as death, as if frozen numb by cold and sorrow.

The general, standing in the cutting wind, looked very pale and sallow, his deep-set eyes circled by dark shadows, his face grim. He stood erect, as solid as a bronze statue.

'Comrades...' he shouted in his hoarse voice. It sounded so unfamiliar that many stopped to listen to him. The old man bent down and unzipped his bag with an effort, revealing black mourning armbands. Raising his head, he uttered, swallowing hard. 'Please...'

There was no need to say any more. People, one by one, took the bands and put them on their arms.

'Whose idea was this?' A hand, its fingers brown from too much smoking, suddenly touched the shoulder of the general. It was the mayor.

The general was silent.

'We've already told you that no one is going to hold any mourning ceremony. What are you up to?'

The general did not even raise his eyes.

Turning round, the furious mayor bellowed at the crowd, 'Don't move, any of you! Take off your arm-bands!'

But no one complied.

'Disobeying, eh? Old tailor, you take it off first!'

The tailor was stunned. Looking at the mourning arm-band and then at the mayor's angry face, he trembled for a second. Before dawn, the general had knocked at his door and given him a roll of black cloth. The bad news had upset him dreadfully, but he had realized at once what his visitor wanted him to do. Together, they sat down to work, grief-stricken.

Now this indignant petty official was trying to force him to throw his band on the ground in shame. But it was not merely a matter of an arm-band, but of a heart loyal to the late premier. Could anything be more insulting? Clever, scrupulous and law-abiding, he never did anything harmful to others. Though he had bitter memories of being insulted and humiliated, none was worse than this. He would not swallow it.

He looked up and met the general's burning eyes, which scorched his heart. With quivering lips, he said slowly, 'Is it against the law to mourn Premier Zhou? Do what you like to me. I'm a tailor. I won't die of hunger wherever I go. Sorry, I won't take the arm-band off.'

'To mourn Premier Zhou isn't against the law!'

'We won't take our arm-bands off!'

Those docile, unambitious people had gone mad! They stood united in rebellion! The sense of justice, buried in their hearts, had been aroused by a general in exile, shattering their traditional timidness and humility.

Nonplussed, the mayor turned to the general.

But the old man did not even glance at him. Calm and concentrating, he seemed to be commanding a battle.

Only his wife knew the mental and physical pain racking his frail body. Despite his strained nerves and aching muscles, he stood erect. She dared not say anything, though her heart was torn.

'You'll pay for this!' snarled the mayor, his face distorted by rage. Then he took to his heels and disappeared round a corner.

Suddenly, the general gasped, short of breath, and collapsed.

A few days later, the barber heard the shocking news that the general would live in the town for the rest of his life as an 'honorary' general, because of his new 'mistake'. This was the first time that the barber kept a piece of news to himself. He had no heart to pass it on.

*

Just like the changeable weather in early spring, the people became depressed once more after their few days of happiness.

Ringworm Hill was again silent. Crowds came to see the general every day, their faces showing no trace of joy.

The general never again left his bed after his collapse. In and out of a coma, he sometimes ran a high temperature, staring at the ceiling with glazed eyes, raving deliriously or muttering away.

One day, suddenly his mind cleared. Scanning each anxious face, which showed momentary delight and surprise, he said with difficulty yet distinctly, 'I ... I will not leave you. I'll look after the park and ... you must plant trees ... repair the roads ... dig a canal. You won't drive me away, will you? Good...'

The general died. But his noble character had left an indelible impression on the people.

Then came an order from the authorities: the body of the general was to be cremated on the spot. No notice was to be given to his relatives or friends and there was to be no obituary, no mourning ceremony. It was a stupid decision, but they wanted to have everything under their control. In fact, no one complied with it.

The people were calm, yet stubborn, and did it their way. A

mourning committee was elected, and it decided at once to hold a traditional, grand funeral. Quickly, the townsfolk went into action.

The oldest citizen contributed his cypress coffin, the only one still remaining in the town; the tailor made the shroud that night; the barber spent a long time giving the general a face-lift. When the corpse was put into the coffin, incense and an oil lamp were lit. The boy, whose life the general had saved, and his parents had tramped thirty *li* to join the funeral. Dressed in mourning, he served as a filial son. People not only from the town but also from the surrounding villages came to present their wreaths and mourning streamers. The huge wreath sent by the nearby garrison, whose cook had once been scolded by the general, was particularly eye-catching.

The dawn sky was overcast on the day the funeral took place. Heavy clouds hung low over the town and open country. According to his will, the deceased wanted his ashes to be scattered over the hillside. However, the long funeral procession first headed for the town. With the bier at the head, carried by sixteen stalwart young men, people marched through both short streets, which nevertheless took them the whole morning. Finally they stopped under the camphor tree, and many people made memorial speeches expressing their grief, regrets and vows.

But two people were strongly against such a funeral. One was the general's wife. She argued that her husband had been a Communist and a revolutionary soldier and had asked in his will to be cremated. Before she could finish, people pleaded with tears in their eyes. 'The general would understand. He wouldn't complain. We've no objection to his being cremated later. But please let us have our way for the time being.' She closed her eyes with an effort, fighting back her tears. The other was the mayor, but he could do nothing except peep through his screened window. Furiously, he vowed through clenched teeth, 'Wait till I deal with you!'

One year later, the 'Gang of Four' fell. It was not the barber or the old tailor, but the mayor and his followers, who were disgraced at last.

When the people began to modernize their small town, they first put the general's wishes into practice.

In the last three months of that year, pits for tree-planting were dug all over Ringworm Hill and some other hills near by; the rubbish dump by the stream was removed; and the two streets were given a tarmac surface. Diverting the stream was already included in the town's water conservancy plan, and the first phase of the project worked on by several thousand people was completed before the Spring Festival.

Everything went well and smoothly but, of course, there were occasional quarrels, too. Once, however, there was a bitter one which shook the whole town.

It was about whether or not they should build a monument in memory of the general under the camphor tree. The porter and his mates were all for it, while the barber was in two minds. As people argued heatedly, the tailor picked his way into the crowd. Raising his hand, he pointed to the tree and said in a choked voice, 'Look here, what's better than this tree in memory of him? It's old and its bark has peeled, but its roots are still alive. Look at the new twigs and the lush leaves...' He faltered, swallowing hard.

Suddenly the townsfolk felt as if the tree had turned into the general wearing his green uniform buttoned at the collar, with a bright red star on his cap and red insignia on his collar. Leaning on his stick, he stood erect and blinked his eyes from time to time, silently watching the changes in the small town.

Imagining this, they forgot all about their disagreement.

1979

Anonymous translation

Liu Xin-wu

Black Walls

SUMMERTIME. Sunday.

A courtyard in an alley. Three fruit trees, five or six households.

Early morning. 7:30 a.m.

The room at the eastern end of the courtyard is the Zhou's. Actually there is just one certain Mr Zhou, about thirty years old, who lives there on his own. One might assume that he has never been married, though he uses a basin with a large, red double happiness design. One might also assume that he had been married and divorced but then why does he lower his head, study the ground and walk off in the other direction when he sees an unmarried woman in the courtyard? He only recently moved in and his work unit has a long and complicated name so his neighbours have not been able to work out exactly what he does for a living. By reckoning on their fingers they can work out that at his age, having been sent to the countryside for eight years, he can only have been working for about seven years at the most. Consequently, the amount of money in his monthly wage packet is not interesting enough to keep them guessing for long. Since he moved in he has never caused any trouble. He never drops in on anyone, nor does he receive any guests. When he meets neighbours in the courtyard they may first ask him: 'How are you?' He will reply neither shyly nor arrogantly: 'I'm very well, thank you'; or he may first ask the neighbour: 'Finished for the day?', and the neighbour will reply: 'Lord no! I'm just sitting in the cool breeze awhile'. But he will not stop and chat. Sometimes when he goes to the communal tap in the courtyard to fetch water, wash his clothes, or wash some rice and he bumps into a neighbour, of course they have to say something to each other. He only speaks when forced to reply to a question. If he answers, he will not follow it with another question. The other families who have lived in the courtyard a long time cannot say that they like him, nor that they dislike him.

He was busy very early one morning. First he moved everything out of his room, then he mixed some sort of liquid in a large wash basin. He must have borrowed a foot operated spray gun yesterday. Clearly, he was going to paint his room.

This began as nothing out of the ordinary. When the neighbours bumped into him at the communal tap, they asked him: 'Are you painting your room today?' 'Yes, yes I am.' Then they asked him politely, 'Do you need some help?' He thanked them: 'I've got a spray gun so it should be an easy job! Thank you anyway.' After collecting the water he calmly walked away. A calling cicada was hiding in the umbrella-like crown of a scholar tree whose trunk was only as wide as the mouth of a bowl. The noise was getting louder, but they had all grown accustomed to it and so did not find it annoying anymore.

7:46 a.m.

'Chi – chi – chi...'

It was a new sound but it was clear what it was. Zhou had started spraying his room.

7:55 a.m.

Several of the young people from the courtyard had the day off and went out one by one. Naturally they were all dressed up in the latest fashions, each one different from the next. One girl, a meat cutter during the week, was wearing imitation jewel earrings and cream coloured high-heels. As she left the courtyard, she opened a blue-flowered, nylon, automatic umbrella. There was also a young man who worked in the foundry's workshop. On his upper half, he was wearing an Indiana State University T-shirt, printed in English. On his legs, he wore grey corduroy hunting trousers originally made for export. He put on a pair of large-framed, purple sunglasses as he walked out, pushing a small-wheeled bicycle. A second girl hurried out of the courtyard. She studied business management at the local branch of the university. She was wearing a pale green dress, loose at the waist, which she had made herself, and was carrying a round, rattan hand-bag. The events which followed may have occurred because they all went out, but it is hard to say if things would have been different if they had not done so, as there was still one young person who remained behind the entire time. This young man sold glassware in the local market and was enjoying a day off. After breakfast, he lay on his bed, reading *The Lamp Without Light*. When his mother called him to join in the following events, he smiled, lay back down and continued to read his book.

8:15 a.m.

The atmosphere in the courtyard was heating up. It is not quite correct to say 'in the courtyard'; it would be better to say 'in the room'. It was not in every room, but it was in the north room in the middle of the courtyard. That was where the Zhao family lived. Mr Zhao was fifty-six years old. He had retired early so his second daughter could take over his job. Soon after his retirement, he went to another work unit to 'fill in' for a time. Recently, that unit began making cutbacks, leaving Mr Zhao out of work. Currently, he was trying to arrange another job in a different work unit.

Several of the neighbours gathered at his house. They told Mr Zhao the news: Mr Zhou was not spraying his walls white but black! He was actually spraying his walls black! They did not know what kind of paint he was using but it was black as ink! Pitch black!

Mr Zhao was both astounded and strangely pleased at the same time. Ten years before, he had been the deputy-in-charge of the Workers' Propaganda Team in a song and dance troupe. At that time when some 'activists' came to inform him about some 'new trends', his manner and tone were just as they were now. Mrs Zhao felt much

as her husband did. Eight years before she had been the head of a
'socialist neighbourhood committee'. Once when some people told
her about the remains of a reactionary slogan written at the base of
the wall behind the date tree, the atmosphere was much as it was
now. Who could guess that something would happen to bring the
dead issues of a decade or so ago back to life again?

'That's just not right,' Mr Zhao proclaimed.

'How dreadful,' said Mrs Zhao indignantly.

8:25 a.m.

'Ch – chi – chi . . .'

Mr Zhou was still spraying his room.

Newsflash: He had sprayed the ceiling black, too!

Mr Zhao asked them all to sit down, giving the room the feeling of
a meeting hall. Meetings can take on all forms: at some, everyone is
bored; at others, only you are interested; at still others, it is you who
is bored. Mr Zhao enjoyed the present meeting. He put forward the
motion: 'In this sort of situation we should inform the police as soon
as possible.'

If this were eight or ten years ago, this would not have been a mere
proposal but a conclusive decision; not just a man giving his own
opinion, but a leader's directive.

But, this was the present, not the past. Tall, thin Mr Qian went so
far as to immediately oppose him, saying, 'As I see it, we shouldn't go
to the authorities . . . that is, we have no basis. What can we tell the
police?'

Mr and Mrs Zhao both stared hard at him. They were both thinking:
Damn tailor! Years ago when he was an entrepreneur he never dared
to open his mouth, much less oppose our suggestions, but now he
does some private business at home, buys a colour television and his
whole tone of voice changes.

Mr Qian sat up straight and began fervently expressing his opinion:
'Brother Zhou may be suffering from a recurring illness. There are

such diseases; I've read about them in the paper. Sufferers have been known to behave strangely under stressful conditions ... Young Zhou was airing his quilt outside his front door last Sunday. Perhaps no one noticed but the quilt cover was made of bright red silk while the underside was duller red. Really, very odd! So I say we should not go to the police but fetch a doctor instead. Although I have heard that traditional medicines don't work on these kinds of illnesses, it would not hurt to consult him.'

Not many people responded to Mr Qian's words because as he talked they could not help gazing out of the window, through the shade of the scholar tree, to where they could see 'Brother Zhou'. Perfectly calm and collected, he continued to spray his walls. Faintly, they could hear him humming a song. Was this the manner of a sick person?

Mr Sun, who was sitting by the door, passed his little finger through his thinning hair and suggested: 'Shouldn't we just go and ask him why he is spraying his walls black? If he can't give a good reason, we can just forbid him – no, advise him not to – yes, advise him not to do it any more.'

Another neighbour, Mrs Li, who was sitting in the middle of the crowd, took the opportunity to say, 'Why don't you go and ask him for us.'

Everyone agreed to this suggestion.

8:36 a.m.

When Mr Sun made his suggestion he thought it would naturally be Mr and Mrs Zhao who would confront Mr Zhou. He never imagined it would be he who would be sent to ask. He regretted sitting by the door. For the past thirty years, he had worked in a primary school in charge of general affairs. He had not taught a class in his life. Consequently, he had picked up many of the mannerisms of a teacher but, now faced with a situation where he had to straighten his back and go to investigate a 'strange phenomenon', he felt as though he had been forced to the front of a podium to deliver a speech. His hands and knees shook uncontrollably and he was completely tongue tied.

8:37 a.m.

'Chi – chi – chi...' The spraying continued.

'Bzzzzzzz...' Inside the room, they continued talking in hushed voices.

Mr Sun flicked the long nail of the little finger on his left hand and stared at the tips of his shoes. He was not willing to go to question 'Brother Zhou'. How could he ever face them again if he received a brash refusal? How could he explain such a failure? What if the idiot said something incriminating? Should he report it directly and be responsible for the unknown consequences, or should he keep the information to himself and risk being accused of protecting Mr Zhou? And what if some evidence came to light in the future...

He gave it tremendous thought. Beads of sweat broke out on his forehead as he said, 'Maybe ... maybe Mr Zhao could go and ask instead?'

As no one else wanted the job, everyone agreed and said in chorus, 'Yes! Let Mr Zhao go!'

Mr Zhao did not make any immediate move, but waited for them to stop urging and start pleading with him. Only then did he abruptly stand up and declare, 'I'll go and ask!' He turned and left the room.

Everyone gazed out the window and watched the receding figure of Mr Zhao walking straight towards Mr Zhou's front door. They all listened attentively, hoping to catch a part of the conversation. All they could hear was the incessant call of the cicadas, high in the scholar tree.

8:41 a.m.

Ashen-faced, Mr Zhao returned to the room and reported, 'That rascal says he will come and explain to me when he has finished. I knew he would pull some trick. He doesn't respect us, his neighbours.

Mrs Zhao pointed out of the window and said, 'That's the man come to read the water meter, isn't it? He'll go and look in Mr Zhou's room! He'll probably spread all kinds of rumours about black paint and our courtyard, and give us all a bad name!'

Mrs Li, whose job was fluffing cotton into quilts, had a very placid nature and so put forward an explanation to make them all feel better, 'Perhaps the black paint is just the undercoat. When it's dry he'll spray a top coat of white paint.'

8:43 a.m.

'Chi – chi – chi...' The noise from the spray gun continued. Looking towards the room all they could see was blackness. No one really believed Mrs Li's explanation. The more Mrs Li looked, the more she could not help despairing.

What could one say? Black walls! In this very courtyard! Mr Zhou is not afraid of doing evil things himself, but he should not get others involved.

8:45 a.m.

Everyone in the room agreed about one thing: he should not spray his walls black! How could anyone spray his walls and ceiling black? Most people would not dare even think of such a thing. He did not just think about it, he actually did it! Extraordinary! Weird! Half-mad! Reactionary!

Mr Zhao still thought the police should be informed. Just as he was about to go and do so, he had second thoughts: The police station is not the same as it was eight or ten years ago (at that time there was not a police station but a 'group to smash the leaders of the judicial and public security institutions'. It was in the same courtyard as the present-day police station). Today the police are not as extreme nor do they think themselves as important as in the past. They always talk about 'going by the book' but once you start doing things 'by the book' then problems like the black wall dilemma will drag on and possibly never be resolved. Mr Zhao hesitated. He felt strongly about it and really did want to report it. It was a responsibility he could not shirk, a duty he had to take quick action to deal with. Could he be doing it for his own good? But what possible benefit could come of reporting it?

Mrs Zhao realized what her husband must be feeling and felt very bitter. How different it was eight or ten years ago! Her husband was actually suffering now because he lacked any real skills, and could only work as an assistant or warehouse watchman. Was it because he had not tried to learn a trade? Certainly not. For the past thirty odd years he had been transferred to work in various campaigns. The campaigns had come and gone, so now he had no way of earning a living. Formerly all his pride had come from his political sensitivity. Now he had a chance to display this talent, but his eyes, wrinkled face and the corners of his mouth showed hesitancy. Why was it? What was all this exertion for today? Could it be just for the good of his own family?

More and more, Mr Zhao believed that 'Brother Zhou' was suffering from a recurring illness. He admitted that what he had just been thinking was wrong. Traditional doctors were unable to treat this sort of illness. Could he not just let the doctor take his pulse? Not really. He would still have to get a Western doctor. But doctors didn't make house calls nowadays. It would be extremely difficult. Who could persuade him to go to the out-patient's department?

Mrs Li wanted to go home and get her lump of a son to stop reading his novels and think of what to do. Perhaps he could bring Mr Zhou to his senses, and even help spray the walls white again. White is so nice! Why should anyone want anything different?

Mr Sun wanted to go home but was too embarrassed to make the move. In this sort of situation a person ought to make clear his position on the matter, so in the future he could not be accused of 'sitting on the fence'. Of course a person should not leave it so that in any future situation he could not be accused of having played a part in a 'misjudged case'. Ideally one would avoid any sort of criticism in the past, present or future. He had already shown enough 'intention' to go to Mr Zhou's, so he should now make an early retreat. But it would be hard to slip out without being noticed...

8:48 a.m.

Mr Zhao had a grandson affectionately known as 'Little Button' who was not much more than ten years old. At the start of all this he had been painting in the back room. At length, he came and leaned on the doorway between the two rooms, curiously listening to the adults' discussion. He thought the room crowded, muggy, hot and disordered. Why did adults have to torment themselves like this?

Once again they began to discuss the matter and once again the atmosphere heated up. Little Button stood before his grandfather, turned his head and asked: 'Grandpa, what are you all doing?'

Mr Zhao said to him firmly, 'Off with you! Go and play! There's nothing for you here!'

Little Button was not convinced and thought to himself: Are you angry with Uncle Zhou for spraying his walls? Uncle Zhou is a very nice man. He's such fun. Once he called me to his room. He took some pieces of card from a drawer. The pieces were of every colour under the sun and were as big as the *Evening News*. He kept changing them and pressed them up to my eyes so that all I could see was that colour. Then he asked: 'Do you like it or not? Does it feel hot or cold? Dry or wet? Pleasant or nasty to smell? Does it make you want to go to sleep or go out and play? What does it make you think of? Or does it make you think nothing at all? Does it make you feel frightened or calm? Does it make you thirsty or not? Do you want to go on looking at it or not? He jotted down every reply that I made. See how much fun he is! If you don't believe me, go over to his place and see for yourselves!

Little Button thought this far, then raised his head and said loudly, 'Grandpa, you still haven't finished your discussion. You must be awfully tired. Can I say something now?'

There was nothing for it but for everyone to stop talking. They all looked at him.

Mr Zhao waved his hands as if he had been wronged and said, 'Right, right! Go ahead!'

Little Button asked: 'When Uncle Zhou has finished his room, will he go from door to door spraying everyone else's rooms as well?'

8:49 a.m.

Everyone went blank.

8:50 a.m.

Mr Zhao blurted out: 'I'm sure he'd dare!' Mrs Zhao echoed, 'He'll try! Mrs Li and Mr Sun said at once, 'He wouldn't, he'd never...' Mr Qian thought carefully before saying, 'He doesn't look like a trouble-maker. His illness only seems to recur in his own home...'

8:51.30 a.m.

Little Button turned round, blinked his round, black eyes, blacker even than the walls, shining black. He smiled innocently and said in a shrill voice: 'So that's settled! Uncle Zhou is spraying the walls of his own room, and it has nothing to do with us, so what are you all going on about?

8:52 a.m.

Everyone went silent.

The 'chi – chi – chi...' of the wall spraying drifted over, mingling with the sound of the cicadas, becoming even more pronounced.

Summer 1982

Translated by Alice Childs

Wang Ceng-qi

Big Chan

Big Chan was the porter at Fifth Prime, the county's Fifth Primary School. The porter was what we would now call a janitor or caretaker. In any case, in those days Big Chan was known as the porter. This old form of address gradually went into disuse, but when it did so nobody knew.

Big Chan was enormous. Very fat, and very white. In the summer he wore nothing but a vest, with his shoulders and belly exposed, wobbling on every step. This had the effect of making him look even fatter and whiter. Occasionally he would drink a little, lose his temper a little, and then his cheeks would go pink, turning him into a big white fat fellow with pink cheeks.

The headmaster Zhang Yunzhi and the teachers all called him Big Chan. But the children insisted on using his full name: Big Fat Chan. Fat Chan would have done equally well of course, but they preferred Big Fat Chan, not skimping on a single word.

A fat porter was surely unheard of? But all the pupils thought that Big Chan was exactly the way he should be. They couldn't imagine having a thin porter. If Big Chan wasn't fat, somehow things wouldn't have been the same. He was an integral part of the school, having worked there for many years. Perhaps he had always been a porter, ever since he was born.

Big Chan's main responsibility was to ring the bell at the beginning and end of each lesson. Otherwise he was to be found in his room. He had his own small quarters behind the main gates at the southernmost part of the grounds. Originally this room was intended to be the reception, for guests to check in and messages to be sent. But Fifth Prime didn't receive many messages, and visitors had always walked straight through since Big Chan would never dream of stopping anyone. By and by this little room became the porter's private domain.

Mostly he would sit there, giving his wall clock an occasional glance. There were two of these clocks – the other one hung in the school office. The first thing Big Chan did when he got up in the morning was to wind them both up, clack-clack, after which he would open the school gates. Then he would look at his clock again, and at exactly the right time emerge ringing the school bell, ding-dong, ding-dong, traversing the grounds from the south side all the way up to the north.

Time for class. After the initial rush, the students were fairly disciplined, seating themselves in their own classrooms. At the end of the lesson he would ring the bell again, lifting everyone's spirits. Whoosh – the children would come running into the playground, towards the swings, to kick a ball, play hopscotch, or toss bean bags ...

Big Chan had worn down quite a few bells in his time.

Some years later, a few of the students in the final year decided to pool resources and buy a small brass bell as a school-leaving present. That was how Big Chan graduated from the old hand bell to a proper suspended bell.

It was a beautiful bell, made of shiny yellow brass.

The brass bell hung by a thin metal chain between two parasol trees on one side of the small school yard. A clapper dangled from the centre of the dome which was in turn tied to a long piece of rope. Big Chan tugged at the rope and the bell would go dong, dong, dong, dong. When not in use, the end of the rope was knotted loosely round one of the branches.

As the parasol trees grew taller, so did the bell.

The children in Fifth Prime grew taller too.

Big Chan had another responsibility, which was to trim the ilex trees. Quite a few hedges had been planted around the school grounds. There was one on either side of the hall, one just outside the gates, and one on each side of the entrance to the kindergarten. These hedges grew very quickly, with new twigs climbing into a tangle at the top. Every so often Big Chan would wield a pair of gigantic scissors which he had to hold with both hands. Clip-clip-clip he went, paving the ground with leaves. When the hedges were neat and tidy, the air would be filled with the fragrance of fresh young ilex.

Trimming the hedges was something Big Chan was obliged to do several times each term. Hence his main function in the school was to ring the bell and cut the hedges.

Big Chan was fat, no doubt about it, but when it came to cutting and pruning he was always very energetic, attacking the trees as if he hated them, or perhaps it was because he loved them.

He also watered the flowering plants.

The school yard was not very big. Twisting among the ilex branches were some Goat's Beard. There were also two peach trees, two pear trees, one willow, some Ten Sisters, and a wisteria. In the centre of the round pond grew a rare Iron Tree. One year it flowered, and many people came from the town to admire it. Dotted around the play ground were also campions, corn poppies and peonies. Big Chan watered them all with a large can sprouting an enormous shower head.

In the autumn Big Chan had to sweep the fallen leaves from the many parasol trees planted in the school grounds. After a storm leaves were scattered everywhere, making a rustling sound underfoot once they were dry. Big Chan liked to use a big broom made of bamboo, swishing the leaves into a huge pile and then setting fire to it. Black smoke, red flames.

What else did he do? He boiled water for the teachers on a charcoal stove in the school office – both for drinking and for washing their faces. The fire was lit every day, and then whish-whish, Big Chan would fan a palm leaf to keep it going. On top of the stove stood an iron kettle.

Now and again he also helped copy exam papers, operating the mimeograph roller while one of the teachers turned the pages. When they were all done, Big Chan put a match to the stencil. The odour of the burning ink floated out of the windows so that sometimes you could smell it even in the classrooms.

During the winter and summer breaks, Big Chan had extra responsibility delivering school reports to the families of each of the two hundred students in the school. He went from house to house carrying report cards in large envelopes. On the left-hand side was written the student's name and address. A stamp in the centre announced in red: 'For the Perusal of the Parents'. On the lower right-hand corner was another rectangular seal which said 'The Fifth Primary County School'. Parents always attached great importance to these reports, tearing open the envelopes in haste to find: Literature, 98 per cent, Arithmetic, 86 per cent... When they had finished reading they would give Big Chan a tip.

Apart from ringing the bell before and after class, something else brought Big Chan into direct contact with the children: he sold peanut and sesame snaps from his little room. These sweets were kept in a rectangular box with a glass top. After the bell had gone, some of the children would sneak into his room to buy sweets.

Big Chan was very bad. His sweets were dearer than the ones sold on street stalls – much dearer, in fact! But the pupils at Fifth Prime had no choice but to go to him since they were not allowed to leave the premises during school hours.

The purchasing of sweets on school grounds was strictly forbidden by Headmaster Zhang Yunzhi. Summoning Big Chan to his office one day he said: One, pupils are not permitted to eat snacks in school, two, these sweets are unhygienic, and three, making money out of the children is immoral.

Big Chan was forced to continue his business on the sly. When he rang the bell, he would secrete some sweets inside his left sleeve. Pupils who approached him were answered with a wink which indicated some secluded spot away from the prying eyes of both headmaster and staff. There money and sweets would change hands.

Almost every student at Fifth Prime had done business with their porter at some point. After they had grown up and left, they would reminisce about their school days, always remembering Big Chan and his peanut and sesame snaps.

This was how Big Chan passed his time, peacefully, year after year. Apart from the winter and summer vacations when he went home, the rest of the year was spent at the school. During the winter break the building was usually empty, the grounds covered in white after a couple of snowstorms. In the summer however, a handful of students sometimes came back to play among the tall uncut grass.

Every day after school, when teachers and pupils had all gone home, two people were left in the building, three on occasion. Big Chan aside, the female teacher Wang Wenhui would be there. Sometimes the headmaster Zhang Yunzhi also stayed over.

Wang Wenhui came from Huxi but she had no immediate family. From time to time she would go home to visit relatives, but mostly she stayed behind in a south-facing room by the kindergarten. She taught arithmetic to the first and second grades, and was not bad-looking despite a few pock-marks on her face. She had a way of skimming the ground when she moved, and she had smiling eyes. It had to be said it was rather strange the way she smiled to herself while walking along. What was there possibly to smile about? Some male members of staff made the suggestion that she was not quite right in the head. Apart from this habit, there didn't seem to be anything wrong with her. In fact she seemed perfectly normal in every other respect – the way she conducted a class was much the same as everyone else, teaching addition, subtraction, leading the pupils in the recitation of their multiplication tables:

> One one is one,
> One two is two,
> Two twos are four ...

After class, she usually returned to her little room to mark the day's homework, sometimes stopping to listen to the children singing:

> Good little lamb
> Please open the gate,
> Let me in quickly,
> Don't let me wait ...

At night, she lit a paraffin lamp to read by. She read *The Dream of the Red Chamber, Tragic Love Stories, Tale of an Aristocratic Lady* by Zhang Henshui, and poems by Li Quingzhao. Some nights she would softly recite the poem 'The Song of Wulan' to herself:

> Whirr turns the spindle,
> Wulan sits and weaves ...

Other evenings she might choose to write a letter to an old friend at the teacher's training college, telling them about the school, the Ten Sisters, the wisteria, how lovely the children were, how happy she was. Or she might remember an outing they had shared long ago in the spring, and sigh about the passage of time. These letters were always very long.

Headmaster Zhang Yunzhi was not particularly fierce, but the pupils were all afraid of him, mostly because he had the power to expel. If a student committed a serious offence, a notice would go up outside the school office: 'Student so-and-so has committed such-and-such an offence and will be expelled forthwith.'

Then in the next paragraph: 'This notice is hereby given in observation of school regulations and as a warning to others not to repeat the error.'

The headmaster's seal appeared below bearing his signature – Zhang Yunzhi. Zhang Yunzhi as a name possessed an invisible but terrible power.

He taught one of the classes too, literature in the fifth or sixth form. Whenever he recited a text, his head would sway and roll and nod according to the rhythm of the prose, his voice modulating with drama and expression, not unlike an old character actor on the opera stage. 'In the Jin Dynasty, during the reign of the Emperor Taiyuan, lived a man from Wuling, a fisherman by profession...' or '*En route*, I passed through autumnal hills with turning leaves, dried fields and withered flowers, before I knew it I was in Jinan, where springs sprang from every courtyard, and willows wept in every garden...'

Composing elegiac couplets was one of his favourite pastimes. Once he had finished a pair, he would pin them up on the wall where his colleagues could properly appreciate them. All the teachers would crowd round, pointing and gesticulating, praising the turn of a phrase here, the vigorous choice of a word there. Zhang Yunzhi would be rather pleased with himself, but never so pleased as to lose his composure. He almost wished sometimes that more of his relatives would die, so that he could compose something suitably mournful, to be displayed somewhere suitably eye-catching.

He had a family. Sometimes he went home, sometimes he elected to stay in the school. Apparently his children were too noisy at home and that the quiet of the school suited him better. After all he had to read, to write.

When the last bell had gone, Big Chan often found himself alone with Zhang Yunzhi and Wang Wenhui.

Wang Wenhui sometimes took a solitary walk around the school grounds. On the way back to her room she would come across Zhang Yunzhi standing on the front steps of the school office. Wang Wenhui would give him a smile and a nod, and Zhang Yunzhi would return with a smile and a nod. Wang Wenhui then headed back towards the kindergarten, while Zhang Yunzhi stared after her until she disappeared through the doors.

Zhang Yunzhi often studied at night. He read classics like *The Strange Tales of Liaozai, Conversations on the Edge of the North Pool, A Rainy Autumnal Retreat, Letters Home from Zeng Guofan, The Poetry of Zheng Banqiao, Spirits in the Wilderness, Life Among the Floating World...*

Separated by the length of the playground, the north window in the headmaster's room faced directly onto the south window of the teacher's room. The playground contained swings, see-saws, and a slide. The paraffin lamps in the two rooms stood face to face across the distance.

One night, Zhang Yunzhi went over to Wang Wenhui's room to borrow her dictionary. Wang Wenhui handed over the volume but he didn't leave. Instead he lingered to talk about nothing in particular, alluding to the classic love poem from *The Dream of the Red Chamber*, where the heroine buries a flower, and also to Li Qingzhao's famous verse, 'This aimless endless search, cold, alone and sad and mad...' Wang Wenhui didn't know what it was that the headmaster wanted, but her heart started to pound. All of a sudden, 'puff!' – and the light was blown out.

Since then Zhang Yunzhi often crept into Wang Wenhui's room late at night.

This did not escape the notice of Big Chan. Anxious about burglars taking the mimeograph, the brass bell, the iron kettle, he often came out in the middle of the night to have a good look round.

Big Chan was angry. In the privacy of his own room he would swear to himself: 'Zhang Yunzhi you bastard! You have a wife and a family and yet you are behaving like an animal! This is a young woman all on her own, how is she going to face her future? How will she ever be able to marry!'

The affair did not escape the notice of the staff either, partly because Wang Wenhui often stared at Zhang Yunzhi with undisguised affection, but also because she had started to wear perfume. Walking around, her smile was brighter than ever.

One day, after school, a member of staff named Xie went past the porter's lodge and invited himself in. 'Big Chan,' he said, 'would you mind coming over to my house this evening?' Big Chan didn't know why.

This teacher called Xie was something of a playboy, and was nicknamed Gentleman Xie. The students had made up a ditty:

> Gentleman Xie
> catches a rat
> the rat is fat
> but Xie's no cat.
> The rat squeals
> Xie swoons.
> His mother calls him
> an old buffoon!

Gentleman Xie lived very close to the school, no more than a few paces away.

That evening, he made conversation for a while and then asked Big Chan a question:

'Does Zhang Yunzhi often visit Wang Wenhui's room?'

Big Chan understood at once – Gentleman Xie wanted to get rid of Zhang Yunzhi so that he could become headmaster himself! He replied, 'No, of course not! You mustn't make things up.'

Big Chan was not protecting Zhang Yunzhi, he was protecting Wang Wenhui.

Since that evening, however, he started to sell his peanut and sesame snaps quite openly, no longer bothering to avoid the head-master.

Big Chan continued to be a porter, ringing the bell, trimming the hedges, selling sweets.

Later, Zhang Yunzhi became the headmaster of Fourth Prime, and Wang Wenhui went to teach in a town a long way away.

Then Zhang Yunzhi died. Wang Wenhui also died (she never married). Fat Chan died too.

In fact, many people in the town died.

Translated by Peng Wen Lan and Carolyn Choa

Deng You-mei

Han the Forger

He hadn't walked down this road for more than thirty years. Now it was asphalted and lined with buildings and a school. In his youth Gan Ziqian used to come along here to Taoran Pavilion Park to sketch. Now, standing beside the historic lake, he felt lost. 'Where on earth can Han be?' A man who would be useful for the country's modernization, Han had been ousted from the antiques trade decades ago. Like a sputtering candle, Gan knew his days were numbered. If he didn't find Han he wouldn't find peace even after death.

The misunderstanding between Gan and Han had started with a prank. Gan could paint well in the traditional style, and sometimes copied old works. Seeing a masterly copy of an early painting one day tempted him to do likewise. On an impulse he made a painting called *The Cold Food Festival* and attributed it to the celebrated 12th-century artist Zhang Zeduan, using a well-preserved sheet of Song paper and ink. Originally he did it just for fun, never expecting his copy would attract a newspaper correspondent, Na Wu, who came from an impoverished Manchu noble family. Na Wu took it away and asked a famous craftsman to mount it, colour it with tea and then fake the seal of the Qing emperor Qianlong. When this was done he brought it back to Gan saying, 'Look, it exceeds even Master Zhang's skill. And it's certainly as accomplished as Han's.'

As a dealer, connoisseur of paintings and well-known copyist, Han had been appointed assistant manager of the Gongmao Pawnshop.

'You flatter me. I don't think my skill is nearly as great as Han's,' he protested.

'Flatter you? Never!' retorted Na Wu. 'If you don't believe me, let's put it to the test.'

'How?'

'I'll take it to Gongmao Pawnshop. If Han tells me it's a fake, then I'll say we were only joking. But if I can fool him, then it proves that you do have a remarkable skill. What's more we can share the money between us. Then you can treat me to a roast duck.' With this, he carried the painting away wrapped in a blue cloth.

At first Na Wu had only wanted to pawn the painting in order to make the bet with Gan and it was only when he actually had it in his hands that he changed his mind. To fool people he needed to be dressed in his finest clothes, since the pawnshop looked first at the customer and then at the goods. So on the appointed day, he wore his silk gown, a fashionable waistcoat, black satin slippers and white silk socks. Between his fingers he balanced an exquisite cigarette-holder with a fine cigarette, lit but unsmoked. Placing the painting on the counter, he asked a price of a thousand yuan and then turned away to look at the wall. From his appearance, Han assumed that he must be a ne'er-do-well from an impoverished Manchu family and that he had stolen the heirloom to pawn. Men of his ilk never sold things and usually never redeemed what they pawned.

Fooled perhaps by Na Wu's appearance, frightened by the high asking price or owing to sheer negligence, Han, after haggling for a long time, chanted in his Shanxi accent, 'An antique painting. We can loan you six hundred yuan ...' In those days, a bag of flour was only two yuan and forty fen so six hundred yuan was an enormous sum. When Na Wu returned and told the story, Gan laughed heartily. But on second thoughts, he was scared stiff. If the story got about, it would discredit him with his friends, and offend them as well. Although the relationship between them was not particularly close, they were still friends. And both were fond of Beijing opera, especially of perform- ances by Sheng Shiyuan. Whenever an opera was staged starring

Sheng, they would both go to see him. As a result of their frequent attendance and vocal support, Sheng was convinced that if they were not at the theatre cheering, his performance would be below par.

Seeing Gan's misgivings, Na Wu coaxed, 'Don't get so worried about it. Everybody already knows Han makes a living from forged paintings. It's time he got his comeuppance. If you're worried about your reputation, we won't do it again. Nobody will find out if neither of us let on. What we did this time wasn't to make money but to put your technique to the test. Now that he's offered us money though, we mustn't be so foolish as to turn it down. Are you really going to pay it back with interest and redeem the painting?'

'I can't afford to.'

'You couldn't even if you had the money since the pawn ticket belongs to me now.'

Gan had no choice but to give him three hundred yuan. Finishing his duck, Na Wu declared, 'Now I'm going to take the ticket to the Japanese pawnshop. I should be able to bluff him out of two or three hundred yuan. So let me pay the bill.'

'You're a little too clever at times,' remarked Gan.

'Well, don't you agree that to cheat a Japanese is patriotic?'

And soon Gan heard others gossiping, saying that Han was used to cheating people with his fakes, but that he had never expected to be swindled himself. Shortly thereafter Gan received an invitation from Han to celebrate his birthday on August 16.

When the day arrived, Han rented the Listening to Lotus Hall overlooking a lake in a garden behind Beihai Park and set ten tables under a corrugated iron shade to treat his friends. Gan expected to find a dispirited Han but instead he looked more cheerful than ever. After three cups of wine, he stood up and bowed to the guests with his hands folded, saying, 'It's not only because it's my birthday that I invited you here today. I also want to tell you that I've made a blunder.'

'I'm sure you've already heard – I've been taken in by a fake. When I was poor, I lived on fake paintings. Now I've been caught myself. It is a sort of retribution, and I've no one to blame but myself. But I think all of us are basically honest men, so to save you from suffering a similar loss, I've brought it here for you to have a look at. Bear this lesson in mind and don't make mistakes yourselves.' Then he ordered the painting to be brought out.

With this, his two apprentices approached, one holding the painting, the other carrying a pole with a double-pronged tip which he used to hang the painting on to a bronze hook. All the guests gathered round to examine the work. 'Looks genuine all right. How amazing!'

'Don't you be taken in by it. Try to spot its weakness and then we will learn something from it.' Turning to look at Gan, Han smiled, adding, 'Ziqian has a good eye. You try first.'

Gan's face had already turned crimson, but since he had been drinking, no one became suspicious. Moving forward, he first looked at the lower left-hand corner of the painting and spotted his thumbprint, positive proof that the work was his, but he was unable to detect any discrepancies. Had he known of any, of course, he would have corrected them in advance. Secretly he admitted that his brushwork was not up to that of the original painting. He commented, 'The brush strokes are weak, and the style a little vulgar. Mr Han's really been deceived by the fact that the artist has used 12th-century paper and ink.'

Han laughed saying, 'I was duped this time not because the faker was so skilful but because I was too conceited and negligent. So today I'd like to advise you all, don't follow in my footsteps and always keep your eyes open. The painting looks genuine but if you're observant enough, its weakness can be easily detected. For instance, the subject is *The Cold Food Festival* and that takes place in spring. The painter Zhang Zeduan lived in Kaifeng where at that time of year people would have been wearing spring clothes. But look, the boy in the painting is still wearing a cotton-padded hat with flaps. Do you think Zhang would have made such a mistake? For another thing, the young woman by the grave is weeping over her dead husband. The word "husband" has a closed syllable at the end, but her mouth is open saying "ah". Judging from this, I would venture to suggest that this painting is not by Zhang Zeduan.'

It was an explanation that won everyone's admiration, even Gan's.

At this, Han threw a cup of wine over the fake, struck a match and set fire to it. Then he laughed again, saying, 'Getting rid of it saves anyone else from being swindled. Now let's have another drink before the opera begins.'

With the destruction of the painting, Gan felt greatly relieved and calmly sat enjoying the entertainment. As a gesture of friendship, Sheng Shiyuan appeared and performed especially well. Han, on his part, cheered loudly and Gan couldn't refrain from following suit. When the performance was over, Han went backstage to express his appreciation. Sheng asked, 'The man who often accompanies you to the theatre hasn't come to see me for a long time. Who is he? Won't you introduce us next time he comes?' Since he'd been cheated, Han had felt so miserable that he hadn't been to the theatre for several days and consequently wasn't aware that Gan had also been staying home. Sheng's words startled him. He knew that the forger must be someone from the same trade and had therefore invited a number of them in order to watch what would happen during dinner. However, he had never been even remotely suspicious of Gan. Immediately he looked around to find him but was told by his apprentice that Mr Gan had just been called away unexpectedly.

Later, called to the side door of the garden by Na Wu, Gan was annoyed. 'What the devil did you come here for?' he growled.

'I apologize but I must tell you. I went to pledge the pawn ticket with the Japanese but he asked me to let him inspect the painting first. Dare we run the risk? If it passes, then there's no problem. If the

Japanese spots anything wrong with it though, he won't be as easy to deal with as Han – we'll be sent to prison.'

'You're too greedy!' Gan scolded. 'In any case, the painting has already been destroyed by Han.'

At first Na Wu was stunned by the news. Then all of a sudden he slapped his thigh and exclaimed, 'Wonderful! It's time Han got what was coming to him.'

'What are you going to do? We've already made him lose six hundred yuan. Don't be so cruel! He and I are friends and see one another frequently.'

'Friends? No. Business is business. It's foolish to let a good opportunity slip through your fingers. Come, stay awhile. I'll treat you to some crabs.'

After Na Wu's departure, Gan was uneasy. Han was a better man than Na Wu and even if he himself had nothing further to do with this, he didn't have the heart to let Na Wu extort any more money from him. So he made up his mind to visit the pawnshop and inform him of Na Wu's intention in order to avoid any further trouble.

When he arrived at Gongmao Pawnshop, Han came out to meet him and graciously ushered him into a private room behind the accountant's office. Shortly an apprentice appeared bringing Gan a cup of tea. Han puffed at his hookah for a while before breaking the silence, 'I haven't seen you lately. Where've you been?'

Before Gan could reply, the accountant, looking upset, scurried in and stuttered, 'Something's wrong, sir.'

'What's wrong?' Han asked nonchalantly.

'There's a man here to redeem his pledge.'

'Redeem his pledge? What's wrong with that? It's natural that people come here to redeem their pledges.'

'But he wants to redeem the...' The accountant glanced at Gan, then approached Han and whispered.

'Speak up!' ordered Han. 'Mr Gan is not a stranger.'

The acountant couldn't help blurting out, '... that painting!'

'Which one?'

'*The Cold Food Festival* that you burnt yesterday.'

Gan, shocked, felt a shiver run down his spine, for he had never expected that Na Wu would carry his trick so far.

But Han said calmly, 'Tell him the painting he pawned is a fake and that he should be content with the sum he got from me. If not, I'll take him to court.'

'I'm sorry, sir. But you can't speak to a customer that way. He came here to redeem his pledge and even if the pledge was a bit of toilet paper, we are still supposed to return it to him. If we can't, then we should pay him twice the loan. Even if we do, I'm not sure he'll take it. How can I tell him we'll go to court?'

The accountant's argument reduced Han to silence. Just then they heard a commotion outside. Na Wu shouted, 'What! You want to keep my heirloom, do you? If you're not going to return it to me, you'd better pay me a proper price for it!'

'Outrageous! I'd better go and see what's happening,' said Han. 'Excuse me, Ziqian.'

Angry and embarrassed, Gan ignored protocol and followed Han out of the room.

The shop's counter was over a foot higher than the customer. Behind the counter stood Han, surrounded by his accountant and assistants, all looking down at Na Wu, who challenged, 'If you have the painting here, then return it to me. If not, we'll have to settle the matter another way.'

Gan peered out from behind Han and saw a swarthy, heavy-set fellow standing behind Na Wu. He was dressed in grey clothes, his sleeve cuffs covering his hands. Beneath his unbuttoned jacket Han could see a white calico vest edged with black trimming, and recognized him immediately as a police detective. It certainly looked as though Na Wu was determined to continue hounding Han. Winking at him, Gan began tentatively, 'Oh, it's you, Mr Na. Well, we're all friends here. Why do you want...'

'Mr Gan, what we're talking about is no laughing matter. Please don't get mixed up in this. I pawned a scroll painting inherited from my forefathers. Today I've come here to redeem it. First they tell me it's a fake. Then they promise I can get it back another day. Does it surprise you that my patience has run out?'

As Gan was about to try and coax him out of continuing, Han edged forward saying to Na Wu, 'So you've run out of patience, have you? Well, I'm much more impatient than you are. I reckoned you'd be here as soon as the shop opened. Why did it take you so long? You want to redeem the painting, do you? Then first please show me the money!'

'So you're afraid I haven't brought it.' With this, Na Wu threw a white packet on to the counter containing the principal and interest, amounting together to over eight hundred yuan. Having counted the sum and placed the interest to one side, Han handed six hundred yuan to the accountant, then removed a package from under the counter and handed it downwards.

'Here. Now take it away.'

Hearing this, Gan and the assembled assistants were taken aback. Na Wu stood stunned before nervously reaching out for the package, his hands trembling so much that he could not even hold it. The detective reached out and steadied him, saying, 'You'd better have a look. Is it the one you pawned?'

No sooner had he untied the bundle than the sweat stood out on his brow, and his lips trembled. Pretending to talk to himself, he said so that Gan could hear, 'Wasn't this burnt yesterday?'

'If I hadn't burnt it yesterday, would you have come here today?' replied Han sarcastically.

'So there are two such paintings in existence!' uttered Na Wu.

'If you like, I'll produce another one for you tonight,' added Han.

Incredulously Gan asked, 'What on earth is it, Mr Na? Won't you let me have a look?'

Holding the painting, Gan blushed scarlet with shame. First of all, he examined the lower left-hand corner, and looked hard at the thumb-print, which though very pale could barely be distinguished from that in the destroyed painting and had they been placed together in front of him, he would have been unable even to identify his own work. It was said that some craftsmen were so skilful they could peel off the top layer of a painting to make two. 'Can Han do that?' he wondered.

'It looks like there's nothing for me to do here.' The detective was growing impatient. 'Settle with me and I'll be off.'

Paying him, Na Wu turned towards Han with a contrite smile and folded his hands in a gesture of respect, 'I've learned a lesson from you and paid two hundred yuan for the privilege.'

'Take the interest back!' Han handed it over to him and laughed. 'It was you who brought the painting here and I imagine your slippers must be worn out, so you'd better use the money to buy a new pair. By the way, please tell the man who made the fake...' With this he turned to the dumbfounded and embarrassed Gan before going on, 'Does he think he's clever enough to fool me? Not until he can fool the painter himself with his fakes, will he be properly qualified. So I suggest he study for another couple of years.'

Ashamed, Gan slunk out of Gongmao Pawnshop, head bowed, and from then on never appeared when Han was around. Although Han was a man of good reputation, his master dared not run the risk of losing any more money and in the first month of the following year he was dismissed. Later he was reduced to working as a junk dealer for two years, but since business was bad, he finally supported himself by collecting and selling scrap. Gan, despite suffering a temporary loss of credibility, got a good job restoring damaged paintings.

As a result of his background, clear record, progressive ideology and loyalty to the Party, Gan was elected to the leadership of the antiques trade after Liberation and became vice-chairman of the trade association during the socialist transformation of capitalist enterprise.

To reinforce the leadership after the changeover, someone suggested that they should appoint Han to a job. The authorities did not know much about his past and asked Gan for his opinion. Gan was evasive, saying he didn't know much about him and asked them to wait until he found out a little more. Returning home, he turned the affair over in his mind. Though he hadn't intended to cheat Han, he certainly wouldn't be able to explain it easily. 'If Han isn't hired, then no one will rake up the past,' he thought. 'If he is, however, he may raise it against me. What's more I'm applying for Party membership. Why should I bother to recommend him?' But Gan also couldn't lie to the authorities. When asked for his opinion, he said, 'Han lived on fakes and used to be an assistant manager in a pawnshop. He was quite well-off before Liberation. On his birthday the famous Beijing opera actor Sheng Shiyuan even performed at his home . . .'

'It's said that he's an able man. What do you think about our employing him?'

'The decision rests with you,' Gan replied evasively. 'My political experience is low, and I'm not sure.'

In the end Han was rejected.

According to the conventions of the antiques trade, people who had been vetted could do anything except assess or deal in antiques. From that day on Han sank into obscurity.

Many years passed. Gan didn't feel guilty and, as time went on, forgot about Han.

During the 'cultural revolution', Gan was deeply wronged. After the fall of the 'Gang of Four', he was rehabilitated and had his savings, which had been confiscated, returned. What pleased him most was that he was able to go and work at an antiques studio, where he could put his knowledge to full use. But time takes its toll. When he was elected a people's representative, he was given a medical certificate stating that if he didn't rest, his chances of recovery were nil. At length he called Han.

In the antique world some old craftsmen had died, and others had fallen ill. During recent years few talented successors had turned up, and a shortage of able people became a big problem. The international antique market was brisk. Han was good at both assessing and copying ancient paintings and should have had a position which would have given full play to his unique skill. Instead, the man had been barred for many years.

Gan was so filled with remorse that he confessed everything to the Party committee. The secretary praised him and asked him to try and locate Han.

But Beijing was so big, where was Han? First Gan was told that he was a boilerman for a teahouse at Tianqiao, but when he got there he found the place had closed down. Then he was told that Han and another old bachelor had rented a house to breed goldfish near the Goldfish Pond. When he went to look for him, the house had been razed. Half a month passed but Han was nowhere to be found. All Gan knew was that he was still alive, and sometimes went to Taoran Pavilion Park to practice shadow-boxing at dawn.

He was determined to find him. Despite the doctor's warnings, he went with his cane first thing in the morning to the park. As the sun had not yet risen, only a few dim figures could be discerned running along the edge of the lake. Others were singing, walking or fishing. But whom should he approach?

Just then an old man with a beard and a cane, wearing traditional-style clothes, came towards him. He was so absorbed in humming a Beijing opera aria that he didn't notice the people around him. Out of habit, Gan spontaneously cheered, 'Wonderful!'

The old man stopped to look up towards the shaded trees by the lake. 'Why, that cheering sounds familiar to me, but I haven't heard it for more than thirty years.'

'I haven't heard such a sweet voice for over thirty years either,' Gan chimed in. 'Aren't you Mr Sheng?'

'Oh my goodness!' The old man stepped forward, and grasped Gan by the hand. 'It's you, the man who used to come with Han to see my performances.'

'Yes. My name is Gan Ziqian.'

'I've heard of you. Once after a performance, I wanted to meet you, but you had already left. Thirty years have passed since that day. How are you getting along? Where do you work now?'

Told that Gan was an adviser at an antiques studio, Sheng said, 'I'm with a Beijing opera company now. I lost my voice in 1945 when the Japanese surrendered and was jobless. But after Liberation, the government showed a lot of concern for us and gave us the opportunity to use our talents, so I became a teacher at a Beijing opera school, but that was interrupted by the "cultural revolution".'

'Mr Sheng,' Gan cut him short, 'you mentioned Mr Han to me just now. Do you know where he is?'

'Why yes. He lives with me.'

'Eh?' surprised, Gan stared at him for a long time before he asked cautiously, 'Really?'

'Of course. Anybody who comes here to practice shadow-boxing knows he's lodging with me. During the "cultural revolution" the teahouse where he worked closed down. Since he couldn't earn a living, I told him not to worry and to stay with me for the time being. My wife died and my son was transferred to another province, so I was alone. I told him he could come and keep house and that as long as I had an income, he wouldn't go hungry. So he's been living in my place for the past ten years.'

'If he's there now,' Gan said impatiently, 'may I go with you to see him?'

'No.'

'Why?'

'Because he's gone into hospital with a stroke.'

Gan heaved a sigh.

'Don't worry,' Sheng added. 'He's out of danger, but the doctor won't let him have any visitors yet.'

Relieved, Gan asked again, 'What caused it?'

'Overwork. Last year the doctor insisted that he take it easy, but he was busier than ever with his work. He said that his ancestors were connoisseurs of paintings, and had the knack of being able to tell genuine works from fakes. While he was able, he wanted to write it down so that the knowledge would not be lost.'

Gan sighed. 'If only he could have done it earlier!'

'Years ago he used to complain to me that the higher-ups in the antique world were a bunch of laymen who'd insulted him and that he would rather die with his skills than teach others. However, in the last couple of years, since I've been cleared of the false accusations made against me in the "cultural revolution" and we've had a bit more money, he's changed his mind. Now he says he won't withhold his knowledge any longer and has decided to write it all down. I was delighted and provided him with paper, ink, fine tea and tobacco, but I forgot to remind him to take care of his health.'

Hearing this Gan was moved. 'You really have been a loyal friend!'

'Oh, I owe a great deal to the way things have improved since those chaotic years, otherwise I couldn't have afforded to help him.'

With a heavy heart Gan walked silently beside Sheng for a while before asking, 'Is he able to talk?'

'Yes, but his tongue gets a little stiff sometimes.'

'So he can still be cured.' Gan was cheered, thinking he should suggest sending someone to Sheng's house to have Han's speech recorded. When the next National People's Congress opened, someone should propose helping old scholars and craftsmen to pass on their knowledge.

Saying goodbye to Gan, Sheng promised, 'As soon as I have the doctor's permission, I'll take you to see him.'

On his way home, Gan felt much more at ease; at long last he had found an opportunity to make amends for his error. Now he could die with a clear conscience.

1981

Translated by Song Shouquan

Zhang Jie

Love Must Not Be Forgotten

I am thirty, the same age as our People's Republic. For a republic thirty is still young. But a girl of thirty is virtually on the shelf.

Actually, I have a bona fide suitor. Have you seen the Greek sculptor Myron's Discobolus? Qiao Lin is the image of that discus thrower. Even the padded clothes he wears in winter fail to hide his fine physique. Bronzed, with clear-cut features, a broad forehead and large eyes, his appearance alone attracts most girls to him.

But I can't make up my mind to marry him. I'm not clear what attracts me to him, or him to me. I know people are gossiping behind my back, 'Who does she think she is, to be so choosy?' To them, I'm a nobody playing hard to get. They take offence at such preposterous behaviour.

Of course, I shouldn't be captious. In a society where commercial production still exists, marriage like most other transactions is still a form of barter.

I have known Qiao Lin for nearly two years, yet still cannot fathom whether he keeps so quiet from aversion to talking or from having nothing to say. When, by way of a small intelligence test, I demand his opinion of this or that, he says 'good' or 'bad' like a child in kindergarten.

Once I asked, 'Qiao Lin, why do you love me?' He thought the question over seriously for what seemed an age. I could see from his normally smooth but now wrinkled forehead that the little grey cells in his handsome head were hard at work cogitating. I felt ashamed to have put him on the spot.

Finally he raised his clear childlike eyes to tell me, 'Because you're good!'

Loneliness flooded my heart. 'Thank you, Qiao Lin!' I couldn't help wondering, if we were to marry, whether we could discharge our duties to each other as husband and wife. Maybe, because law and morality would have bound us together. But how tragic simply to comply with law and morality! Was there no stronger bond to link us?

When such thoughts cross my mind I have the strange sensation that instead of being a girl contemplating marriage I am an elderly social scientist.

Perhaps I worry too much. We can live like most married couples, bringing up children together, strictly true to each other according to the law ... Although living in the seventies of the twentieth century, people still consider marriage the way they did milennia ago, as a means of continuing the race, a form of barter or a business transaction in which love and marriage can be separated. Since this is the common practice, why shouldn't we follow suit?

But I still can't make up my mind. As a child, I remember; I often cried all night for no rhyme or reason, unable to sleep and disturbing the whole household. My old nurse, a shrewd though uneducated woman, said an ill wind had blown through my ear. I think this judgement showed prescience, because I still have that old weakness. I upset myself over things which really present no problem, upsetting other people at the same time. One's nature is hard to change.

I think of my mother too. If she were alive, what would she say about my attitude to Qiao Lin and my uncertainty about marrying him? My thoughts constantly turn to her, not because she was such a strict mother that her ghost is still watching over me since her death. No, she was not just my mother but my closest friend. I loved her so much that the thought of her leaving me makes my heart ache.

She never lectured me, just told me quietly in her deep unwomanly voice about her successes and failures, so that I could learn from her experience. She had evidently not had many successes – her life was full of failures.

During her last days she followed me with her fine, expressive eyes, as if wondering how I would manage on my own and as if she had some important advice for me but hesitated to give it. She must have been worried by my naiveté and sloppy ways. She suddenly blurted out, 'Shanshan, if you aren't sure what you want, don't rush into marriage – better live on your own!'

Other people might think this strange advice from a mother to her daughter, but to me it embodied her bitter experience. I don't think she underestimated me or my knowledge of life. She loved me and didn't want me to be unhappy.

'I don't want to marry, mother!' I said, not out of bashfulness or a show of coyness. I can't think why a girl should pretend to be coy. She had long since taught me about things not generally mentioned to girls.

'If you meet the right man, then marry him. Only if he's right for you.'

'I'm afraid no such man exists!'

'That's not true. But it's hard. The world is so vast, I'm afraid you may never meet him.' Whether married or not was not what concerned her, but the quality of the marriage.

'Haven't you managed fine without a husband?'

'Who says so?'

'I think you've done fine.'

'I had no choice...' She broke off, lost in thought, her face wistful. Her wistful lined face reminded me of a withered flower I had pressed in a book.

'Why did you have no choice?'

'You ask too many questions,' she parried, not ashamed to confide in me but afraid that I might reach the wrong conclusion. Besides, everyone treasures a secret to carry to the grave. Feeling a bit put out, I demanded bluntly, 'Didn't you love my dad?'

'No, I never loved him.'

'Did he love you?'

'No, he didn't.'

'Then why get married?'

She paused, searching for the right words to explain this mystery, then answered bitterly, 'When you're young you don't always know what you're looking for, what you need, and people may talk you into getting married. As you grow older and more experienced you find out your true needs. By then, though, you've done many foolish things for which you could kick yourself. You'd give anything to be able to make a fresh start and live more wisely. Those content with their lot will always be happy, they say, but I shall never enjoy that happiness.' She added self-mockingly, 'A wretched idealist, that's all I am.'

Did I take after her? Did we both have genes which attracted ill winds?

'Why don't you marry again?'

'I'm afraid I'm still not sure what I really want.' She was obviously unwilling to tell me the truth.

I cannot remember my father. He and Mother split up when I was very small. I just recall her telling me sheepishly that he was a fine handsome fellow. I could see she was ashamed of having judged by appearances and made a futile choice. She told me, 'When I can't sleep at night, I force myself to sober up by recalling all those stupid blunders I made. Of course it's so distasteful that I often hide my face in the sheet for shame, as if there were eyes watching me in the dark. But distasteful as it is, I take some pleasure in this form of atonement.'

I was really sorry that she hadn't remarried. She was such a fascinating character, if she'd married a man she loved, what a happy household ours would surely have been. Though not beautiful, she had the simple charm of an ink landscape. She was a fine writer too. Another author who knew her well used to say teasingly, 'Just reading your works is enough to make anyone love you!'

She would retort, 'If he knew that the object of his affection was a white-haired old crone, that would frighten him away.' At her age, she must have known what she really wanted, so this was obviously an evasion. I say this because she had quirks which puzzled me.

For instance, whenever she left Beijing on a trip, she always took with her one of the twenty-seven volumes of Chekov's stories published between 1950 and 1955. She also warned me, 'Don't touch these books. If you want to read Chekov, read that set I bought you.' There was no need to caution me. Having a set of my own why should I touch hers? Besides, she'd told me this over and over again. Still she was on her guard. She seemed bewitched by those books.

So we had two sets of Chekov's stories at home. Not just because we loved Chekov, but to parry other people like me who loved Chekov. Whenever anyone asked to borrow a volume, she would lend one of mine. Once, in her absence, a close friend took a volume from her set. When she found out she was frantic, and at once took a volume of mine to exchange for it.

Ever since I can remember, those books were on her bookcase. Although I admire Chekov as a great writer, I was puzzled by the way she never tired of reading him. Why, for over twenty years, had she had to read him every single day? Sometimes, when tired of writing, she poured herself a cup of strong tea and sat down in front of the bookcase, staring raptly at that set of books. If I went into her room then it flustered her, and she either spilt her tea or blushed like a girl discovered with her lover.

I wondered: Has she fallen in love with Chekov? She might have if he'd still been alive.

When her mind was wandering just before her death, her last words to me were: 'That set...' She hadn't the strength to give it its complete title. But I knew what she meant. 'And my diary ... "Love Must Not Be Forgotten" ... Cremate them with me.'

I carried out her last instruction regarding the works of Chekov, but couldn't bring myself to destroy her diary. I thought, if it could be published, it would surely prove the most moving thing she had written. But naturally publication was out of the question.

At first I imagined the entries were raw material she had jotted down. They read neither like stories, essays, a dairy or letters. But after reading the whole I formed a hazy impression, helped out by my imperfect memory. Thinking it over, I finally realized that this was no lifeless manuscript I was holding, but an anguished, loving heart. For over twenty years one man had occupied her heart, but he was not for her. She used these diaries as a substitute for him, a means of pouring out her feelings to him, day after day, year after year.

No wonder she had never considered any eligible proposals, had turned a deaf ear to idle talk whether well-meant or malicious. Her heart was already full, to the exclusion of anybody else. 'No lake can compare with the ocean, no cloud with those on Mount Wu.' Remembering those lines I often reflected sadly that few people in real life could love like this. No one would love me like this.

I learned that toward the end of the thirites, when this man was doing underground work for the Party in Shanghai, an old worker had given his life to cover him, leaving behind a helpless wife and daughter. Out of a sense of duty, of gratitude to the dead and deep class feeling, he had unhesitatingly married the daughter. When he saw the endless troubles of couples who had married for 'love', he may have thought, 'Thank Heaven, though I didn't marry for love, we get on well, able to help each other.' For years, as man and wife they lived through hard times.

He must have been my mother's colleague. Had I ever met him? He couldn't have visited our home. Who was he?

In the spring of 1962, Mother took me to a concert. We went on foot, the theatre being quite near. On the way a black limousine pulled up silently by the pavement. Out stepped an elderly man with white hair in a black serge tunic-suit. What a striking shock of white hair! Strict, scrupulous, distinguished, transparently honest – that was my impression of him. The cold glint of his flashing eyes reminded me of lightning or swordplay. Only ardent love for a woman really deserving his love could fill cold eyes like those with tenderness.

He walked up to Mother and said, 'How are you, Comrade Zhong Yu? It's been a long time.'

'How are you!' Mother's hand holding mine suddenly turned icy cold and trembled a little.

They stood face to face without looking at each other, each appearing upset, even stern. Mother fixed her eyes on the trees by the roadside, not yet in leaf. He looked at me. 'Such a big girl already. Good, fine – you take after your mother.'

Instead of shaking hands with Mother he shook hands with me. His hand was as icy as hers and trembling a little. As if transmitting an electric current, I felt a sudden shock. Snatching my hand away I cried, 'There's nothing good about that!'

'Why not?' he asked with the surprised expression grown-ups always have when children speak out frankly.

I glanced at Mother's face. I did take after her, to my disappointment. 'Because she's not beautiful.'

He laughed, then said teasingly, 'Too bad that there should be a child who doesn't find her own mother beautiful. Do you remember in '53, when your mother was transferred to Beijing, she came to our ministry to report for duty? She left you outside on the veranda, but like a monkey you climbed all the stairs, peeped through the cracks in doors, and caught your finger in the door of my office. You sobbed so bitterly that I carried you off to find her.'

'I don't remember that.' I was annoyed at his harking back to a time when I was still in open-seat pants.

'Ah, we old people have better memories.' He turned abruptly and remarked to Mother, 'I've read that last story of yours. Frankly speaking, there's something not quite right about it. You shouldn't have condemned the heroine ... There's nothing wrong with falling in love, as long as you don't spoil someone else's life ... In fact, the hero might have loved her too. Only for the sake of a third person's happiness, they had to renounce their love ...'

A policeman came over to where the car was parked and ordered the driver to move on. When the driver made some excuse, the old man looked around. After a hasty 'Goodbye' he strode back to the car and told the policeman, 'Sorry. It's not his fault, it's mine ...'

I found it amusing watching this old cadre listening respectfully to the policeman's strictures. When I turned to Mother with a mischievous smile, she looked as upset as a first-form primary schoolchild standing forlornly in front of the stern headmistress. Anyone would have thought she was the one being lectured by the policeman. The car drove off, leaving a puff of smoke. Very soon even this smoke vanished with the wind, as if nothing at all had happened. But the incident stuck in my mind.

Analyzing it now, I realize he must have been the man whose strength of character won Mother's heart. That strength came from his firm political convictions, his narrow escapes from death in the revolution, his active brain, his drive at work, his well-cultivated mind. Besides, strange to say, he and Mother both liked the oboe. Yes, she must have worshipped him. She once told me that unless she worshipped a man, she couldn't love him even for one day.

But I could not tell whether he loved her or not. If not, why was there this entry in her diary?

'This is far too fine a present. But how did you know that Chekov's my favourite writer?'

'You said so.'

'I don't remember that.'

'I remember. I heard you mention it when you were chatting with someone.'

So he was the one who had given her the *Selected Stories of Chekov*. For her that was tantamount to a love letter. Maybe this man, who didn't believe in love, realized by the time his hair was white that in his heart was something which could be called love. By the time he no longer had the right to love, he made the tragic discovery of his love for which he would have given his life. Or did it go deeper even than that?

This is all I remember about him.

How wretched Mother must have been, deprived of the man to whom she was devoted! To catch a glimpse of his car or the back of his head through its rear window, she carefully figured out which roads he would take to work and back. Whenever he made a speech, she sat at the back of the hall watching his face rendered hazy by cigarette smoke and poor lighting. Her eyes would brim with tears, but she swallowed them back. If a fit of coughing made him break off, she wondered anxiously why no one persuaded him to give up smoking. She was afraid he would get bronchitis again. Why was he so near yet so far?

He, to catch a glimpse of her, looked out of the car window every day straining his eyes to watch the streams of cyclists, afraid that she might have an accident. On the rare evenings on which he had no meetings, he would walk by a roundabout way to our neighbourhood, to pass our compound gate. However busy, he would always make time to look in papers and journals for her work. His duty had always been clear to him, even in the most difficult times. But now confronted by this love he became a weakling, quite helpless. At his age it was laughable. Why should life play this trick on him?

Yet when they happened to meet at work, each tried to avoid the other, hurrying off with a nod. Even so, this would make Mother blind and deaf to everything around her. If she met a colleague named Wang she would call him Guo and mutter something unintelligible.

It was a cruel ordeal for her. She wrote:

We agreed to forget each other. But I deceived you, I have never forgotten. I don't think you've forgotten either. We're just deceiving each other, hiding our misery. I haven't deceived you deliberately, though; I did my best to carry out our agreement. I often stay far away from Beijing, hoping time and distance will help me to forget you. But when I return, as the train pulls into the station, my head reels. I stand on the platform looking round intently, as if someone were waiting for me. Of course there is no one. I realize then that I have forgotten nothing. Everything is unchanged. My love is like a tree the roots of which strike deeper year after year – I have no way to uproot it.

At the end of every day, I feel as if I've forgotten something important. I may wake with a start from my dreams wondering what has happened. But nothing has happened. Nothing. Then it comes home to me that you are missing! So everything seems lacking, incomplete, and there is nothing to fill up the blank. We are nearing the ends of our lives, why should we be carried away by emotion like children? Why should life submit people to such ordeals, then unfold before you your lifelong dream? Because I started off blindly I took the wrong turning, and now there are insuperable obstacles between me and my dream.

Yes, Mother never let me go to the station to meet her when she came back from a trip, preferring to stand alone on the platform and imagine that he had met her. Poor mother with her greying hair was as infatuated as a girl.

Not much space in the diary was devoted to their romance. Most entries dealt with trivia: why one of her articles had not come off; her fear that she had no real talent; the excellent play she missed by mistaking the time on the ticket; the drenching she got by going out for a stroll without her umbrella. In spirit they were together day and night, like a devoted married couple. In fact, they spent no more than twenty-four hours together in all. Yet in that time they experienced deeper happiness than some people in a whole lifetime. Shakespeare makes Juliet say, 'I cannot sum up half my sum of wealth.' And probably that is how Mother felt.

He must have been killed in the Cultural Revolution. Perhaps because of the conditions then, that section of the diary is ambiguous and obscure. Mother had been so fiercely attacked for her writing, it amazed me that she went on keeping a diary. From some veiled allusions I gathered that he had questioned the theories advanced by that 'theoretician' then at the height of favour, and had told someone, 'This is sheer Rightist talk.' It was clear from the tear-stained pages of Mother's diary that he had been harshly denounced; but the steadfast old man never knuckled under to the authorities. His last words were, 'When I go to meet Marx, I shall go on fighting my case!'

That must have been in the winter of 1969, because that was when Mother's hair turned white overnight, though she was not yet fifty. And she put on a black arm-band. Her position then was extremely difficult. She was criticized for wearing this old-style mourning, and ordered to say for whom she was in mourning.

'For whom are you wearing that, Mother?' I asked anxiously.

'For my lover.' Not to frighten me she explained, 'Someone you never knew.'

'Shall I put one on too?' She patted my cheeks, as she had when I was a child. It was years since she had shown me such affection. I often felt that as she aged, especially during these last years of persecution, all tenderness had left her, or was concealed in her heart, so that she seemed like a man.

She smiled sadly and said, 'No, you needn't wear one.' Her eyes were as dry as if she had no more tears to shed. I longed to comfort her or do something to please her. But she said, 'Off you go.'

I felt an inexplicable dread, as if dear Mother had already half left me. I blurted out, 'Mother!'

Quick to sense my desolation, she said gently, 'Don't be afraid. Off you go. Leave me alone for a little.'

I was right. She wrote:

You have gone. Half my soul seems to have taken flight with you.

I had no means of knowing what had become of you, much less of seeing you for the last time. I had no right to ask either, not being your wife or friend ... So we are torn apart. If only I could have borne that inhuman treatment for you, so that you could have lived on! You should have lived to see your name cleared and take up your work again, for the sake of those who loved you. I knew you could not be a counter-revolutionary. You were one of the finest men killed. That's why I love you – I am not afraid now to avow it.

Snow is whirling down. Heavens, even God is such a hypocrite, he is using this whiteness to cover up your blood and the scandal of your murder.

I have never set store by my life. But now I keep wondering whether anything I say or do would make you contract your shaggy eyebrows in a frown. I must live a worthwhile life like you, and do some honest work for our country. Things can't go on like this – those criminals will get what's coming to them.

I used to walk alone along that small asphalt road, the only place where we once walked together, hearing my footsteps in the silent night ... I always paced to and fro and lingered there, but never as wretchedly as now. Then, though you were not beside me, I knew you were still in this world and felt that you were keeping me company. Now I can hardly believe that you have gone.

At the end of the road I would retrace my steps, then walk along it again. Rounding the fence I always looked back, as if you were still standing there waving goodbye. We smiled faintly, like casual acquaintances, to conceal our undying love. That ordinary evening in early spring a chilly wind was blowing as we walked silently away from each other. You were wheezing a little because of your chronic bronchitis. That upset me. I wanted to beg you to slow down, but somehow I couldn't. We both walked very fast, as if some important business were waiting for us. How we prized that single stroll we had together, but we were afraid we might lose control of ourselves and burst out with 'I love you' – those three words which had tormented us for years. Probably no one else could believe that we never once even clasped hands!

No, Mother, I believe it. I am the only one able to see into your locked heart.

Ah, that little asphalt road, so haunted by bitter memories. We shouldn't overlook the most insignificant spots on earth. For who knows how much secret grief and joy they may hide. No wonder that when tired of writing, she would pace slowly along that little road behind our window. Sometimes at dawn after a sleepless night, sometimes on a moonless, windy evening. Even in winter during howling gales which hurled sand and pebbles against the window pane ... I thought this was one of her eccentricities, not knowing that she had gone to meet him in spirit.

She liked to stand by the window, too, staring at the small asphalt road. Once I thought from her expression that one of our closest friends must be coming to call. I hurried to the window. It was a late autumn evening. The cold wind was stripping dead leaves from the trees and blowing them down the small empty road.

She went on pouring out her heart to him in her diary as she had when he was alive. Right up to the day when the pen slipped from her fingers. Her last message was:

> I am a materialist, yet I wish there were a Heaven. For then, I know,
> I would find you there waiting for me. I am going there to join you,
> to be together for eternity. We need never be parted again or keep

at a distance for fear of spoiling someone else's life. Wait for me, dearest, I am coming—

I do not know how, on her death bed, Mother could still love so ardently with all her heart. To me it seemed not love but a form of madness, a passion stronger than death. If undying love really exists, she reached its extreme. She obviously died happy, because she had known true love. She had no regrets.

Now these old people's ashes have mingled with the elements. But I know that no matter what form they may take, they still love each other. Though not bound together by earthly laws or morality, though they never once clasped hands, each possessed the other completely. Nothing could part them. Centuries to come, if one white cloud trails another, two blades of grass grow side by side, one wave splashes another, a breeze follows another ... believe me, that will be them.

Each time I read that diary 'Love Must Not Be Forgotten' I cannot hold back my tears. I often weep bitterly, as if I myself experienced their ill-fated love. If not a tragedy it was too laughable. No matter how beautiful or moving I find it, I have no wish to follow suit!

Thomas Hardy wrote that 'the call seldom produces the comer, the man to love rarely coincides with the hour for loving.' I cannot judge them by conventional moral standards. What I deplore is that they did not wait for a 'missing counterpart' to call them. If everyone could wait, instead of rushing into marriage, how many tragedies could be averted!

When we reach communism, will there still be cases of marriage without love? Perhaps ... since the world is so vast, two kindred spirits may never be able to answer each other's call. But how tragic! Could it be that by then we will have devised ways to escape such tragedies? But this is all conjecture.

Maybe after all we are accountable for these tragedies. Who knows? Should we take the responsibility for the old ideas handed down from the past? Because, if you choose not to marry, your behaviour is considered a direct challenge to these ideas. You will be called neurotic, accused of having guilty secrets or having made political mistakes. You may be regarded as an eccentric who looks down on ordinary people, not respecting age-old customs – a heretic. In short they will trump up endless vulgar and futile charges to ruin your reputation. Then you have to succumb to those ideas and marry regardless. But once you put the chains of an indifferent marriage around your neck, you will suffer for it for the rest of your life.

I long to shout: 'Mind your own business! Let us wait patiently for our counterparts. Even waiting in vain is better than a loveless marriage. To be single is not such a fearful disaster. I believe it may be a sign of a step forward in culture, education and the quality of life.'

Translated by Gladys Yang

Zhou Libo

The Family on the Other Side of the Mountain

Treading on the shadows of the trees cast on the slope by the moon, we were on our way to a wedding on the other side of the mountain.

Why should we go to a wedding? If anyone should ask, this is our answer: sometimes people like to go to weddings to watch the happiness of others and to increase one's own joy.

A group of girls were walking in front of us. Once girls gather in groups, they laugh all the time. These now laughed ceaselessly. One of them even had to halt by the roadside to rub her aching sides. She scolded the one who provoked such laughter while she kept on giggling. Why were they laughing? I had no idea. Generally, I do not understand much about girls. But I have consulted an expert who has a profound understanding of girls. What he said was 'they laugh because they want to laugh' ... I thought that was very clever. But someone else told me that 'although you can't tell exactly what makes them laugh, generally speaking, youth, health, the carefree life in the co-op, the fertile green fields where they labour, being paid on the same basis as the men, the misty moonlight, the light fragrance of flowers, a vague or real feeling of love ... all these are sources of their joy.'

I thought there was a lot of sense in what he said too.

When we had climbed over the mountain we could see the home of the bridegroom – two little rooms in a big brick house. A little ancient red lantern was hung at the door. The girls rushed inside like a swarm of bees. According to local tradition, they have this privilege when families celebrate this happy event. In the past, unmarried girls used to eavesdrop the first night of a friend's marriage under the window or outside the bridal chamber. When they heard such questions as 'Uh ... are you sleepy?' they would run away and laugh heartily. They would laugh again and again the next day too. But there were times when they could hear nothing. Experienced eavesdroppers would keep entirely silent on their own first night of bliss and make the girls outside the window walk away in disappointment.

The group of girls ahead of us had crowded into the door. Had they come to eavesdrop too?

I had picked several camelias to present to the bride and groom. When I reached the door I saw it was flanked with a pair of couplets written on red paper. By the light of a red lantern one could make out the squarely written words:

> Songs wing through the streets,
> Joy fills the room.

As we entered, a young man who was all smiles walked up to welcome us. He was the bridegroom, Zou Maiqiu, the storekeeper of the co-op. He was short and sturdy with nice features. Some said he was a simple, honest man but others insisted he wasn't so simple, because he found himself a beautiful bride. It is said that beautiful girls do not love simple men. Who knows? Let's take a look at the bride first.

After presenting the camelias to the bridegroom, we walked towards the bridal chamber. The wooden lattice of the window was pasted with fresh paper and decorated in the centre with the character 'happiness', cut out of red paper. In the four corners were charming paper-cuts of carps, orchids and two beautiful vases with two fat pigs at the side.

221

We walked into the room. The girls were there already, tittering softly and whispering. When we were seated they left the room in a flock. Laughter rang outside the door.

Then we scrutinized the room. Many people were seated there. The bride and her matron, who was her sister-in-law, sat on the edge of the bed. The sister-in-law had brought her three-year-old boy along and was teaching him to sing:

> In his red baby shoes a child of three,
> Toddles off to school just like his big brother
> Don't spank me, teacher, right back I shall be
> After going home for a swig of milk from mother.

I stole a glance at the bride, Pu Cuilian. She was not strikingly beautiful, but she wasn't bad looking either. Her features and figure were quite all right. So we reached the conclusion that the bride-groom was a simple and yet not too simple man. Though everyone in the room had his eyes on the bride, she remained composed and was not a bit shy. She took her nephew over from her sister-in-law, tickled him to make him laugh and then took him out to play for a while in the courtyard. As she walked past, she trailed behind a light fragrance.

A kerosene lamp was lit. Its yellowish flame lit up the things in the room. The bed was an old one, the mosquito-net was not new either and its embroidered red brocade fringes were only half new. The only new things were the two pillows.

On the red lacquer desk by the window were two pewter candle-stands and two small rectangular mirrors. Then there were china bowls and a teapot decorated with 'happiness' cut out of red paper. Most outstanding of all the bric-a-brac presents were two half-naked porcelain monks, with enormous pot bellies, laughing heartily. Why did they laugh? Since they were monks they should have considered such merry-making as frivolous and empty. Why had they come to the wedding then? And they looked so happy too. They must have learned to take a more enlightened view of life, I suppose.

Among the people chatting and laughing were the township head, the chairman of the co-op, the veterinarian and his wife. The township head was a serious man. He never laughed at the jokes others cracked. Even when he joked himself, he kept a straight face. He was a busy man, he hadn't intended to come to the wedding. But since Zou was on the co-op's administrative staff and also his neighbour, he had to show up. As soon as he stepped into the door, the bridegroom's mother came up to him and said:

'You have come just at the right moment. We need a responsible person to see to things.' She meant that she wanted him to officiate.

So he had to stay. He smoked and chatted, waiting for the ceremony to begin.

The head of the co-op was a busy person too. He usually had serious talks. He also had to work in the fields and was often scolded by his wife for coming home too late at night. He worked hard and never complained. Indeed he was a busy man, but he had to come to congratulate the union of these two young people however busy he was. Zou Maiqiu was one of his best assistants. He had come to express his goodwill and to offer his help.

Of all the guests, the veterinarian talked the most. Talking on all subjects, he finally came to the marriage system.

'There are some merits to arranged marriages too. You don't have to take all the trouble of looking for a wife yourself,' said he, for he had obtained his beautiful wife through an old-fashioned arbitrarily arranged marriage, and he was extremely satisfied. With his drink-mottled pock-marked face, he would never have been able to get such a beautiful wife by himself.

'I advocate free choice in marriage,' said the chairman. His wife, who married him also in the old-fashioned way, often scolded him, and this made him detest the arbitrary marriage system.

'I agree with you.' The township head sided with the co-op chairman. 'There is a folk song about the sorrows caused by the old marriage system.'

> My old marriage system promises no freedom.
> The woman cries and the man grieves.
> She cries till the Yangtse River overflows,
> And he grieves till the green mountain is crested white.

'Is it as bad as that?' laughed the co-op chairman.

'We neither cry nor grieve,' said the veterinarian proudly, looking at his wife.

'You are just a blind dog who happened on a good meal by accident,' said the township head. 'Talking about crying reminds me of the custom in Jinshi.' He paused to light his pipe.

'What kind of custom?' asked the chairman.

'The family who is marrying off a daughter must hire many people to cry. Rich families sometimes hire several dozen.'

'What if the people they hire don't know how to cry?' asked the veterinarian.

'The purpose is to hire those who do. There are people in Jinshi who are professional criers and specialists in this trade. Their crying is as rhythmic as singing, very pleasing to the ear.'

Peals of laughter burst forth outside the window. The girls, who had been away for some time, evidently were practising eavesdropping already. All the people in the bridal chamber, including the bride, laughed with them. The only people who did not laugh were the township head and the veterinarian's beautiful wife who knitted her brows.

'Anything wrong with you?' the veterinarian asked softly.

'I feel a little dizzy and there's a sick feeling in my stomach.'

'Perhaps you're pregnant?' suggested the township head.

'Have you seen a doctor?' the bride's sister-in-law asked.

'She's in bed with a doctor every night! She doesn't have to look for one,' laughed the chairman.

'How can you say such things at your age!' said the veterinarian's beautiful wife. 'And you a chairman of the co-op!'

'Everything is ready,' someone called. 'Come to the hall please.' All crowded into the hall. With her little boy in her arms, the bride's sister-in-law followed behind the bride. The girls also came in. They leaned against the wall, shoulder to shoulder and holding hands. They looked at the bride, whispered into each other's ears and giggled again.

On one side of the hall were barrows, baskets and bamboo mats which belonged to the co-op. On the table in the centre, two red candles were lit, shining on two vases of camelias.

The ceremony began. The township head took his place. He read the marriage lines, talked a little and withdrew to sit beside the co-op chairman. The girl who acted as the conductor of ceremonies announced that the next speaker was to be one of the guests. Whoever arranged the programme had put the most interesting item, the bride's turn to speak, at the very end. So everyone waited eagerly for the guests to finish their chatter.

The first one called upon was the co-op chairman. But he said:

'Let the bride speak. I have been married for more than twenty-years and have quite forgotten what it is like to be a newly-wed. What can I say?'

All laughed and clapped. However the person who walked up to speak was not the bride but the veterinarian with his drink-mottled pock-marked face. He spoke slowly, like an actor. Starting from the situation in our country before and after Liberation and using a lot of special terms, he went on to the international situation.

'I have an appointment. I must leave early,' said the township head softly to the co-op chairman. 'You stay to officiate.'

'I should be leaving too.'

'No, you can't. We shouldn't both leave,' said the township head. He nodded to the bridegroom's mother apologetically and left. The co-op chairman had to stay. Bored by the talk, he said to the person sitting beside him:

'What on earth is the relation between the wedding and the situation at home and abroad?'

'This is his usual routine. He has only touched on two points, so far. There are still a lot yet.'

'We should invent some kind of device that makes empty talkers itch all over so that they have to scratch and cannot go on speaking,' said the chairman.

After half an hour or so, the guests clapped hands again. The veterinarian had ended his speech at last. This time the bride took the floor. Her plaits tied up with red wool, she was blushing crimson in spite of her poise. She said:

'Comrades and fellow villagers, I am very happy this evening, very, very happy.'

The girls giggled. But the bride who was saying that she was very, very happy didn't even smile. On the contrary, she was very nervous. She continued:

'We were married a year go.'

The guests were shocked, and then they laughed. After a while they realized that she had said married instead of engaged because she was so nervous.

'We are being married today. I'm very happy.' She paused and glanced at the guests before continuing. 'Please don't misunderstand me when I say I'm happy. That doesn't mean I shall enjoy my happiness by sitting idly at home. I do not intend to be merely dependent on my husband. I shall do my share of work. I'll do my work well in the co-op and compete with him.'

'Hurrah! And beat Zhou down too.' A young man applauded.

'That's all I have to say.' The bride, blushing scarlet, escaped from the floor.

'Is that all?' Someone wanted to hear more.

'She has spoken too little.' Another was not satisfied.

'The bride's relative's turn now,' said the girl conductor of ceremony.

Holding her boy of three the bride's sister-in-law stood up.

'I have not studied and I don't know how to talk.' She sat down blushing scarlet too.

'Let the bridegroom say whether he accepts the bride's challenge,' someone suggested.

'Where is the bridegroom?'

'He's not here,' someone discovered.

'He's run away!' another decided.

'Run away? Why?'

'Where has he run to?'

'This is terrible. What kind of a bridegroom is he?'

'He must be frightened by the bride's challenge to compete.'

'Look for him immediately. It's unbelieveable! The bride's relative is still here,' said the co-op chairman.

With torches and flashlights people hurried out. They looked for him in the mountains, by the brooks and pools and everywhere. The co-op chairman and several men, about to join in the hunt, noticed a light in the sweet potato cellar.

'So you are here. You are the limit, you...' A young man felt like cursing him.

'Why have you run away? Are you afraid of the challenge?' asked the chairman.

Zhou Maiqiu climbed out of the cellar with a lantern. Brushing the dust from his clothes he raised his eyebrows and said calmly in a low voice:

'Rather than sit there listening to the veterinarian's empty talk, I thought I might as well come to see whether our sweet potatoes are in good condition.'

'You are a good storekeeper, but certainly a poor bridegroom. Aren't you afraid your bride'll be offended?' said the chairman half reproachfully and half encouragingly.

And escorting the bridegroom back, we took our leave. Again treading on the tree shadows cast by the moonlight, which by now was slanting to the west, we went home. The group of girls who had come with us remained behind.

In the early winter night the breeze, fragrant with the scent of camelias, brought to our ears the peals of happy open laughter from the girls. They must have begun their eavesdropping. Had they heard something interesting already?

November, 1957

Translated by Yu Fanqin

Zhao Da-nian

Three Sketches

IQ Test

A TV station organized an entirely new sort of IQ test, planning to broadcast it nationwide once they had finished making it. First they took their cameras and recording equipment to a bureau to test the officials there.

The host drew a chalk circle on the blackboard and asked, 'What's this, everybody?'

The high-voltage mercury vapour lamps were on, and the cameras were panning across the faces of the bureau officials. Reporters carrying baton-like mikes waited to stick them in front of the mouth of anyone who spoke. The bureau officials stared at the chalk circle on the blackboard in bewilderment. What on earth did it mean? Uncertain what to do, they dared not answer. But the cameras kept panning back and forth. Could no one answer? That would be too embarrassing. The staff members started to look to their section heads for instructions. The section heads eyed the department heads for advice. The department heads fixed their clever eyes, which were so attuned to inferring leaders' intentions, on the bureau head. As was his wont, the bureau head looked to his secretary for help. However, this time the pretty secretary was completely stumped, and so she went over and whispered in the bureau head's ear. She had forgotten that the cameras were running. Only after hearing his secretary's report through did the bureau head protest, 'Sorry! I wasn't informed of the matter beforehand, and it hasn't been deliberated, so how can I answer your question just like that?'

The comrades from the TV station went to the second group of subjects for the IQ test – in the classroom of a university Chinese department. The lights were on and the cameras and recorders were running. As before, the host drew a chalk circle on the blackboard and asked, 'What's this, everybody?'

There was an awkward silence for half a minute. Then the proud students burst out laughing, and shouted:

'What sort of a question's that? You want to test us university students?'

'It's too condescending! It's a joke!'

'Only a fool would answer your question!'

'Don't yell, they're still taping!'

Junior middle school students formed the third group. An outstanding student, who often came top in exams, put his hand up politely, then stood up, and pointing at the chalk circle on the blackboard, replied:

'It's a zero.'

'Is he right?' asked the host.

'Yes!' the students chorused.

'Are there any other answers?' asked the host.

'Is there a second way of answering the question? Please think it over carefully, everyone.'

'O! O, like in the English alphabet!' shouted a mischievous student, not even daring to stand up.

The class teacher gave him an angry look, but the host hastily said, 'He's right, very good!'

The fourth group was composed of first grade primary school students. Once they saw the chalk circle on the blackboard, the classroom burst into life, all the little hands going up, and everyone trying to answer first:

'It's the moon.'

'Why's it the moon?' asked the host, delighted.

'The blackboard is the sky, it's dark, and the moon is white and round!'

'It's a ping-pong ball.'

'A sesame seed cake.'

'An egg!'

'Li Guyi's mouth – she's singing!'

'No, it's one of teacher's eyes, and she's mad!'

The IQ tests came to a satisfactory end. When the TV station broadcast the programme, they added a subtitle: 'How do people lose their powers of imagination?'

Impression of Drunkenness

The young painter Xiao Du had a habit – before he composed a work, he would drink two *liang* of *Erguotou* liquor. When he drank to the point where his head was heavy, his feet were light and his eyes were drowsy, where people looked as though they were seen in a distorting mirror, and scenery looked as though it was seen through a kaleidoscope, then, at that point, ideas of style and content would pour out of his head like a stream.

The theme he'd selected at the time was drunkeness.

He began to read poetry. The ineffable beauty of poetry and painting combined. Poetic painting and painterly poetry. In my *Drunkenness*, I will paint the essence of poetry. 'Li Bai's hundred verses in a single pour.' Great! 'Lady Yang in her cups.' Even better! 'Drink makes not man drunk; man makes himself drunk.' Excellent! 'Drowning sorrows in a drink only makes you feel more sorrowful.' Best of all!

Although he'd got his theme and some ideas on it, he still didn't have any images. What can I paint that will express my thoughts?

In January, he painted a drunk as drunk as a lord. It was priced at 10 yuan, but no one wanted to buy it. They said it lacked dynamism.

In February, he painted a drunken lout attacking someone, the liquor jug flying through the air. It was full of dynamism. The price was 50 yuan, but still no one wanted to buy. They said it lacked refinement.

In March, he painted a crazy drunk, dipping and weaving like a disco dancer. His posture was very refined. It was priced at 100 yuan, but still no one wanted to buy. They said it was too shallow.

In April, he painted a beautiful liquor jug, with an agate cup and a big, tasty crab beside it. It was priced at 200 yuan, but the critics shook their heads. They said they couldn't see the meaning of the objects.

Xiao Du didn't know what to make of it. His wife Xiao Hu lost faith in him, too. Putting one hand on her hip and pointing at his nose, she would curse him out loud: 'Can't you paint something else? A panda? A big factory? A satellite launch? Fake medicine from Jinjiang County? The rising price of cabbages? Reagan's visit to China? Something that has to do with real life now! And don't ignore me! Let me tell you, if you don't come back with some money next time, this liquor jug stays empty for good!'

The more Xiao Du worried, the more Xiao Hu pointed at his nose and cursed. She was in the habit of putting her left hand on her hip and raising her right arm high. She cursed and cursed until, eureka, she aroused his inspiration! Xiao Du suddenly noticed that his wife's body was shaped like a liquor jug! Her left arm on her hip was the handle, and her raised right arm was the spout. Thank the lord!

It was May already, and the weather was boiling hot. The sweat pouring off him, using thick ink and deep colours, Xiao Du painted *Impression of Drunkenness* all in one go. The picture was of a young woman in a charming pose, her left arm on her hip like a handle, and her right arm raised like a spout. She was wearing a gauzy green dress transparent as a cicada's wings, the curves of her body swelling out, hemisphere-like. The whole resembled a captivating, intoxicating liquor jug. It was priced at 500 yuan, and sold the day it was hung in the gallery.

Even better, Xiao Du's mind was unblocked at last, and masterpieces came pouring out one after another. The prices went up from 500 to 800, then 1,000, 1,500, and 2,000. Next it was francs, US dollars and pounds. He became famous far and wide, and critics in China and abroad all praised him as 'the best of the Far East Impressionist School'.

His charming wife Xiao Hu didn't curse him anymore, either.

Breaking an Eagle

The playwright Lao Chen was so tired that in the end he became sick. His film script, after having been gone over, picked at, criticized, discussed, consulted upon, worried at, passed, rejected, tampered with, cooperated on, resuscitated, passed again, reneged upon again, turned against, rejuggled, rejected again, indicted, taken to court, scrapped over, given the cold shoulder and sweated over by ninety-nine people over three years, three months and three days, with twenty-seven revisions, big and small, screenwriters increased from one to six, and combined efforts from north, south, east, west, above and below, had had the rejection rejected, finally been approved and gone into production.

However, Lao Chen was so tired that in the end he became sick. Both physically and mentally exhausted, he went to recuperate on the remote Inner Mongolian grasslands. There he could get a change of air, and see blue skies, white clouds, soaring eagles and boundless stretches of green grass. Green is the source of life, and by seeing it one can get back to nature.

He met an old hunter called Zamrin, and stayed in his 'one-storey Beijing house'. It was said that this sort of house, with red-brick walls and a flat roof made of concrete slabs, came from the suburbs of Beijing. Lao Chen preferred those of the Mongolian yurts and ox-carts that hadn't been abandoned yet.

Zamrin rode his horse out hunting every day, taking his eagle with him. His hunting eagle was very ferocious. It could not only catch hares, foxes and weasels, but also claw out the eyes of Mongolian gazelles. What puzzled Lao Chen was why the eagle didn't fly away. And why didn't it eat its prey once it caught it? Why did it wait to be fed by Zamrin after coming home?

'Why won't it eat the food I offer it?' asked Lao Chen.

'It's broken in!' replied Zamrin proudly.

One day, Zamrin took two lengths of wild hare gut, and using lots of hempen rope and string, tied them fast in the middle of a big, flat basket, which he then placed on the roof.

'What's that for?' asked Lao Chen.

'My hunting eagle's getting old,' Zamrin said with a wink.

Before long, there was a young cock eagle circling above the roof. It wanted to eat the hare gut, and after taking good aim, dived down like a fighter plane, skimmed across the roof, grabbed the gut with its powerful talons, and dragged the five-foot-across basket up into the sky, too.

The young eagle had been thoroughly taken in. First, its feet were knotted up, and the talons themselves were tangled in the rope, so it couldn't let go. Besides, it was so stubborn and hungry, it wouldn't let go anyway. But trying to carry a basket aloft was really tiring. Even worse, it couldn't see the hills, prairies, trees and villages below, so it didn't dare descend, but could only go on desperately trying to fly upwards. It flew and flew, the sweat pouring off its back, panting like an ox, seeing stars before its eyes and foaming at the beak. The air between its wings and the basket included irregular currents, eddies, countercurrents, updrafts, and mixed currents. Even if you had invited the air current expert Dr Qian Xuesen, it would have taken him thirty years to figure out the laws governing those currents. The eagle was failing. Once its tail lost the ability to maintain balance and steer, it was in great danger.

Lao Chen was fascinated. The view from below was no less than wondrous. The eagle couldn't be seen; there was only the basket, flying by itself, like a UFO or a flying saucer. It was even more like a headless fly buzzing about, flying around in circles in the air above Zamrin's house, unable to escape from Buddha's palm.

And like Buddha, Zamrin narrowed his eyes, smoked a cigarette, had a cup of milk tea, and didn't even look once. He was completely confident: 'A young eagle will struggle for an hour at most, then it'll fall.'

It was just as he said. The basket fell less than a hundred paces away. The eagle was soaked in sweat like a wet chicken. It was so exhausted it allowed itself to be handled.

Zamrin put it on a perch, and tied one talon down. The perch consisted of a wooden stick hanging like a swing from two lengths of hempen rope in the room. He gave it a push every now and then, and it would swing back and forth for a few moments. Because it was not stable, the eagle did not dare to sleep, exhausted though it was. Instead, it gripped the perch tight, and flapped its aching wings in an effort to balance itself. At night, Zamrin hung an electric light by the perch. The eagle was terrified, scared that its feathers would be burned, and so it dared even less to sleep. The real breaking in had begun. The next day, it couldn't keep its eyes open, but every time it dozed off, Zamrin lashed it with a switch of willow. The eagle had never been harrassed like this before! It stared with wide-open eyes, wanting to take on the switch. On the third day, its eyes were bloodshot and it was beside itself with hunger. It began to cry pitifully, and open its beak, begging for food.

A neighbour of Zamrin's came to help. He took a ball of hemp string about as big as an egg, soaked in sesame oil and fed it to the eagle. The starved bird didn't care what it ate anymore, and swallowed it right away. However, one end of the string was still in the neighbour's hand. After a moment, he started to draw the string out. Ow! The eagle's eyes rolled white with the gut-wrenching pain as the string clawed the fat and blood out of its innards.

Eagles can distinguish people. When that neighbour came to feed it again, it didn't dare eat. A different neighbour came, but fed it a ball of string again, and pulled it out again. After a few repetitions, the eagle began to refuse food no matter who tried to feed it. Only at this point did Zamrin take the stage, parting the eagle's beak and stuffing a piece of bloody mutton in. It tasted good and there was no excruciating pulling out of hemp string. Eagles are not overintelligent, so it gave thanks to God, and tearfully recognized its saviour.

From then on, the young wild eagle was broken in as a tame hunting eagle, following its master Zamrin out to catch hares, foxes and weasels every day. The hungrier it got, the keener it was to fly back home, because only the food master gave it was not a ball of hemp string.

Soon, the old hunting eagle died and was sold to an exhibition hall as an animal specimen. Once he was better, Lao Chen the playwright also seemed to have understood something, and left the vast grasslands.

Translated by Wu Ling

Feng Ji-cai

The Tall Woman and Her Short Husband

1

Say you have a small tree in your yard and are used to its smooth trunk. If one day it turns twisted and gnarled it strikes you as awkward. As time goes by, however, you grow to like it, as if that was how this tree should always have been. Were it suddenly to straighten out again you would feel indescribably put out. A trunk as dull and boring as a stick! In fact it would simply have reverted to its original form, so why should you worry?

Is this force of habit? Well, don't underestimate 'habit'. It runs through everything done under the sun. It is not a law to be strictly observed, yet flouting it is simply asking for trouble. Don't complain though if it proves so binding that sometimes, unconsciously, you conform to it. For instance, do you presume to throw your weight about before your superiors? Do you air your views recklessly in front of your seniors? When a group photograph is taken, can you shove celebrities aside to stand swaggering and chortling in the middle? You can't, of course you can't. Or again, would you choose a wife ten years older than you, heftier than you or a head taller than you? Don't be in a rush to answer. Here's an instance of such a couple.

2

She was seventeen centimetres taller than he.

One point seven five metres in height, she towered above most of her sex like a crane over chickens. Her husband, a bare 1.58 metres, had been nicknamed Shorty at college. He came up to her earlobes but actually looked two heads shorter.

And take their appearances. She seemed dried up and scrawny with a face like an unvarnished ping-pong bat. Her features would pass, but they were small and insignificant as if carved in shallow relief. She was flat-chested, had a ramrod back and buttocks as scraggy as a scrubbing board. Her husband on the other hand seemed a rubber rolypoly: well-fleshed, solid and radiant. Everything about him – his calves, insteps, lips, nose and fingers – were like pudgy little meatballs. He had soft skin and a fine complexion shining with excess fat and ruddy because of all the red blood in his veins. His eyes were like two high-voltage little light bulbs, while his wife's were like glazed marbles. The two of them just did not match, and formed a marked contrast. But they were inseparable.

One day some of their neighbours were having a family reunion. After drinking his fill the grandfather put a tall, thin empty wine bottle on the table next to a squat tin of pork.

'Who do these remind you of?' he asked. Before anyone could guess he gave the answer. 'That tall woman downstairs and that short husband of hers.'

Everyone burst out laughing and went on laughing through the meal.

What had brought such a pair together?

This was a mystery to the dozens of households living in Unity Mansions. Ever since this couple moved in, the old residents had eyed them curiously. Some registered a question mark in their minds, while others put their curiosity into words. Tongues started wagging, especially in wet weather when the two of them went out and it was always Mrs Tall who held the umbrella. If anything dropped to the ground, though, it was simpler for Mr Short to pick it up. Some old ladies at a loose end would gesticulate, finding this comic, and splutter with laughter. This set a bad example for the children who would burst out laughing at sight of the pair and hoot, 'Long carrying-pole; big, low stool!' The husband and wife pretended not to hear and kept their tempers, paying no attention. Maybe for this reason their relations with their neighbours remained rather cool. The few less officious ones simply nodded a greeting when they met. This made it hard for those really intrigued by them to find out more about them. For instance, how did they hit it off? Why had they married? Which gave way to the other? They could only speculate.

This was an old-fashioned block of flats with large sunny rooms and wide, dark corridors. It stood in a big courtyard with a small gatehouse. The man who lived there was a tailor, a decent fellow. His wife, who brimmed over with energy, liked to call on her neighbours and gossip. Most of all she liked to ferret out their secrets. She knew exactly how husbands and wives got on, why sisters-in-law quarrelled, who was lazy, who hard-working, and how much everyone earned. If she was unclear about anything she would leave no stone unturned to get at the truth. The thirst for knowledge makes even the ignorant wise. In this respect she was outstanding. She analyzed conversations, watched expressions, and could even tell what people were secretly thinking. Simply by using her nose, she knew which household was eating meat or fish, and from that could deduce their income. For some reason or other, ever since the sixties each housing estate had chosen someone like this as a 'neighbourhood activist', giving legal status to these nosey-parkers so that their officiousness could have full play. It seems the Creator will never waste any talent.

Though the tailor's wife was indefatigable she failed to discover how this incongruous couple who passed daily before her eyes had come to marry. She found this most frustrating; it posed a formidable challenge. On the basis of her experience, however, and by racking her brains she finally came up with a plausible explanation: either husband or wife must have some physiological deficiency. Otherwise no one would marry someone a whole head taller or shorter. Her grounds for this reasoning were that after three years of marriage they still had no children. The residents of Unity Mansions were all convinced by this brilliant hypothesis.

But facts are merciless. The tailor's wife was debunked and lost face when Mrs Tall appeared in the family way. Her womb could be seen swelling from day to day, for being relatively far from the ground it was all too evident. Regardless of their amazement, misgivings or embarrassment, she gave birth to a fine baby. When the sun was hot or it rained and the couple went out, Mrs Tall would carry the baby while Mr Short held the umbrella. He plodded along comically on his plump legs, the umbrella held high, keeping just behind his wife. And the neighbours remained as intrigued as at the start of this ill-assorted, inseparable couple. They went on making plausible conjectures, but could find no confirmation for any of them.

The tailor's wife said, 'They must have something to hide, those two. Why else should they keep to themselves? Well, it's bound to come to light some day, just wait and see.'

One evening, sure enough, she heard the sound of breaking glass in their flat. On the pretext of collecting money for sweeping the yard she rushed to knock on their door, sure that their long hidden feud had come to a head and avid to watch the confrontation between them. The door opened. Mrs Tall asked her in with a smile. Mr Short was smiling too at a smashed plate on the floor – that was all the tailor's wife saw. She hastily collected the money and left to puzzle over what had happened. A plate had been smashed, yet instead of quarrelling they had treated it as a joke. How very strange!

Later the tailor's wife beame the residents' representative for Unity Mansions. When she helped the police check up on living permits, she at last found the answer to this puzzle. A reliable and irrefutable answer. The tall woman and her short husband both worked in the Research Institute of the Ministry of Chemical Industry. He was chief engineer, with a salary of over 180 yuan! She was an ordinary laboratory technician earning less than sixty yuan, and her father was a hard-working low-paid postman. So that explained why she had married a man so much shorter. For status, money and an easy life. Right! The tailor's wife lost no time in passing on this priceless information to all the bored old ladies in Unity Mansions. Judging others by themselves, they believed her. At last this riddle was solved. They saw the light. Rich Mr Short was congenitally deficient while poor Mrs Tall was a money-grabber on the make. When they discussed the good luck of this tall woman who looked like a horse, they often voiced resentment – especially the tailor's wife.

3

Sometimes good luck turns into bad.

In 1966, disaster struck China. Great changes came into the lives of all the residents in Unity Mansions, which was like a microcosm of the whole country. Mr Short as chief engineer was the first to suffer. His flat was raided, his furniture moved out, he was struggled against and confined in his institute. And worse was to come. He was accused of smuggling out the results of his research to write up at home in the evenings, with a view to fleeing the country to join a wealthy relative abroad. This preposterous charge of passing on scientific secrets to foreign capitalists was widely believed. In that period of lunacy people took leave of their senses and cruelly made up groundless accusations in order to find some Hitler in their midst. The institute kept a stranglehold on its chief engineer. He was threatened, beaten up, put under all kinds of pressure; his wife was ordered to hand over that manuscript which no one had ever seen. But all was to no effect. Someone proposed holding a struggle meeting against them both in the courtyard of Unity Mansions. As everyone dreads losing face in front of relatives and friends, this would put more pressure on them. Since all else had failed, it was at least worth trying. Never before had Unity Mansions been the scene of such excitement.

In the afternoon the institute sent people to fix up ropes between two trees in the yard, on which to hang a poster with the name of Mr Short on it – crossed out. Inside and outside the yard they pasted up threatening slogans, and on the wall put eighteen more posters listing the engineer's 'crimes'. As the meeting was to be held after supper, an electrician was sent to fix up four big 500-watt bulbs. By now the tailor's wife, promoted to be the chairman of the neighbourhood's Public Security Committee, was a powerful person, full of self-importance, and much fatter than before. She had been busy all day bossing the other women about, helping to put up slogans and make tea for the revolutionaries from the institute. The wiring for the lights had been fixed up from her gatehouse as if she were celebrating a wedding!

After supper the tailor's wife assembled all the residents in the yard, lit up as brilliantly as a sportsground at night. Their shadows, magnified ten-fold, were thrown on the wall of the building. These shadows stayed stock-still, not even the children daring to play about. The tailor's wife led a group also wearing red armbands, in those days most awe-inspiring, to guard the gate and keep outsiders out. Presently a crowd from the institute, wearing armbands and shouting slogans, marched in the tall woman and her short husband. He had a placard hung round his neck, she had none. The two of them were marched in front of the platform, and stood there side by side with lowered heads.

The tailor's wife darted forward. 'This wretch is too short for the revolutionary masses at the back to see,' she cried. 'I'll soon fix that.' She dashed into the gatehouse, her fat shoulders heaving, to fetch a soapbox which she turned upside down. Mr Short standing on this was the same height as his wife. But at this point little attention was paid to the relative heights of this couple facing disaster.

The meeting followed the customary procedure. After slogans had been shouted, passionate accusations were made, punctuated by more slogans. The pressure built up. First Mrs Tall was ordered to come clean, to produce that 'manuscript'. Questions and denunciations were fired at her, hysterical screams, angry shouts and threatening growls. But she simply shook her head gravely and sincerely. What use was sincerity? To believe in her would have made the whole business a farce.

No matter what bullies sprang forward to shake their fists at her, or what tricky questions were asked to try to trap her, she simply shook her head. The members of the institute were at a loss, afraid that if this went on the struggle meeting would fizzle out and end up a fiasco.

The tailor's wife had listened with mounting exasperation. Being illiterate she took no interest in the 'manuscript' they wanted, and felt these research workers were too soft-spoken. All of a sudden she ran to the platform. Raising her right arm with its red armband she pointed accusingly at Mrs Tall.

'Say!' she screeched. 'Why did you marry him?'

The members of the institute were staggered by this unexpected question. What connection had it with their investigation?

Mrs Tall was staggered too. This wasn't the sort of question asked these days. She looked up with surprise on her thin face which showed the ravages of the last few months.

'So you don't dare answer, eh?' The tailor's wife raised her voice. 'I'll answer for you! You married this scoundrel, didn't you, for his money? If he hadn't had money who'd want such a short fellow!' She sounded rather smug, as if she alone had seen through Mrs Tall.

Mrs Tall neither nodded nor shook her head. She had seen through the tailor's wife too. Her eyes glinted with derision and contempt.

'All right, you won't admit it. This wretch is done for now, he's a broken reed. Oh, I know what you're thinking.' The tailor's wife slapped her chest and brandished one hand gloatingly. Some other women chimed in.

The members of the institute were flummoxed. A question like this was best ignored. But though these women had strayed far from the subject, they had also livened up the meeting. So the institute members let them take the field. The women yelled:

'How much has he paid you? What has he bought you? What has he bought you? Own up!'

'Two hundred a month isn't enough for you, is it? You have to go abroad!'

'Is Deng Tuo* behind you?'

That day you made a long-distance call to Beijing, were you ringing up the Three Family Village?†

The success of a meeting depends on the enthusiasm worked up. The institute members who had convened this meeting saw that the time was ripe now to shout a few more slogans and conclude it. They then searched Mrs Tall's flat, prizing up floorboards and stripping off wallpaper. When they discovered nothing, they marched her husband away, leaving her behind.

---

* Deng Tuo (1912–1966), historian, poet and essayist, was the Party secretary of Beijing in charge of cultural and educational work, who was considered a counter-revolutionary after the start of the 'cultural revolution' in 1966.

† In 1961 Deng Tuo, Wu Han (a historian) and Liao Mosha (a writer) started a magazine column 'Notes from the Three Family Village' and published many essays which were well received. During the 'cultural revolution' the three writers were falsely charged as 'The Three Family Village'.

Mrs Tall stayed in all the next day but went out alone after dark, unaware that though the light in the gatehouse was out the tailor's wife was watching her from the window. She trailed her out of the gate and past two crossroads till Mrs Tall stopped to knock softly on a gate. The tailor's wife ducked behind a telegraph pole and waited, holding her breath, as if to pounce on a rabbit when it popped out of its burrow.

The gate creaked open. An old woman led out a child.

'All over, is it?' she asked.

Mrs Tall's answer was inaudible.

'He's had his supper and a sleep,' the old woman said. 'Take him home quickly now.'

The tailor's wife realized that this was the woman who minded their little boy. Her excitement died down as Mrs Tall turned back to lead her son home. All was silence apart from the sound of their footsteps. The tailor's wife stood motionless behind the telegraph pole till they had gone, then scurried home herself.

The next morning when Mrs Tall led her son out, her eyes were red. No one would speak to her, but they all saw her red, swollen eyes. Those who had denounced her the previous day had a strange feeling of guilt. They turned away so as not to meet her eyes.

4

After the struggle meeting Mr Short was not allowed home again. The tailor's wife, who was in the know, said he had been imprisoned as an active counter-revolutionary. That made Mrs Tall the lowest of the low, naturally unfit to live in a roomy flat. She was forced to change places with the tailor's wife and moved into the little gatehouse. This didn't worry her, as it meant she could avoid the other residents who snubbed her. But they could look through her window and see her all alone there. Where she had sent her son, they didn't know, for he only came home for a few days at a time. Ostracized by all, she looked older than a woman in her thirties.

'Mark my words,' the tailor's wife said, 'she can only keep this up for at most a year. Then if Shorty doesn't get out she'll have to remarry. If I were her I'd get a divorce and remarry. Even if he's let out his name will be mud, and he won't have any money.'

A year went by. Mr Short still didn't come back and Mrs Tall kept to herself. In silence she went to work, came back, lit her stove and went out with a big shabby shopping basket. Day after day she did this, the whole year round… But one day in autumn Mr Short reappeared – thinly clad, his head shaved, and his whole appearance changed. He seemed to have shrunk and his skin no longer gleamed with health. He went straight to his old flat. Its new master, the honest tailor, directed him to the gatehouse. Mrs Tall was squatting in the doorway chopping firewood. At the sound of his voice she sprang up to stare at him. After two years' separation both were appalled by the change in the other. One was wrinkled, the other haggard; one looked taller than before, the other shorter. After gazing at each other they hastily turned away, and Mrs Tall ran inside. When finally she came out again he had picked up the axe and squatted down to chop firewood, until two big boxes of wood had been chopped into kindling, as if he feared some new disaster might befall them at any moment. After that they were inseparable again, going to work together and coming back together just as before. The neighbours, finding them unchanged, gradually lost interest in them and ignored them.

One morning Mrs Tall had an accident. Her husband rushed frantically out and came back with an ambulance to fetch her. For days the gatehouse was empty and dark at night. After three weeks Mr Short returned with a stranger. They were carrying her on a stretcher. She was confined to her room. He went to work as usual, hurrying back at dusk to light the stove and go out with the shopping basket. This was the same basket she had used every day. In his hand it looked even bigger and nearly reached the ground.

When the weather turned warmer Mrs Tall came out. After so long in bed her face was deathly white, and she swayed from side to side. She held a cane in her right hand and kept her elbow bent in front of her. Her half-paralysed left leg made walking difficult. She had obviously had a stroke. Every morning and every evening Mr Short helped her twice round the yard, painfully and slowly. By hunching up his shoulders he was able to grip her crooked arm in both hands. It was hard for him, but he smiled to encourage her. As she couldn't raise her left foot, he tied a rope round it and pulled this up when she wanted to take a step forward. This was a pathetic yet impressive sight, and the neighbours were touched by it. Now when they met the couple they nodded cordially to them.

5

Mrs Tall's luck had run out: she was not to linger long by the side of the short husband who had loved her so dearly. Death and life were equally cruel to her. Life had struck her down and now death carried her off. Mr Short was left all alone.

But after her death fortune smiled on him again. He was rehabilitated, his confiscated possessions were returned, and he received all his back pay. Only his flat, occupied by the tailor's wife, was not given back to him. The neighbours watched to see what he would do. It was said that some of his colleagues had proposed finding him another wife, but he had declined their offers.

'I know the kind of woman he wants,' said the tailor's wife. 'Just leave it to me!'

Having passed her zenith she had become more subdued. Stripped of her power she had to wear a smile. With a photograph of a pretty girl in her pocket she went to the gatehouse to find Mr Short. The girl in the picture was her niece.

She sat in the gatehouse sizing up its furnishing as she proposed this match to rich Mr Short. Smiling all over her face she held forth with gusto until suddenly she realized that he had not said a word, his face was black, and behind him hung a picture of him and Mrs Tall on their wedding day. Then she beat a retreat without venturing to produce the photograph of her niece.

Since then several years have passed. Mr Short is still a widower, but on Sundays he fetches his son home to keep him company. At the sight of his squat, lonely figure, his neighbours recall all that he has been through and have come to understand why he goes on living alone. When it rains and he takes an umbrella to go to work, out of force of habit perhaps he still holds it high. Then they have the strange sensation that there is a big empty space under that umbrella, a vacuum that nothing on earth can fill.

January 16, 1982

Translated by Gladys Yang

Cai Ce-hai

The Distant Sound of Tree-felling

Over Gumu River was carried the intermittent sound of tree-felling. The sound, merging with the gurgling river, seemed as lasting as the flowing water.

Gumu River was ancient. Below the calamus, moss reached to the edge of the water and the rock river-bed was masked by the ever-flowing water, which had bored a cave over five kilometres long in a big stone mountain.

By the river stood a tiled-roof cottage resembling the pavilions and towers found in the gardens of Suzhou and Hangzhou, though it was not quite so splendid. The cottage, simple and sturdy like all other buildings in the vicinity, was a special feature of this mountain area. In this cottage lived a carpenter, Old Gui, who was in his sixties, his daughter Yangchun and his apprentice Qiaoqiao, who was betrothed to his daughter. Their life was solemn and gloomy as Old Gui observed strict formality and discipline as a father and master. Even the river seemed less lively at this part, its wild shoals having changed into deep pools.

Some observant people felt it was high time that Yangchun and Qiaoqiao, both in their twenties, got married. If Old Gui continued to put off the wedding something untoward might happen. Though a master of his trade, his knowledge of such matters was inferior to a woman's.

But Old Gui, being Old Carpenter Gui, had his own plans.

He was known in the area by the tools he carried in a basket on his back and the ruler in his hand, the insignia of his status like the epaulettes of a general. Despite the load, he strode with firm legs and a straight back. His face, shaved clean except for a goatee five inches long, was as expressionless as a smooth boulder. By nature taciturn, when he did open his mouth it was to talk about work. Therefore, to all unruly youths, elders would say, 'Two years of apprenticeship to Old Carpenter Gui would do you a world of good.'

The skill Old Gui learned from his forefathers brought him great prestige. His ink marker and ruler, handed down from his great-great-grandfather, made him the master carpenter who marked out planks for others to work on. He was the expert. All the new houses in the area had been built by him.

Unlike other craftsmen, who worked according to how well they were fed, he took pains with all his jobs even if certain employers only fed him sweet potatoes. He cherished his craft. He had not grown up on good food, and his strict father had not spared the rod. The ruler had become the personification of his father. When he took that over, he followed in his father's footsteps as a man and craftsman.

Old Gui had no son as his successor, his wife having died after Yangchun's birth. And he liked none of the apprentices he trained until Qiaoqiao appeared. Now there was someone to inherit his ink marker and ruler and take care of his daughter.

Qiaoqiao, the son of a distant relative, was apprenticed to Old Gui at the age of seven. His character, as if mapped out by the ink marker, followed his master's design in every way. Though a ruddy-cheeked, strapping young man, a head taller than his master, he was reticent and never bantered with the young men and girls when he was working. He worked nonstop doing a better and faster job than Old Gui. But he retained his early obedience to his master, acting and moving only as he indicated. At home, when Old Gui reclined on a chair with a fan, he would sharpen the blunt tools or make a stool or some other object.

Thinking the world of his apprentice, Old Gui decided he should be his future son-in-law. Every evening, Old Gui and Qiaoqiao retired to their rooms in the eastern part, leaving Yangchun stitching a shoe sole by the fire in the kitchen. The change in Qiaoqiao's status had wrought other changes. The three of them no longer shared the same room, but had one each. Yangchun, having to get up early to light the fire and cook, slept in the kitchen. Qiaoqiao was on the second floor, and Old Gui beneath him. The children had grown up, Yangchun's breasts had filled out and her eyes sparkled. Qiaoqiao's chin was a darker shade, his voice husky. This was another responsibility borne by Old Gui – that of father-cum-master-cum-father-in-law. It was one that all parents had when their children grew up. Like other fathers, Old Gui nurtured his fledglings in his heart and felt desolate as they grew ready to fly. But unlike other fathers, he would not have to face his daughter leaving the nest. His son-in-law would live in his house. When the time came, they could have a simple wedding without ceremony and guests. Grand-children would be raised in this cottage to take over his ink marker.

But the time was not ripe yet, so Old Gui made Qiaoqiao move in with him, knowing that some modern young people had no morals when they got carried away. Though honest, Qiaoqiao was, after all, a young man.

Qiaoqiao tucked his master in and lay down beside him, as immobile as a log all night. Old Gui's heart went out to this dutiful youth, promising apprentice and reliable future son-in-law.

Old Gui had his reasons for postponing his daughter's wedding.

In her presence, Old Gui had said to Qiaoqiao, 'The day you're ready to take over the ink marker, I'll let you marry Yangchun. I'll use my skill to make you a set of furniture with the best quality wood.'

Her heart turning a somersault, Yangchun quickly picked up a sieve. Qiaoqiao listened as if his master was giving him an assignment, as if waiting for him to mark the planks.

Yangchun stole a glance at the solemn Qiaoqiao, a carpenter

moulded by her own father. Her heart returned to normal and the sieve in her hands slowed down. Then she stopped and put chaff into the stove, smothering the flames which smokily leapt up again a minute later. Choked, Yangchun hurried out.

On the other side of Gumu River, explosives were detonated, sending rocks and yellow smoke into the sky to merge with the clouds. The rocks dropped on to the ground and grass and into the river making big splashes. What did this mean? Were people burning lime? Who had come deep into the mountains to burn lime? But Old Gui's family were never curious, even if there were explosions right in front of their door.

After a while Yangchun returned to the house.

A song floated over the river, drifting into the cottage.

> The sun climbs on top of the rocks,
> Where a girl airs her embroidered shoes.
> I don't love the pretty shoes
> But the beauty who's sunning them.

Old Gui grumbled, 'Those are grown boys and girls. Who's howling such nonsense?'

'I didn't hear anything,' said Yangchun.

Surely her denial betrayed her? Year after year, the boatmen sang such songs as they passed by, but Yangchun was not supposed to listen and Qiaoqiao was not supposed to sing them. Sometimes Yangchun thought if Qiaoqiao started singing, she would join in humming the tune. But Qiaoqiao would never sing such songs.

Qiaoqiao went out. The boatmen had stopped to tighten their rafts. Cupping his hands to his mouth, Qiaoqiao shouted, 'Hey, you over there on the water, you can't be mooring so far from your destination?'

The answer was, 'Mind your own business. No one has touched your wife.'

All three heard the remark. None uttered a rebuke.

The chopping sound was carried over. Who were felling trees to build new houses? The two carpenters pricked up their ears while Yangchun put down her sewing. When the two men went off to work, she would be all alone in this house far away from others.

The silence was so great that a small noise in the distance sounded like a rumble of thunder.

Everything resumed its slumber. On both sides of the river the precipices rose to block out the sky except for the strip above the water, which flowed quietly into the valley and on to Changde, Hankou and the sea. The boatmen were on their way to a bigger world.

The sound of tree-felling, now subsided, had brought music here. Old Gui, reclining in his sling chair with his eyes closed, was snoring quietly. But he had not fallen asleep. He had business with all the cottages in the villages on both sides of the river. A new cottage rising beside an old one added honour and glory to Old Gui and the mountain villages. His prestige would continue to grow, for people must build houses. A carpenter's trade was indispensable and secure.

Opening his eyes he said to Qiaoqiao, 'Learn the trade well, Qiaoqiao, and you'll have a better future than I.'

That was quite true. He had been a bachelor half his life while Qiaoqiao already had Yangchun. He had no son, while Qiaoqiao and Yangchun might have one.

Qiaoqiao nodded, as he always did. Not that he understood every word the old man said, but he wanted him to believe he did.

Yangchun glanced at them wondering what they were up to. Their business didn't concern her. She cooked three meals a day and when the two men were away, she didn't bother much. In the evenings she had taught herself to sew while other girls had their mothers teach them. She was skilled at it, working without a pattern. Everything she did was exquisite. The flowers she embroidered were beautiful, their composition good. In the mountains, all one saw were the clouds in the sky and their reflection in the water. Flowers bloomed and withered, the mountain turned green and yellow. But in the past two years, the river had become noisy at night. Quite often, even if she didn't sew, Yangchun would sit up till midnight and rise very early in the morning. The water pot would often be empty and need filling again. Hearing his daughter filling the pot so many times, her father would demand, 'What are you doing? Cooking an ox?'

Yangchun would retort with a giggle, 'Get up and have some.'

This cheeky answer jarred on the ears of the old-fashioned carpenter. He heaved a long, unfathomable sigh.

Old Gui didn't mind her answering back as long as there was no impropriety. Yangchun was a sensible and prudent girl who would not make a mistake. But a father doesn't know his daughter as well as a mother, so he had to be vigilant.

He told Qiaoqiao, 'I've betrothed Yangchun to you. The day I give my ink marker and ruler to you, you can get married. At the moment you're still an apprentice, not a qualified carpenter.'

A head taller than his master, Qiaoqiao bent down when he talked to him. Yes. He must be a qualified carpenter.

Yangchun knew nothing about carpentry and the old man didn't bother telling her, but he kept a stricter eye on her. When Yangchun went to gather firewood where Qiaoqiao was working, Old Gui would go to inspect his apprentice's work, lingering as long as Yangchun. When Qiaoqiao went to wash clothes in the river, Yangchun went too to wash vegetables. Qiaoqiao turned his back on her. The stupid youth had become duller and dumber as he grew older. As children, they had gone to catch birds together. Qiaoqiao got red beaks or thrushes every time. He could skip a stone farther than she too. Qiaoqiao would lie on the water with his stomach above the surface showing Yangchun his navel, while she flung mud at him until he dived under.

Now he was an apprentice and couldn't play games any more. He had become inhuman. The old man liked him and had retained him, after throwing out all the others.

Taking pity on the simple-minded Qiaoqiao, Yangchun called out to him, 'Give me your laundry, Qiaoqiao. I'll do it for you.'

'No,' Qiaoqiao buzzed like a mosquito, his back still turned to her.

Her glance falling on her reflection in the water, Yangchun blushed at her full breasts. She quickly plunged her vegetables into the water, stirring up many ripples which carried her reflection farther and farther away.

'Haven't you two finished washing?' called Old Gui.

Qiaoqiao rose and left. Yangchun stared into the water, lost in her thoughts as her reflection took form again.

'Watch out for an explosion,' someone called from the other side of the river.

Yangchun returned to the cottage.

*

The days slipped past as calmly as the flowing water in front of the house. Those who had predicted that something might happen in this family admired Old Gui's control over his children.

Old Gui and Qiaoqiao were always sent off on a new assignment with good food. Yangchun cooked some pig's trotters with fungus she had gathered. She herself preferred edible water plants mixed with chilli powder.

They would be away for a month at a time building new houses. Yangchun had mixed feelings about their leaving.

Old Gui and Qiaoqiao went away again. Someone had come to fetch them. Yangchun was no longer interested in the fungus and mushrooms when she gathered firewood on the mountain. Her heart was disturbed by the flowers blooming all over the slopes.

From somewhere a loud sound was carried over. Not a sound of tree-felling, but of someone building a new house. Setting up a new house was quite complicated. One needed to buy a stove, chest of drawers and lots of other things. And if they had a girl as old as Yangchun, they needed an extra bed too.

Yangchun let her thoughts wander.

No more explosions on the other side of the river. Yangchun made for the bank and saw men piling up rocks. No smoke. They were not making lime. Building a fortress? Her father had told her that in the past people had guns and built fortresses against bandits. Now, thirty years after China's Liberation, there were no bandits. What were these people doing?

She must find out. If her father were home, she could ask his permission. Since he wasn't, she made up her own mind.

She unfastened a little raft from a chestnut tree and crossed the river. She halted some distance away and watched the men laying the walls. Yangchun knew that they were building houses.

The men had strong arms and legs as if born to lift big stones. They were careless and casual, laughing and whistling, putting the irregular stones into neat walls which were growing like a honeycomb.

What they were doing was more interesting and grander than the houses her father and Qiaoqiao built. She wanted to lift a stone too, imagining that she was one of them.

She had been curious about her father's and Qiaoqiao's work, which she sometimes made fun of. But these people worked in an entirely different manner.

She walked over. Not wanting to be laughed at if she didn't ask the right question, she addressed an elderly man, 'You're putting up many buildings here, who'll be living in them?'

At the sound of her ringing voice everybody stopped to scrutinize the girl who had descended like a goddess of the woods.

'She's as lovely as Zhangjiajie.'

Yangchun was being compared to a recently discovered scenic spot in the mountains.

The girl standing before these strangers was really a beauty. Her melon-seed-shaped face was as pretty as peach blossom. A constant smile hovered around her dimples and her bright innocent eyes sparkled continuously. Her figure was not as thin as those city girls in their tight clothes, nor as plump as those of country girls in their loose shapeless ones. Her hair was straight, and she wore no earrings. She was pretty, elegant and healthy.

'If she's an actress, she'll be more famous than Zhangjiajie.'

'Not really. Zhangjiajie has been featured in magazines and films. It's known abroad...'

Yangchun lowered her head in embarrassment. It was the first time she'd stood before so many people. She addressed the elderly man again, 'I asked you a question, uncle.'

Rubbing the mud from his hands, the man answered with a smile, 'You'd better ask our leader.'

The person who had been measuring with a ruler turned around. Wasn't it Shuisheng? The thing in his hand, which Qiaoqiao had called a snail ruler because it curled back after being pulled out, had made Old Gui see red. He had snatched it and tossed it away and then kicked Shuisheng out calling him a rebel. Shuisheng had picked it up and left without a word.

Why hadn't she said something then? A single word would have carried a lot of weight at such a time.

Of course Shuisheng shouldn't have been so mean as to sneer at Qiaoqiao's country ways. And he shouldn't have sung the boatmen's songs. If she had put in a word for him, it might have made things worse.

Yangchun greeted him shyly.

Shuisheng did not answer her. He hated her father, that inhuman, old-fashioned man who had thrown him out and kept that block-head Qiaoqiao. It was an insult to him. He had vowed never to see him again. There were many professions beside carpentry. The world was big. One could get ahead anywhere.

Working across the river, he didn't call on his former master. He preferred to camp with his friends. Men are equal when no favours are involved.

And bygones were bygones, and Shuisheng was now a bricklayer. Besides, the girl was not to blame for what had happened.

Kindly Shuisheng spoke to the new grown-up daughter of his former master. 'Hello. After your dad made me leave, I had good luck. I'm in charge of the group here.'

Yangchun was bolder when her father was not around. 'Without the blessing of Lu Ban,* the ancient master carpenter, these stone houses will collapse.'

'But I'm not doing carpentry. And the stone houses belong to the county government. We're building a hydro-electric power station. With glass windows and plaster, it will look like a palace.'

'You're just bragging.'

'Come back in two months and you'll see.'

Yangchun caught sight of some girls in checked blouses. She became envious. 'You've picked this job right across the river from us just to show off.'

'I'm not that mean. I got this for our team because we'd just finished one and were looking for another.'

Hunger gnawed at Yangchun, reminding her to go home and cook. As she left, she told Shuisheng, 'Drop in when you have time. Our home isn't out of bounds and our water doesn't taste bitter.'

Yangchun walked with a light step. The world had become livelier

---

* Lu Ban – a legendary master craftsman worshipped by Chinese carpenters as their patron.

with Shuisheng and his group here. Every house would have electricity soon like in the cities. What were cities like anyway?

Shuisheng gazed at the pigtail swinging behind Yangchun. Her printed blouse, which might seem gaudy in other parts, was bright and arresting in the green valley. But when the image of Qiaoqiao rose in front of him, Yangchun faded from his thoughts. Yangchun returned home, a girl with new knowledge and experience.

The young man who had been driven away by her father with all his training wasted was now the head of a group constructing an electric power station. He must have lots of bright ideas. Yet her father had promised his ink marker and her to Qiaoqiao, who was not as promising as Shuisheng. Was he being unfair to Qiaoqiao? She was more unfortunate than he, cooking and looking for firewood daily like a sparrow seeking food. She recalled two bricklayers, a husband and wife, from Sichuan who had stayed with them for a while one year. They called each other 'master'. Even her old-fashioned father had to laugh.

Never had so many thoughts crammed her mind. Overnight she had matured. She was, in fact, almost twenty-three. But to her father, she would always be a child even if she was a hundred.

The following day, Shuisheng crossed the river and shouted outside the door, 'Give me some vegetables. I'll pay you back with kelp tomorrow.'

Yangchun emerged from the cottage. Shuisheng's grim face made her laugh. 'Vegetables are good enough for us,' she said. 'We don't want your delicious seafood. If you like our greens there's lots in the garden.'

She gathered two bundles and some spring onions which she gave to Shuisheng.

Something was on the tip of Yangchun's tongue. She blurted it out only when Shuisheng was about to leave, 'Brother Shuisheng, do you take girl apprentices?'

'Sure.'

'Qiaoqiao . . .' Yangchun blushed and lowered her head.

'That fine future son-in-law of your father's? Let him stay and inherit your father's ink marker.' Shuisheng burst out laughing.

'I'm serious, Brother Shuisheng. I'll come to work with you if he comes too.'

'You? We can't afford to have you.'

'I can cook. I can mix lime too.'

Her eyes reddening, she almost wept.

Feeling sorry for her, Shuisheng compensated by saying, 'Qiaoqiao is an honest boy who's extremely loyal to your father. But your father'll never give him his ink marker as long as he can work. Getting somewhere as a carpenter is difficult. When a man finally becomes a master, his prime is behind him.'

Shuisheng was speaking the truth. Sadly Yangchun began to miss her dead mother. She'd been neglected by her father who'd set his heart on training Qiaoqiao.

When Yangchun wanted to ask Shuisheng something else, he was already down by the river. 'Take care, Brother Shuisheng,' she called after him.

The raft bobbed. Shuisheng lost some of the vegetables. The river turned dark green as if tinted by the leaves.

One night, after Yangchun had retired, there came a knock at the door. It was Qiaoqiao.

Yangchun got out of bed, stoked up the fire and opened the door. Qiaoqiao had come to fetch some tools. Yangchun put them in a satchel, lit a torch and saw him to the door.

The sky was pitch dark and the steps were moist. It would soon rain.

'The torch will go out in the rain and there are leopards and wolves in the valley. Why don't you stay the night?'

As lightning streaked across the sky, Qiaoqiao turned back and retired to his room while Yangchun shut the door and sat down by the fire.

As soon as his head touched the pillow, Qiaoqiao began to snore. His work was really hard, thought Yangchun. Qiaoqiao used to snore as a kid. When they had all slept on the same bed, Yangchun used to push him with her feet until he touched the plank wall.

Shame. Where were her thoughts leading? Blushing, Yangchun raked the fire and went to bed.

She woke up after a while. When rain was imminent, it became especially muggy. Yangchun felt as if a cat was clawing her heart. Qiaoqiao was still snoring.

He must have kicked away his covering, thought Yangchun. He might catch cold when the temperature cooled down after the rain and be unable to work. Yangchun rose again, lit a pine twig and headed for the eastern part of the house. The door gave at her touch. Qiaoqiao hadn't bothered to bolt it as that was Old Gui's job. Yangchun entered and found Qiaoqiao sleeping stretched out on top of his covers. Yangchun quickly turned away in embarrassment, her heart thumping.

When she collected herself, she became as calm as a windless moonlit forest where no leaf stirred. She approached the bed and covered Qiaoqiao who groaned and continued to snore even louder. Yangchun pulled out some straw from under the bedspread and tickled his nose.

Rubbing his nose, Qiaoqiao opened his eyes, his gaze falling on Yangchun.

What was she doing there?

In this room there seemed to be an invisible though tangible demarcation line, as straight as the marks his master made on planks. Qiaoqiao would be at a loss if he crossed it. That was what made Qiaoqiao nervous. He trembled at the sight of Yangchun and almost cried out for his master.

Remembering he was away, Qiaoqiao shouted, 'You shouldn't be in here, Yangchun.'

'Of course I should, Qiaoqiao.'

She sat down at the edge of the bed and put her hand on his bare cool shoulder.

Qiaoqiao became as docile as a lamb. He took Yangchun's hand and put it on his solid warm chest, his heart thumping at her touch.

All of a sudden, he pushed her hand away as if it was a biting centipede and cried, 'It's dawn, I must go.'

The change in him startled Yangchun.

Steadying her quivering body, she smoothed her hair with her fingers. Tearfully, she said, 'Don't be so stupid, Qiaoqiao. My father betrothed me to you which means I belong to you. Let's go to the commune office and get married. I'm a poor motherless girl. Please turn around. You're even more miserable. I want to make you happy.'

Qiaoqiao stopped her. 'The master gives the orders. You go back to your room right now.'

'Listen to me, Qiaoqiao. For the sake of our future, you must leave my dad. He's a strict old man who hangs on to his ruler. Shuisheng left him.' Yangchun tried to persuade him.

Qiaoqiao voiced her disapproval of Shuisheng. 'He's a crook. I don't want to be like him.'

'He's taken the right road. Now he's in charge of construction work. Not just somebody's house but an electric power station for the whole county. He's smarter than my dad.' After a little pause, she continued, 'Please don't sulk. Shuisheng is just across the river. Go and see him tomorrow morning. Let's work with him . . .'

'Anyone who forsakes his master will come to a bad end.'

With that Qiaoqiao pulled the cover over his head and held it tightly around him.

Yangchun sobbed beside him.

The rain had let up and a puff of wind drifted in through the window. Crying made Yangchun feel better. Laughing and crying always helped. Yangchun was a little dizzy.

She said to Qiaoqiao, still under the quilt, 'I feel sorry for you.'

She returned to the kitchen and stoked up the fire until the flames hissed and leapt up to rise with the smoke, dancing.

'A dancing flame heralds a special guest.' She poked the fire until sparks shot up furiously.

'Don't be so wild,' she scolded.

The water in the river rose, surging ahead louder and faster as if racing against the night.

The next morning, Yangchun slipped some boiled eggs into Qiaoqiao's satchel and when he was leaving hurriedly caught up with him and said, 'When you and dad return I'll have made each of you a pair of cloth shoes and a pair of padded ones.'

She was crazy, thought Qiaoqiao. Girls only give their fathers and brothers two pairs of shoes when they were getting married.

Yangchun added, 'I'll put them by your bed.'

Buildings like the palace of the goddess of the moon had descended from the sky and planted themselves beside the river.

It was the work of Shuisheng and his group.

They had left for some distant place. People saw them leaving after the buildings were finished, saying that they were going to the county town to build a cement factory. Then people could build houses with cement. Goodness! The uniform tiled-roof cottages would be looked down upon in the future.

Many thoughts crowded into Yangchun's mind as she stood before the brand-new buildings. She saw another kind of life, another world. A strange, strange attractive world.

*

More rafts passed along Gumu River. The machines on some of them were bigger than Old Gui's cottage. They really were constructing an electric power station.

The old-fashioned cottage across the river was as sturdy as ever, not even creaking in a big gale. It stood imposingly opposite the new buildings, its grandeur diminished only by the withering bristlegrass on its roof.

A senile old man lingered under a chestnut tree to gaze after the rafts. It was Old Gui.

Outside the new buildings someone was telling a young boatman who'd stopped for a rest that Old Gui had an only daughter as pretty as a pheasant who was once betrothed to a carpenter as good as Old Gui. But some odd things had happened, and that lovely girl had gone away on a raft.

'Where to?'

'To a bricklayer in the county town.'

'You're joking. That bricklayer must be a rogue.' The young boatman stood up for the fiancé.

'No. He's an honest fellow. When he and his people were ready to leave after completing those buildings, the girl begged him on her knees to take her with him.'

'Really!'

'Ask the river if you don't believe me. Strange things happen here.'

'And then?'

'Who knows what happened then?'

The boatman left. And the gossip flowed away with the current.

Translated by Yu Fanqin

Bai Xiao Yi

Six Short Pieces

Romance

A friend had taken it upon himself to find me a wife. He put in a lot of effort, handed over a telephone number and told me to 'get on with it'. I thought at the time that this was an outrageous way to meet people but I made the call – I have a weakness for all things outrageous.

She had a beautiful voice, so I immediately imagined that she would also have a beautiful face, even though one attribute does not necessarily guarantee the other. She said she understood my situation, and suggested that she should come over to my place at once. Her school was a long way from where I lived and it meant changing buses at least three times. Naturally I could not allow her to do anything so tiring so I urged her not to come, but instead to wait for me at her school gates.

She insisted on coming. I thought it best if I went to her. At this point the telephone went dead.

I dialled her number again, but now it was engaged. I didn't know what to do – we had not resolved our disagreement. Was I going? Or was she coming? I pondered the question for a long time and decided that since this was the first time we had spoken, it was best to go along with her wishes.

As a result, I waited all afternoon.

The next day I called her again –

'I waited for you for a long time,' she said.

I explained in detail what had happened. I was determined she should decide where we would meet that day before the phone was cut off again.

'I don't see the necessity to meet anymore,' she said.

'Why not?'

'It would appear that we are both a little too clever. If we had both gone over to the other's place and waited in vain that would have been so much better. Don't you think?'

I agreed that would have been an incredibly moving scenario.

She did not say anything else and hung up.

That day we missed each other in exactly the way that she had described.

The following day she called in a temper and said that it was clearly impossible for her to marry somebody who was as foolish as she was.

Normal

Her husband kept suspecting that there was something between her and Xiao Lin. She didn't know whether to be angry or to be amused. Xiao Lin and she shared an office, but they hardly ever spoke. Xiao Lin was something of a cold fish and she often found it quite boring spending time with him.

Nonetheless her husband was undeterred and insisted there was 'something not quite right' in her demeanour.

At first it was not too bad, he would only make a sly comment occasionally. Gradually, interrogation became the order of the day, often laced with threat. He insisted that she should 'clarify her position'. She began to find the atmosphere more and more oppressive, until she got a headache every time she approached her home.

One day after office hours she remained seated at her desk. Xiao Lin had already left but came back. He asked her in a formal manner if there was anything he could do to help. She stood up, walked out of the door and said, 'Take me home.'

Xiao Lin escorted her in total silence.

'It is right you should accompany me. You don't know how every day I am punished because of you . . .' she mused.

Usually she took a bus home, but today she did not want to. Walking along, she discovered that the man next to her was big and warm. She could not stop herself melting into him. It was only then that she realized here was a heart which was pounding because of her.

That evening, her husband did not interrogate her. She waited calmly until midnight. Eventually she could not sleep, so she decided to ask him, 'Why didn't you ask me to clarify my position today?'

'I don't have to ask anymore. The devil in your heart is gone. You have never looked as normal as you do today.' The expression on his face was that of a living buddha.

Suspicion

I was just making a phone call when I heard the key turn in the front door. Ah, he's back. I stopped dialling and put the phone back on the hook just as the door opened.

'Were you phoning somebody just now?' The minute he came in he asked.

'Yes.' I plopped into the sofa, looking at my clever, strong and talented husband.

'So . . . why did you put the phone down again?' His sensitivity is so loveable. He is like a big detective.

'Because you've come back,' I said.

'Why did you have to stop just because I'm here?' He sounded a little worried now.

'Because I was calling you.'

His face went bright red and then he smiled, trying to change the subject. I could not tell for sure if he really believed me.

No Title

If anybody asked me what I hated the most, I could answer without hesitation: curiosity. This is absolutely true. It was damned curiosity that turned me, a quiet and gentle young girl, a well behaved high school student, into a sinner...

It was drizzling. The tarmac shone. I was on my way to school. The reflection of my floral-patterned umbrella was bobbing up and down on the wet surface of the road, like an early branch of peach blossom mirrored in a stream. A bookshop. Multi-coloured covers reflected in the water, disturbing the shadow of my beautiful spring flowers. A shop window. Comics, school texts with sombre expressions. I raised my head and saw a poster on the window – 'New Arrival – *The Knowledge of Sex*. $0.19. Available for Sale!'

Sex? What is there to learn about sex? I flicked back my pig-tail, drawn by the possibility of discovering something I was completely ignorant of. This was the beginning of my downfall. If I had known then what I know now, I would not have walked into that cursed bookshop.

'Ai ... let me have a look at that ...' For some reason I was not able to get out all the words.

'What?'

'That!' I pointed at the book across the counter.

The middle-aged woman sitting on the other side of the counter squinted at me.

Ah! What is that in her eyes – a smirk, something sour; electricity! I was electrocuted. My cheeks sizzled like a hot ring on a stove.

The worst thing was the mysterious expression on the corner of her mouth as she handed me the book. A cold smile, the kind of smile that delighted in someone else's misfortune. In any case it was extremely unappealing. A man browsing in the shop now darted a sidelong glance in the direction of my book, then at me and pursed his lips. I could see that he was mocking me. This was another weird smile, full of insinuation, a smile designed to give one goose pimples all over.

Suddenly, I was no longer innocent about sex. At least I knew then that it was closely associated with shame.

Coming out of the bookshop, I quickly stuffed the book into my satchel, letting out a sigh of relief. At least I had managed to hide my 'shame'.

School. There weren't many lessons this afternoon. Chemistry was followed by a study period. As usual, our teacher paced up and down with his hands behind his back and his head hanging.

Plop. When I reached for my exercise book, another book fell out – directly into my teacher's path.

He stooped down to look at it and did not straighten up for a very long time.

Oh God, I knew it must have been that book. Oh heavens. My 'shame' had been exposed! What should I do? I shut my eyes.

'Huh!' My teacher grunted somewhere near the top of my head. It was a soft but meaningful grunt. He stood up. I heard the sound of my book dropping back into my bag, and then the sound of footsteps retreating.

I opened my eyes and stole a quick glance at his back. How serious is this going to be, I wondered. Ugh, look at that neck turning red, the steam emerging from the back of his head; I couldn't see his face, but it was probably going through some sort of chemical change. He didn't know where to put his hands, as if his fingers too had been touched by shame. Teacher, my omniscient teacher, what is the matter with you? No, it's not over yet, look, teacher is weighed down with grief, shaking his head. What is the matter with me?

At that moment, more than ever, sex was no longer something I didn't comprehend. I now knew that it was closely linked with not only shame but degeneration.

After school. I stuffed the book into the bottom of my satchel. It was heavy, containing the weight of both shame and degeneration. I was hardly able to breathe under the pressure.

Home. Evening. I felt restless. My curiosity once again urged me to take out the volume. I had to see what rubbish it contained within its pages.

Father strode in, trailing a breeze behind him. He saw that I was reading and his manner softened immediately. He took off his oil-stained work-clothes, smiling at me. Yes, he loved to see me read. He was harbouring ambitions for me to go to university.

Suddenly – oh dear! Father saw the cover.

'What? What is this! Oh – my god. Wah! I thought you were being diligent, instead you are looking at this … stuff! Is there a university in the world which offers this subject as a degree? Arghhh!'

My face turned red. *The Knowledge of Sex* equals shame and degeneration. 'This is a total disgrace! You … have no shame!'

Another new discovery. Shame, degeneration and on top of that, disgrace. This – is the knowledge of sex.

Sobs. Tears. An inexplicable sense of shame. Degeneration that had appeared from nowhere. Nineteen cents had bought me disgrace. I hated the book! Even though I still didn't know what lay between the covers.

The sound of pages being ripped to pieces. Tiny bits of paper dancing around me like a snowstorm. I had torn it all up – shame, degeneration, disgrace. All torn.

The depth of night. Dreams. The wet shimmering surface of the road, drizzle, rain bouncing off the window of the bookshop. An advertisement I could just about make out – 'New Arrival – *Shame and Disgrace*. $0.19. Available for Sale!'

The next day. Back to school. The news had by now spread through the entire class. Wherever I went people turned away. Strange looks, mocking faces, giggles, astonished stares, looking, watching, glaring, squinting... As if Shame, Disgrace and Degeneration was written all over my face. All over me was written the Knowledge of Sex.

Madness

In my memory, the craziest, most romantic love I had ever experienced somehow coincided with the most difficult days I had ever known. There were three different divisions in our youth group. We were stationed in the remote countryside, living side by side with the peasants, undergoing a re-education programme. I didn't belong to any of the groups. They didn't want me, and I couldn't be bothered with them. There was only one person who was sympathetic to me and that was a girl. The reason I became a public target was also because of her.

Her name was Xiao Mei. In the tiny place where we lived she was the most beautiful girl anyone ever saw. Everybody had their eyes on her. At that time the younger boys had not yet learnt that love was nothing to be ashamed of. When Xiao Mei and I started going out with each other in earnest, my status amongst the group was immediately elevated beyond the reach of mere mortals. The others would give me strange looks while at the same time keeping a respectful distance. Soon this turned into something else, and they started to regard us with angry, sour faces. If the object of my love had been a plain-looking girl, no doubt the situation would have been better. But Xiao Mei was too eye-catching, and the others understandably all wished they were in my shoes. In a way I sympathized with them – if someone else had got to Xiao Mei first, I would have burnt with jealousy. These flights of fancy gave me a kind of private pleasure.

I suppose I ought to be thankful for the public scrutiny. Because of the attention, the love between Xiao Mei and I grew strong and dignified. The difficulty of meeting with so many eyes on us also meant that our secret trysts were full of sweetness.

Our romance matured over the long days of a hot summer. A canopy of pale green cornfields stretching into the distance became our paradise. Perhaps because of our lack of imagination, we never did anything which overstepped the mark. The way we felt about each other meant that even a little time spent quietly sitting together was enough to intoxicate us.

But the corn was ripening. Soon our Garden of Eden would come under the blade of a scythe, and grey clouds begin to gather in our hearts.

The harvest season finally arrived. The ears of corn were systematically broken off leaving the dried stalks standing. Our furtive meetings became even more of a thrill – we knew we were fighting a losing battle with the season and the scythe, so we took on the recklessness of a soldier confronting his final combat, the madness of an addicted gambler.

Sometimes it felt as if our passion had become a mystery even to ourselves. By then people were beginning to guess at our secret and tried to ambush us with great determination. Our rendezvous seemed not to be a private matter anymore, but something central to the survival of the whole community. Our happiness and their frustration had somehow become inextricably linked.

The older people in the village commented on the fact that they never knew a year when the corn-stalks had remained standing for so long.

Eventually the day came when the stalks had to be cleared. We all became depressed – Xiao Mei and I lost our paradise and the others lost their sport. This was a difficult time for everybody. We were compelled to live through a period of temporary truce.

Nobody anticipated an earthquake.

We were all asleep. The first tremor did not wake many people. Those not particularly blessed with sensitivity took it upon themselves to laugh at others who were worried enough to alert the police. It was then that the second wave hit us. This was a much bigger shock than before, and the structure which was our home started to shake. All of a sudden people were in a panic, running for their lives – the scene was unbearably tragic...

Standing outside, we could see our building beginning to keel over. The beams were exposed, and large cracks appeared on the walls.

There was nothing to do except to hang around in the open. A few of us went over to look at some of the old farm houses in the village. They were in a similar state to ours – still upright but not safe enough for anybody to go back in to sleep.

As there were no casualties, the fear hanging in the air was gradually imbued with a sense of jolly playfulness. To those of us who were young and single and without responsibility, the evening turned out to be oddly festive. It was hot, and nobody bothered to go inside to fetch their clothes. We were all fooling around in the courtyard in our vests and shorts. Even the girls were less shy than usual. When natural disaster struck, more than ever they seemed to need the protection of men.

When I found Xiao Mei, she was sitting on a pile of dried twigs, her hands round her knees. She was in her underwear. She saw me walk towards her, but remained where she was.

'Are you all right,' I said.

She did not say anything. Her breathing was uneven, getting shorter and shorter.

I too was unable to move. Gazing at her, my heart started to pound.

All around us people were rushing around, shouting, having fun. They had clearly forgotten all about us.

We stayed staring at each other, then without a word we walked towards a block which had pitched onto one side.

This was the biggest of our dormitories, usually reserved for meetings. Inside were two large mattresses which slept more than twenty people.

That night only Xiao Mei and I shared one.

It seemed to me as if innumerable earthquakes took place that long night. Even now I recall the beams shaking and groaning above our heads. The roof and the walls were moving against each other like somebody grinding his teeth. The noise it made was a mixture of terror and ecstasy, seeping into the core of our bones.

At sunrise Xiao Mei and I came out together. The others were just stirring from the haystacks which had served as their beds. When they saw us, their mouths dropped open. All eyes focused on us in disbelief. Xiao Mei wore a lazy, nonchalant expression on her face; my heart was as peaceful as if I were dreaming.

After that nobody resented us anymore.

Diplomatic Relations

On the north-west corner of the campus there was a beautiful little building which accommodated thirty odd foreign as well as Chinese students who studied alongside them. Each room was shared by two residents of different nationalities but the same sex. The untrustworthy chaps from abroad were forever trying to bend the rules about single-sex accommodation, but thanks to the presence of wardens with strong moral fibre, their efforts were largely frustrated. Very often it came down to a battle of wits as well as courage.

Lian Dong had volunteered to share a room with Mark, a student from America, with a view to improving his English. Unfortunately, apart from when he talked in his sleep, Mark would only speak in

Chinese. Furthermore he had picked up some cheeky colloquial phrases from God knows where, which he would spring on Lian Dong from time to time, usually in the most inappropriate manner and completely out of context, rendering his despairing room-mate unsure as to whether he should laugh or cry.

After dinner this evening, Mark told Lian Dong he needed sole occupation of their room for two hours. 'I am engaged in diplomatic relations tonight...' he winked. Lian Dong was not at all happy about this but felt unable to refuse. After repeated instructions for Mark to behave, he resigned himself to a long and lonely evening at the library.

Just as he was coming out of the door Lian Dong ran into the Chinese girl visiting Mark that evening. She was far more beautiful than he had anticipated. His heart sank to the bottom of his shoes. Deliberately lingering at the doorway, Lian Dong tried his best to discourage her with a strong disapproving gaze. The girl paid him no attention whatsoever and ran straight to Mark's side. The bastard suddenly decided to converse in English tonight and the girl's responses were surprisingly fluent.

Lian Dong shut the door with inexplicable fury. He walked down the corridor with a heavy heart, a black cloud hanging over his head.

'Lian, good evening!' A charming and flirtatious voice with a weird accent called out to him. Lian Dong turned round and saw Belinda, an attractive French student, standing there smiling at him.

'Good evening.' Lian Dong stopped in his tracks.

'Are you very busy? I need someone to go over my notes with me – could you, do you think?' Belinda's feet looked like a couple of huge buns, but her movement was light and delicate. In a moment she had curled herself under Lian Dong's arm. 'Why don't we go to my room?'

Lian Dong could not find a reason to say no, but as they walked along, he carefully disengaged himself. She laughed, tilting up her chin, her golden hair dazzling him.

In comparison with the mess of a den which he shared with Mark, this was like a peaceful, cosy nest. Her Chinese room-mate was absent. Before Lian Dong had a chance to steady himself, Belinda's arms were round his waist.

He froze to the spot, at a loss as to what to do.

'Lian, I'm not too much for you am I?' Belinda challenged him, head to one side, without any sense of embarrassment.

Lian Dong felt her body against his, hot and soft and full of raw energy. This was the first time he had stood so close to a woman ... He wanted to struggle free, but could not bear to tear himself from such alluring sweetness.

'Belinda...' Lian Dong managed to clear his head. With a touch of regret in his voice he said, 'Of course you are not too much. But why don't you let me have a look at your notes now.'

Belinda's blue eyes flashed, penetrating his very soul. 'Lian, I have something far better to show you. I'll let you look at me instead, how's that – surely I am a little more interesting than my notes? Here ...' She was now kissing his face, murmuring softly, passionately, 'China boy, do you know how to kiss...'

*

When Lian Dong finally crept out of Belinda's room, his head was reeling. Belinda leant against the door, apologizing profusely. She said she was sorry but she really couldn't begin to understand Chinese men. Lian Dong could only manage a rueful smile.

When he got back to his own room he hesitated outside the door, not knowing whether or not the Chinese girl would still be there. After a short pause he decided to knock.

The door opened softly. Mark was wearing an odd sort of smile. Off-hand Lian Dong was unable to decipher its meaning. He felt a touch uncomfortable, as if anybody looking at him now would immediately guess at his secret.

'She's gone. Lian, you don't have to worry.' Mark made a face. 'Come in.'

Somehow everything looked different in the room. He stepped on something. Looking down he saw Mark's copy of *Playboy* lying on the floor. Lian was glued to the spot, one foot on the magazine.

'Lian, I had terrible luck.' Mark started to whinge. 'I can't understand what it is with Chinese girls.'

Lian suddenly and just as inexplicably felt better. Perhaps what he did with the French student tonight was not unprompted by what he thought Mark might have been up to with the Chinese girl. Casually he said, 'What do you mean?'

'She is terrifying. So very beautiful yet utterly terrifying.' Mark looked the picture of a downtrodden victim. 'All I did was give her a kiss, and she hit me! I was ... I was stunned.'

Lian Dong found himself smiling ruefully again. At the same time his temper was rising. 'You only have yourself to blame! Where do you think this is? New York? Paris?'

'You think this is my fault?' Mark pointed at his own chest with a long, slender finger, his face red, bursting with rage.

'It's probably just a matter of cultural difference ...' Lian thought of Belinda and wasn't entirely sure if he had a leg to stand on. He muttered something under his breath, turned his back on Mark, sat down on the chair by the window, and didn't take any further notice of his room-mate.

Mark was still complaining to no one in particular. 'Absolutely incredible ... this is ... How shall I put it? To borrow a Chinese phrase – what you might call a hot cheek against a cold bottom ...'

Lian Dong smiled his rueful smile.

Translated by Carolyn Choa

Bi Shu-min

One Centimetre

When Tao Ying rides on the bus alone, quite often she does not bother to buy a ticket.

Why should she? Without her, the bus would still be stopping at every stop, a driver and a conductor would still have to be employed, and the same amount of petrol used.

Clearly Tao Ying has to be astute. When the bus conductor looked like the responsible type, she would buy a ticket as soon as she got on board. But if he appeared to be casual and careless, she would not dream of paying, considering it a small punishment for him and a little saving for herself.

Tao Ying works as a cook in the canteen of a factory. She spends all day next to an open fire, baking screw-shaped wheat cakes with sesame butter.

Today she is with her son Xiao Ye. She follows him onto the bus. As the doors shut her jacket is caught, ballooning up like a tent behind her. She twists this way and that, finally wrenching herself free.

'Mama, tickets!' Xiao Ye says. Children are often more conscious of rituals than adults. Without a ticket in his hand, the ride doesn't count as a proper ride.

On the peeling paint of the door somebody has painted the shape of a pale finger. It points at a number: 1.10 m.

Xiao Ye pushed through. His hair looks as fluffy as a bundle of straw – dry and without lustre. As a rule, Tao Ying is very careful with her purse, but she has never skimped on her child's diet. Nonetheless the goodness in his food refuses to advance beyond his hairline. As a result Xiao Ye is healthy and clever, but his hair is a mess.

Tao Ying tries to smooth it down, as if she was brushing away topsoil to get to a firm foundation. She can feel the softness of her son's skull, rubbery and elastic to the touch. Apparently there is a gap on the top of everyone's head, where the two halves meet. If they don't meet properly, a person can end up with a permanently gaping mouth. Even when the hemispheres are a perfect match, it still takes a while for them to seal. This is the door to Life itself – if it remains open, the world outside will feel like water, flowing into the body through this slit. Every time Tao Ying happens upon this aperture on her son's head, she would be overwhelmed by a sense of responsibility. It was she who had brought this delicate creature into the world after all. Although she senses her own insignificance in the world, that her existence makes no difference to anyone else, she also realizes that to this little boy she is the centre of the universe and she must try to be the most perfect, flawless mother possible.

Between Xiao Ye's round head and the tip of the painted digit setting out the height requirement for a ticket rests the beautiful slender fingers of Tao Ying. Since she is in contact with oil all day, her nails are shiny, glistening like the smooth curved back of a sea shell.

'Xiao Ye, you are not quite tall enough, still one centimetre away,' she tells him softly. Tao Ying does not come from a privileged background, and has not read very many books. But she likes to be gentle and gracious, to set an example for her son and make a good impression. This elevates her sense of self-worth and makes her feel like an aristocrat.

'Mama! I'm tall enough, I'm tall enough!' Xiao Ye shouts at the top of his voice, stamping on the floor as if it were a tin drum. 'You told me the last time I could have a ticket the next time, this is the next time! You don't keep your word!' He looks up at his mother angrily.

Tao Ying looks down at her son. A ticket costs twenty cents. Twenty cents is not to be scoffed at. It can buy a cucumber, two tomatoes or, at a reduced price, three bunches of radishes or enough spinach to last four days. But Xiao Ye's face is raised up like a half-open blossom, waiting to receive his promise from the sun.

'Get in! Don't block the entrance! This is not a train, where you stand from Beijing to Bao Ding. We're almost at the next stop...!' the conductor bellows.

Normally, an outburst like this would certainly have discouraged Tao Ying from buying a ticket. But today she says, 'Two tickets, please.'

The fierce conductor has beady eyes. 'This child is one centimetre short of requiring a ticket.'

Xiao Ye shrinks, not just one but several centimetres – the need for a ticket has all of a sudden become interwoven with the pride of a small child.

To be able to purchase self-esteem with twenty cents is something that can only happen in childhood and certainly no mother can resist an opportunity to make her son happy.

'I would like to buy two tickets,' she says politely.

Xiao Ye holds the two tickets close to his lips and blows, making a sound like a paper windmill.

They had entered through the central doors of the bus, but alight towards the front. Here another conductor is poised to examine their tickets. Tao Ying thinks that this man can't be very bright. What mother accompanied by a child would try to avoid paying the correct fare? However poor she would never have allowed herself to lose face in front of her own son.

She hands over the tickets nonchalantly. The conductor asks: 'Are you going to claim these back?' 'No.' In fact Tao Ying ought to have kept the tickets so that the next time there is a picnic or an outing at work she could use her bicycle and then claim back the fare with the stubs. Both she and her husband are blue-collar workers, and any saving would have been a help. But Xiao Ye is a smart boy, and might well question her aloud, 'Mama, can we claim back tickets even when we are on a private outing?' In front of the child, she would never lie.

It is exhausting to follow rules dictated by parental guide-books all the time, but Tao Ying is determined to be the ideal mother and create a perfect example for her son to look up to. She needs really to concentrate – living this way is not unlike carrying an audience with you wherever you go. But her actions are full of love and tenderness. For instance, whenever she eats a watermelon in front of Xiao Ye, she would take care not to bite too close to the rind even though she doesn't actually think there is much difference between the flesh and the skin. True, the sweetness gradually diminishes as you work your way through the red towards the green, but every part of the melon is equally refreshing. In any case the skin of a melon is supposed to have a beneficial cooling effect, and is often used as medicine.

One day, she came across her son eating a melon in the same manner she did. When Xiao Ye looked up, Tao Ying could see a white melon seed stuck to his forehead. She was furious: 'Who taught you to gnaw at a melon like that? Are you going to wash your face in it too?' Xiao Ye was terrified. The small hand holding the melon began to tremble, but the big round eyes remained defiant.

Children are the best imitators in the world. From then on Tao Ying realized that if she wanted her son to behave as if he were the product of a cultured home, then she must concentrate and never fail in her own example. This was very difficult, like 'shooting down aeroplanes with a small gun' – but with determination, she knew that nothing was impossible. With this clear objective in mind, Tao Ying found her life becoming more focused, more challenging.

Today she is taking Xiao Ye to visit a big temple. He has never seen the Buddha before. Tao Ying is not a believer and she does not intend to ask him to kow-tow. That is superstition, she knows.

The tickets cost five dollars a piece – these days even temples are run like businesses. Tao Ying's ticket was a gift from Lao Chiang, who worked at the meat counter. The ticket was valid for a month, and today was the last day. Lao Chiang was one of those people who seemed to know everybody. Occasionally he would produce a battered coverless month-old magazine and say: 'Seen this before? This is called the Big Reference, not meant for the eyes of the common people.' Tao Ying had never seen anything like this before and wondered how such a small rag, smaller even than a regular newspaper, could be called a Big Reference. She asked Lao Chiang but he seemed confused. He said everybody called it that – perhaps if you were to take out the pages and laid them flat they would end up bigger than a normal newspaper. It seemed to make sense. Studying this publication written in large print, Tao Ying could see that it was full of speculation about the war in the Middle East. Foremost on everyone's mind seemed to be whether the export of dates from Iraq to China would continue as it did in the sixties during the famine. In any case, Tao Ying was full of admiration for Lao Chiang. In return for her indiscriminate respect, Lao Chiang decided to reward her with a ticket for the temple. 'Is there just the one?' Tao asked, not without gratitude but with some uncertainty. 'Forget your husband, take your son and open his eyes! Children under 110 centimetres do not need a ticket. If you don't want to go, sell it at the door and you'll earn enough to buy a couple of watermelons!' Lao Chiang had always been a practical man.

Tao Ying decided to take the day off and go on an outing with Xiao Ye.

It is rare to find such a large patch of grass in the middle of the city. Even before they got there, there was something refreshing, something green in the air, as if they were approaching a valley, or a waterfall. Xiao Ye snatches the ticket from his mother's hand, puts it between his lips, and flies towards the gilded gates of the temple. A little animal rushing to quench his thirst.

Tao Ying suddenly feels a little sad. Is the mere attraction of a temple enough for Xiao Ye to abandon his mother? But almost immediately she banishes the thought – hasn't she brought her son here today to make him happy?

The guard at the gate is a young man dressed in a red top and black trousers. Tao Ying feels somehow that he ought to have been in yellow. This uniform makes him look somewhat like a waiter.

Xiao Ye knows exactly what he has to do. Moving amongst the crowd, he seems like a tiny drop of water in the current of a large river.

The young man takes the ticket from his mouth, plucking a leaf from a spring branch.

Tao Ying's gaze softly envelopes her son, a strand of silk unwinding towards him, following his every gesture.

'Ticket.' The youth in red bars her way with one arm, his voice as pithy as if he was spitting out a date stone.

Tao Ying points at her son with infinite tenderness. She feels that everybody should see how lovely he is.

'I am asking for your ticket.' The red youth does not budge.

'Didn't the child just give it to you?' Tao Ying's voice is peaceful. This boy is too young, years away from being a father, she thinks. Tao Ying is not working today and is in a really good mood. She is happy to be patient.

'That was his ticket, now I need to see yours.' The youth remains unmoved.

Tao Ying has to pause for a moment before it sinks in – there are two of them and they need a ticket each.

'I thought that children were exempt?' She is confused.

'Mama, hurry up!' Xiao Ye shouts to her from inside the doors.

'Mama is coming!' Tao Ying shouts back. A crowd is beginning to gather, so many fishes swarming towards a bright light.

Tao Ying starts to panic. She wants this fracas to end, her child is waiting for her.

'Who told you he doesn't need a ticket?' The guard tilts his head – the more onlookers the better.

'It says so on the back of the ticket.'

'Exactly what does it say?' This boy is obviously not a professional.

'It says that children under 110 centimetres do not have to pay.' Tao Ying is full of confidence. She moves to pick up one of the tickets from a box next to the guard and reads out what is printed on the back for all to hear.

'Stop right there!' The youth has turned nasty. Tao Ying realizes she should not have touched the box and quickly withdraws her hand.

'So you are familiar with the rules and regulations are you?' Now the young man addresses her with the formal 'you'. Tao Ying detects the sarcasm in his tone but she simply nods.

'Well, your son is over 110 centimetres,' he says with certainty.

'No he isn't.' Tao Ying is still smiling.

Everybody begins to look at the mother with suspicion.

'He just ran past the mark. I saw it clearly.' The guard is equally firm, pointing at a red line on the wall which looks like an earthworm inching across the road after a rainstorm.

'Mama, why are you taking so long? I thought I had lost you!' Xiao Ye shouts to her affectionately. He runs towards his mother, as if she was one of his favourite toys.

The crowd titters. Good, they think, here is proof, the whole matter can be cleared up at once.

The youth is getting a little nervous. He is just doing his job. He is certain he is right. But this woman seems very confident, perhaps ... that would be awful...

Tao Ying remains calm. In fact, she feels a little smug. Her son loves excitement. This is turning into something of an event so it is bound to delight him.

'Come over here,' the youth commands.

The crowd holds its breath.

Xiao Ye looks at his mother. Tao Ying gives him a little nod. He walks over to the guard graciously, coughs a little, adjusts his jacket. In front of the gaze of the crowd, Xiao Ye is every inch the hero as he approaches the earthworm.

Then – the crowd looks, and sees – the worm comes to Xiao Ye's ear.

How is this possible?

Tao Ying is by his side in two paces. The flat of her hand lands heavily on the little boy's head, making a sound as crisp as a ping-pong ball popping underfoot.

Xiao Ye stares at his mother. He is not crying. He is shocked by the pain. He has never been hit before.

The crowd draws its breath.

'Punishing a child is one thing, hitting him on the head is totally unacceptable!'

'What a way for a mother to behave! So what if you have to buy another ticket? This is a disgrace, hitting a child to cover up your own mistake!'

'She can't be his natural mother...'

Everybody has an opinion.

Tao Ying is feeling a little agitated now. She had not meant to hit Xiao Ye. She meant to smooth down his hair. But she realizes that even if Xiao Ye were bald at this instant, he would still be towering above the worm on the wall.

'Xiao Ye, don't stand on tip-toe!' Tao Ying's voice is severe.

'Mama, I'm not...' Xiao Ye begins to cry.

It's true. He isn't. The worm crawls somewhere next to his brow.

The guard stretches himself lazily. His vision is sharp, he has caught quite a few people who had tried to get through without paying. 'Go get a ticket!' he screams at Tao Ying. All pretence of courtesy has by now been eaten up by the worm.

'But my son is less than one metre ten!' Tao Ying insists even though she realizes she stands alone.

'Everyone who tries to escape paying always says the same thing. Do you think these people are going to believe you, or are they going to believe me? This is a universally accepted measurement. The International Standard Ruler is in Paris, made of pure platinum. Did you know that?'

Tao is flummoxed. All she knows is that to make a dress she needs two metres eighty centimetres, she does not know where the International Ruler is kept. She is only astonished at the power of the Buddha which can make her son grow several centimetres within minutes!

'But we were on the bus just now and he wasn't as tall...'

'No doubt when he was born he wasn't as tall either!' the youth sneers, chilling the air.

Standing in the middle of the jeering crowd, Tao Ying's face has turned as white as her ticket.

'Mama, what is happening?' Xiao Ye comes away from the earth-worm to hold his mother's frozen hand with his own little warm one.

'It's nothing. Mama has forgotten to buy a ticket for you.' Tao Ying can barely speak.

'Forgotten? That's a nice way of putting it! Why don't you forget you have a son as well?' The youth will not forgive her calm confidence of a moment ago.

'What more do you want?' Tao Ying's temper rises. In front of her child, she must preserve her dignity.

'You have a nerve! This is not to do with what I want, clearly you must apologize! God knows how you had managed to get hold of a complimentary ticket in the first place. To get in free is not enough, now you want to sneak in an extra person. Have you no shame? Don't think you can get away with this, go get yourself a valid ticket!' The youth is now leaning on the wall, facing the crowd as if he is pronouncing an edict from on high.

Tao Ying's hands are trembling like the strings on a *pei-pa*. What should she do? Should she argue with him? She is not afraid of a good fight but she doesn't want her child to be witness to such a scene. For the sake of Xiao Ye, she will swallow her pride.

'Mama is going to buy a ticket. You wait here, don't run off.' Tao Ying tries to smile. This outing is such a rare occasion, whatever happens she mustn't spoil the mood. She is determined to make everything all right.

'Mama, did you really not buy a ticket?' Xiao Ye looks at her, full of surprise and bewilderment. The expression on her child's face frightens her.

She cannot buy this ticket today! If she went ahead, she would never be able to explain herself to her son.

'Let's go!' She gives Xiao Ye a yank. Thankfully the child has strong bones, or his arm might have fallen off.

'Let's go and play in the park.' Tao Ying wants her son to be happy, but the little boy has fallen silent, sullen. Xiao Ye has suddenly grown up.

As they walk past an ice-cream seller, Xiao Ye says, 'Mama, give me money!'

Taking the money, Xiao Ye runs towards an old woman behind the stall and says to her: 'Please measure me!' It is only then that Tao Ying notices the old lady sitting next to a pair of scales for measuring weight and height.

The old woman extends with difficulty the measuring pole, pulling it out centimetre by centimetre.

She strains to make out the numbers: 'One metre eleven.'

Tao Ying begins to wonder if she has encountered a ghost or is her son beginning to resemble a shoot of bamboo, growing every time you look at him?

Something moist begins to glisten in Xiao Ye's eyes. Leaving his mother behind and without a backward glance, he starts to run away.

He trips. One moment he is in the air, taking flight like a bird, another and he has dropped to the ground with a heavy thud. Tao Ying rushes over to lend a hand but just as she is about to reach him Xiao Ye has picked himself up and is off again. Tao Ying stops in her tracks. If she gives chase Xiao Ye will only keep falling. Watching her son's vanishing silhouette, her heart beings to break: Xiao Ye, aren't you going to look back at your mother?

Xiao Ye runs for a long time and eventually comes to a halt. He throws a quick glance backwards to find his mother, but the moment he can see her, he takes off once more...

Tao Ying finds the whole incident incomprehensible. She wanders back to the old woman and asks politely: 'Excuse me, these scales you have...'

'My scales are here to make you happy! Don't you want your son to grow tall? Every mother wants her sons to shoot up, but don't forget when he is tall, that means you'll be old! Mine are flattering scales,' the old woman explains kindly, but Tao Ying remains baffled.

'You see my scales are old and not very accurate and they make people seem lighter than they really are. I have also adjusted it to make them seem taller. These days it is fashionable to be long and lean – mine are fitness scales!' The old woman might be kind, but she is not without cunning.

So that is the reason! Xiao Ye should have heard this speech! But he is a long way away, and in any case would he have understood the convoluted logic?

Xiao Ye still looks suspicious, as if Mother has turned into a big bad wolf, ready to eat him up. Later when they are back at home, Tao Ying takes out her own tape measure and insists on measuring him again.

'I don't want to! Everybody says I am tall enough except you. It's because you don't want to buy me a ticket, don't think I don't know!

If you measure me I am bound to get shorter again. I don't trust you! I don't trust you!'

The yellow tape in Tao Ying's hands has turned into a poisonous viper.

*

'Chef! Your cakes look as if they are wearing camouflage uniforms, all black and brown!' a customer queuing in front of her counter shouts out.

The cakes are ruined. They are full of burnt marks, and look like tiny terrapins.

Sorry sorry sorry.

Tao Ying feels very guilty. She is usually very conscientious in her work, but these couple of days she often finds herself distracted.

She must rescue the situation! At night, after Xiao Ye has gone to sleep, Tao Ying straightens his little legs so that he is lying as flat as a piece of newly shrunken fabric. Tao Ying then stretches her tape from the soles of his feet to the top of his head – one metre nine centimetres.

She decides to write a letter to the administrators at the temple.

She picks up her brush but suddenly realizes that this is harder than she thinks! Seeing her deep in thought with knitted brows, her husband says, 'So what do you imagine might happen even if you wrote to them?'

He is right, she doesn't know if anything would come of it. But in order to melt the ice in her son's eyes, she must do something.

At last the letter is done. There is a man in the factory nicknamed 'the Writer'. People say he has had some small articles published at the back of a news rag once. Tao Ying finds him and respectfully offers up her literary work.

'This sounds like an official communication. Not lively enough, not moving.' The Writer traces the letter with his nicotine-stained fingers.

Tao Ying doesn't know what an official communication is but she detects a tone of dissatisfaction in the scholar's voice. She looks at the lines he is pointing to, and nods in agreement.

'What you need to do is this. You must open with a strong and righteous claim, followed by a passage of stunning originality so that your work stands out and grabs the attention of the editor. This would make him pick it out of a large pile on his desk. It has to catch his eyes like a blinding light, an apple in a mound of potatoes. But most important of all, your letter must touch his heart. Have you heard of the saying, grieving soldiers always win?'

Tao Ying keeps nodding.

The Writer is encouraged to continue: 'Let us look at the opening paragraph – it should go something like this: "The power of the Buddha is surely infinite! The foot of a five-year-old boy has scarcely touched the threshold of the temple and he has grown two centimetres; but alas, the power of the Buddha is finite after all – on his return home the boy shrinks back to his original size..." I know this is not yet perfect, but have a think about it along these lines...'

Tao Ying tries to memorize the words of the Writer, but she finds it hard to recall all of it. Back home she makes a few corrections as best she can, and sends out the letter.

*

The Writer comes by her stall at lunch-time. Tao Ying's face is framed in a small window where she is collecting vouchers. She looks like a photograph, staring out at the camera with a sombre expression.

'Please wait a moment,' and she disappears behind the frame.

The Writer suspects the cakes are burnt again. Perhaps Tao Ying has gone to find a few which are less burnt than others, to thank him for pointing her in the right direction.

'This is for you, with extra sugar and sesame,' Tao Ying says shyly.

This is the greatest gift a baker could offer a friend as a token of gratitude.

*

Then comes the long wait.

Tao Ying looks through the newspapers every day, reading everything from cover to cover including small classified advertisements for videos. In the meantime she would listen to the radio, imagining that one morning she will hear her own letter read out by one of those announcers with a beautiful voice. Afterwards she would go down to the post office, in case the administrative department of the temple has replied to her letter, apologizing for their misdeed...

She has imagined a hundred different scenarios, but not what actually happens.

The days have been like the white flour she works with, one very much like another. Xiao Ye appears to have recovered from the ordeal but Tao Ying firmly believes that he has not really forgotten.

Finally, one day, she hears a question, 'Which way is it to comrade Tao's home?'

'I know, I'll take you.' Xiao Ye excitedly shows two elderly gentlemen in uniform through the front door. 'Mama, we have visitors!'

Tao Ying is doing the laundry, immersed in soap up to her armpits.

'We are from the administrative office at the temple. The local newspaper has forwarded your letter to us and we have come to ascertain the truth.'

Tao Ying is very nervous, and somewhat depressed. Chiefly because her house is very messy, and she has not had the time to tidy up. If they think that she is prone to laziness they might not believe her.

'Xiao Ye, why don't you go out to play?' In Tao Ying's fantasies, Xiao Ye would be in the room to witness the revelation of the truth. Now that the moment has finally arrived, she feels uncomfortable having him there. She cannot predict what will happen. These are after all the people who employed the youth in red, so how reasonable can they be?

The younger of the two speaks. 'We have investigated the matter with the party concerned, and he insisted he was in the right. Don't tell the boy to leave, we want to measure him.'

Xiao Ye obeys and stands next to the wall. The white of the wall looks like a virgin canvas and Xiao Ye a painting filling up the space. He leans tightly against the wall as if the act of measuring his height has once again stirred up some terrifying memory in the recesses of his mind.

The men are very serious. First of all they draw a bold line across the wall from the top of Xiao Ye's head. Then they take out a metallic tape and take the measurement from the line to the floor. The metal of the tape glistens like a flowing stream in sunlight.

Tao Ying regains her calm.

'What does it say?'

'One metre ten, just so,' the younger man answers.

'This is not just so. There was a delay of one month and nine days before you came. A month ago he wasn't this tall.'

The two officials look at each other. This is a statement they cannot refute.

They produce a five-dollar bill from a pocket. The note pokes out of an envelope. They have evidently come prepared. Before they left the temple, they must have checked the height of the earthworm, and realized it was not drawn accurately.

'The other day you and your son were unable to enter. This is a small token to redress the situation.' This time it is the elder of the two gentlemen who speaks. His demeanour is kind, so he must be the more senior of the two.

Tao Ying remains still. That day's happiness can never be bought again.

'If you don't want the money, here are two tickets. You and your son are welcome to visit the temple any time.' The younger man is even more polite.

This is a tempting proposition indeed, but Tao Ying shakes her head. To her, to her son, that place will always be associated with unhappy memories now.

'So which would you prefer?' both men ask in unison.

In fact Tao Ying is asking herself the same question. She is gracious by nature – if the youth in red had come in person to apologise today, she would not have made him feel awkward.

So what is it that she wants?

She shoves Xiao Ye in front of the two elderly officials.

'Say Grandpa,' she tells him.

'Grandpa.' Xiao Ye sounds infinitely sweet.

'Dear Leaders, please take back the money, and the tickets. Kindly do not punish the guard on duty, he was only doing his job...'

The two officials are puzzled.

Tao Ying nudges Xiao Ye closer: 'Gentlemen, would you be so kind as to explain to my son exactly what happened on that day. Please tell him that his mother has not done anything wrong...'

1991

Translated by Carolyn Choa

Author Biographies

DAVID SU LI-QUN

Born in Chungking in 1945, David Su Li-qun's family were originally from Suchow. He attended school in Beijing, then enrolled at the National Academy of Drama majoring in acting. In 1967, during the Cultural Revolution, Li-qun was sent to work in the countryside in Hebei. After four years he returned to join the Hunan Provincial Theatre Company as an actor and playwright. In 1980, Li-qun became resident playwright of the National Union Theatre in Beijing, where he remained for the next four years. In 1984 he emigrated to London, and began intermittent work for the BBC World Service while working as a Chinese teacher privately. Since 1987 he has been teaching at the School of Oriental and African Studies (SOAS) at London University. David Su Li-qun has also worked for Channel Four television creating subtitles for programmes made in Chinese.

Plays include the prize-winning *In the Dead of Night* (National Youth Theatre, 1980); *Zhuang Zi Tests His Wife* (National Experimental Theatre in Beijing, 1995; International Festival in Seoul, 1996) and *Years in London* (BBC Radio, 1988–1990).

Film scripts include *The Sinner* (1978) and *The Dream of an Actress* (1985).

Novels include *Red Balloon in a Blue Sky* (1982); *In the Dead of Night* (1984); *The Dead Lake* (1984); and *Beijing Opera* (1994).

David Su Li-qun offers the unique perspective of a Chinese writer who lives abroad but who continues to maintain close links with his country. He is able to explore and develop his interest in the cohabitation of Eastern and Western culture in both countries, a running theme in most of his recent works as a novelist. In this extract from the novel *Beijing Opera*, a young English girl brought up in China attempts to find a teacher who will impart to her the ancient art of Beijing opera.

CHENG NAI-SHAN

Born in Shanghai in 1946. Cheng Nai-shan graduated from the English Department of the Shanghai Education Institute and worked as an English teacher in one of Shanghai's middle schools. In 1979, her first work, 'The Song Mother Taught Me to Sing' was published in the magazine *Shanghai Literature*. Cheng joined the Shanghai Writer's Association in 1983 and has been a professional writer since 1985.

She has published dozens of short stories, including 'The Story of the Happy Goddess', 'The Yellow Silk Ribbon', 'The Poor Street', 'The Clove Villa', 'Daughters' Tribulations', and 'The Bankers'. Medium length novels include *The Blue House*, and *The Three Silver Coins in the Fountain*. In 1982, her collection *The Death of the Swan*, was published by the Jiangsu People's Press.

Cheng Nai-shan often writes about the present-day life of the old Shanghai upper-class who have weathered thirty years of political storm, as well as the lives and thinking of their children. Her writing has a strong local style. It is astute yet without rancour. 'Hong Tai-Tai' is an excellent example of her interest in the way old attitudes are transformed by a new environment.

SHI TIE-SHENG

Born in Beijing in 1951. Shi Tie-sheng was sent to work in the countryside in 1969. In 1973 he was crippled by an accident and returned to Beijing. His works include 'Half an Hour at Lunchtime', 'On a Wintry Evening', and 'My Faraway Qing Peng Wan', which was awarded the National Prize for Best Short Story in 1983. 'Grandmother's Stars' won the same prize in 1985.

In the preface to his collection *Strings of Life*, Shi quotes from one of his own essays and speaks of the three trials that God sends to test us – loneliness, frustration and fear. He goes on to say: 'Perhaps God has in fact given us three potential sources of pleasure ... I think what attracts me to writing is that it helps me transform these trials into a source of delight.'

WANG AN-YI

Born in 1954 in Fujian Province, Wang An-yi is the daughter of the noted woman writer Ru Zhi-juan. Wang represents the generation of Chinese writers whose formal education was disrupted by the Cultural Revolution. Her father was denounced as a Rightist when she was only three, and she was unable to continue her education beyond junior school. At the age of fifteen, Wang was sent to work on a commune in northern Anhui. She began publishing short stories in 1976, and was finally able to return to Shanghai in 1978 where she worked as an editor on the magazine *Childhood*. 'The Destination' and 'The Lapse of Time' are two of the many works that have won literary prizes in China.

Wang An-yi's writing embodies the new resurgence of Humanist literature after the fall of the Gang of Four in 1976. She analyses China with an imagination that is nourished by both pre-revolutionary and post-revolutionary culture. The stories are about everyday urban life, which can be grimy, gloomy, and utterly exhausting. Often we see the underclass struggling with their mundane existence, asserting their will for its own sake as the last and only refuge of control in their lives. The inner passions of her characters do not find expression in raw exuberance, but in quiet and confidential mutual understandings. Commenting on her own work, Wang An-yi once said: 'I hope that my fiction has this effect – that people will read it and say, "Yes ... this is the way things were once upon a time. These are lives that people led."'

SU SHU-YANG

Born in Hebei in 1938, Su was branded a Rightist during the Cultural Revolution. Since the early 1980s Su Shu-yang has written many plays, including *The Simple Heart*, which won first prize in a national competition; film scripts include *Sunset Street*; short stories include the collection, *The*

Wedding Handbook. He has also produced novels, poetry, and a biography of the late Premier Chou En-lai – *Son of the Earth*.

SU TONG

Born in 1963 in Suchow. His father was a machinist, his mother a factory worker. Su Tong grew up during the Cultural Revolution and fell ill with a kidney disease when he was nine. Confined to his bed for six months, he developed a voracious appetite for books, a habit which was to become his all-consuming passion as an adult. He entered secondary school in 1975, where he excelled in creative writing. After school he began to experiment with poetry. In 1980 he left home for the first time, enrolling in the Chinese Department of the Teacher's Training College in Beijing. He began writing earnestly, and found his first poetry and short stories published in 1983 in four different magazines. In 1984, Su Tong went to work in an art college in Nanjing, where he continued to write until appointed editor of the literary magazine *Zhong Shan*. In 1985, his short stories started to appear in reputable publications like *October* and *Harvest* with which he still maintains a strong link. In 1987, *The Shanghai Literary Review* and *Beijing Literary Review* also took note, establishing Su Tong's reputation once and for all.

Short stories and novellas include 'Escape in 1934', 'Raise the Red Lantern', 'The Sad Dance', 'Rice', 'The Decline of the South', 'A Friend on the Road', 'My Life as an Emperor', 'The Divorce Instruction Manual', 'Cherry' and many more.

In his epilogue to the collection *Cherry*, Su Tong sums up his own simple but driven attitude to writing by quoting his friend Yieh Xiao Yin, 'If you are a writer then you should bloody well write.' He adds, 'there is a voice in my head which says, go on writing, don't be distracted, who do you think you are? What else can you do apart from writing? What else, eh?' His modesty conceals a ferocious commitment to his craft which continues to delight readers both in his own country and abroad.

Author Biographies

MO SHEN

Born in 1951 into a family in Wuxi in Jiangsu Province, also known as Sun Shu-gan. After graduating from high school in Baoji County in Shansi in 1968, he spent over three years working in a rural commune, returning to the city in 1972, where he worked as a porter at the Baoji railway station.

Mo Shen was one of the generation of young writers who emerged after the fall of the Gang of Four in 1976. 'Sighs of the People', his first work, was published in 1977 in the literary monthly, *Yangtze River*. The story, about the people's love for the late Premier Chou En-lai, was also broadcast on radio several times. 'The Window' is his best known work to date.

Mo Shen once said that his aim as a writer is 'to echo the voice of the people'.

WANG MENG

Born in 1934 into an intellectual family in Beijing. Wang Meng's love of literature began early. He went to the People's Secondary School in 1945 where he excelled in creative writing, languages and mathematics. He joined the Communist Party in 1948, and, when the city was liberated the following year, he gave up his studies to work in the Communist Youth League.

Wang wrote his first novel, *Long Live the Youth* in 1953, but publication was delayed until 1979. His first published work was in fact a collection of children's stories in 1955. Between 1958 and 1962, Wang was sent to the suburbs of Beijing to do manual work, and his creative life was put on hold for five years. In 1962 he returned to lecture at the Teacher's Training College in Beijing, but was again exiled in 1963, this time to Tibet to do physical labour. Ten years later he was allowed to work as a translator of the Uygur language in Urumqi. In 1976 Wang Meng went back to writing. He was rehabilitated in 1979 and was transferred once more to Beijing where he joined the Federation of Literary and Art Circle. By 1980 there was a notable change of style and the beginning of a very prolific period;

fifteen short stories, five short novels, and a long novel appeared within the next two years.

Known for his ideological insight and humour, Wang Meng has won many literary awards over the years. 'Most Precious', 'The Gentle Heart of the Palm', and 'The Sound of Spring' all won national prizes for Best Short Story; 'A Roomful of Guests' was awarded first prize by the *People's Daily News*; 'The Kite' won first prize in the *Beijing Literary Monthly*; and 'Butterfly' first prize in the *October* magazine, where it was also voted Best Short Story in the national awards.

Wang Meng is more interested in the inner workings of his characters than in narrative. It is through the individual that he explores the social and political milieu which they inhabit. He is constantly experimenting with form and style, pushing frontiers and exerting a deep influence on the literary life of his country. He has worked as editor on several magazines, and has lectured in Germany, the US, and Mexico.

CHEN SHI-XU

Born in 1948 in Jiangxi. On graduation from junior school in 1964, Chen Shi-xu was sent to work in the countryside for eight years. He began writing in 1972 and went back to study in the Chinese Department of Wuhan University in 1985. Upon graduation in 1987, he started doing literary research. He is now an associate fellow in the Jiangxi Literary Research Institute. 'The General and the Small Town' and 'The Angry Waves' both won national short story awards. Among his collections of short stories are: *Shells Bearing Sea Breeze, Beside the Swan Lake*, and *The General and the Small Town*.

LIU XIN-WU

Born in 1942 in Sichuan. Liu Xin-wu began to teach Chinese in a Beijing middle school after graduating from a teacher's training college in 1961. He was to remain a teacher until 1976, when he started work as an editor at a publisher's in Beijing. He had begun to write in 1958, and in 1978 his short story 'The Form Teacher' won first prize in a national short story competition. The following year 'I Love Every Leaf in Green' won the same prestigious award. His novel *The Clock Tower* won the Mao Dun Literary Prize in 1984.

'Black Walls' explores the plight of the individual in a society where to conform was the only acceptable way to live.

WANG CENG-QI

Born in 1920 in Jiangsu, Wang was a pupil of the eminent scholar and writer Shen Chung-wen. In 1939 he enrolled in the South-West Union University in Kwunming, graduating in 1943, when he started work as a schoolteacher. In 1950 Wang moved to Beijing where he became editor of several literary magazines. He began writing in 1940, receiving public recognition in 1947, when his short stories were published in the *Spring Autumn* literary magazine. In 1962, he became resident playwright at the Opera Theatre in Beijing.

Wang Ceng-qi's works include 'The Meeting', 'Revenge', 'The Wang Ceng-qi Collection of Short Fiction', and 'Flowers for Dinner'; Beijing opera scripts include *Fan Chung Passes his Exams*, and *Sha Jia Yau.*

Wang said of his own work, 'When I was young, I had the ambition to destroy boundaries which separated novels, essays and poetry. Prose poems and novels are only divided by a very thin line, and I have always felt that novels should contain an element of poetry.' He aimed to combine the traditional elevated style of the Beijing opera with a modern minimalist approach to romanticism. He went on to say, 'Some of my novels are hardly novels at all. Sometimes they are mere sketches of people. I am not good at story-telling, and I don't really like novels which look too much like a novel, where the narrative dominates. When that happens, the story inevitably loses its own truth.' Wang Ceng-qi was an admirer of the unadorned pared-down quality of folk art. By the 1980s the style in his own writing had evolved to become deceptively simple, as exemplified by the writing in 'Big Chan'. Wang Cen-qi passed away in 1997.

Author Biographies

DENG YOU-MEI

Born in 1931 in Tianjin. Deng You-mei became a messenger in the Chinese Communist Party's Eighth Route Army at the age of eleven. Being too small, he was sent back to Tianjin, where he led an itinerant life until he was forced to go to Japan as a labourer. In 1945 he returned to China and joined the new Fourth Army as a journalist. In 1957 he was criticized for writing 'On the Precipice' and sent to do manual work for over a decade. Following his rehabilitation in 1978, he started writing again and his short stories 'Our Army Commander', 'Three Women Soldiers in Pursuit of Their Troops', and 'Han the Forger' all won national awards. His recent works, including 'Snuff-Bottles' and 'Na Wu' are set in Beijing and have a strong local style.

ZHANG JIE

Zhang Jie was born in 1937 to a primary schoolteacher and is one of the most widely hailed of today's women writers. As a child, she displayed an ardent interest in books and would spend hours poring over fables and fairy tales of such writers as Hans Christian Andersen and Ivan Krylov. Upon finishing high school in 1956, she had hoped to apply to the Department of Literature in Beijing University, but her school authorities recommended economics and she dutifully enrolled in the Department of Economics in the People's University. During her years as an undergraduate, Zhang became an avid reader of philosophy. She later recalled, 'Philosophy played an important role in my understanding of life and in my work.'

On graduation in 1960, she was assigned to the State Bureau of Complete Set of Equipment. During this time, Zhang continued to consume works by both Chinese and foreign writers, though it was not until 1978 that she began writing herself. 'The Child from the Forest', her first piece, was an immediate success, garnering a prize in the national short story competition that year. This began a period of prodigious productivity when a vast number of stories, essays and plays were published. 'Who Knows How to Live' went on to win the National Short Story Award in 1979.

Zhang Jie's style is poetic, with a strong philosophical bent. She has since combined her life as an author with employment at the Editing and Directing Department of the Beijing Film Studio.

Harrison E. Salisbury (author of *The Long March*) comments that she 'writes with a comprehension and sympathy which is certain to appeal across any boundaries of nation or viewpoint'; and Hualing Nieh (Director of the University of Iowa's International Writing Programme) says that Zhang 'is often bravely controversial, and widely appreciated as one of the outspoken and influential writers in China today'.

ZHOU LIBO

Zhou Libo was born in 1908, a native of Hunan. He joined the China Federation of Left-Wing Writers in 1934. After the Anti-Japanese War broke out he went to take part in resistance work serving as editor of a magazine and newspaper. He also worked as a war correspondent, translator and teacher at the Lu Xun Arts Institute in Yanan. After Liberation in 1949, he continued to write, producing such novels as *Hurricane, The Flowing Molten Iron,* and *Great Change in a Mountain Village* as well as many short stories and essays. 'The Family on the Other Side of the Mountain' was written in 1957.

The oldest writer in this collection, Zhou Libo offers the insight of someone who had lived and worked almost continuously both before and after the revolution. Zhou Libo died in 1979.

ZHAO DA-NIAN

Born in 1931 in Beijing, Zhao Da-nian is a Machu writer who owes much boyhood literary influence to his intellectual parents. He studied at Nankai Middle School in Tianjin before joining the Chinese People's Liberation Army in 1949 and became an actor in the modern drama team of the Cultural Troupe. He published his first story in 1950 when his unit was carrying out land reform in western Hunan. In 1959 he was demobilized and transferred to the Agricultural Machinery Research Institute in Beijing, where he continued to produce stories, poems and plays. Among his published works are *Hunting at Lingdingyang,* a collection of short stories, and three novels, *A Grand Retreat, The Fate of Women Prisoners of War* and *The Musk Case.* Here, in 'Three Sketches', we find Zhao Da-nian in an unusually light-hearted mood.

FENG JI-CAI

Feng Ji-cai was born in 1942 and brought up in Tianjin. After completing high school, he became a professional basketball player. An injury curtailed his future as an athlete, and Feng was transferred to the Chinese Traditional Painting Press in Tianjin where he began to paint and write. In 1974 he started teaching Chinese traditional painting at the Tianjin Worker's College of Decorative Art while continuing to write in his spare time. Following the publication of his first novel, *The Boxer,* Feng turned professional and became a member of the Tianjin Writer's Association. Since then he has produced many works, including novels, short stories, scripts, essays and articles. These include 'Magic Light', 'The Miraculous Pigtail', 'The Wrong Road', 'The Figure-Carved Pipe' and 'Ah!', the last two winning awards at the national short story and medium-length novel competitions in 1979 and 1980 respectively.

CAI CE-HAI

Born in 1954 in a mountain hamlet in Hunan, Cai Ce-hai finished middle school in 1966 just as the Cultural Revolution was starting and had to return home to work in the fields then later in railway construction. In 1974 he entered the local public health school, graduating in 1976 to work as an anatomy teacher and then as a doctor in the local hospital. In 1980 he was transferred to the County Cultural Centre and in the following year became a correspondent and editor for the Hunan People's Broadcasting Station. He graduated from the Chinese Department of Beijing University in 1983 and is now a full-time writer.

Since 1979, titles include 'The Mother Boat', 'Through Death' and 'The

Dark Tunnel'. 'The Distant Sound of Tree-felling' won the National Award for Short Stories in 1982.

BAI XIAO YI

Bai Xiao Yi was born in 1960 in Shenyang. He entered primary school in 1968, graduating from university in 1983. While at secondary school Bao pretended to be ill and played truant for a year, until the hospital refused to treat him any further and he was forced to resume his studies. His first work was published in 1981. Since then he has written several hundreds of 'micro' stories, of which six are included in this anthology. He has also produced innumerable short stories, and several medium-length novels. Bai Xiao Yi is the editor of a literary magazine in Shenyang, where he continues to live.

BI SHU-MIN

Bi Shu-min was born in 1952 in Beijing. She joined the army at sixteen and was sent to work in Mongolia. She has been serving her country as a doctor for over twenty years, at the same time obtaining a masters degree in literature in the Beijing Teacher's Training College.

Bi Shu-min is one of the best-known writers currently working in China. Her works have been translated into many languages. She has won innumerable literary awards both in China and in Taiwan. 'One Centimetre' is a fine example of a mature artist working at the height of her powers.

Acknowledgements

The editors would like to thank Mr Wu Cheng-dong, Mrs Shen Jie-ying, Senior Editors at the Chinese Literature Press, and Mr Ji Rong-sheng, Director of the Overseas Department at the Foreign Language Press in Beijing. Without their co-operation this book could never have been put together. We would also like to thank each of the writers in this anthology who allowed us to translate their stories for the first time into English. We hope that we have done justice to their work. We mourn the death of Mr Wang Ceng-qi who passed away in the spring of last year, and thank him for his charming story, 'Big Chan'. Lastly, we thank Annette Lord for her contribution and her grace; Jung Chang and Dzidra J. K. Stipnieks, marketing manager at the SOAS Language Centre, for their kind support; Mary Mount at Picador for her editorial help; Tim Bricknall for his daily assistance; Lee Newman at Judy Daish Associates for her legal advice; and Mr Wang Yi-dong for allowing us to use his exquisite painting, 'Rain in the Meng Mountain', for the cover.

Permission Acknowledgements

Grateful acknowledgement is made to the following for permission to reproduce copyright material:

Extract from *Beijing Opera* by David Su Li-qun. Copyright © 1998 David Su Li-qun. English translation copyright © Carolyn Choa.

'Hong Taitai' by Cheng Nai-shan. Copyright © 1989 Chinese Literature Press. English translation copyright © 1998 Janice Wickeri. Reproduced by kind permission.

'Fate' by Shi Tie-sheng. Copyright © 1991 Chinese Literature Press. English translation copyright © 1998 Michael S. Duke. Reproduced by kind permission.

'Life in a Small Courtyard' by Wang An-yi. Copyright © 1988 Chinese Literature Press. English translation copyright © 1998 Hu Zhihui. Reproduced with kind permission.

'Between Themselves' by Wang An-yi. Copyright © 1988 Chinese Literature Press. English translation copyright © 1998 Gladys Yang. Reproduced with kind permission.

'Between Life and Death' by Su Shu-yang. Copyright © 1984 Su Shu-yang. English translation copyright © 1998 Carolyn Choa.

'Cherry' by Su Tong. Copyright © 1996 Su Tong. English translation copyright © 1998 Carolyn Choa.

'Young Muo' by Su Tong. Copyright © 1996 Su Tong. English translation copyright © 1998 Annette Lord and Carolyn Choa.